The Last Matriarch

Katherine Black

Best Book Editions

Best Book Editions

1 3 5 7 9 10 8 6 4 2

First published in 2023 by Best Book Editions.

Paperback ISBN 9798386766054

Cover by Best Book Editors

A CIP catalogue record of this book is available from the British Library

Contents

Chapter One

2 8th May 1973

He shuffled down the corridor. Clutching his Scooby-Doo lunchbox in his left hand, he looked confused. He always looked confused.

'Late. Late. Late.' He had an empty rucksack on his back. It was his, and because it belonged to him, it was important. He didn't have anything to put in it, but he took it with him always, as a child carries a favourite blanket. The rucksack was all he had. It was his, something that grounded him into who he was, in case he forgot.

At the Great Gables home for special children, he didn't have much. None of them did. Even their clothes got mixed up in the laundry process. Very often, he got Andy Dixon's Y-fronts, and towels were a free for all. Simon never went into the linen cupboard for a clean towel because he didn't like to wash. He didn't like soap—he hated the feel of it, but when he was forced to use it, even that had somebody else's scud on the top.

His cardigan was fastened wrong. An extra hole hung alone at the waistband and, to compensate, a lone button stood out like an on-off switch near his neck. Mrs Quigley had made him his favourite for breakfast –soft-boiled eggs – and his shirt bore testament. His trainers were on the wrong feet, the laces undone and trailing. Every few steps, he stumbled over them.

Gloria shook her head and tutted. 'Simon, look at the state of you.' Simon tried to look, but his chin stopped him from being able to see much of his top half, and his tummy hid everything from the waist down. As for his face, he couldn't see that at all. 'How many times have I told you to stay in your room until somebody comes to check you over?'

Simon thought about it, and his long brow furrowed as he mulled the question over. He gave a triumphant grin. Working around his speech impediment and his jumbled words, he said, 'A millionty-three.' Gloria herded him back in the direction of his room.

He waited there, sitting on the end of his bed and counting to twenty. He got confused and jumped from thirteen to twentitty-one, missing out on his goal of twenty completely. He wanted to hurry up and get to twentitty-one because it was a funny number and made him giggle. He wasn't sure what came after that and was aware that he'd probably got it wrong somewhere. He tried to work it out, and when he got more confused, he decided to go back to one and start again. But before he started the second scale, he forgot about numbers and thought about days instead.

He knew it wasn't Monday because they went swimming on a Monday and he hadn't been swimming. He forgot to allow for the fact that it wasn't nine o'clock yet. And if it was Tuesday, he would have been swimming yesterday, and his hair would smell of chlorine because he didn't like having a shower after he'd been swimming. The water in the pool's showers was too cold, and Jimmy always splashed him and called him Jelly Belly. He liked smelling his hair on a Tuesday. He would remember being in the pool and how much fun he'd had. Swimming, he decided, not for the first time, was one of his favouritest things, but it wasn't as good as eating cream cakes or ice cream. If he could go swimming and eat cream cake and ice cream all at the same time, it would be his favouritest day ever. He wished that there were twentitty-one days in a week because then surely one of them would have swimming and eating cream cakes and ice cream at the same time.

Nobody had come to check on him yet. He wondered if he should go and find somebody. *Because nobody's comed to get me, and someone might be giving away good eats out there.*

Helen always came at quarter to nine. He felt that it must be later than that now. Simon was an optimist. He saw the good in every situation, and if there wasn't any, he'd add the possible element of ice cream or something else nice, and his trademark grin would attach itself to his face. When Simon smiled, nobody could be angry with him for long. Well, except for Mummy, but she was always angry about something. Gloria said he was a sunbeam. Simon liked being a sunbeam. She didn't tell anybody else they were a sunbeam. *Gloria might be missing me by now. It's been such a longer time. I'd better go and find her and tell her nobody's comed yet.*

He shuffled down the corridor again, tripping over his laces, smiling his smile and trying his best to see if he could smell ice cream or even sausages. Sausages were easier to smell than ice cream. Ice cream was a real hard smell to smell, and you had to almost have your nose in

3

it before you could smell it proper. Sausages were good, too, and he'd forgotten that he'd just had his breakfast.

Gloria was still clearing away the breakfast things when Simon reappeared. It was only three minutes since she'd taken him back to his room. She understood that three minutes was a long time for Simon. Gloria understood most things when it came to her kids. She took him back to his room and called him darling. She promised she'd get somebody to come right away and sort him out. She suggested that he might like to draw a picture until Helen came.

Simon thought that was a smashing idea. It wasn't something he'd ever have thought for himself. He had to be told what to do all the time. He didn't just do something. That was one of the things Mummy got annoyed about. Gloria didn't like Mummy much. Simon wouldn't ever think of drawing a picture by himself, but he was clever enough to know that Gloria didn't like Mummy.

Gloria led him to the desk in the corner of his room. All the children had a desk in their room with coloured pencils and paper. It wasn't his, though, like his rucksack. His thick tongue stuck out of his mouth, and he drew a big brown flower with two red leaves at the bottom and a snail climbing up the stalk.

As much as he struggled to work out his routine from one moment to the next, Simon functioned on order. He didn't always know what was right, but he knew if something was changed or different—or just plain wrong. He didn't like anything to be different. It upset him. Because you don't have chips on a Thursday, do you? No, it's smashed potatoes on a Thursday. He thought that something bad might happen if you had chips on a Thursday when it should be smashed potato. Thursday was a smashed potato day.

This morning wasn't right. Two things had happened that upset Simon.

The first was that Helen didn't come into his room to check him over before the bus came to pick him up. Helen always came at quarter to nine because the bus would arrive at five to. Simon couldn't tell the time, and he got anxious that she'd be late and he always went looking for her, but that was all part of it being right. That's the way it was.

That morning somebody new came into his room. She said hello and put out her hand for him to shake. Simon knew how to shake hands. He liked shaking hands. Sometimes he shook hands with Helen or Gloria, and it made him giggle, but not when they were trying to fold sheets. The new Helen said she was called Anna. Anna was pretty and smiled big, but he wouldn't shake hands with her. He wanted to wait for Helen to come. But if he waited for Helen to come, he'd be late for the bus now because it must be after quarter to nine. It was bad. He moved from one foot to the other and wouldn't look at Anna or shake hands with her.

Anna told him that Helen couldn't come just now. She said that Helen was sad about not coming to see him off, but she'd had a bit of a problem with James. Everybody had a bit of a problem with James. He got mad. He got mad a lot more than Simon did, and sometimes he hit people, too. Simon was scared of James.

Anna said, 'I'm sure Helen will be all right, but she's had a nasty knock to the head and has gone to the hospital just to be on the safe side.' All the while she was talking, she was undoing Simon's buttons. That was distressing. He was distressed that Helen was hurt too, also. It wasn't nice that Helen was hurt too, also. If Anna had more experience or knew Simon and his ways, she might have said something different to explain Helen's absence. With every word, he was more agitated. He moved from one foot to the other and made a deep moaning noise in his throat. Anna kept talking to him softly, trying to ease his discomfort, but the foot changing became more insistent, and the moaning was louder.

Gloria rushed into the room without knocking. That was very bad. Simon knew it was very bad because, at Great Gables, people always knocked on other people's doors. That was called good manners. Gloria said so herself, and here she was, coming in without knocking. It was bad, for sure. It was a bery bad day—and that was bery bad.

'It's all right now, Anna. I'll take over here. Thank you for stepping in like that.' They talked in low voices. 'Yes, she'll be all right, I think, but best not to take chances with these things. Head wounds can be funny.'

Simon didn't think head wounds were funny at all. He thought that they probably hurt a lot, and that was nothing to laugh about. Gloria coming in like that without knocking was distressing, but not as distressing as a new helper sending him off or Helen getting hurt. It was still one more thing to get upset about, and Simon moaned louder. Without warning, he brought his left hand up and hit himself hard on the side of the head. Gloria caught his arm as it raised a second time. 'No, you don't. Come on, my bonny lad, let's get you sorted. It's all right now. I know that was scary, but everything's back to normal now.'

'Not back normal now,' Simon said. 'Late bus now.'

'It's okay, Simon. The bus will wait for you. It doesn't matter, don't worry. We're only a couple of minutes behind.'

'Not five to nine.'

'No, Simon, it's not five to nine. It's three minutes to. What's two minutes between friends, eh? It's no biggie. Tom's holding up the bus for everyone.'

'Bad, bad,' Simon said in his upset voice. 'Not five to nine. Late to bus. Big bad. Big bad. Bad for sure.'

Gloria gave up on fastening his shoes, intending instead to distract him from his tantrum by walking him to the bus, hair uncombed and laces trailing. Better to have that this morning than face another one throwing his fists around. Simon was only thirteen, but he was a big lad with plenty of bulk to fling his weight behind. Gloria thought he was probably the gentlest soul on earth, but, like many Downs Syndrome sufferers, he could fly off the handle if he was frustrated or frightened.

During the first lesson after lunch, it dawned on him what day it was. They had PE that day. It took almost half of the lesson to get all the pupils into their blue shorts and white vests and then almost the other half to get them back into their normal clothes. The actual lesson only lasted ten minutes. Simon knew that Mummy came on the day they had PE, and that distressed him.

Simon loved his Mother. She was always there waiting for him in his room when he got off the school bus, but she distressed him. He was agitated, as always, in the Wednesday PE lesson. His mood would worsen throughout the afternoon and only subsided into a quiet stillness when the visit was over, and his mother was gone. He worried a lot on PE day. PE day was bad for worry.

After PE, they had an activity lesson before home time, and Simon tried every week to learn to be clever really fast so that his mummy would like him. He tried so hard to do well in that lesson but only seemed to succeed in covering himself in glue or paint or flour, which made his mummy even more cross.

He made her a clay pot that he baked in the oven and painted. She said it was lop-sided. He made her a flower out of tissue paper and glitter. She said it was ugly. He made her a love heart and decorated it with real daisies. She forgot to take it home with her, and Simon found it on the floor. The daisies had wilted, and he was sorry for picking them and making them die.

That day they made biscuits in class. It was a lot of fun, and they smelled really good when they were baking. It made all the children hungry, and Miss Brown said that if they were very good and made a great job of decorating them with icing and Smarties, they could each have one to take home. Simon really, really wanted to eat his biscuit with the other kids on the way back to Great Gables. There were only enough for them to have one each. Simon wanted to eat it a lot but saved it for his mummy.

She was waiting in his room when he got back. She was always waiting in his room. She didn't like it in the lounge or along the corridors where she might see the other children. She said they made her feel sick. Simon sometimes wondered if he made her feel sick, too. Simon had felt sick once, and it wasn't very nice. He shuffled down the corridor a little faster than usual. His big moon face had a huge grin, and his tongue protruded from his smiling mouth.

He walked into his room. 'Mummy biscuit,' he announced, shuffling towards her and holding the present out with pride.

She pulled a twisty face and put it straight in the wastepaper basket. Simon was sad. He would like to have eaten it himself.

'Really, Simon, you can't expect me to actually eat that. Where have your hands been?'

Simon thought about that. He thought about all questions seriously but sometimes couldn't work out an answer. He looked at his hands—they were on the ends of his arms, the same as they always were. He wondered if Mummy meant to ask, 'What have you been doing with your hands?' which was a different question altogether. He remembered that he had put one of his hands down his trousers quite a lot that afternoon because he had an itch, but he couldn't remember which one it was that he'd scratched his private parts with. None of this seemed to have anything to do with his biscuit that was now in the wastepaper basket. He was still pondering his hands and his biscuit, looking sad and confused, when his mummy slapped him on the arm. It wasn't a hard slap, but it made him jump. Maybe she slapped him because his hands had wandered off on their own for a little bit when he wasn't looking, and that's what she meant by her question.

'Will you pay attention? I'm talking to you, Simon.'

He looked up. His tongue bulged over his lower lip, and his big almond-shaped eyes looked empty. That was the expression that his mother said she hated most of all. She told him she couldn't bear to look at him and focused on her watch.

Only another hour and fifty minutes and she would escape her son and his smell of maternal neglect.

Chapter Two

3 rd November 1960

3 rd November 1960
   Some might argue that an infant returning to the Lord deserves rays of brilliant sunlight and the Hallelujah Chorus sung by the angels. This wasn't that kind of funeral. It was a sombre occasion, a ceremony in black, as only a Catholic funeral knows how.

Violet Postlethwaite was still a young girl, though the strain of the past week and the black clothes and veil had given her the appearance of a woman fifteen years older. She was called Woods now and had been for the past five months, but people around those parts took to change in their own time. So, to them, she was, and pretty much always would be, little Vi Postlethwaite.

She had elevated opinions of herself and very firm opinions about her name. She shuddered if anybody dared to call her Vi to her face. 'My name,' she'd declare icily, 'is Violet. Vi-o-let, three syllables. It is the name I was given, and had my parents wanted me to be called Vi, I'm sure they would have seen fit to christen me thus, in the sight of God.'

Her grievance with the name Postlethwaite was even worse. She hadn't been married long to Donald Woods, and on returning from their honeymoon, they'd moved into the small public house just outside Windermere, run by Donald's parents. Local dialect was very neatly divided through the middle of Windermere. Anything Bowness and south was still Cumberland until Cumberland leaked into Lancashire, but north of Windermere, the Cumberland dialect really kicked into its wellies. Violet had been horrified the first time she'd heard Postlethwaite contracted to produce the sound Postlethut and was glad that she'd taken her new name of Woods. Even these yokels would find it difficult to tamper with that. Donald wasn't good for much, but at least he'd had the sense to be born with a dependable surname.

She wasn't thinking about names as she stood beside the damp hole watching the tiny coffin being lowered. She wept into a fine lace handkerchief and threw a small amount of earth onto the top of the white casket lid.

'God bless, my darling,' she sniffled before throwing her head back and wailing, 'My baby. My poor, dead baby.'

Molly Davis, the Woods' cleaning lady, sobbed even louder. 'It was a lovely service,' she told everybody later.

Georgina and Arthur, Violet's parents, were the epitome of dignified mourning. They stood shoulder to shoulder with their daughter, lending her their support and strength. Donald was pushed out. He loitered, apart, ashen and confused. In his turn, he dropped a handful of earth into the grave, but only after Monsignor Burton had urged him to. Donald had expected the soil to sprinkle like icing sugar on the top of a sponge cake, but Windermere earth is clay, and it clumped in his sweaty hand and fell to the coffin lid like a stone, landing with a resounding thump, and Donald jumped as though he had been hit in the chest by a torpedo.

Georgina's head shot up, glaring at her new son-in-law. Her lips pursed, and her black eyes peered at him. She looked startled, like a malevolent crow, as she shook her head in exaggerated movements. Again Donald had disappointed. Donald felt that Georgina blamed him for the mud on her new court shoes, for the escalating price of home-cured ham and for the fact that it was raining. But what she could never blame him for was the death of the child.

Donald didn't want to get married. And he'd never wanted to put Violet in the unfortunate position that they had had to get married. If truth be told, he didn't like her very much. He hadn't liked her on sight, and his opinion of her had never warmed. He'd been pushed into taking her out by his enthusiastic parents. Violet had made all the other decisions. He just went along with them because he found that, where Violet was concerned, that was best. What upset Donald was standing beside that gave, with those people, on that day with his own mother smiling at him. It was one of those smiles that were meant to encourage, but it said, 'I'm sorry, I don't know what to say.' Perhaps what Donald hated the most was the fact that his parents were hurting. They didn't deserve this. They were good people.

Violet told everybody that the baby was brought to his burial in what would have been his christening gown. 'Yards of pure white lace,' she said to anybody who would listen, 'adorning his poor tiny little body. What was Our Lord thinking?' She repeated this many times that day, along with, 'How could He take our angel, our sweet, precious angel?'

Whispers carried back through the church from pew to pew. It was the tradition in these parts to go for open-casket funerals. Why, then, had they chosen to keep the baby's coffin closed? But nobody dared mention it to the family. 'It wouldn't be right to ask, would it?' Maisy Roach said.

'Mebby's it were a really ugly babby,' Jack Dawson said.

'Aye, or 'appen it 'ad summat right wrong with it like. 'Appen it were that spiral biffica, there's a lot a that abart. Deformed, I reckons, proper unsightly like.' Maisy sucked in air through her teeth and tutted, and they all nodded their heads in solemn agreement.

No expense had been spared on the funeral. Usually, Arthur clung to his wallet as Georgina ripped it from his hand with vigour, but that day, he just looked shifty and sad—and scared.

Willoughby's had taken care of the funeral. The family rode in a black Rolls Royce with red brocade curtains at the windows to shield their tears from curious eyes. The coffin was brought to the church in a carriage with a glass mantle. Four ebony stallions, with black plumes on their heads, pulled the carriage, their hoof beats tolling perfect time along the cobbled streets. Mister Willoughby himself headed the procession. He walked in front of the carriage, stamping the tempo into the road with his cane, and raindrops reflected in the calyx patterns from the crystal orb on the top. He wore a black coat to his knees, a claret cravat and a black top hat, but mostly he wore dignity and respect. It was what the family had paid through the nose for.

Monsignor Burton ran out of prayers. His hands ached from being spread, upturned to God at chest height. His thin, reedy voice sang the final lament, and his left knee throbbed with deep arthritic pain from

13

the damp weather. 'God be with you,' he said for the third time. 'Go in peace to serve the Lord.' For the most part, the mourners had dispersed. They left fast with a taste for sherry and salmon sandwiches that had their crusts cut off. The family didn't seem to know what to do. They looked down at the tiny coffin, shaking their heads and searching their hearts for guilt.

Jack Murray gave an apologetic cough, his hand fisted at his mouth. He didn't know how best to disturb them, and he was terrified of Georgina Postlethut, but time was getting on. Stinging Nettle was running in the three o'clock at Chepstow.

'Jack,' Donald said, turning to shake the large man's hand, but he couldn't look him in the eye. 'Thank you for coming. And please, thank everyone at the lodge for the floral tribute. It's right grand.'

'It's nothing, my man. Nothing,' Murray grunted. His eyes examined the same pebble that Donald found interesting. 'Terrible business, terrible. Of course—'cough'—we've had another whip round—'cough'—For you. There's a small monetary gift for Violet. It'll be presented at the lodge on Monday. We'll see you there, yes?'

Donald heard raindrops bouncing off the lid of the coffin.

They shook hands, and, without another word, the president of the Windermere branch of the Freemasons Society walked away, wiping the shaken hand on the seam of his suit trousers in case it infected him.

Like the family, and because of his part in the scandal, he wouldn't sleep easy in his bed that night.

Chapter Three

After the funeral, life settled down for Violet and Donald. Violet wasn't happy to rest on her laurels for long. Before meeting Donald, she had a life plan mapped out. Getting pregnant at nineteen wasn't part of that schematic. It wasn't even in the small print at the bottom that said she should always be able to rely on her mother and father for financial help in any unexpected eventuality. Nowhere was unexpected and unfortunate pregnancy mentioned, and Violet felt violated.

Donald had worked at Borrowdale Quarry for eight years. He was happy. His friends were there, and he got to work outside in the fresh air. He always joked that he had a full membership to the cheapest gym in the country. His work wasn't far from Derwent Water Lake, and he spent eight hours a day playing Peeping Tom to nature at her most alluring. He was a worker, and both management and his co-workers respected him. His body was brown and taut, and his job made going home to Violet just about bearable.

As soon as it was seemly after the funeral, Violet arranged meetings with estate agents in a thirty-mile radius. They looked at the bed and breakfast establishments, public houses, and hotels at the cheaper end of the market. Violet saw no reason at all why they shouldn't commit to four hundred thousand pounds worth of mortgage right away. They were young. They had their whole life ahead of them to pay it off, and with a sizeable down payment from Daddy as a late wedding present, they'd manage. Donald's head swam. Four hundred pounds was more than he'd ever owed anybody in his life. Four hundred thousand wasn't a millstone. It was an entire mill house—and the town surrounding it—tied about his neck. It was in the days when being a millionaire still meant something, and four hundred thousand pounds was a tremendous amount of money. Donald's protests fell on grit and concrete. He couldn't make Violet see sense. However, the mortgage companies fared better by refusing to fund her whims. She alienated several brokers who'd been willing to allow them a more manageable mortgage before she agreed to downgrade her ambition with the bank's money.

Luck was with them the day they found the small hotel on the outskirts of Windermere. It wasn't on the lake edge as Violet wanted. Otherwise, it was beautiful. Structurally it was sound, but it needed a lot of work and modernisation. Mrs Finch, the vendor, was an old widow with money. Since her husband died, she'd found it difficult to manage alone, and the good reputation of the hotel declined. Her glass back was telling her it was time to hang up her apron and let Glenridding Mount go.

For all her bombastic nature, Violet was canny. Instinct told her she needed to get the old girl on her side, so she turned up her charm oven to four hundred degrees and coated her natural brusqueness with honey. Each room seemed to her more old-fashioned and dingier than the last. The only place she felt an ambience to the place was in the kitchen, which was fitted with a huge Aga. She was bursting with a need to voice her plans. Walls out, décor changed, complete overhaul, Little Bird Finch thrown on the scrap heap. But she held herself in check, cooing in all the right places and complementing the vendor on her charming home.

One thing that was genuine was her instant love for the place. Glenridding Mount had Mrs Violet Woods' name written all over it. She soon had the old crow eating out of her hands.

Donald went along to the viewings reluctantly. He was happy with his work. The thought of spending his leisure hour and his workday close to the bosom of his delightful wife appalled him. To an outside eye, Donald Woods was a wimp, the blueprint of the stereotypical hen-pecked husband. However, anybody taking time to study the dynamics would see that he gave his lady so much rope, and when he was ready to reel her in, he held her on a short tether—and a muzzle. When the farce of buying a business property was mentioned, he wasn't going to give up his job to learn a new trade as a hotelier. It was an occupation he was untrained for, and he hadn't the first clue about how to operate it. Some might say it was cruel to let his wife look for something he had no intention of buying for her. But the way Donald saw it, Violet was a woman who needed something to occupy her mind. She bored with ease, and an idle Violet would turn to gossip and spouting malice around the town. This way, Violet got to play with her fantasy, and Donald got some peace and avoided the relentless nagging about a hotel that they couldn't afford to buy.

It surprised him more than anybody when he fell in love with the Glenridding Mount. He was caught up in and enthused with Violet's plans and added his own ideas. Violet had an eye for detail and good taste—which came as a surprise. Donald saw through the old-lady mustiness to polished floors, restored oak beams and a new bar that he might feel at home behind. He was caught up in the moment, and he rode piggyback on Violet's excitement. The frugal and reticent husband couldn't believe what he was saying when he heard himself putting in an offer on the first viewing, standing in the kitchen beside the old blue Aga.

Violet couldn't believe it either. She hadn't expected that. If she decided to change their brand of toilet roll, Donald's way was to go home and talk it over. He'd been outside in the sun too long, but she wasn't knocking it. She squealed like a little girl when their modest offer was accepted. She wasn't quite twenty yet but seemed much older. Donald had never met this side of her. She threw her arms around his neck and hugged him right there in front of Mrs Finch.

Donald wondered as if it was the first time he'd seen them if Violet was named for the colour of her eyes. Her plain, ruddy complexion looked softer and pinker. Maybe it was just the lighting in the old kitchen. He surprised himself again with a genuine feeling of affection for his wife. He hugged her to him and felt that, just maybe, they would be happy there.

The hotel sale went through. They'd secured it for way below the market value. But even in the busy and exciting months ahead, the Wednesday and Sunday rituals were rigid. Violet wouldn't waver and wouldn't relent. Every Wednesday afternoon, she went out at noon and didn't return until after six. Sunday's belonged to God. Violet attended Mass twice on a Sunday, and Donald refused to be hauled along with her more than once a day. For appearance's sake and to make his wife happy, he gave up his Sunday morning lie-in to attend early Mass, but that was it. That was as far as his religious devotion would extend, and he refused to budge. The other Sunday ritual he would have no part in at all, and nothing Violet said would change his mind.

Right through the bitter, cold winter months, through the delights of spring and into the blossom-laden summer, Violet went to the cemetery with flowers every Sunday after lunch. She would spend an hour at the grave throwing out the previous week's blooms and arranging the new ones. Grieving relatives often talk to their lost loved ones, telling them their news and feeling close to them. Violet never uttered a word unless to speak to a passerby. She did what she had to do and then knelt at the graveside in prayer. She stayed only as long as she needed to be seen doing her duty, and then she left, returning home hours later after attending to her private business.

Despite being spoiled and entitled, hard work came easily to Violet. She had exacting standards, and soon after opening, the hotel was booked up months in advance. They were in a position to take on more staff. Violet hired and fired with gusto. But, as hard as she drove her staff, she drove herself more, in a manic need for absolute perfection.

After their second year, they surpassed breaking even, and their bank balance was healthy enough for expansion. Violet was ambitious. She could never be satisfied with enough and always wanted more. They extended their property once in that year and twice more in the following three years.

Donald found his niche, but not as the hotel manager. He took on the role of a groundsman. He loved the land and tended the acreage with pride. He entered competitions with his flowers and vegetables to bring recognition to the hotel, and his work and hobby intermingled. Violet hired a chef and a manager with experience and a reputation. The Glenridding Mount Hotel gained a star a year for three consecutive years.

While the Woods' empire was busy building, things weren't slacking on the domestic front. Almost nine months to the day of the funeral, Violet bore a son. She saw this as a solo endeavour. If she had to admit to Donald having any role to play, then it was as an extra, a cameo role, soon done with, and the unpleasantness of it forgotten. Violet wouldn't have wanted him there, getting in the way and making the place look untidy. Having babies was a woman's work.

She gave the almighty heave that propelled the infant into the world. Apart from a few grunts of exertion, the labour was silent. She bit down on her fists when the cramps chewed into her raw nerve endings and made her want to scream. She felt the procedure was unbecoming enough without wailing and gnashing of teeth. But as she felt her second child slither into the world, she was overcome with hysteria. She cried out for her husband, terrified that it might be like the last one.

'It's a boy, love,' the midwife said.

'Take it away,' Violet whimpered. 'I don't want to see it until I know it's normal.'

Donald was brought into the delivery room. He barely noticed the blood and amniotic waters on the floor. He didn't look at the child. His first concern was for his wife, who needed him for the first time ever—and would never need him again. She groped for his hand and clung to him, vulnerable and pale. She couldn't cope if it was like last time.

When the midwife had cleaned the baby and convinced her that he was beautiful—and beautifully normal, Violet took her son into the crook of her arm.

She examined the grizzling face. She looked at his forehead, peered into the baby's eyes and followed the contours of his tiny face to his mouth. Without care or gentleness, she ripped away the blanket the midwife had wrapped her son in, exposing him to her. She had to know. She needed to be sure.

The midwife urged Violet to put him on her breast, but she ignored the woman. She spread the baby's hands, scrutinising each one, back of the hand, palm, back of the hand again. She wasn't counting the fingers or marvelling at the beauty of something so delicate and tiny as new mothers do. This wasn't her son—not yet. Not until she was sure. She was looking for a larger-than-normal space between the fingers and thumb. And for a thicker-than-usual tongue. She was looking for hooded, myopic eyes.

'Vi, love, he's perfect. He's our boy,' Donald said.

'You said that about the last one,' she spat at him. Her eyes never left the child crying in her arms.

Donald cradled his wife and son until he felt the tension leave her body in a flood. He was perfect. She wept silent tears onto his soft head.

This was her son.

She named him Simon Peter, after the first Apostle. It was a name befitting a child who would mature to greatness, for Violet had no doubt of this. Simon Peter was the rock of Jesus.

Simon Peter was her rock.

Two and a half years later, another son was born. Violet was disappointed. He should have been a girl. She'd planned for a girl and expected a girl. Violet and Georgina blamed Donald for producing a son instead of the daughter they both expected. It takes a real man to make a girl. Violet took a few days to love this one. But she reasoned he could be great too. Her Andrew, the second Apostle of Jesus.

Less than a year later, in her compulsion for a daughter, Violet gave birth to twins, both boys. She was resigned to having sons now. They were her boys, her beautiful, perfect boys. A girl would be different. She would stand out and make for an untidy parade.

Yes, she decided, boys were best, all uniform, and all wonderful in their own special way—Violet's apostles. Jesus had no time for girl apostles, and neither, she decided, did she. The twins were called James and John after the third and fourth disciples of Jesus. A tradition was set. Donald was scared. He was often seen pulling at the corners of his moustache, a sure sign that something troubled him. Where was it going to end, this churning out of children? Did she plan on going for the full twelve? He hoped not. Dear Lord, he joked, please make her stop before we get to number ten. Surely not even Violet could christen a child Labbaeus Thaddaeus.

Violet completed her family two years later with her last son, Philip. She was a staunch Catholic and didn't believe in birth control. When she came out of the hospital after the birth of her fifth son, she moved into her own bedroom. She had lain down and made her children, and she was done with all that undignified stuff now. Sex was a perfunctory business, and she'd never taken to it. Donald sighed, having to accept what he couldn't change. It was nice while it lasted, he thought.

Violet felt as though she'd been pregnant forever. Now that she was finished with it—and sex, she needed a new challenge. She went back to hounding the estate agencies and took to viewing grand Lakeland hotels way beyond their budget. The difference this time was that she had a history. The Woods had an excellent record of accomplishment, and their reputation preceded them. The brokers fell over themselves to throw money at them.

Violet was viewing, but she wasn't buying. She knew what she wanted and was determined to wait to get it. She viewed many and found them all lacking. She knew when she saw it that would be the one for her. And when she saw it, she was right. Donald had no say in the matter. His voice was a chirp in her ear. It wasn't just the name of the hotel, but that did seem like the hand of God pointing their way ahead. The Halcyon Woods Hotel stood on the water's edge of Windermere in twenty acres of its own woodland and lakeside splendour. Violet waited for news of harsh times in the hotel industry, and when an outbreak of foot and mouth disease hit Lakeland ground, slaughtering tourism in the summer of sixty-six, she pounced.

They made an initial offer of four million and settled on £4.8m. It was a colossal amount of money, and while Donald took to night sweats and insomnia, and the brokers pulled at their ties and wiped a thin film of grease from their collective foreheads, Violet slept well and dreamed of chintz coverlets.

Financially, things were tight for the next few years. It had been a tremendous gamble, but one that only Donald lost sleep over. Violet was far too occupied making it work to have time to fret.

The boys grew under a strict regime of firm discipline. Violet treated her children in the same way that she treated her staff. She expected things to be done when she first asked and for them to be done properly. The hardest thing her staff, her children and even her husband had to live up to was Violet herself. Everything had to be done to her rigorous standards.

The boys had the perfect playground to grow up in. There were always guests' children to make friends with, and yet Violet's boys—always Violet's boys, never Donald's—were given no time to play and were discouraged from engaging with the guests.

She dressed them alike and expected them to be spotlessly clean at all times. 'Appearance,' she said, 'is of the utmost importance in our profession. And you, my darlings, are my ambassadors. Remember your position at all times and make Mummy proud.'

The Woods boys grew to love Wednesday afternoons in the school holidays. Donald had shorts and tee shirts hidden in his garden shed for them to change into the minute Violet left. She still went out every Wednesday, and while she was gone, the boys would fell trees with their father or play football on the lawns. On a Wednesday afternoon, they were allowed to get dirty on the strict understanding that they cleaned up before Mother's return. Violet was too preoccupied on those evenings to notice that they collected most of their scrapes and grazes on Wednesdays.

But into every week, a Sunday must fall. What they enjoyed mid-week, they paid for on the Sabbath.

They rose at five-thirty to bathe. Violet filled the enormous tub in their quarters, and a conveyor belt system was operational. As one got out of the bath, the next was ready to step in, starting with Philip because he was the youngest and therefore needed the most help. James, the more dominant of the identical twins, always made John go after Philip because the youngest boy often peed in the bath out of sheer wickedness. John still had to get in the bath water, now, slurried by another brother's scum and by his turn, the water was too cloudy to see if James had peed as well, but it wasn't so bad if you didn't get in straight after Philip.

By the time it was Simon Peter's turn to get in the bath, the water was black and cold. SP, as the lads called him when their mother wasn't listening, perfected bathing without ever getting into the bath, but every so often, Mummy would check behind his ears, and then he'd be for it.

The boys hated their Sunday outfits. Violet faced down the tears and tantrums, the screaming and bawling. She never raised her voice much, but she spoke to them in a tone three parts ice to two parts venom. They didn't refuse her wishes. It wasn't done.

They presented for inspection at six thirty. Being Catholics, they weren't allowed anything to eat until after Mass which tortured them from seven-thirty and could go on for two hours if Monsignor Burton had a fire in his belly to preach about. The brothers stood in line looking miserable, but that wasn't allowed either. Violet chided them to straighten their hats and their faces before leaving the house. 'And for goodness sake, men, smile.'

She had earned the nickname Mother Duck around town. She was a regular sight on a Sunday morning, marching down the street in her stout church brogues. Her five children marched behind her, in single file, starting with the eldest and ending with little Philip, who found it hard to keep time and sometimes had to run a bit to catch up.

The matronly woman and her five offspring were a remarkable sight, and if ever somebody compiled a list of the Windermere eccentric, Old Mother Duck would be right up there at the top of the list. Violet was proud of her standards.

'Standards,' she said, 'are everything.'

She felt that she was a respected member of the highest Lakeland society. And indeed, she was respected as a shrewd and determined businesswoman. But when it came to the way she treated her children, it was a different matter. There wasn't a mother in town who wouldn't like to take those poor lads into her arms for a cuddle.

She wore black for church, right down to the brogues on her feet and the lace veil on her head, folded back for marching, ready to pull over her face when she entered the House of God. Childbirth had not been kind to her, and Violet was broad in beam and bosom. By comparison, her boys were all slim and gave the appearance of being easily broken.

She had their clothes handmade. They hated the straw hats the most, but only marginally more than the burgundy and grey striped blazers with the tacky gold buttons. Their outfits were finished off with grey knee-length shorts with creases you could cut paper with, long grey socks and black shoes, which the boys would clean on a Saturday night until Violet could see her face in them.

Nobody knew for sure whether the boys learned to walk first or to march. They had a car, so Donald could have driven them to church, but Violet wouldn't hear of that. Regardless of the weather or temperament, every Sunday, those boys would be marched through the town to Our Lady of the Lake Catholic Church. When they passed the house of their paternal grandmother, Violet would order, 'Eyes right, boys, and salute to Grandma.' The children would dutifully turn their heads as one, raise their right hands and salute in unison into their grandmother's lounge window.

Donald's mother hated it. She loathed seeing her grandchildren demoralised and had begged Violet not to do it. 'They're only children, Violet. Let them be.' But Violet saw it as her duty to the town to show that her boys were the best behaved and the most beautifully mannered children ever raised. Grandma Mary had long since made sure that she was never in the proximity of her front window on a Sunday morning. Violet saw that as no deterrent and commanded the boys to salute regardless.

As children do, the boys learnt to adapt to their mother's ways. They were well fed, almost never spanked and had musical and holiday privileges that most boys their age didn't. Violet loved them even more than she loved her double string of cultured pearls and showed them off to all the right people just as often.

She groomed them to be altar boys, and if Monsignor Burton was too busy to see how good they were, then Violet was sure he would hear about it.

Chapter Four

M ass was over for another week. The Woods boys were starving, and Violet ordered the meal to be brought to her quarters. Sunday lunch was as religious as seven thirty Mass. No menial waiter was allowed to serve this meal. It had to be brought by the head chef himself.

Succulent pink beef, roast potatoes—crispy on the outside with a hot and fluffy centre—red wine and garlic gravy made with the juices from the tenderloin and infused with thick double cream. The meal could have been good, it should have been good, but hanging over them was the Sunday curse. The boys drew out the feast as long as possible while the meat turned to cardboard in their mouths. Anything to avoid the ritual.

After getting home from Mass, the whole family changed out of their Sunday best before sitting down to eat. Endless prayers were said over the tureens, and Marcus, the head chef, with his eyes rolling, rubbed his lower back when it ached. If the meal cooled, it would be sent back to the kitchen amid a torrent of screaming abuse from the Madonna Violet.

When Philip, who was the star of the show when it came to holding up the proceedings, had shovelled the last Brussels sprout into his unwilling mouth, the second course was over. He screwed up his face and chewed until the food turned to water in his mouth because he couldn't face the thought of swallowing the foul vegetable. Violet didn't allow anybody to leave the table until every plate was empty and the cutlery laid neatly to rest, side by side like a little old couple in their grave. There was no table chatter. Children should be seen and not heard. Apart from polite requests for the cruet set to be passed, the meal was taken in silence. Sunday lunch was a chore for the boys and their father.

Only Donald rose from the table with a joyful heart. He'd attended Mass with his wife and sons. He had smiled dutifully as he paraded her around on his arm and passed time with the wealthier parishioners. When he rose from that table, he stood up a free man. Donald didn't hold fast to much, but from day one, he had refused to go through the Sunday afternoon ritual with the rest of his family. He felt sorry for his sons, but they were spared the worst part of all. They didn't know what he knew, so it wasn't so bad for them. When it came to Sunday afternoons, Donald was of the opinion that it was every man for himself, and he was far too concerned with getting his own backside into the sunshine, or breeze, or even snow if that's what the weather had in store for him. Donald found peace in his gardens. While his wife lived life in the fast lane, wired on nervous energy and flying into rages over un-Brassoed brasses, Donald breathed. He had two gardeners under him now. The new hotel was too big for one person to cope with. He was a thinker, sitting on his bench by the water's edge for long periods and planning his perennials and herbaceous borders. For the most part, he was a content man.

Lunch finished, they would file out of the room while Marcus waited, still standing to attention, ready to call his team in to clear the table and relay for afternoon tea.

The boys would change out of the gabardine slacks they had worn for lunch and back into their Sunday best. They would get their emerald cushion, crafted in the finest crushed velvet with a leather underside and embroidered with their name. Violet had them handmade for a purpose. They would march back to the church in procession and with all same pomp and formality.

On a good day, the sorry pantomime would be over in an hour, but if there was an audience, Violet would wallow, dabbing her eyes with a lace handkerchief. Once, when dignitaries from the Bishop's party had visited, she had wilted in a faint to the nearest bench and, when attended to, she told them how her heart breaks for her Lovely Angel returned to the Lord Above. But not before she'd made the boys sing a rousing chorus of *All Things Bright and Beautiful*, in four-part harmony, around the graveside.

'Philip, don't be so tone-deaf, dear,' she hissed over the headstone. 'Mime, dear, mime.'

Gerald Sawkins had walked his dog through the cemetery that day, and Andrew suffered weeks of torture at school. Children couldn't forget watching a band of little soldiers, in straw boaters and striped blazers, singing *All Things Bright and Beautiful* while their mother waved her walking cane at them like a baton.

Beginning with Simon Peter and ending with Philip, the boys were expected to come forward and tell their Lovely Angel all about the week just passed. Once, Andrew had asked what their Lovely Angel was called.

'What's he really called, Mummy?' It had been puzzling him. Apart from around the grave on a Sunday afternoon, the boys weren't encouraged to talk about their Lovely Angel.

Violet had turned stricken eyes on him that day, they shone with unshed tears, but beneath the watery sheen, there was something akin to malice. Andrew wasn't sure what the look was, but he knew well enough when to leave it alone.

'When the good Lord, in His infinite wisdom, decided he couldn't bear to be without our Lovely Angel beside him, he reclaimed him. We had him only a second before he was gone. He is, and always will be, our Lovely Angel, taken back to heaven to look down upon us. He is too good to have an earthbound name.'

John was dying to point out that even Jesus had an earthly name and that surely their Lovely Angel wasn't gooder than Jesus, but he'd seen the look in his mother's eye. He bit the words back before they sprawled out of his mouth and got him a slap around the head. It was as well he held his counsel because he'd have got the slap and a hundred lines illustrating the correct use of the words better and good for his trouble.

The prayers came next. Prayers for their Lovely Angel and prayers for the starving children in Africa, though Violet never did approve of Negroes much and felt that starvation was their punishment for having the audacity to be born coloured. But one had to be seen to be doing one's bit, and one never knew who was passing when one had their eyes shut in supplication and prayer. She was just thankful that Windermere had not been invaded by any Negroes. That would be unthinkable, and as for the Chinese—she would swoon at the thought.

The boys always had to sing, *The Old Rugged Cross* before leaving because Mother said it was such a rousing song to leave their Lovely Angel with. She said that he would be warm and snug in his grave, wrapped in the lyrics like a shroud. The boys didn't like to think of their Lovely Angel lying in his grave. John was the most inquisitive of the boys. He wondered how long it took a body to decompose. What would our Lovely Angel look like now, he wondered, if we dug him up and opened his coffin? How would he smell? They were questions that haunted him at night, and he woke from nightmares, convinced he'd see the stain of earth on his hands.

The boys were agreed that Sundays were the worst day of the week.

Chapter Five

The church brogues were too big. The leather was stretched and shapeless from water-retentive feet being forced into them every week. The tweed skirt had to be held up and cinched tight with a belt. The double string of pearls hung almost to the waistband of the skirt.

'It's so difficult getting clothes to fit these days,' said the false, cultured tone.

Makeup lay strewn across the glass top of the kidney-shaped dressing table. 'Now, then, which lipstick shall I wear today? Something subtle, I think. Oh dear, I don't have anything subtle. Cherry Bomb Explosion number sixteen. Yes, that sounds about right. It'll just have to do.'

The evening meal was ready. The boys were assembled at the table and standing to attention behind their chairs until grace was said, and they were given the instruction to sit. Violet pursed her lips in irritation. She was always tense on a Wednesday evening. What made her mood black this week was the fact that Donald had refused to come in to eat again. This was the third meal he'd missed that week. Violet was a staunch believer in the adage, 'A family that eats together, stays together,' and she had no intention of letting any of her family escape. She glared at her husband's place setting, then at the only other chair that didn't have a boy standing behind it. Where was he? He was her most sensitive son, the one with an artistic personality but prone to tantrums and flares of temperament. He was the one who would go off by himself to find somewhere to read. He liked to be alone—and loved cooking.

'Oh, for goodness sake. Go and get him,' she said irritably and to nobody in particular.

The child nearest the door replied with a courteous, 'Yes, Mummy,' and left the room, remembering not to run like a hooligan in his mother's presence. The boy, who would one day be a hippy and a master forger, knew his brother would be for it because he was late for the meal. Violet didn't hold with people being late to her table. She didn't hold with anything on a Wednesday. He wanted to find his older brother and bring him to the dining room fast. Once he knew he was out of his mother's earshot, he called his name and ran down the corridor, his slippers flapping time on the cool Mediterranean tiles.

The foundation was messy and took a while to rub in. It stuck to his hands, and he had nothing to wipe them on. If he left handprints on any of his mother's fine bathroom linen, she'd know somebody had been in her room. That would be crime enough, but Lord forbid she ever discovered what he did on a Wednesday afternoon when he knew she was out for hours. It didn't bear thinking about. He went into the ensuite bathroom and washed his hands in the basin. He covered the top of the soap in Autumn Glow foundation and then had to wash the soap as well as his hands. That got soap all over his hands again, so he had to wash and rinse several times until he was rid of all the suds. He could see that it wasn't all glamour being a girl.

He sat back at his mother's vanity unit and applied a layer of pressed powder. He chose pale blue eye shadow; it brought out the lilac of his eyes. He kohl'ed his inner eyelid with black liner, rouged his cheeks with pink blush, reddened his lips with Cherry Bomb Explosion and finished the look with a thick application of black mascara. The end result looked sultry and feminine. He didn't look like a boy playing with makeup, but a girl with a practised hand. His high cheekbones and full lips made the perfect canvas for his art. Anybody seeing him for the first time might have queried why she was wearing her mum's clothes, but they would have thought she looked beautiful.

He lamented his mother's lack of fashionable clothing. Serviceable tweeds and polyester slacks were the norms for Violet Woods. She had a large selection of special eveningwear for socialising with the Lakeland elite, but they were stored in polythene from the dry cleaners. How he longed to get hold of those dresses with the black lace and sequins.

He'd been doing this for months. It was more than just an urge. It was a compulsion. He twirled in the full-length mirror, satisfied with his look. Now that he'd finished with the intense concentration of putting the makeup on, another part of his mind was taking over. Mother had just one fine item, one piece of feminine clothing that he adored.

Donald, hoping to rekindle their love life, had brought home a pair of delicate French knickers one Valentine's Day. Violet was appalled. It wasn't a man's place to buy underwear. It wasn't seemly. They had a terrible row. After forcing him to tell her where he'd bought them, Violet said that she wouldn't be able to shop in Kendal ever again. Donald argued that a large place like Debenhams in Kendal was hardly likely to remember one nondescript man buying a pair of knickers for his wife.

'Donald.' Violet had admonished. 'Please don't use that word. It's vulgar and most unchristian for a gentleman to be talking about a lady's undergarments in such terms.'

Violet was shocked by her husband's behaviour. Valentine's Day—what piffle, she thought as she stuffed the baby pink knickers into the back of her drawer and out of sight. She was happy with her Marks & Spencer underwear in a hundred per cent cotton with a breathable gusset. Anything else just wasn't hygienic.

The cross-dressing boy had no idea where the knickers had come from, but he was delighted that they had. He wore them under the frumpy old skirt. They felt decadent, and the heavy silk lining under the tweed was forcing the smooth satin of the panties against his young body. His penis, on the cusp of puberty, was rock hard, and his heart raced as he posed. He felt the cold material moving against his turgid penis, and it felt wonderful.

He lay on his mother's bed and pulled the skirt high on his slim thighs so that he could see himself grown under the sheer material of the French knickers. They were just like boxer shorts, really, but without the fly. But boxers had never felt this sumptuous. He fantasised about wearing the satin under his school uniform. The thought was dangerous and exciting. He could only do it on days when he wouldn't have to change for PE. It would be his special secret. He would never have the courage to actually do it, but just the thought of it was enough to make him want to touch himself. He did, tentatively at first. But instinct overtook him and taught him how to manipulate himself within a fistful of baby pink satin. And that's when the new fantasy was born. It was an idea so wrong and so sinful that it put interfering with oneself into the baby-sins bucket. It was wrong. It was dirty and wrong, but it drove him mad at the thought of doing it. His whole body tensed as his hand flew. He felt a strange tightening in his stomach, and seconds later, he experienced a sensation that was new, a bit scary and all-encompassing. He had his first-ever ejaculation, and it left him shocked and quivering.

His mind was in turmoil. He'd made a mess in his mother's panties. Surely, he would go to hell for such a sin. His penis was flaccid now, but his mind was still turgid. The idea that formulated as he interfered with himself wouldn't leave. He cleaned the mess and washed the underwear under the tap. What was he going to do with it now? He couldn't put them back in her drawer, soaking wet. He couldn't put them on the radiator to dry.

In desperation, he flushed them down the toilet. Imagining them getting stuck in the piping and flooding the entire hotel. He was scared as he tried to cover his tracks. What if Mother found out? He felt guilty and dirty, but he lamented the loss of the satin knickers. He put his own pants back on. He was shaking and hadn't had time to replay and think about what had just happened. He needed to take the makeup off, but he had to sit down for a moment. He lay back on the pillows of his mother's bed, still in her blouse, wearing her pearls and her makeup. He closed his eyes to think, and seconds later, he drifted into sleep. He dreamed of hotel rooms filled with sensual female clothing, and in his sleep, his body reacted again.

He heard somebody calling his name. In his dream, he was dressed in lace underwear, a sable fur coat and high heels. The voice was pulling him out of the soft fur, but he didn't want to come out of sleep. It was nice. He heard his name again and opened his eyes. He was awake. The bedroom door was opening. He panicked. He mustn't be caught like this.

The brothers stared at each other. Neither of them spoke. The cross-dresser with the painted face and pearls dangling in his lap was the first to drop his eyes. He looked at the erection pushing through the skirt, alerting his brother so that his eyes, too, focused there.

The forger tugged his hair the way he always did when something upset him. His brother could see that he was shocked and disgusted. And the fact that he didn't mock or tease the cross-dresser showed that it went too deep for that.

'Get out,' the cross-dresser hissed as though the intruder was the one in the wrong. He was angry, the rouge on his cheeks standing out on his pale face, his bright red lips pursed in temper. His blue, lidded eyes flared in anger.

'I'll cover for you. Hurry up and come down. You're late for dinner, and Mother's furious.' The forger closed the door behind him and walked to the dining room, buying himself as much time as possible to make up an excuse for his brother's absence. He could have stayed a few moments to help tidy up the room so that his mother wouldn't know anybody had been in, but he didn't want to see his brother taking off the painted face. It was obscene, and seeing it come off would have been too reminiscent of it going on, and he wanted no part of that.

The cross-dresser arrived at the table, grey with fear and apprehension. Was his dirty secret out in the open and exposed for them to make of it what they would? Or was his brother as good as his word? His pallor served its purpose well and backed up the story that he had been sick. Mother showed maternal concern for half a minute, asking if he was all right before firing a barrage of questions at him to find out what he'd been eating while she was out. Had he been at the fruit trees in the orchard? Had he taken sweets from one of the guests? Had he been associating with dirty children from the estate who might have countless untold and horrendous viruses and illnesses? She was hungry and impatient to eat and finished her inquisition by telling him how disappointed she'd be with him if he vomited at the dining table. The matter, as far as she was concerned, was closed. He was well enough to walk. Therefore he was well enough to eat the meal the good Lord—and the kitchen staff—had provided for him.

When Mother turned her attention to the tureen of roasted parsnips, two pairs of eyes met over the table. The forger touched the ridge

39

of his own temple to indicate a missed smudge of makeup and then dropped his gaze. And the secret that was shared between them remained just that, a secret. A third pair of youthful eyes caught the look. The youngest was the eavesdropper and realised something had happened. He made a mental note to find out what it was from his brothers later, but a game of cricket was organised for the evening, and the vibes he had seen crossing the table were forgotten by the time the meal was finished.

Over the following week, the cross-dresser's mind was congested with the fantasy of going into the guests' rooms to steal clothes and makeup and some nice jewellery, too. It was the middle of the summer holidays, the hotel was booked solid, the weather was hot, and the women were walking around in flimsy dresses and shorts that showed their thighs. He took to sitting in one of the Chesterfield armchairs in reception. He watched the women passing through the foyer, his penis pushing hard against the material of his shorts. He wasn't interested in the women and girls, only in how they dressed and carried themselves. He studied their styles and how they moved. The way he wanted to look and move. He made notes about which guest occupied which room, and the fantasy of sneaking through them and stealing their pretty things turned into a burning desire.

The following Wednesday took an age to come. He sat at breakfast with two spots of high colour on his cheeks and an uncomfortable erection hidden under the table. It was still a dream. He had no intention of actually doing anything. For another hour and a half, it was just a fantasy borne in the mind of a young pubescent discovering himself.

His brothers were cycling to Fell Foot Park for the day. It was perfect. They'd be gone for hours. That left him alone to trawl the corridors of the vast hotel undetected. He'd learned that young boys have an uncanny knack for passing unnoticed among adults. He could check in the register to see which guests had left their keys and had gone off for the day. It would be easy to take his mother's master key from the hook in her private office, and nobody would notice. But it was just a dream. The others tried to get him to go with them, but he said he wanted to finish the book he was reading. The forger looked at him accusingly, and he slopped orange juice from his glass. His mother was too preoccupied with her own Wednesday thoughts to notice.

He waited for a long time after the other boys had gone. His mother left before them, and he checked that his father was still taking fresh produce to the local market that day. He walked around the upper storeys of the hotel for the first hour, talking to the chambermaids and marking their progress along the corridors. He saw a couple leaving room 506. They were full of chatter about sailing on *The Swan* across Lake Windermere. He watched them go around the corner, listened to the lady's clicking heels descending the stairs, and his heartbeat quickened in his chest. He walked by their room and tried the door. It was locked. This was the defining moment. It was the second that turned his fantasy into reality.

He was going to do it.

Getting his mother's key was as easy as expected. Checking the hotel keyboard proved more difficult, but he bided his time until the receptionist was called away. He slipped behind the desk and into the general office, where an enormous board with hanging keys covered the back wall. Guests were encouraged to leave their room keys at reception when they left the hotel in case of loss. The pegs were two-thirds occupied with room keys, and a volt of adrenaline shot through his body.

He contemplated cycling into town to have a copy of the master key made, but he had no money. He had lots of time but didn't want to waste any of it by going out. He had far more exciting things to do. And anyway, he promised himself this was a one-time deal. It would be too risky to do it again, just today, just once. Only today. He'd have to make sure he found lots of the right things the first time.

It would have served his purpose well to be able to jot down the vacant room numbers, but that would be dangerous. If he was seen, difficult questions would have to be answered. He contented himself with writing to memory the first five numbers under the pegs with keys hanging from them.

Making sure the chambermaids were nowhere in sight and that the corridor was clear of guests, he rapped on the first door. He hadn't a clue what he would say if anybody answered and was ready to run at any noise from inside. He was terrified. His mouth was dry and tasted metallic, and he could feel his heartbeat through the artery in his throat.

There was no answer. With trembling hands, he let himself into the room. It was empty. The bed was made, and everything was neat and tidy, despite the chambermaids not having got that far on their cleaning rounds yet. The only sign of habitation was the towelling dressing gown hanging on the back of the door and the neatly folded, *Observer* newspaper beside the bed.

He was disappointed. A quick search of the drawers showed that, despite it being a double room, only one person inhabited it, a man.

He rifled through the guest's belongings, making as little disturbance as possible. In the shallow bedside cabinet drawer, he found some lose money, about eight pounds in coins. He almost took it. He picked it up and felt the weight in his hand. There might be enough to pay for a duplicate key, but it would be stealing. He was going to steal. He had every intention of stealing, that's what he'd come for, but he wanted to keep his sins down to a low number, and taking actual money seemed worse and more sinful than taking somebody's old clothes and stuff. He put the money back, checked to see that nothing was out of place and after peeping around the door to check the corridor was empty, he slipped back out of the room, locking the door behind him.

The second room was better. The bed was made, but the place wasn't as tidy as the last room. Damp towels were thrown on the end of the bed. Mother wouldn't approve of that. He picked them up, folded them and put them on the towel rail in the ensuite bathroom. He stepped over a pair of tiny black panties that were scrunched up and had been worn. He felt a jolt at the thought that if there was one pair, then there would surely be more. He didn't like the thought of touching underwear that was dirty. What kind of lady left her dirty linen on the bathroom floor? He crossed the room, but the thought of those tiny panties drew him back. He picked them up. He rubbed them through his hands, liking the soft feel of them. His fingers found the double layer of the gusset. His penis jerked and rose in his pants as his thumb was the first digit to find the stuff. It had stiffened in the crotch of the panties, and it cracked as he bent the material. He saw the white staining, and a tiny flake of something that had once been wet but had recently dried fell onto his hand. He pulled the underwear up to his nose and rubbed the stained part across his nostrils. The smell wasn't strong, almost undetectable. He had no idea whether it was female stuff or male stuff that had leaked from the woman, but he knew that it was the smell of sex. He'd pulled on himself every day since that first time. He wanted to do it now. He had to squirt his own stuff on top of the stain that was already there. The need to do it was unbearable, but he might be caught. He stuffed the panties into his pocket, forced his mind back to the real job in hand, and breathed hard as he waited for his boyhood to shrink into itself.

The room was an Aladdin's cave of treasures. Bottles of exotic creams and lotions, shampoos and bubble baths filled the shelves in the bathroom. The vanity unit had perfume in fancy bottles and makeup left out. Bracelets and necklaces were strewn amidst the lipstick and blusher. The people in this room had left in a hurry. The wardrobe was hung with shimmering dresses and elegant trouser suits. And, the joy of joys, the top drawer of the dresser was filled with nylon stockings and sinful lingerie.

That first day he only took a few small things. He took a necklace with pretty blue stones set in a crescent-shaped pendant, a chiffon scarf that smelled of a sophisticated perfume, two pairs of sexy panties and a pair of stockings. It was only later, in his own room, that he discovered that you had to have something to hold the stockings up, and he had no idea what that something was.

From another room, he took more panties and a black lacy bra. And from a third, he took a broach in the shape of a heart and a pink underskirt. He was tempted by a bottle of perfume. It looked expensive and had a French name. The bottle was so pretty he wanted it, but when could he wear it? Somebody would notice that he had ladies' perfume on. He didn't have to wear it, though, did he? Just having it, owning it, knowing that it belonged to him would be enough. It would be there. It would be his. He could smell it and imagine what it would be like to dab some on the pressure points of his neck. He felt the stirrings of sexual arousal again and hovered with the bottle in his hand. If he was lucky, the things he had taken might not be noticed straight away. He reasoned that the jewellery might be expensive. He had no way of knowing what was good and what wasn't. But jewellery was so small that somebody might not notice that a piece was missing until they came to want it. He knew his mother wore the same perfume every day. *J' Taime* by Estée Lauder. She would notice if a bottle was stolen, but then his mother would probably notice if a hairgrip was out of place. He wanted the perfume. It was so pretty, so feminine—and too risky. He left it, taking instead some loose change that had been thrown into an otherwise empty trinket dish on the vanity unit and a pale pink lipstick. He didn't take all of the money there and hoped that three-pound coins and fifty-three pence would be enough to have the key replicated.

That was the year that The Halcyon Woods Hotel experienced a spate of thefts. The proprietor, Mrs Violet Woods, made several statements to the police and to the local press, saying that she would not rest until this despicable thief had been caught and taken to book. It had to be a member of staff. The police were ruling nothing out, and at that stage, they had to assume, by the nature of the articles stolen, that it was a female member of staff, probably one of the chambermaids. The staff were all fingerprinted and released without charge. It was a terrible business and not good for the hotel's reputation.

The day the police came to take statements and fingerprint all the staff, he was ill. He vomited several times, guilt rising with the gorge from his stomach. He waited in his room, expecting the police to come for him at any moment, but they didn't come at all.

They returned several times over the following months. He assumed that the police hadn't worked out that the spate of thefts coincided with the school holiday, but they had. The focus of the investigation shifted to the casual staff that Violet employed in the holidays to help out with the seasonal rush. They tracked the school holidays for several terms, and then, when the Windermere secondary school let out for their summer break, there were no thefts. It blew the police theory out of the water. There were a few small incidents two weeks later when Guildmarten Head public boys' school had their term end. These rose to another full-on assault of guests missing property as the long summer months unfolded. The case was never solved.

He felt invincible. The stupid police were too dumb to catch him. He changed and taunted them. He was purposefully sloppy, leaving clues for them to pick up, but they never associated the thefts with the son of the proprietor. He was beyond reproach, and the Woods boys were never formally questioned.

He was caught once, though. That had been hairy. He was in somebody's room and rifling through the woman's knicker drawer when her stupid husband walked in.

He'd been marvellous. All the guests knew the children of Mrs Woods. The man recognised him. While he demanded to know what was going on, the *cross-dresser* stood up and stammered, pretending to be confused. He wasn't frightened. This was the first time he'd ever been caught since his brother found him in his mother's clothes, and yet he was calm and composed. He fed the man a line about his mother asking him to come up to Mrs Burton-Graham's room for her spectacles. He said he was very sorry and could see that he had mistaken room 432 for 423 in his haste. The man clapped him on the back and said what a fine boy he was, how he was a credit to his mother. And that was the end of it. He was concerned that the tale would get back to Mother—but it didn't.

He was untouchable.

It was after that incident that he used the facilities. He would shower in the rooms, take long bubble baths and use the guest's cosmetics in situ. He dressed in their clothes, ate whatever edibles were left in their rooms and made himself tea with the tea-making facilities.

That year he took possession of his own secret dressing room, too. The attics in the hotel were immense. Room after dingy room sat at the top of the house, most of them empty and unopened in years. The boys were forbidden from going up to the attic since they were caught playing hide and seek up there. Mother considered it a dangerous place for them. And then they grew up, and although some of the rooms were used for storage, most of them were empty. He'd taken one of those right at the very back of the attics in a room leading off another room. During the police investigations, only the staff were suspected. None of the workforce lived in, so the hotel was never searched. He had fixed external and internal locks to the door in case it was ever found. He had the only keys. It was risky, and he knew that one day his room would be discovered, but nobody would ever link it back to him.

He couldn't believe his luck the day he found his greatest treasure. He entered a guest's room and almost hit the ceiling with shock. There was somebody there, sitting at the dressing table. It was only when the shock faded that he saw it wasn't a person. It was a polystyrene head with a long auburn wig attached. It was beautiful. He had to have it. He'd become selective over the months. He had stopped taking indiscriminately. Clothes had to be designer labels. Perfume had to be the best. He never used it but had a collection of fine fragrances that he knew would be his to wear one day. His tastes in jewellery had refined. He took only gold and precious stones. He would have traded his entire collection for that one wig.

He put it on and felt the long curls cascade down his back. He masturbated on the woman's bed, naked apart from the fabulous wig and her heels. In that wig, he was a woman.

His need for danger and excitement was enhanced too. He had stolen for over three years. He was fifteen, and his mother didn't terrify him the way she used to. Part of him wanted to be caught, but another part still craved his mother's love and pride. He hated the fact that he yearned for her approval.

Two weeks before he left to begin his chef training, he went out with a bang. He'd be caught, but he needed the excitement. Just as he'd played with his ideas that first week before he committed any crime, he fantasised about the way his coming out as a cross-dresser would go.

They had a talent contest scheduled for that night. The entire hotel would be there. His mother in her finery, his father in a suit, all his brothers, the ones with stubble would shave, the ones without, would have their faces scrubbed until they gleamed. It was a charity bash, and Mother was so good at charity.

The boy dressed with precision. He wore stilettos and walked on them with more grace than many women he'd seen. He wore stockings and a short skirt, a bat-winged top that was currently popular and a wide belt, almost as broad as the skirt underneath it. He spent more time than usual putting on his makeup, and when he donned the wig, he felt like a natural-born woman.

He walked through the hotel, and heads turned. Everybody looked at the stunning girl. It was that kind of look. He walked past his mother's table. Looked right into her eyes. She glared her disapproval. She didn't hold with hussies flaunting their bodies for men to be tempted. She didn't like strumpets in her hotel. Two of his brothers were talking to girls at another table. They looked up as the stunner passed by. The other two brothers were standing at the bar. They stared as he walked between them with a polite, 'Excuse me, please.' It was a buzz. Nobody recognised him. He was a butterfly in the light, a chameleon—he was untouchable.

Chapter Six

1 8th July 1979

The residents didn't go on trips very often.

They weren't called children on Hathaway wing. Simon didn't like moving to Hathaway when he was eighteen, and he was happy on Brontë. He was very worried that Mummy wouldn't be able to find him. She always waited in his bedroom. But it wasn't his bedroom anymore. It belonged to somebody else. He worried that his mummy belonged to somebody else, too. Maybe part of him even wished she did, and that made him feel bad. Simon loved his mummy and was a bad boy for thinking bad things. Sometimes, when she was shouting at him, Simon imagined his mummy burning in a big orange fire. He tried really hard not to think bad things about her because she often seemed to know what he was thinking, and if she knew he was watching her burn in a big fire, she would be mad at him again. She pinched him sometimes when his tongue flopped out, and he couldn't help that. Simon couldn't imagine what she'd do if she knew about the fire. He was good at imagining fire stuff but not good at knowing what Mummy would do. He just knew that she was always mad at him.

They were going on a big bus. But it was Tuesday. They always banged drums and tangerines and sang *This Old Man He Had One* on a Tuesday. Simon didn't want to go on a big bus. He wanted to go on the school bus to school and bang drums and sing *This Old Man He Had One*. Sharon Peat always got sick on big buses that went far. Gloria said they weren't going far, only to Lancaster and that Sharon would be fine because she'd given her a tablet. She said he'd like it at Williamson's Park. But it was Tuesday. He moved from one foot to the other, and Gloria sighed and gave him a tablet, too.

David, one of the helpers, pushed Simon from behind while Gloria and Helen pulled him from the front. He didn't want to sit on the fifth row back. He always sat on the second row. That's where he sat when he went to school. Mike didn't mind moving from the second-row seat. He couldn't talk, and he didn't mind about anything much. Simon sat quietly on the bus. His eyes glazed, and his tongue lolled out of his half-open mouth. He thought about drums and hummed *This Old Man*. Gloria sang it, and some people joined in until Sharon got sick. It wasn't the same without drums and his blue tangerine, anyway.

Williamson's Park was lovely, but there were too many hills and lots of steps and his legs hurt. Gloria said he'd complain about the colours in paradise. Simon had never been there so didn't know if he'd like the colours or not, but he knew that he was hot and that his feet were hurting.

They had a picnic in the shadow of the Ashworth Memorial building. It was a beautiful day. Sharon had stopped being sick and wanted lots to eat, but Gloria wouldn't let her have lots because they still had to go home on the big bus. Simon thought that Sharon should walk home because she made the big bus smell really bad.

After lunch, they went to see the butterflies. The butterfly house had some lizards and bats and was hot. Simon liked them but was glad they couldn't get out of their homes. Gloria was fascinated by all the plants, but Simon didn't like the way the butterflies were just there, not fastened up or tied down or anything. He wondered what it would be like if one of them fluttered near his face. He gave his low moaning noise that sometimes came just before and during an epileptic fit, but sometimes he did that noise anyway, so Gloria held his hand and promised him that nothing would hurt him. Up to that point, they had only seen little butterflies. Rounding a corner, there was an orchid, but the beauty of the flower faded next to the enormous butterfly resting on it. Simon couldn't understand how something so big didn't make the flower bend all the way over until its head fell off.

Gloria was in her element. She scrambled through the guidebook that had a section on identifying all the species of butterfly. It cost her three pounds ninety-nine, and Simon thought that was probably more than a pound. He wasn't impressed. Gloria was his care assistant, but she let go of his hand to find the big butterfly, and Simon didn't think that was very caring at all. Simon was scared. If the big monster fluttered near his face, it would cover him completely, and he might not be able to breathe. It was hot in the butterfly house, and he could feel his chest tightening and thought that he'd drown.

A man called Callum was taking them around. He was a guide and told them all about the different species of animals and flowers. He was very interesting, and Gloria listened to him while scrabbling through the book for a picture of the massive butterfly. She liked to do things herself sometimes and didn't wait for the man to tell them about it. Simon was bored. He was hot and uncomfortable, too, and he was uneasy and nervous, all symptoms that led to his agitation.

'Here we are,' Gloria said, grinning like a fool. Couldn't she see the danger? 'It's a Goliath butterfly, and guess what, Simon? It's the second biggest species in the world and has a wingspan of almost a foot. They can only be found in Indonesia. Aren't we lucky to see such a beautiful thing right here in Lancaster?'

The butterfly chose that moment to flex its wings. It fluttered, once, like a tablecloth lifting in a breeze, and then it rose resplendent into the air. As it lifted, Simon saw its ugly little face and realised that butterflies aren't pretty at all. It's just an act they put on to fool people they want to drown. The butterfly had the face of a bluebottle, only much, much bigger. Its beady eyes peered into his, and the long black things called antennae twitched towards his face.

They hadn't seen the birds yet. As if on cue, there was an enormous batting of wings that Simon thought was coming from the butterfly. Simon didn't like wings. They sounded dry and feathery. The hot house smelled bad. It smelled old and green and rotten. He knew the butterfly was big, but he couldn't understand that it could make so much noise just by flapping its wings. If he'd looked up, he would have seen the real culprits, but Simon was transfixed on the butterfly that was coming to suffocate him.

The miniature murmuration of starlings rose as one. They did a circuit of the hothouse before looping the loop and swooping down on the visitor's heads. People squealed in delight as the birds landed on them, hoping for pickings from the specially prepared bags of birdfeed. The cheeky birds were gentle but greedy, and they dive-bombed the visitors with aeronautical precision, never missing their mark.

Simon didn't have a bag of food. He was frightened and waved his arms in the air, and that attracted the bird's attention. Three of the starlings flew towards him. He wasn't moaning now. He was screaming. The birds landed on him, two on his arms and one on the top of his head. They were screeching. The noise was cacophonous, echoing in the stillness of the hothouse.

Gloria tried to calm him, but he was a large man-child in a frenzy of terror, and he fought her off. People stopped what they were doing to watch the Downs bloke having some sort of fit. Mothers grabbed their children to them. The world slowed down.

Callum ran towards Simon. Their female Goliath was right in front of the Mongol's face. She was their rarest and most valuable exhibit. He made three steps while Simon thrashed. The starlings took flight and rose into the air, adding to the mayhem, their wings beating, beating, fluttering, and beating. The noise was too loud, amplified by his rush of adrenaline. Simon beat them off, catching one on its tail feathers and knocking it into a spin. It landed safely on the floor, shook itself and rose again to perch somewhere high up and safe. Still, there was the beating in his ears, loud droning. Too hot. The place was too hot. He couldn't breathe.

His arm came down fast, smashing into the valuable Goliath. She fluttered to the floor and lay twitching for a second, broken. Simon didn't notice. He was too immersed in his panic to see. His feet pounded on the dying butterfly, ripping its delicate wings and turning it to dust on the floor.

The crowd gasped. Gloria moaned just the way Simon did when he got upset. A piece of the green wing with a black eye blot looking towards him hung over the front of Simon's shoe.

Callum reached out to Simon. His fingers connected with the sleeve of his shirt. Simon batted him away as though he was just another butterfly.

He was running for the exit. He didn't mean to knock the children over. He didn't see them. All he could see were wings flapping around him. All he could hear was the beating, thrumming boom of wings. All he could feel was his terror. He pushed a little girl. She lost her balance, and her father's arm shot out too slowly to catch her. She teetered for a moment on the brink of the edge before falling into the Koi carp pool with a loud splash. A warder jumped in to save her before she was hurt or suffered any physical harm. Simon came into contact with four children, innocent children, and several adults, all of them with wide, frightened eyes, all fighting to get out of his way. The children were knocked to the ground, into water or bashed into walls. Adults screamed about assault and yelled for the police to be called.

Callum was chasing him. He saw his beautiful Goliath, so gentle and serene, cut down and killed by the Mongol. People like that shouldn't be allowed out in public. They should be locked up and kept away from decent folk. He had cared for and tended to all the butterflies for four years, but the Goliath was his favourite. He didn't tell any of his mates, but he called her Lotus, sometimes she'd rest on him, and he talked to

55

her. People would say he was mad, but he liked to think she knew him and waited for him to come in every morning.

He was so mad that when he got hold of him, he was going to punch that stupid fat face. All Lotus ever did was make people happy. What had that thing ever done to make anybody happy with his fat body and moony face? Where was the beauty in that great useless lump of humanity?

He caught up with Simon by the face painting stall. Clowns and tigers, monkeys and vampires, turned to stare with wide, innocent eyes. A second throng of panicked parents, sensing danger, drew their young into their embrace.

Callum had tears of anger and loss stinging his eyes. He let out a bellow and flew through the air towards Simon's legs. He caught him in a rugby tackle, and Simon turned to face his danger before going down on his back. The rucksack he always wore protected his spine from the hard concrete, but his head made contact with a sickening crunch. Again the world slewed, and Gloria was in time to see Simon's head bounce off the paving. He'd bitten his tongue, and a line of spittle and blood hit Callum in the chest. Simon's eyes were wide and pleading for mercy.

People screamed, and a crowd formed a circle around the action. They were ghouls moving forward to see what was happening better. Callum straddled Simon and drew his right arm back to punch him in the face.

He stopped mid-swing and looked appalled at what he was about to do. Beating a disabled person was a sin. Simon knew that, but Callum didn't. All the fight left him, and his fist fell to his side. People jumped at him to pull him away. He rolled off Simon and held out a hand to help the boy to his feet.

It was too much. Simon's eyes flickered erratically before turning up and rolling backwards until only the whites showed. His body jerked and spasmed. Pink, foamy spittle frothed out of the corners of his mouth. He made the low cow noise. It looked as though a demented puppeteer was pulling his arms and legs to make them jerk. But Simon was away from it all. He was in his peaceful place.

He woke up several times in the hospital. He'd taken a nasty knock to the head and done more damage during the seizure. He asked for his mummy, and Gloria promised to get her.

But Mummy was too busy to come. It was Tuesday, not Wednesday, so she didn't have a window.

When she did come, she was angry. She called him names and said that if she'd known what he was, the good Lord could strike her down stone, stiff dead, but she'd never have had him.

Simon didn't blame his mummy for not wanting him for what he was. It was horrible being a butterfly killer.

Chapter Seven

Violet hated watching her boys grow into men. One at a time, they slipped through her fingers and weren't just her boys anymore. They were people in their own right, and she hated that. She had held them to her, protected them from the world. They were projections of her, innocent but in need of firm management.

She stood open-mouthed and speechless the first time one of them had risen in front of her and defied her command. He knew his own mind, that boy of hers. He was her strong one. He was a fifteen-year-old hippy the first time he stood, hands on hips, furious points of crimson on his cheeks and said, 'Mother, I will not have time to practise my trombone tonight. I have other plans.' Where was the wheedling voice? 'Aw, do I have to?' It was the most rebellious thing any of them had ever said to her.

He didn't sound like her son, this gruff-voiced man-becoming with determination blazing in his eyes.

'You will do whatever I tell you to do, my boy.'

'I'm sorry, Mother, I don't want to argue with you. But I've had enough of practising my trombone every night, followed by another hour on the violin, followed by a third of homework before bed. From now on, I'll play when I want to play. I've put in the practice. Since I was eight years old, I've practised my music for two hours a night, five days a week. Surely music is supposed to be a passion, something inside you. I'm coming to detest it. You are driving me to hate it.'

'How dare you hurl your unfounded accusations? Do you have any idea how much I've spent on you and your brothers so that you can attain the high standard you have as a competent musician? All I ask is a little hard work in return. Is some dedication from you too much to wish for? I expect loyalty from my flesh and blood. That awful rock and roll babble that you try and call music is rotting your brain, child.'

It was the same old tired guilt trip, she knew she relied on aged material, dredged up every time one of them dared to disagree with her, but it had always worked before.

'And, what's more, I think it's time we had our own bedrooms. All our lives, we've had to share. Will you please at least think about it, Mother?' He left the room with his too-long-for-his-body legs taking giant strides across the Axminster carpet. His broadening shoulders were flung back and defiant. He left her standing, mid-lecture, without waiting at attention to be dismissed. 'Bitch,' he said, too far from her and too low to be heard.

'Come back here right now. Don't you dare walk away from me. You just wait until I tell your father,' she yelled after him. That was a first, too. Violet had never relied on Donald for backup in any situation. She'd never needed to.

She lost him that day. In standing up to her, he made the transition from boy to man. He stayed until he was sixteen, and school was finished for good, but he was the first of the Woods boys to leave home. He knew the day he left that he'd never live under his mother's smothering control again. He went to college and, from there, to university studying mathematics and the sciences. Watching him leave home broke his mother's heart for ten minutes, but she recovered nicely in time for the seven-thirty pensioners' bingo.

On the day of the argument, he stormed to his room, resolute and determined that he'd make a stand against Violet's bullying. He hadn't thought past winning the fight and had no idea what to do with his allocated music practice time. He took a transistor radio apart that had broken months before. He loved anything technical or with working parts, and he broke down every component of the radio that could be taken to bits. He cleaned each piece on a soft cloth and lined them up in front of him. He gave thought to putting it back together and the intricate assembly. His fingers worked with a sure deftness and instinct, more than memory, told him where each component belonged. In a short time, he was turning the dial on the old-fashioned radio to find a station. His mood was calm and tranquil. He was doing what he loved. This boy was a fixer of broken things.

The first station he found came alive beneath his fingers in a hiss of sibilant static. A song was playing that he didn't know. He wasn't listening to it. He was too busy being pleased with himself for fixing a radio that half an hour earlier had been destined for the dustbin. Something happened to him that afternoon, sitting on his knees on the bedroom floor, his eyes glowing with calm and quiet pleasure. The words came out of the radio and engulfed him. They were sung just for his ears. He straightened and listened.

If I could save time in a bottle,

The first thing that I'd like to do,
Is save every day 'til eternity passes,
So I could spend each day with you.

That single verse held his future in its melody. As though a light had shone through the ceiling and slapped him on the head, he knew what he was going to do with the rest of his life. The hippy, who that day had stood up to his domineering mother, was going to make time.

Violet was wary of him from that afternoon. He was different. He had grown-up confidence and wasn't as malleable. She was frightened that this newfound independence would rub off on the rest of her children. She had their futures written and their careers mapped out. They would follow their parents into the family business. She wanted all of her boys to work in the hotel, all in positions of responsibility, pulling together to make it better than it was. The Halcyon Woods Hotel was a family affair, and she intended to keep it that way. Her boys would be allowed to go off and finish their education at university. She would even permit them a year to play on the continent—and find themselves—if she had to. That was the fashionable thing. But it was always understood that the boys would return after their year out, funded by Violet as a bribe, to take their rightful positions in the business. They had been groomed for it since they were old enough to stand. One day, Violet and Donald would hand over the reins of the company to their children. It was already written.

The thief was her clever boy with a penchant for fraud. He was the eldest and was happy to slot into the role his mother carved out of the lodestone for him. He didn't have any ambition or dreams of his own and was willing to float on the prophecies of Violet. After all, it was in his best interests to do so. The fraudster did all his wrongdoings well away from his mother's sight. He never challenged her. He passed from boy to man without an angry word, and it was never threatened that he would be struck from the parental heritage. He worked hard at manipulating his mother while all the time keeping her sweet. He went from public school to university, reading mathematics and science like his brother, but alongside those subjects, he crammed hard to fit in an accountancy course and a degree in hotel management. His life road was charted, and he saw no valid reason to veer from it.

Like one of the twins, the chef with a preference for pink, he took stupid chances. Sometimes, when the bar areas were deserted, the fraudster swooped in, as calculating as a magpie, and steal from the till. It was two years before security cameras would be installed, but by the time they were, the first four Woods boys were all pursuing their education elsewhere. There were sackings and raised indignant voices when the tills were down. Violet had no time for the innocent until proven guilty clause that the rest of Britain clung to as our birthright. If money couldn't be accounted for in a Halcyon Woods till, then whoever had control of that till, at that time, was removed from her employment. Along with the other spate of thefts, the finger of accusation never stuck its bony presence in any of her children's faces.

The eavesdropper was her thoughtful boy, but he didn't care for others. Thoughtful was the only adjective she could find to suit this son, who wasn't always a nice person—sly would have fit him better, but Violent stuck with thoughtful. She didn't like to see any unpleasant traits in her little men. Sly and cunning were two words that fit equally well, but she didn't like those. This boy flapped his ears at private conversation, pressed himself against closed doors to listen, and told tales out of school. He held no allegiance to anybody and was often labelled a grass and a turncoat by his brothers. The first sign of trouble, and without any form of discipline or torture, this one would sing like a canary in spring for the pure joy of doing it. He had a head for facts but never used it for storing anything useful. All his learning was deleted in favour of an empty head in which to store gossip and salacious tittle-tattle. When he was twelve, he kept a journal. He was obsessed with filling it. Book after book was written and then locked away in his personal safe. For three years, when asked what he wanted for Christmas and Birthdays, he said he wanted a safe to keep his personal stuff locked away. The others wanted one, too, but for them, it was only a whim. Violet sent men to manufacture a hole in the wall big enough to hold a small safe. He kept a picture of his mother over it and joked that it would deter any would-be safebreakers. His brothers all had a crack at opening the combination on the safe. They were never fewer than three numbers away from success.

He knew things.

And what he knew, he wrote in his journals.

He was the youngest and her favourite boy. She smothered him the most, the one who would never leave her. He was devoted to his mother. He wanted to be like her in strength and character. His childhood wasn't easy, but he felt that it had made him the fine man that he came to be. In truth, he wasn't a fine man. He was a Mummy's boy, precious and pathetic. He debated at the debating society and came out with a swelled head after shouting everybody down until he was hoarse. It didn't matter if his opinion was a valid one, only that he was heard. The other members stopped attending the society because they couldn't stand being in the same room as him.

He made patches for clothes and wanted to be a hippy like his brother, but his mother wouldn't let him grow his hair past his collar. He wasn't allowed to sew the patches he made onto his clothes either, so he made them with the intention of selling them to other people at festivals around the country. But his mother wouldn't let him go to festivals—rough places, full of dirty dropouts, she said—so he made his patches and kept them in a bag in his wardrobe. He liked to sit in the hotel foyer cutting pieces of felt and sewing them together, but Mother said he looked like a sissy sitting in public sewing, so she made him go to his room, as though making patches was something to be ashamed of. He collected things, too. Beer mats and beer towels, stamps and patches, pin badges and dead insects, Super Cars cards and later, real supercars as they hit the market.

He took eggs from the nests of roosting birds.

He would have made the perfect bookworm, but he didn't like books. He liked blackmail. Reading took too much of his attention, and he had no opportunity to voice his opinion. The only other thing he liked doing was talking at the guests. He'd hang around reception and then pounce. Sometimes he saw them poking their heads around the graphite pillars in reception before running out of the door and down the drive to freedom. It didn't matter, and he wasn't offended. He'd catch them on their return.

Violet would stand at reception, glowing with pride as she watched her friendly son, deep in conversation with a party of hotel guests. He was her ambassador, and his arms would gesticulate with enthusiasm as he signalled the air or slapped the table for emphasis. This was the last of her children still at home. She wouldn't let him go—she wouldn't. He was such a good boy, this one.

* * *

The gambler liked to play cards. What started as a bit of fun was soon a nuisance. He had to be stopped from looking for likely people to trap into a game of Newmarket for pennies. The gambler liked two things. He liked girls, and he liked money, the latter because he discovered that money could buy him girls. He was fourteen when a five-pound note and ten fags bought him his first blowjob. Suzie Philips met him after their last period of the day. They found a quiet place in the woods at the back of the hotel. She'd never done it before, but that was okay because the gambler had nothing to compare it to, and he blew like Old Yeller under a high-pressure build.

She tried to kiss him afterwards, but he didn't want any of that. 'I've got to go now,' he said, backing away and putting distance between them. 'I'll see you in school tomorrow.' He was disgusted when he saw her clearing her throat by making little coughing noises, but if the price was right, he'd do it again.

'Hey, what about my fags and money?'

He walked back to her, pulled the crumpled fiver out of his trouser pocket, and handed it to her. He took a ten-pack of Embassy No. 1 from the inside pocket of his school blazer, opened the cellophane, took a cigarette out of the pack, and lit it, 'One for the road, babe.' He'd heard James Dean say that in a film. He thought it was cool. 'That was great, by the way. I need a fag after that. See you tomorrow.'

He threw the packet with the other nine cigarettes to her. She tried to catch them but failed and had to scramble in the fallen leaves to find them. He swaggered as he walked away and never looked back until he was sure that she'd left. He doubled back and met Pete Walker and Jamie Dodd at the clearing. They'd come out of the cover of the trees.

'You jammy bastard,' Pete said. 'I can't believe she just did that. She went with Robbie Jones and wouldn't even let him touch her tits.'

'I've still got a hard-on,' moaned Jamie. 'It's not fair, you get a blowie, and we have to pay for it.'

'Don't bet with the best if you can't afford to lose. And speaking of which, gentlemen, I do believe you have some settling up to do.' The gambler was smiling. This was one of the best days ever.

The boys dug in the pockets of their school pants and pulled out their money. They coppered up two pounds fifty each and handed it to the gambler. Jamie put his hand into his blazer pocket and brought out ten fags. He took the cellophane off, took one out of the packet and lit it.

'One for the road, mate. I need a fag after that,' The gambler snatched the lit cigarette from between his friend's lips and put it in his mouth. 'Some men are born to win, and others will always be losers. Fool.' He grinned, turned his back on his mates and walked away, making sure that his strut was cool and his manner confident.

At the other side of the clearing in the woods, a fourth boy was sitting with his back against a tree. The eavesdropper was writing, his hand flying across the page. He had a sly smile on his face.

Violet was in her office. Mornings were a time of brisk efficiency where none of the staff dared to breathe out of line. It was her custom, from nine until luncheon, to review the mail, deal with customer complaints, and meter out staff discipline.

Thumbing through the post, one envelope caught her attention. It was plain white, household brand stationary and unremarkable in itself. What made it stand out was that it was typed—badly. The margins hadn't been set properly, and the formatting of the address was mis-aligned. Whoever had typed this wasn't proficient in clerical skills. If it was a job application, it would go straight into the bin.

She read the single sheet of paper as the colour drained from her face.

I know about your disabled son.

Put fifty quid, in used ten-pound notes, in an empty After Eight *box. There's a bin outside the nut house, just by the bus stop.*

*On Wednesday, when you visit, put the box with the cash inside the bin
just before you get on the 5-15 bus.*

Do not tell nobody.

Do not go to the police.

If you ignore this letter

I will ruin you.

Violet pushed the letter into her pocket and took the rest of the day
off. She read it many times over the day. But the thing that she couldn't
get her head around was the sum of money that the blackmailer had
demanded. Fifty pounds was a ridiculous amount. Violet assumed
that the letter meant fifty thousand pounds, but it was specific— fifty
pounds. Could the imagination of the blackmailer really be so limited?
It had to be one of the staff at Great Gables. It couldn't be anybody
else. They'd promised to protect her identity from the menial staff. It
was enough that they had to know she was the boy's mother. She would
have them all sacked. They were useless anyway. But she didn't—when
the time came, she didn't say a word. She treated herself to a small box
of *After Eight* mints and gorged on them until she felt sick, but she
couldn't stop until the box was empty. She wanted to feel sick.

The Eavesdropper was in the park across the road. There was a
man-sized concrete tube artfully arranged on the grass, whether the
council felt it constituted modern art, or it was some flight of fancy
of a psychologist's idea of stimulation for young people, or if, indeed,

the council workmen had just dumped it when their job was done, wasn't clear. Youths smoked in it at night, and it smelled of urine, but that didn't matter. He had a clear view of the bus stop from where he crouched.

Violet looked agitated. She had her crocodile skin handbag hooked over her arm and was holding her white gloves in the same hand. Every few seconds, she looked up the street into the windows of the care home as if they held the answers she sought. As the bus came around the corner, she opened her bag as though she was taking out her fare. She pulled the package out and put it into the waste bin beside her before boarding the bus. The eavesdropper watched it pull away and saw his mother's gaunt but fleshy face pressed against the window, staring towards the home.

Three weeks later, he sent a second letter, this time asking for a hundred pounds, a week after that— a thousand. It was more money than he'd ever seen before. He took it out of his safe and counted it at night. He loved the feel of it, the sound of it, even the smell. He imagined buying his own hotel. It was his dream.

During this period, Violet was distracted. She wasn't eating properly, skipping meals and then gorging on chocolates and biscuits long into the night. She'd purge her shame into the toilet bowl and then go for another litre of ice cream from the hotel freezers. She didn't sleep and often got up an hour after going to bed to walk the corridors and sometimes the grounds at night. Every payment had escalated. It was well within her means for now, but if it continued, she'd be ruined. She had to go to the police. It couldn't go on. She'd be publicly outed as the mother of one of those damaged people—and she was Violet Woods. She couldn't stand it.

The gambler knew his brother was up to something. The eavesdropper was always shifty, it was inherent in his DNA, but he'd been playing up and was acting odd. The forger had noticed it too. He was scribbling in his stupid diaries more. On Wednesday afternoons, he didn't walk home with the others anymore. He said he had somewhere to be. The gambler thought he had a secret girlfriend until he found a crumpled typewritten envelope on the floor by his bed. It was addressed to their mother. That night, after dinner, the Eavesdropper sloped away to his room. The gambler followed him and waited for the familiar, beep, beep, beep of his safe mechanism opening. He held his ground for another few minutes and then burst into the room.

The eavesdropper was sitting on his bed surrounded by money. More money than the gambler had ever seen. The eavesdropper tried to cover his stash with his quilt, but it was too late.

'Will you look at all that money? Where did you get it?' He looked at his brother. 'What are you up to?'

He wouldn't say. The gambler dragged him off the bed and straddled him on the floor, picking his head up and banging it onto the carpet. He wouldn't tell. He looked as though he saw stars and was crying, but he wouldn't utter a word about where he'd got the money. The gambler wanted in. He helped himself to most of it anyway but needed to know the source. He left the eavesdropper a few quid, but not much. 'Can you get more?'

The eavesdropper shook his head. He hated the gambler. He wanted to kill him. But mostly, he was relieved that it was only his very stupid brother, the chef. He could get more. He'd almost been caught, but all he lost were his most recent hauls. They'd soon be replenished and more besides. The gambler still asked where the money had come from, and he bullied him to find out if there was any more. The eavesdropper knew how to make money. It was so easy, but he wouldn't do it to his own family again. That was just his launch pad. He was honing his art and turning his attention to the outside community and the richer, most influential hotel guests. He wrote everything he saw and everything he heard in his diaries.

Chapter Eight

Andrew knew the day he left for University that he never wanted to come back to the hotel as a live-in occupant. He was going to complete his education. And he'd take a year out after his second year, but it would be done on his terms and under his own steam. He'd broken away from his mother on the day of the argument over music practice, and they both knew it. Andrew turned into a man that day, and there was no going back.

It wasn't long before he wished he could be a little boy again, protected and coddled by his overbearing mother.

When he came home in the summer holidays of 1984, he'd finished his second year at university. He was worn and troubled. Violet didn't know that look. She was used to the hungover, cannabis-induced appearance of him and his brothers when they came home, usually with an entourage of hangers-on for summer break, but this was different. Andrew was edgy and introverted. He looked frightened but wouldn't talk to his parents about his problems.

He was a man weighed down with guilt and secrets.

Andrew left home, and Violet and Donald didn't see their son again for five years.

It was the Thirteenth of October 1989. Everybody knew the date. It was branded into all the staff's brains because it was Violet's birthday. Simon Peter—SP— was stomping around in a foul mood. He was on the warpath, and everybody was wary of crossing him. Everything had to be perfect, all arrangements adhered to, the staff beautifully turned out and looking fresh and efficient. Every attention to detail was considered and acted upon. SP's shrapnel voice rang through the kitchen, the dining hall, the ballroom and reception. The man gave the impression of being everywhere. He held a clipboard under his arm, ticking off jobs as they were done and adding new ones at an alarming rate as they occurred to him. Cigarette breaks were foregone, and coffee cooled in staffroom mugs as another bouquet of flowers arrived and needed arranging.

Julia Morgan was working in reception that afternoon. She was sick of being told, 'This isn't right. That is wrong.' Julia prided herself on doing a good job, as she kept telling Linda Bell, who was working the reception desk with her.

'If he shouts at me once more, I'll ram his clipboard so far up his arse that he'll be chanting out his orders falsetto without needing to look at it.'

Linda laughed. 'You'll have a job, mate. I bet his arse is so clenched it would take a JCB to prize it open.'

The girls were still laughing when they saw the couple who'd wandered in from the street. They were used to the hippies. Violet didn't like them. Windermere, although exclusive in Lakeland society, still had its element of undesirables. People who, according to Violet, lived in packs like wolves and roamed the streets in their beards, beads and peculiar odours. She had put a large sign on the hotel entrance, next to the one that said *No hikers: boots and backpacks must not be brought into the hotel*. The hippy sign said *No Hippies: Patchouli oil must not be worn in the hotel. Anybody caught in possession of illegal substances will be prosecuted*.

The Halcyon Woods Hotel did not encourage hippies.

The couple looked tired, as though they'd travelled a long way. She was heavily pregnant, and he supported her and their possessions, which were packed in the forbidden backpacks. Either they'd been too weary to see the sign, or they'd chosen to ignore it. She had two plaits and wore men's boots, and he had dirty hair past his shoulders and an unkempt beard that covered most of his face and chest.

'May I help you?' Julia asked stiffly in a different voice from the one she'd been talking to Linda in. She didn't add, 'Sir,' and there was no welcoming smile to accompany the clipped words. Snobbery, along with malice, is an emotion that spreads like an infection, but Julia was too caught up in her position of assumed power to notice it.

The man opened his mouth to speak, but SP was already homing in like a torpedo.

'You people can't come in here looking like that. We have a dress code. There's a sign,' he finished, as though that explained everything.

The hippie's narrow eyes opened wider, and the sun-bronzed crows-feet wrinkled into his hairline. 'Well, SP, you pompous old bastard. I see the old lady has taught you well.' Despite the insult, the words were warm, and the man smiled through them.

SP stood with one arm, half raised, a barrier as he tried to herd the couple back to the main entrance. He furrowed his brow and then burst into laughter. People quietly reading *The Times* in the Chesterfield sofas looked up in irritation. They were amazed to see the cause of the unruly commotion was one of the Woods' blokes.

'Andy? Is it you?' he grabbed the filthy traveller in a suit-crumpling bear-hug. 'Where the hell have you been, you sod? We hoped you were dead.' They laughed. 'What the hell are you doing here?' He held Andrew at arm's length and looked at him, checking that it really was his brother and not an impostor hoping to take his place. 'Come on, come into the kitchen quick.' Julia and Linda looked at each other with open mouths as SP shouted at them over his shoulder, 'Not a word to anyone.'

'Yes, Mister Woods,' they chorused. Old Witchy Woods wasn't going to like this.

James was still the head chef at the time. It would be another two years before the court case and shame, and Violet would send him to exile in London. SP was dragging the man by the arm towards the kitchen, yelling James' name at the top of his voice. 'This is going to be the best present ever for Ma. She'll be stoked. James, James, look who I've got.' They disappeared through the swing doors. 'You are going to have a shave before the party, though, aren't you, mate? You niff a bit.' These were the last words the receptionists heard from SP and the stranger.

The pregnant woman was left standing in the middle of reception with the two overstuffed backpacks at her feet. 'You'd better sit down, I suppose,' Julia said. 'Can I get you a glass of water or anything?'

And that was how the prodigal son returned.

Andrew and his new wife were hidden until the present giving, and for once, Violet was speechless, and her tears were genuine. Violet was delighted to have her son returned to her and thanked the Lord many times that evening. Andrew refused the tuxedo that SP tried to insist he wore. 'My days of being told how to dress are long over, bro,' he said, thinking back to the straw boater and striped blazer days. He wore the least creased and dirty of his own clothes, a pair of khaki shorts and a cheesecloth shirt that bore the merest olive stain from their fruit picking in Greece the previous summer. He wore battered Jesus sandals, but his feet were clean, his toenails clipped, and his beard partially tamed.

Like SP, Violet didn't recognise Andrew as he was led to her table during the party. Her lip curled with disgust.

'And here's the biggest surprise of all. Look who's come home for your birthday.'

'Hello, Mother. Surprise.'

And then there was hugging, crying, and more hugging. Mother duck had her little ducklings all present and not quite correct, but they were around her again. John was home on holiday from his work in London, and that night the champagne flowed. All ills were forgotten, old scores laid to rest, and misdemeanours brushed under the red carpet for the evening.

Violet hated Beth, Andrew's wife, on sight, not least because of the huge swelling that she carried and flaunted in front of her. 'You're going to be a Grandma, Mother,' Andrew said, glowing with pride. The girl was in her final month. Her breasts were swollen and heavy, readying themselves to nourish the infant to come. She wore a thin sundress and no bra. Her panties were visible through the sheer material, and the way she flaunted her condition was shameless. She wore flat espadrilles on her feet, the laces climbing bare sun-browned legs. Violet even managed to find fault with them and said they were indecent and the type of things that only a shameless hussy would wear. But, for this night only, though her expression said it all, she kept her opinions hushed and shared them with only a select few.

'So, am I to assume that you're married?' she asked with ice in her tone.

'You may indeed, Mother. You may indeed. Been married for the past three years. May I introduce you to Mrs Bethany Woods? Your daughter-in-law, my wife, and the mother of my children, of which there are several and will be many more. And long may I hope to enjoy making every one of them.'

'Really, Andrew, there's no need for that kind of talk,' Violet said, shocked. Andy grinned at Beth, who was shy and blushing. He'd always loved winding his mother up.

'You have children? I'm a Grandmother, and you never bothered to so much as send us a postcard. Shame on you, boy.'

'Come on now, Ma. This is a day of celebration. Save the recriminations for another day. We've come a long way to be with you tonight.'

'Tell me about your children.' Her voice was frosty and hurt, but her eyes burned with curiosity.

'Let me see if I can remember them all. It'll be a first if I can reel them off without missing anybody out. We have Rainbow Viola. She's the eldest. She's almost five. We call her Raino, and I tell you, Ma, bossy? She's a madam.' He gave a little laugh and winked at James, sitting on his right.

'She's a lot like you, and you'll love her.'

Violet did the maths and bristled. She shot a revolted look at the illegitimate girl's mother. A grandchild or not, it would be impossible to love a child conceived out of wedlock.

'And then there's the twins, Denim Sky and Storm, both girls and both, not surprisingly, four years old.'

More of them thought Violet. It's a bastard epidemic. 'What kind of names are those for children?' She nearly said innocent children, but they were hardly that with being born on the wrong side of the brush. 'There's nothing wrong with good strong names out of the holy book. What are you going to call this poor child when it's born? Sludge?'

Even Andrew had to admit that was witty for his caustic mother.

'Touché, Ma,' he replied with a good-natured grin.

Opposite him, Beth seethed. 'We worship the elements, Mrs Woods. We see it as an honour to name our children from nature.'

Andrew cut in before she could say more. Beth was opinionated when it came to their beliefs. It was one of the things he loved about her. That, he thought, and the ability to give the best blowjob in the civilised world. But his mother had a lot to get used to, and their lifestyle was just one thing. 'Ladies, let's drink to life, love, and togetherness.' They lifted their glasses. Beth's was filled with orange juice, everybody else's with champagne, and while the two women sharpened their tongues, the toast was made.

Philip, ever the peacemaker, tried to break the tension in the room. 'Wow, another of my brothers, all grown up and married. James was the first. He married a lady from London, didn't you mate? And just last year, SP tied the knot. He and Ros are coming up to their first anniversary.' Everybody ignored him. Violet hadn't finished grilling her second son and his loose wife.

'You must show me your wedding photos, Bethany. I'd love to see them, seeing how Andrew's father and I weren't invited on the day.' She gave Beth a sickly smile.

'There aren't any photographs, Mrs Woods, it wasn't that kind of a wedding, and we only invited people who we really wanted to be present.'

Let it go, *Beth,* thought Andrew. Please just let that one go. Violet opened her mouth to speak. Oh well, here come the fireworks.

'We had a special and unique ceremony, Mother,' he cut in. 'We married on the top of a volcano in spring.'

Violet's mouth fell open, and she sat for a full ten seconds resembling the laughing clown at Blackpool Pleasure beach. She turned her head with her mouth still open. She moved it from side to side, but there was no laughter coming from her. For those few seconds, she even forgot to breathe. 'You weren't married on consecrated ground? What in the name of the Lord was the priest thinking?'

'Actually, Ma, there was no priest. We were married by an elder of our commune.'

Even Beth could see that he wasn't explaining things well. She was passionate about her beliefs, maybe as passionate as Violet was about her Catholicism. 'Andrew and I are Pagans. He denounced all ignorant religion when we purified in a sweat lodge together at the winter solstice. We don't hold with bowing to false Gods. We worship in the old ways before modern religion was founded. Our Gods are the sun, moon, tides, and seasons, not a ridiculous omnipotent fairy story. We were married by pagan law in a ceremony of light and petals.' At this point, her eyes were dreamy as she remembered the breeze blowing the fragrant petals over them. 'It's not called marriage, in the traditional sense of the word. Our ceremony was a hand-fasting. We are joined in the ceremony for one year and one day or for as long as both partners want to remain so. 'We were naked too, so photographs would have cheapened it.'

Violet lost her dignity. She screamed and ranted. Each time she ran out of insults, she returned to her favourite. 'You witch. You evil, horrible witch. You took my God-fearing son and made him believe in your rubbish. You took my innocent boy and seduced him, you Methuselah.' Beth sat quietly and didn't say a word. She didn't agree with raised voices.

At this point, Violet swooned and had to be helped to her bedroom.

The boys suggested Donald should go to her. She'd had a shock after all, but Don was having none of it. He knew that somehow, at some point, and in some way, the fact that they had produced a heathen son would boil down to being his fault. Sometimes Violet was best left to her own devices, and he figured this was one of those times. Besides, his son is home, and he had some partying to do.

The night was a tremendous success, from everybody's point of view except Violet's. They partied late into the night and had a drunken singsong, huddled around a fire that Andrew insisted on building on the lakeside. 'What about the mess?' Donald said. 'It'll burn the ground. Oh, sod it, let the fire commence,' he slurred. There'd be plenty of time to lament his singed grass tomorrow.

Things were tense again when bolshy with ale, James teased Phil. 'That's it now, Phil, we've all succumbed to the spell, except you. You're the only one left who isn't married. We've never even seen you with a girl. You know what I think, don't you? I think you're gay.'

'Get stuffed, James,' Phil said. 'Just because you like to go around in a dress,' James coloured. It was a subject that the family avoided talking about. James was married, and all of that unpleasant stuff was behind him. He had Rhona, and it settled any silly confusion that he'd suffered in his youth. Nobody knew what he got up to when Rhona was out. Philip felt guilty for bringing it up again, but he'd had his mother whining at him about grandkids earlier. Then SP asked him if he was seeing anybody yet. He felt left out and secluded at family gatherings. He was always the one on his own. The brothers had man talks, moaning about their wives. Phil wanted a woman to complain about, too. It wasn't the first time that James had called him gay. He looked up, about to apologise, as James jumped him, and the brothers sprawled onto their backs in the grass.

The party dispersed after that. The cold night air drove them into the cosy warmth of the hotel. Watching their breath dance in the air made the guests long for warm beds with fluffy duvets and central heating. Soon only, Donald, Philip and Andrew were left. Philip sensed that Donald wanted to talk to his son alone. They had a lot of catching up to do, so after shaking Andrew's hand and reiterating how good it was to have him home, Philip went to bed in the early hours.

Left alone, the two men sat in companionable silence. Andrew took rolling tobacco and papers out of his shorts pocket and rolled a cigarette. He would have preferred a joint, but in deference to his father, he

81

contented himself with a roll-up. He concentrated on the task while his thoughts drifted. He licked the paper and made sure that the finished product was smooth and even before putting it to his lips and lighting it. He offered the pouch of tobacco to his father, and although Donald hadn't smoked for over twenty years, he took it from him and tried to roll a cigarette. The paper tore under his callused hands, and tobacco spilt to the floor. They both laughed. 'It's been a while since I've done this, son.' Andrew took the fixings from him and rolled a second cigarette. 'Your mother would kill me if she knew.' They laughed again.

'It's going to freeze tomorrow, lad. Look at that rag around the moon.' The conversation was sparse and held no substance, but it wasn't stilted or awkward. The two men sat by a fire in the moonlight, happy with each other's company.

'So what are your plans, son?' asked Donald as he stubbed the end of his smoke out on his precious grass. 'Are you staying awhile?'

'No.' He was in no hurry and took the last draw on his smoke before elaborating. 'No, we're not staying awhile. This is home, Dad. I've seen the world, seen some fantastic places and lived some crazy dreams. And now I've come home,' he finished. 'If you want us, we're back for good.' He emphasised the word 'us', letting his father know that if his wife and children weren't accepted into the family, then this wasn't the home he was looking for. 'She's a good woman, you know.' Nobody had mentioned Beth since she'd kissed her husband goodnight hours earlier. He wasn't asking his father to like her. He was stating a fact in the same lazy way that they'd talked about the weather.

'Aye lad, aye. I reckon she is.' Donald put his hand on his son's knee and gave it a little pat. He coughed, embarrassed, and moved his hand to the grass, picking at an imaginary weed. 'I reckon your mother's just going to have to look beyond her blinkers. So, what are you going to do? Any ideas?'

'We're looking at a property tomorrow. We've left the kids at the commune in France. We need to arrange collecting them. Home has to be right, Dad, you know? It has to have the right feel, to sit well with nature. I need a place with outbuildings that can be used as workshops. I've built a name as a pretty good watchmaker. I do clocks, too, and Beth's an artist. We need a studio for her, space for the kids, and a barn to turn into a shop. I'm looking at buying a working farm so that we can put something back into the land.'

Donald didn't answer for a second or two. 'Sounds expensive,' he said at last. 'Clockmaker, eh? That's a fine occupation, lad, but I wouldn't have thought it'd put much into the bank for grand ideas.'

'Oh, we've got money, Pops. That's not a problem. And I don't mind if the property needs work. We'd like that, doing our own place up the way we want it. We're in no rush to have it done, and we'll be comfortable while we work.' At this point, his voice turned bitter. There was a hardness to it, something below the words that Donald couldn't work out. 'We've got more money than we'll ever need.'

Donald was about to press his son to explain. Andrew was troubled. He had something on his mind, but the heavens opened, and raindrops the size of pennies dropped from the sky, soaking them through in seconds. The rain would take care of the dying embers of the fire. They ran drunkenly for the hotel laughing like kids.

Andrew's words came back to Donald as he waited for sleep to take him. The lad seemed to be doing okay. He had a lovely, feisty wife and a family, and yet something wasn't right. The way Andrew spoke, it was as if his money was a curse.

We've got more money than we'll ever need.

Chapter Nine

'Where's the damned artichoke? Morley, you snivelling moron, stop playing with yourself and get the artichoke here now. I told you to prepare it ten minutes ago.'

Keith Morley wiped his nose on his kitchen whites and blushed to the roots of his ginger hair. 'Yes, Chef.'

'Yes Chef, yes Chef,' mimicked James in a whiney voice. 'Just get it here now, dickhead. If you're not up to the job, get out of my kitchen and don't come back.' He was screaming at the top of his voice, and every sentence contained at least two F-words and a C for good measure. 'Bloody hell, it's not as if I ask you to do anything challenging, is it? Did your mother shag the village idiot to have you?'

The young boy with the tear-stained face crossed the busy kitchen carrying a bowl of prepared vegetables. James snatched it from his hands, and Keith Morley scuttled back to the safety of the prep area.

James poked the artichokes. 'What the hell is this? Oi, Moron, get back here. Do they look crisp to you? They're as limp as your tiny dick. You've taken so bloody long doing them that they wilted. You're a waste of breathing space.' James had taken Morley's surname and morphed it into Moron, and the nickname stuck from day one.

Keith approached the enraged chef as though he feared for his life. He was crying and hung his head.

'Look at you. You're like a whipped dog. Why are you so soft? It's not a rhetorical question, Moron. Answer me, you pathetic cretin. Why are you so bloody soft?'

'Don't know, Chef.'

'Prepare another bowl. Go on, get out of my sight.'

'Yes, Chef.'

James threw the bowl of artichokes at him. The stainless steel smashed into the middle of his back and fell with a clatter on the tiled floor. The food spilt and fanned in a semicircle around him.

'Clean it up, arsehole.' James was red and sweating with the exertion of his tantrum, and for the time being, he'd run out of expletives.

The new boy had suffered the fourth hour of the first day in his second week at The Halcyon Woods Hotel. He didn't think he could take much more.

***

Head chef, Marcus, had taken to James when he met the lad as a rebellious three-year-old. In busy periods, the Woods' children weren't allowed in the bustling hotel kitchen, but between shifts, when it was quiet, Marcus had time for them. He would give them cake and tease them as he prepared the bread for the next shift. Sometimes he'd give them a piece of pastry to roll or a bowl with cake ingredients to hand-mix. It was a passing fancy for all of the boys except James. The kid loved being wrist-deep in butter and flour. He'd learned to knead the dough before he could recite the alphabet, and Marcus enjoyed teaching him new things as his ability matured.

As a teenager, it was easy to see that he had a flair for cooking that couldn't be learned. Marcus said true chefs were born with flour in their blood, and even at that age, James had the makings of a remarkable chef. It was obvious he'd go straight into the kitchen when he left university, just as Simon Peter went into hotel management. The difference was that the eldest Woods' boy had been groomed to take over the family business from the day he could walk. With James, it was a gift that he already possessed. He knew how to make food sing and could elevate the dullest ingredients.

Marcus was happy to take him on as his apprentice, but his pleasure was short-lived. The cheeky young lad who'd been a joy to teach had grown into a surly, bad-tempered thug. From day one, James was difficult. He was eager enough to learn the rudiments of his trade from Marcus and was a keen and able student but prone to fits of temper the likes of which the kitchen had never seen. He loved baking bread and cakes and produced some fine and exotic pastries. He had flair and imagination, often marrying flavours that only the foolish or incredibly brave would think of putting together. He was creative and temperamental, both signs of a good chef. However, what he couldn't do, was take criticism or discipline. After his regimented upbringing, he should have been used to following orders, knowing his place, and observing the rules of his rank. But he wasn't.

After nineteen years of being repressed, first by his mother and then by masters of school and university, the boy was done with being told what to do. He was the son and heir, if not of the hotel, then of the kitchen within it. Because he was Violet's son, he considered himself to be the master and Marcus a lowly employee. It caused heated debates and bruised egos on both sides.

Violet bribed Marcus to stay during the first year. A dramatic increase in his salary meant he could cope with his apprentice's inflated ego. On a weekly basis, he flew into Violet's, and later SP's office, threatening to walk out, but he never did. A bonus always slaked his feelings of being undermined.

With SP inducted as the hotel manager, he and James fought bitterly until SP learned not to interfere with running the kitchen. Distinct boundaries had been laid between the two domains. At their mother's insistence and a vicious black eye from his brother, SP stopped querying invoices and left James and the head chef to sort out their hierarchy.

After two years, and at the same time Violet and Donald gave running the hotel to their eldest son, they called a meeting with Marcus. The chef who had served them loyally for many years was one cook too many in the broth. He was given a hefty golden handshake and two months' notice to leave. His last day coincided with bringing forward an official end to James' apprenticeship. Mother knew everything and decreed that he'd learned enough.

Marcus had saved for years to buy his own restaurant, a dream that contentment in his work had always kept on the fringe of his fantasies. Now there was nothing holding him back, and while he was sad to leave the restaurant and the two Michelin stars he'd been awarded, he was okay about going.

James walked out of his apprenticeship and into the head chef position at his parent's hotel with two Michelin stars above the door, and he claimed instant ownership of them as a personal achievement.

Marcus had taught him well. By the end of the second year, he'd learned everything that he should have in his third. Marcus was an excellent chef—but James was better. The transition was a smooth one.

With the certificate of power and ownership, James was a bully. He persecuted everybody who came into his kitchen. What had been controlled while Marcus was in charge was left to run wild when James took the reins. The turnover of staff in the hotel kitchen was rapid. Only the strong-willed survived more than a couple of weeks. The pay was above most in the county, but it had to be to keep the few loyal staff that could tolerate working for James. He was an artist of extreme highs and volatile lows. The kitchen ran like clockwork, standards were everything, and anybody who couldn't keep pace was dispensed with. He had inherited his ambition and willingness to work hard from his mother. But like an unwatched pan, James was never far from boiling over.

Things came to a head the day after the artichoke incident. Day two, week two for Morley, and the last day he would ever enjoy the beauty of nature. James was in a foul mood. A fillet of veal had been returned to the kitchen with a complaint about it being tough. James wasn't working the mains pass that day, but he took every complaint personally and saw it as an attack on him. The kitchen staff were in line to catch the fallout, and he didn't single Keith out. Morley just managed to irritate him more than the other staff.

James resented the apprentice. Morley flew through catering college as a grade-A pupil. During his first day in the kitchen, he'd suggested that James might prepare a skate the way Morley was shown at college. James couldn't believe the audacity of the little bastard. How dare he come into his kitchen showing off his school-taught ways? Morley had the makings of a decent chef. He should, by right of his qualifications, have gone into the kitchen on a second-chef salary, but James made it company policy to start all of his staff at the bottom. If they had what it took, they rose through the ranks in a matter of weeks. If they didn't—they were out.

Keith didn't mind starting on pot washing and then veg prep. He knew about James' reputation and wanted to please him and rise to the second chef's position on merit. He had the knowledge and all the skills. What he lacked was the flair and impulsiveness that makes a great chef.

From that first hour, and after Keith's fatal error, James decided he didn't like the lad and would bring him down.

Morley knew what hotel kitchens were like. He'd done his placements. It was screaming and temperament one minute and then best buddies in the bar when the shift was over. James was in the bar talking to some guests after Morley's first shift. The new kitchen lad, in baggy jeans and an Adidas tee shirt, excused himself and tapped James on the shoulder.

'I'd like to buy you a drink, James, just to show there are no hard feelings and to say I understand why you were so tough on me today.'

The lad was only two years younger than the head chef. In other circumstances, they could have been friends or drinking buddies. The look on James' face told Morley he'd made his second big mistake. From that moment on, war was declared.

On the second day, James took Morley apart one cog at a time. He broke his spirit first and then his will to live. By the time the shift ended, Morley didn't know if he could face another day working for the spiteful bully. He saw the week out in misery, becoming more withdrawn with every shift. By day four, he had no confidence left. He'd been making stupid mistakes in the kitchen, things he would never have done in college. He was emotional, burst into tears several times during every workday and wanted to turn things around and prove himself worthy of the job. It wasn't about pleasing James anymore. It was showing that he could do what he'd been trained for. He stopped sleeping and had headaches from the stress and exhaustion. By the first day of the second week, he was a shadow of the boy he'd been eight days earlier.

The last day of Morley's life wasn't a happy one. He'd been at the biting end of Chef's temper several times.

'Moron, get the eggs on.'

'Yes, Chef.'

'Moron, you gay boy, prepare the garnish.'

'Yes, Chef.'

'Moron, do me some onions. Did you hear me? I said, chop some bloody onions.'

'Yes, Chef.'

'Moron, Where are the tuna? Get them over here now.'

'Yes, Chef.' Keith took the pan off the hob and hurried across the kitchen. He was about to put it on the board next to James when the head chef turned around and collided with Morley and the hot pan.

'You stupid, dumb, halfwit. What have I told you about walking around with hot pans? You're a useless tosser, aren't you? Get me some spinach.'

'Yes, Chef.'

Morley was preparing the spinach when an almighty roar echoed around the sterile cavern of the immense kitchen. 'You stupid, incompetent wanker. You useless little queer.' James ran behind Morley and grabbed him at the back of his jacket collar. Knocking the boy off balance, he dragged him across the kitchen to the range of cooking rings. One glowed an intense red, throwing out a blanket of heat. 'Look at it. You've left it on, you imbecile. Surely, basic kitchen safety tells you that you don't wander off and leave a ring burning. You need to spend less time in bed with your boyfriend at night so that when you come to work, you're aware of what you're doing.' He grabbed the sobbing boy's left hand and forced it onto the burning ring. There was a fizz of burning flesh. Keith screamed. His hand was in contact with the ring for a split second, but it was long enough to burn into his palm's meat. James had lost it. He was out of control. Sheer bloodlust clouded his vision and his rationale.

'You're finished in this hotel. Do you hear me? I'll see that you never work again.' He pulled Morley away from the stove and rammed him against the seven-foot freezer. Morley was holding the wrist of his burned hand and screaming in terror and agony. Lucy, the third chef that day, ran to get SP, while Dave, the commis chef, and Darren, the kitchen porter, tried to pull James away from Morley. James turned, punching Dave Hill in the face. Pandemonium erupted in the kitchen.

SP came in ranting at his brother, and SP and James fought like savages, knocking dishes and utensils onto the floor.

Lucy looked for Morley. She wanted to check his hand, assess the damage and call for an ambulance. He had slipped out when the violence distracted everybody's attention. She assumed he'd gone home to lick his wounds.

Morley ran from the kitchen and out of the rear entrance of the hotel. He didn't stop running until the cool greenness of trees surrounded him. The woods were deep. Tears rolled down his face, and he was white and shaking. The pain throbbed in the palm of his hand and up through his arm to the shoulder. He was in agony, with his body and mind abused and debilitated. James had taken the last of his confidence and made him believe he was useless. His feeling of failure hurt more than the circles of pain radiating from the centre of his palm.

With his good hand, he slid the knife from the sleeve of his kitchen whites. He'd taken it when SP and James were arguing. He listened for any sign that he'd been followed. All he could hear was birdsong. A squirrel stopped in the path ten feet in front of him to watch this trespasser to his territory. Even here, Morley didn't belong. He backed against the trunk of a tree and slithered down until his buttocks came into contact with the cool base moss. He worried about staining his whites. James would go ballistic if he marked them. Morley gave a rueful laugh. What could he do to him now that he hadn't already done?

He sat for two minutes contemplating the eight-inch blade and solid wooden shaft of the knife. He wasn't frightened. What he was going to do meant nothing. He'd gone beyond worrying about something as meaningless as his death. His concern was that he'd be found before it was over. His only fear was that he'd have to see James Wood's face again.

He cut professionally. He might be useless, but he could prepare a cut of meat. He bit deep into his wrist just below the base of his hand. He winced, but the pain from the incision was nothing compared to the pulsating throb of the burn. His arm was resting against his thigh, palm up. The knife was so sharp and his compulsion so strong that he cut clear through his arm and into his leg with the force of penetration. The knife tore through muscle, tendon and cartilage. He had to wrench it back to make the downward pull. He grunted with the exertion of removing the point of the knife from his femoral artery on the inside of his upper leg. That was a mistake but an added bonus nonetheless. The cut to his leg was insufficient to do much damage, but it gave him the idea to improve on it. He stabbed the knife into his thigh, doing incredible damage with the butcher's blade. This time it did hurt and was worse than the throb of it going into his arm. He cried out, clamping down on the noise in his throat so he wouldn't be heard. He made a second cut to his wrist, weakened this time. There was no pain. Shock had gone to his brain and shut down the valves that sent messages to the nerve endings. His cutting hand was weak. He even forgot about the agony of his burned flesh. He was concentrating. There was a lot of blood. His knife hand was trawling through it, and the shaft of the blade was slipping. His whites spread with a deep crimson stain that washed through the material the way a wave washes up a shale beach. The blood was warm and pleasing. Satisfying. He was mesmerised as it poured from his leg and bubbled through the wound in his wrist. He wondered if he had done enough but didn't want to take any chances.

The knife was the best. Eight inches of brutal stainless steel could cut through a rabbit's neck, releasing bones from their anchorage with a single chop. Going through the underside to the back of his arm had been no trouble. But now, he felt the weakness enervating him. His eyes had black spots dancing somewhere to the left of his vision. He went to work fast. It only took one more movement. The knife was already home, He drew it through the flesh of the inside of his lower arm from wrist to elbow, neatly separating his meat into two fillets, attached only by the layer of skin on his outer arm and the bones. As delirium claimed him, his final thought was of suitable herbs and sausage meat to stuff in his arm before cooking. He died beneath the bough of an oak tree, with the disgruntled squirrel his only witness.

Violet took over and did what Violet always did when James went too far. She bought everybody off. Silence cost her dearly that day, and even she had to admit that James was a liability. SP wanted to force James into anger management counselling, but Violet wouldn't hear of it. The Woods family did not air their dirty laundry in public. The inquest heard that Keith Morley had been suffering from depression. Girlfriend trouble was hinted at, subtly suggested by Morley's best friend, who worked at the Halcyon and was bribed by Violet. A verdict of suicide was heard, and that was the end of it. Everybody has their price. Violet knew this as a statement of fact. She bought loyalty, and after Morley's death, she bought silence. 'Dinky' Johnston, Morley's friend, hated himself, he hated the hefty bonus cheque in his back pocket, but he couldn't stop a smile playing at the corners of his mouth as he dreamed of the hi-fi he was going to buy with his spoils. And then, he remembered that his best friend would never listen to it with him. He was dead, and Dinky was weighed down by the solace of his thirty pieces of silver.

James was finished at The Halcyon Woods. It would be years before he could return. Mother funded his first solo venture, a nice restaurant of his own. 'Somewhere near Marcus. You like Marcus, don't you, dear?' Yes, London would be far enough away. Violet cried as she waved him away in his Jaguar XJS. She'd packed him some nice macaroons for the journey. He liked those.

Chapter Ten

A two-pound deficit and an eight-pound gain were to blame for Julie's bad mood. The two pounds was a couple of quid she was short on the fantastic jeans she'd just tried on, and the eight pounds was the half a stone—at least—that she had gained, which prevented her from doing the buggers up. What's a girl to do when trauma as gigantic as that blights her life? She might be fatter, but she wasn't stupid. The answer was obvious. She had no alternative but to go to Salvanna's for the lunchtime special. Once her diet was broken enough to indulge in spaghetti bolognaise drowned in melted cheese, what harm would a full-fat latte on the side do? It took her half a minute to talk herself into it, and half of that was spent asking if she had the guts to eat alone. Once she got there, she'd ring her sister and offer to treat her to lunch. She'd provide the pig-out moral support.

The restaurant was busy but not oppressive. Wimmin-what-lunch and the business exec crowd filled three-quarters of the clientele capacity. Julie saw another woman sitting alone, and that made her feel better until her companion came back from the toilet. What the hell? She was hungry, they served food, and it was less shameful than throwing herself off the dock's bridge and expecting the recovery divers to lift her and her extra half-stone out of the slimy green water.

She squeezed herself between a table and a pushchair, pausing to glare at the child with the mitt-full of deep-pan Margarita. His wide blue eyes were a striking contrast to the tomato red of the rest of his face. He looked as though he'd been massacred—a self-proclaiming prophesy if the brat touched her camel-coloured jacket with either of those filthy hands. She caught the mother's eye and changed her expression into one of those sickly smiles. The kind reserved for the parents of young children and said she'd probably like one of those too, one day.

She felt as if she'd shot up from a size fourteen to a sixteen overnight, and there was no way she was going to a size oh-my-god-how-did-that kid-get-in-there.

The bloke at the next table was eating alone. As she sat down, he looked up from his newspaper with a half-interested glance of curiosity. He didn't look at her, and they certainly didn't make eye contact, so she had no need to smile or say anything. A weary waitress was manoeuvring through the tables towards her. She had menus tucked under her arm and a pencil and jotter at the ready. Julie ordered her latte to fight away the afternoon chill and the weight gain depression. She said she'd order food when her sister arrived.

Emma, her sister, declined the offer of a free lunch. She had a man coming to fit blinds. Julie pleaded desperation due to the gained weight and tragic demise of the jeans that had never been hers. But she was aware that the man at the next table was within earshot of their conversation. She could lean over and snog him without lifting more than her left butt cheek. Vanity demanded that she only suggested once that

Emma leave the blind man to it, and go AWOL. After wasting precious phone credit, she resigned herself to eating alone.

The man at the next table was causing problems. Apart from an initial glance, he hadn't lifted his head from the newspaper, but even so, his presence made her moderate her choices. If he hadn't been there, she could have put the hard word on Emma, and she could have had spaghetti bolognese for lunch. However, there was no chance of eating that in public now. Only a fool would choose spaghetti when there was a potentially eligible man close enough to hit with a stray string of pasta. She wouldn't call herself a messy eater, but she was clumsy. And spaghetti was notoriously wilful. She opted for the safer risotto. It still came smothered in melted cheese, so that was good. Her mood demanded heaps of melted cheese today.

The table was getting on her nerves. It was wobbly, and every time she shifted position, the short leg rocked to the floor. Maybe leprechauns escaped from Ireland and roamed restaurants in the night, cutting an inch off every fourth table leg. It was the grand plan the Irish had to overthrow the British. By jimminy, we'll bring them down by way of their wobbly tables, so we will, Paddy. She was smiling as the waitress returned with her lunch.

The food looked good, but the table was driving her nuts. She folded a cardboard coaster and, being careful not to dangle her hair in the food. She leaned over to put it under the wobbly leg for balance.

As she bent down, she caught the edge of the table with her elbow making it tilt towards her. She was aware of the plate of hot food sliding forwards but couldn't get up fast enough to stop it.

She watched, horrified, as the dish slid towards her face. At the last second, instinct drove her to drop her head. The food emptied into her hair. She was aware that she was screaming as she brought herself upright in the chair.

The man at the next table leapt from his seat, and less than a second after the contents of the dish spilt over Julie's head, he emptied his pint of lager on top of it. He let the glass go, and it dropped to the floor, shattering in a ricochet of broken shards. Less than a second had passed since the first splash of hot food hit her. He was in with his hands, Holding the scalding food away from her skin and clearing the mess from the top of her head before the burning got through her thick hair to her scalp.

'Keep still. I'm a first aider,' he said it to Julie before addressing the room in general. 'Get me water. I need to cool her head.'

When the food dropped, the place had erupted into activity. Waitresses hovered, and people vacated their seats at the tables nearby as glass and food splashed towards them. As if to add to the humiliation, a second drink was thrown over Julie's head, followed by a jug of water. She stopped screaming. There was no heat or pain, only fluid and mess. She peered at her world through two strands of lank, dripping cheesy hair as the man, with a penchant for drowning strangers in restaurants, pulled lengths of the stringy mess away from her.

She was embarrassed, humiliated and pathetic. At a loss for what else to do, she started to cry.

The restaurant worried about the legal comeback, but they were wonderful. They helped mop up the debris, waived the bill and gave her complimentary vouchers for dinner for two, with wine, on the house. The man, not satisfied with initiating the first public drowning in Barrow-in-Furness for a hundred years, insisted, despite her protestations, on taking her to the hospital to be checked over. 'Head burns are serious things,' he said several times. 'You can't be too careful.' Julie just wanted to escape the curious eyes and was too upset to argue. She let him lead her into the street, looking like hell and still snivelling into a Salvanna's serviette. If the child wearing the pizza mask was impressed that a grown-up could get more food on them than he could, she didn't notice.

People looked at them as they walked the short distance to his car. He had his arm around her shoulders, the taboo of intimacy between strangers broken with the competence of the New Samaritan.

He insisted on going in with her when she got to the hospital. Worse, he insisted on staying until she had been given the all-clear. 'Might as well see the job through to the end,' he said.

Who the hell does he think he is?

Julie was grateful for what he'd done but smarted with indignation about the way he'd done it.

When she saw the registrar on A&E duty, she found out how lucky she'd been. He said she would be left seriously burned if it hadn't been for two intervening factors. She had long, very thick hair, which had protected her head from the scalding. And the Samaritan's quick-witted reaction stopped the food from burning through the hair to her scalp. If it hadn't been for these saving graces, she would have been scarred for life and would never have been able to grow hair over the scar. She walked away from the incident humiliated, wet and dressed in risotto and cheese—but completely unharmed. The enormity of what could have happened hit her, and she trembled.

The man introduced himself as Philip Woods and said he'd see Miss Spencer safely home and insisted that she have a calming brandy to steady her nerves. Despite being commended by the doctor and nurses, he was self-effacing. He said anybody would have done the same thing.

He saw her into the house and insisted she showered and changed into her night clothes even though it was only four o'clock in the afternoon. 'You've had a nasty shock and need to rest,' he told her, still playing the role of medical competent to the hilt. Here was a stranger fussing around, making coffee in her kitchen and opening the bottle of brandy he'd bought on the way over, as though it was all perfectly normal. She felt uncomfortable showering with him in the house. He could be anyone. And here she was at her most vulnerable, naked and covered in soapsuds. He didn't seem the type to be anything but a gentleman, but what type is an axe-murdering pervert? She didn't feel at risk, but she locked the bathroom door and tested its strength against attack. She didn't linger. Normally, she wore a short silk dressing gown for lounging, but despite the mild weather, she chose her heavy, hooded velour gown and made sure it was belted over her Pooh-Bear pyjamas.

Julie didn't have any brandy glasses. She'd had some disasters with glasses over the years, and the option was one half-pint glass or coffee mugs. Philip was appalled that they were drinking brandy from chipped mugs, and that set Julie off into peals of irrational giggles. Philip saw nothing funny about the situation and put her silly hysteria down to delayed shock setting in. He only had a drop of brandy because he was driving. His personality was stiff, and he was uptight, but he was kind. She was grateful to him for what he'd done for her.

It seemed right that she invite him to join her for the complimentary meal, and that was how their relationship began. There were no fireworks or love at first sight. And no wild palpitating heartbeats. Just soggy risotto awash with lager and brandy sipped out of chipped Easter bunny mugs.

Chapter Eleven

He looked at her and changed the subject. 'Should we go out for a drink tonight?'

She wasn't letting him off the hook this time. 'Phil, why do you always look so uncomfortable when I ask about your family?'

'I don't.' His eyes shifted, and he couldn't meet her gaze.

'Yes, you bloody well do.'

'Julie, please don't swear. It makes you sound common.' He could look at her now. He wasn't the one in the dock anymore. He'd done a clever sleight-of-hand illusion, and she was standing, with her right hand on the metaphorical bible, under the steel grey eyes of the prosecution.

Julie Sandra Spencer, it is alleged that on the sixteenth of May, nineteen ninety-one, you did utter a profanity that proves, beyond any shadow of a doubt, that you are the common, sewer-mouthed trollop that he suspected you would prove yourself to be. How do you plead?

'I'm sorry,' she said, hating herself for rolling over and showing her belly. This was her house, dammit, and she could say what she sodding well pleased. What she said was a big, fat nothing. She lowered her eyes to her plate and ate in silence. Phil didn't like a lot of chatter when he was eating. She forgot that sometimes.

Her father broke wind from the sitting room. Her mother whined in a half-hearted protest. And Phil didn't comment.

He looked at his food and forked through the cheese and coleslaw on his baked potato. She wasn't sure whether the look of disgust on his face was for the food or for the woman so beneath him that he'd taken as a girlfriend.

Her plate was almost empty when he spoke again. 'Are you going to eat all that? You've put on weight since I met you.' It was a statement with no tone, but the rebuttal stung like a slap. Putting her cutlery down and remembering, as an afterthought, to sit them side by side, she took their plates to the sink. She scraped leftovers into the bin and ran water to wash up. He didn't like plates left after a meal. Better to wash them straight away, he always said, and then it's done with. She almost didn't hear what he said next.

'Perhaps it is time you met my people,' he mused. Just that, no more. He was watching the news on the portable television in the tiny dining room. Wiping her hands on a hand towel, not a tea towel—never a tea towel, she opened her mouth to say something, but he put his hand up for silence, palm facing her, a barrier and brick wall, a command. My people? Pompous bastard. Who does he think he is? Jesus?

'You know what, Philip? Why don't you get up off your sanctimonious arse and do the washing up yourself.' She flung the towel at him and flounced upstairs for a bath, but she remembered not to slouch in her temper. He hated a sloppy posture.

'We'll go to Mother's house on Saturday,' he shouted up after her. 'Find something suitable.' Find something suitable for what? To wear? To give as a gift? Or to murder my boyfriend? What did one wear for a first meeting with one's bloke's posh parents anyway? And would she have to keep all this one's one oneing up for long?

Philip was impatient. he wanted to get away before the tourists blocked the road. Julie insisted they stop off at a florist to buy his mother a large bunch of chrysanthemums, a fitting flower to give on a first-time meeting with the parents. Phil explained to her that Violet and Donald lived at the hotel, though Violet had delegated most of the day-to-day running of the place to Simon Peter when she made him the hotel manager. Violet spent her days playing bridge and chatting with affluent guests over coffee. She and Donald had a suite of rooms overlooking the lake, and life was comfortable.

The first thing Julie noticed as they were invited in were the vases of fresh flowers dotted all over the place. It seemed the lady of the house had a passion for delicate orchids and elegant lilies. The flowers that Julie brought looked bulky and bulbous. They didn't fit in with the ambience and delicacy of the place.

'Hello, Mr and Mrs Woods, nice to meet you.' She tried for a warm smile, but it died on her lips under the scrutiny of the other woman. She gave Violet the flowers. The older woman thanked her stiffly, and her face cracked momentarily in a forced smile, but Julie felt no warmth under the cool gaze.

'So, you're our Philip's bit of stuff then, eh?' Donald said.

He had changed during the time he'd been married to Violet. It was a slow and subtle change, but he bore little resemblance to the mild man who plodded along and was happy with his lot. His wife's views and opinions had rubbed off on him. After years of sharing a life, if not his bed, with her, some of her manner and attitude must have leaked onto his crisp, starched shirts and contaminated him. Donald had contracted an unpleasant dose of Violet and was a more outspoken man.

He didn't bother to mask his top-to-bottom scan of her. It wasn't the leery body scan of a middle-aged letch. It was a sizing up of his son's girlfriend to see if she was worthy of a welcome into the Woods' social circle. He shook hands with her, but it was noncommittal. 'Hardly a slip of a lass, are you? Like your grub, do you? Well, it could have been worse. You could have been a darkie. Don't like them, I don't. Ought to send them all back to where they came from.'

Julie perched on the edge of the sofa and almost choked on what she wanted to say to stop it from leaving her mouth. Violet made tea. Julie hated tea. Phil knew she hated tea, but he didn't say anything to his mother, and Julie felt that it would be rude to ask for coffee instead. Phil and his dad, sitting on opposite armchairs, made small talk, and Julie was ignored as Donald told Phil about some work that he wanted a hand with on the hotel grounds. They discussed when it would be done, what tools they'd need and how long it would take. Julie was invisible.

Violet returned with a tray. The tea set was Royal Doulton, fine China, with a small-handled cup that rattled on her saucer. She handed Julie a dinky cup and said, 'We don't have smoking in here. I can show you to the terrace if you'd like to smoke.' The words were hard and clipped, with disapproval slipping from the back of every syllable.

Julie laughed. It was a nervous reaction. 'Thank you, Mrs Woods, but I don't smoke.'

'You don't smoke? Oh, you look as though you would.' In the last seven words, Violet summed up what she thought about the girl in front of her. The insult was barbed and deliberate.

Tea was served, and as if on cue, they peppered her with questions about her background. She told them about her home, a modest council house on a Barrow estate where she lived with her parents and two sisters. She had never been ashamed of her roots and was proud of the way her family helped one another through difficult times. Her mother was a dinner lady at the local primary school, and her father had taken voluntary redundancy from the shipyard five years before when his back was bad. He hadn't been able to work since and liked to drink more than was good for him. They were good parents, and Julie was happy.

Donald asked Julie about her work, but she was sure Phil had already been well-grilled on that and pretty much every other subject. She told them about her job as an assembler of electrical components at Oxley's in Barrow.

'Factory work? Really?' Violet looked at her son as though he'd suffered a loss in his common sense. 'Never mind, dear. Perhaps something better will come along one day. Didn't you do well at school?'

Julie was a good guest. She was well-mannered and polite. But she was getting fed up with having one thinly disguised put down after another flung at her while her boyfriend sat by and didn't say a word in her defence.

'No, Mrs Woods, I didn't do very well at school. I messed around when I should have been learning, and I wasted every opportunity I was given.' She could see Phil cringing. He was flashing eye signals at her to shut up. This wasn't what she was supposed to say. 'I might regret the time I wasted. I could feel stupid for not having any qualifications, but I enjoy my job. I work a full week and earn my living honestly. I've got some fantastic friends, and I'm happy. Phil and I haven't talked about the future, so for the time being, I'm happy and don't see any reason to change.'

'Philip. His name's Philip. We don't hold with name shortening here. And I think it's far too early to be thinking about the future, dear. You're only—what? Nineteen, wasn't it? You haven't begun to live yet, child. I'd like to think Philip would marry one day, but there's plenty of time yet. And I'm sure that you'll meet a boy your own age and want to settle down, too.' Julie thought she detected a hint of panic in her adversary's eyes at the thought that this cuckoo in the nest might have designs on her son. She disguised a smile and was about to wind the woman up when Phil spoke in her defence.

'Don't underestimate Jules, Mother.' Julie could have kissed Phil right there in the drawing room. 'She's very bright. She can play the piano and guitar and has a lovely singing voice. She's a wonderful artist, too, and can draw just about anything she puts her mind to. You'll have to show Mother some of your portraits, love. She made that dress she's wearing today.'

Violet sniffed. 'Yes, I can see that. You should have lined it, dear. It would have been a nice dress if you'd lined it and had chosen a better print and fabric.'

Julie was impressed that Phil had spoken out in her defence. It was lovely to hear him put into words the things he admired about her. But as he went on, his voice took on a wheedling, beseeching quality, and she realised he wasn't defending her but himself and the choice he'd made in a girlfriend.

'The others all have wives and girlfriends. Why shouldn't I have one, too?' Julie was shocked. The opinionated and insensitive man had turned into a five-year-old child, desperate for his mother's approval.

'Really, Philip.' His mother's tone was sharp. 'You do get the silliest notions. Of course, we're not saying you can't have a friend. You're twenty-six years old. It's not up to us what you do. I'm sure Julie is a nice girl in her own environment. We just feel that she's a little young for a man of your age.'

'We have a reputation,' Donald cut in. 'A certain social standing to be upheld. You running round with a slip of a girl, well, it doesn't look right, that's all. No offence, lass,' he finished, glancing at Julie.

'None taken,' Julie said, nonetheless offended.

They didn't stay long after that. The atmosphere was tense, and Violet kept throwing furious looks at Phil. He made the excuse that they were calling in on friends on the way home and that time was getting on.

'Thank you for your hospitality, Mr and Mrs Woods. It's been nice meeting you,' she lied.

She shook hands with them both. It was stiff.

'Goodbye, lass. I hope your dad finds work soon.' Donald was openly relieved that she was going, but his wishes sounded sincere.

'Goodbye, Julia, dear. Do come again,' Violet gushed insincerity from every pore.

'It's Julie, Mrs Woods. Just plain Julie.'

'Quite, dear.'

Chapter Twelve

Three months later, they bought a house.

It was a good house on Jesmond Avenue. A nice neighbourhood in the upper-middle range of the price bracket. Philip was pleased with his purchase. He fronted most of the deposit, and as the security credit checks were all run on him, the house went in his name. That was okay. Julie didn't care about money and paperwork. Philip assured her it would be his house but their home. They were going to be happy there.

There was only one black cloud marring their horizon. Philip couldn't find the courage to tell his parents he was leaving home. Through the exhilarating and tense weeks of the house sale, he was borne down by the worry of how his parents would react. He put it off for days, weeks, and the full three months it took for the house to be theirs. She said they would face his parents together. How bad could it be? But Phil wouldn't hear of it. He knew all about waving red rags in front of raging bulls.

They picked up the keys together. It was the day they were moving in, but there was a hold-up with the other people, and instead of picking up the keys at nine in the morning, it was three in the afternoon before they took possession of the little pieces of brass that would let them into their new home. It was the perfect excuse for Philip.

'You move in today, love, and make everything nice. I'll talk to the folks tonight and join you tomorrow.' She hated the idea. This was the start of the rest of their lives. They would go into that house together or not at all. It was more than that, though. Instinct told her that if she moved in alone, he might never join her. She didn't see the benefit of the arrangement. They only had two days booked off work, and one had been wasted. Common sense, and Philip bringing his greater will to bear, said that they'd leave the house move until the weekend and move in then. They celebrated with a champagne dinner that night, but the mood was broken, and a tense atmosphere lay between them. Julie wouldn't care if they had to work all night. She'd looked forward to this day for so long, and now she was going home to sleep in the same single bed that she'd slept in every night of her life.

Phil didn't talk to his parents on the Monday night. He couldn't find the right moment. He didn't talk to them on Tuesday or Wednesday, or Thursday. They were moving into the house on Friday.

Each of those evenings, they hit the shops and spent money lavishly, giggling as they piled the house high with beautiful things. Every night the bubble burst, and they went back to their own homes. Julie's parents were diplomatic. They said it was a big thing for him and to give him time and be understanding. She tried, but it was difficult. Julie gave him the, them or me, ultimatum.

113

He told his parents on the Friday morning, blurting it out over the breakfast table. It didn't go well. He left his mother sobbing and his father yelling. He'd never defied them before.

Julie didn't have a lot of money, but when her Auntie had died, some money had been put in a trust fund for her. She hadn't touched it when she turned eighteen, she had no need of extra money, but she drew every penny out to spend on the house. Philip was broke. All his money had gone on the house deposit, so Julie's inheritance was spent furnishing it. She had good taste and was amazed when Philip took a back seat and gave her free rein when it came to buying furniture and fittings. It was out of character for him. He could be demanding, and she hated to use the word because once said it couldn't be withdrawn, but Phil was controlling. With something as big as his first house, Julie expected him to be picky to the nth degree, but on the contrary, he let her buy whatever she wanted. It was the spending spree of a lifetime carried out over several weeks. They did move in that Friday, but the fight with his parents marred their special day. As Phil's wages came in those first few happy months, more was added to the pot. He was generous, denied her nothing, and she had the time of her life spending money like water.

Phil was twenty-six, and Julie was nineteen. Neither of them had lived away from home before. Once the novelty of keeping house had worn off and the pin money had run out, things were difficult. They had to tighten their belts, and the first sign of things to come insinuated its way into their paradise.

They would get home from work tired and fractious. Phil was used to a meal on the table, but Julie had never cooked in her life. When he was on the early shift, Phil would do all the housework. He finished at three, and when Julie walked in at half five, she would be greeted by the smell of pledge and home cooking. On these days, Phil ran his home like an army base, everything just so and done properly.

When he worked a full day and didn't get home until late, the weave of his ordered life unravelled at the seams. Julie wanted to sit and relax when she got home from work. Phil wanted his tea and a clean house, just as his mother had always provided the staff at the hotel. But this wasn't the hotel. This was a house with dust on the units and the breakfast dishes still in the sink. He found it difficult living in a normal environment where they had to do everything for themselves. He relied on Julie, who didn't do things the way he wanted them done. The washing piled up. He hated that. He could see the sheen of dust on the units. It enraged him. Julie was in the habit of leaving clothes on the bedroom floor. He couldn't tolerate it.

They fought.

Things didn't improve between Phil and his parents. He didn't see them at all for the first idyllic three months before the money ran out and the arguments started, but one day he had to ring them about some paperwork he needed to collect. He said he and Julie would call at the hotel that evening. He always picked Julie up when they finished work. They'd go to Windermere together. He saw no reason why there had to be any animosity.

'Don't you dare bring that gold-digging tart to my home? Don't you dare, you little bastard,' Violet screamed down the phone.

115

Phil sat down on the chair beside the telephone. He was rocked. He couldn't believe what he was hearing. His mother had never sworn at him. He hung up in a daze. He didn't go for his paperwork. But the row with his mother coincided with the first big fallout with his girlfriend.

The next time Phil spoke to Violet was when he rang to tell them he was getting married.

And there was the S-word. Julie was confused and didn't understand. He knew that, but when she came to him, with her ripe body insinuating that she wanted to be intimate, he froze. Her curves disgusted him, and the thought of doing it terrified him.

It was much later when he told her that's why he proposed.

It was only to buy him some time.

In the first days of their courtship, she desired him. It shamed him and made his cheeks burn the way her chaste kisses had become open-mouthed and demanding. He made it obvious that he didn't like that. He once said her sour mouth might swallow him.

Sometimes when they said goodnight, she'd rub her body against him, her breath harsh and her eyes wanton. 'Don't, Julie. You're scaring me. I don't like the feel of your breasts pushing into me. I can feel the hard points of your nipples against my body when you embrace me, and it's filthy out of wedlock. It's a dirty sin.' He said he'd noticed she wasn't even wearing a bra.

He was horrified when she brought the subject of sex up. She said the word like a strumpet.

'Don't you want to make love to me?'

He certainly did not and couldn't have recoiled any further. 'Of course, I do.' The thought was abhorrent.

He felt hot. The room was stifling. He wanted to run, aware that his testicles contracted and his limp penis tortoised inside his body. He'd heard that it was wet down there and that a woman was slimy and smelled of fish. Why the hell would anybody want to subject themselves to that?

'Of course, I want you, baby. It's just that I'm a Catholic. It's not allowed.'

She eased off after that and didn't get herself so het up. He was relieved, and maybe that's why he let her push him into buying the house. He didn't want it and certainly never wanted to live with her. He didn't really like her that much. Maybe he thought the problem of the S-word had gone away, and she wouldn't expect to do it. They could have their own bedrooms, and it would be fine. He felt that he'd made his feelings on the subject clear.

He was wrong. It was obvious the day they went to buy beds. He didn't mind her having a double bed. It was okay when she talked about the bedroom. Of course, she could have the biggest room. That was fine by him. He'd already picked the attic room with the sloping roof and skylight that would shine shafts of bright sunlight down on him in the mornings, and it framed the beautiful vista of the stars at night. He suspected that she had other ideas, but he hated confrontation. He never voiced his opinions on the bedroom arrangements. Like telling his parents about moving out, he felt that the sleeping together issue was something that he'd have to work up to.

He never said a word until bedtime on their first night of living together. She went up for a bath, and while she was preening and pampering herself, he crept up the second flight of stairs and got into the snug single bed that she had bought for guests.

It's better this way. He reasoned to himself, no embarrassing scenes. She'll get the message.

But she didn't get the message. She said she was hurt and confused to find him fast asleep in the attic. She didn't understand.

'What are you doing in here?' she asked, tears forming in her eyes. 'Aren't you coming to bed?'

It was obvious that he was already in bed, and he would have to talk to her about knocking before she entered his room. He needed his privacy.

She was almost naked in a thin white negligee, and he could see her form, even in the pale moonlight coming through the window. Her breasts were full, and the nipples stood out against the cold. They were enormous. His eyes betrayed him by travelling lower to the patch of darkness, pushing against the fabric of the nightdress. His small penis shrivelled smaller and lay flaccid against the cushion of his testicles. He flattened his arms against the duvet, hiding himself from her.

She smelled of shampoo, shower gel, talc, deodorant, and some cloying, sickly perfume. He just wanted her out.

'Go to bed, Julie. We'll talk things through in the morning when you're decent.' Her head hung. She went to the door and was closing it behind her when he called her back.

'Julie?'

A smile came to her lips, and the tears froze on her eyelids. She was framed in the doorway, backlit by light from the hallway and spotlighted in the glow of the moon. He saw her completely then, the swell at her breast, stomach and hip, the thatch of dark hair between her legs, the want in her eyes.

He was repulsed.

'In future, would you mind knocking before you come into my room?'

The next morning, he came to breakfast as though nothing had happened. Julie was curled into the plush armchair with her legs pulled under her. She'd been in the chair all night and was miserable. Her face was puffy with red eyes from crying most of the night and the double bed had been left undisturbed. She was confused and unhappy, she felt unwelcome in his house. Julie wanted her mum.

She wanted to talk it through. Didn't she understand that he didn't want to do that? For the second time he fell back on his religious beliefs and said that he couldn't have sex out of wedlock. She pushed and wheedled and before he was aware of what he was doing, he'd agreed they should get married so they could make love. She said she understood, and he bought another few months in his single bed looking at the stars.

'Jules and I are getting married, Mother.'

Chapter Thirteen

Her answer was a long time coming. He knew she was still there. He could hear her inhaling on the other end of the telephone connection. The silence was laden with disappointment, her disappointment in him, and his feeling of being small and useless. He thought he was going to have to break the nothingness between them and be the first one to speak. He had cleared his throat and even stammered the first syllable of, 'Say something, please, Mother,' a couple of times when she cut in on his ineptitude at managing basic vocabulary.

She spoke quietly. 'Put her on the line.' There was no, please. The ice in her voice froze any argument he might have put forward. A bigger man could have tried to protect his wife-to-be, but he pointed the handset towards Julie.

'She wants to speak to you,' he mumbled in the voice of a chastised child.

She took the telephone from him. It was slick with the sweat from his clammy palm. 'Hello.'

'Are you pregnant?' Julie winced at the attack in the form of words. Four syllables, three words, and yet she felt as though the woman, who was going to be her mother-in-law, had punched her in the face and knocked her to the floor with a single blow. It was words that she'd been struck with, and yet she straightened her posture and clung on to the door beside her for support against the assault.

'No, Mrs Woods, I am not pregnant.'

'Liar,' Violet spat. 'You must be pregnant. Why else would you be rushing into this ridiculous notion of marriage? My son's not a fool. He won't marry a low-grade trollop. Or is it just that you're scared, Missy? Is that it?'

Although she had asked a question, she had no intention of giving Julie an opportunity to reply. Barely pausing for breath, she launched into a full-blown rant, spitting out accusations like poisoned darts from a blowpipe. 'Are you scared? That's it, isn't it? You're scared that any day now, my Philip will look at you and see what you are. He'll look at you and see filth, won't he? And we know what will happen then. He'll kick you into the same gutter that he pulled you up from. I see your game face. You saw my son, and your greedy eyes lit up. You saw a great big pound sign, and you grabbed it as any common whore would.'

Philip was hovering across the room, tugging his hair the way he did when he was upset. Although he was over ten feet away from Julie, and the words were tinny and distorted by the telephone line, he could hear every word his mother said. She had called him a bastard the last time they'd spoken. Now she was flinging insults at Julie. He tried to hold the telephone and lowered his head so that his mouth was close to the receiver, but Julie wouldn't let go.

'Really, Mother. I think that's too much.' Julie didn't try to excuse herself from the tirade on the other end of the phone. She spoke to Phil without covering the handset for privacy.

121

'No, it's all right, let her speak. She needs to do this. Let her get it all off her chest.' Phil let the tension go from his body with an audible sigh. He was relieved that he didn't have to get between the strong women. Better to let them sort it out themselves.

'Let me speak? You condescending bitch. How dare you assume that I need your permission to speak? Who do you think you're talking to? I could buy and sell your stinking family a thousand times over.'

'Stop. You can say what you like about me but leave my family out of this.'

Violet cut her off as though she'd never spoken. 'You know that if you don't get a ring on your finger, my son will see you for the gold-digging tramp you are. Don't think I don't know what's going on. He's a meal ticket. And you're going to take him for every penny you can, bleed him dry and then cast him aside when you move on to your next victim. I'm telling you, girl, this wedding will not take place. It isn't going to happen. Do you hear?' Her voice had risen to a shrill screech.

'Right, Mrs Woods, you've had your say now let me have mine.'

'Over my dead body. Do you hear me? Do you hear me?' Violet was screaming into the telephone, the last remnants of self-control lost in the rage of her tantrum. 'Don't mess with me, girl, because I'll crush you like a woodlouse.'

In other circumstances, Julie would have found this funny. Even in the drama of the moment, her mind wandered, and she wondered how a woodlouse would crush. She missed the final barrage of the bitter woman's threats and was brought back with Violet screaming at her to put her son back on. Phil lolled beside her, looking diminished.

'I want you to go to Dr Watkins to be tested for AIDS,' were the first words she spoke when Phil muttered hello into the handset.

'Mother, you're being silly.'

'She could be riddled with disease. You don't know who she laid down with before you. I'd hate to think that you've caught something dirty from her. Oh, Philip, please go and get yourself checked out. You've always been such a sensible boy. Why are you doing this to me? How could you hurt me after what I've sacrificed for you?' Phil's eyelids drooped, and his posture slumped as he settled in for a heavy dose of Violet's pain and disappointment. 'You said you'd never leave me. You were the one who was going to stay home and look after me. We've always been so close, Philip. How could you let this trollop come between us? I swear, this marriage will not happen. I forbid it. Now tell the girl to go back to where she came from and come home. We can sort out the mess you've got yourself into buying that silly house. Come back to your family and be forgiven, son, because if you don't, you're going to lose us all. What is so good about this fat, low-grade bitch that you'd give up your family for her?'

'Mother, please. It doesn't have to be like this. If you'd just give Jules a chance.'

'Never. She will not set foot over my door, and if you are with her, neither will you. I hope you'll think it's worth it, son because you've broken my heart. Your father, brothers, and I will not be attending this sham of a wedding.'

She ranted, sobbed and feigned illness, but the latter was only a momentary hiatus while she restocked on unused insults. Philip learned that his mother had a talent for profanity and gutter talk. Julie listening to the tinny voice spouting poison, willed Phil to stand up to his mother. She heard the names the foul woman called her but remained seated, breathing slowly and thinking about the flowers she wanted to plant in the garden. If we marry in early May, she thought, the cherry and apple blossom will be out. That'll be nice for photographs. She said nothing, hoping that Phil would fight for her. And then Violet got started on Julie's family again.

'The father doesn't work, and the mother's a domestic, Philip. They're scum, scrounging off the state and living a life of filth and squalor.'

It was as though a bomb had been planted under the pink cherry blossom tree. Julie, sitting pretty beneath the boughs in a white dress, saw the blossom explode, and she was on her feet wrenching the telephone out of her fiancé's hand.

'You are a nasty, venomous old cow,' she screamed, slamming the telephone into its cradle hard enough to cause a tremor to ripple through her carpal tunnel.

They argued. Phil said in a cold voice, 'I won't have you speaking to Mother like that,' and the fight finished sometime after midnight when Phil stormed to his bedroom in a sulk.

Julie didn't feel lonely lying in bed on her own that night. She didn't cry into her pillow, confused and rejected. She seethed, furious with Phil for taking his mother's side. Sleep was a long time coming.

The distance between them was tangible the next morning, the air thick with resentment. Julie made plans for her wedding, wondering if she wanted to get married, and Phil sulked. As she leafed through a brochure of wedding cakes, she paused and examined her reasons for going through with a wedding to a spineless man who would never protect her when she needed him to. She loved her new lifestyle. She loved her house. After living on a rough council estate all her life, she'd tasted a better one. She didn't want to go back to what she had been. She was ashamed to recognise that her motive was more mercenary and sheer bloody-mindedness than love. There was no way she was going to let the old cow win. She, Julie, was going to marry Philip, and if that pissed on Violet Woods' parade, then great. Somebody had to stand up to the evil old trout, and if her future husband couldn't do it, then she was going to marry him and teach him how.

Philip was great at sulking over short distances but couldn't go the mile. 'I'm making a coffee. Can I get you one?' he said at three-thirty the next day. The frost was still in the air, but she sensed some slush dripping from the edges. She hadn't made any lunch, so they both did without. At teatime, he went to the kitchen and made chicken with pasta and a cracked pepper sauce. It was her favourite, and they ate from trays in the lounge, something Phil hated. That evening they picked out a honeymoon in Corfu, but Julie still went to bed alone.

The following day she finished washing up after their evening meal, and they were settling down to watch TV. Julie went into the lounge to answer the phone, but Phil was already there, pulling a face at being disturbed. His telephone voice was in place by the time he'd put the handset to his ear.

'Hello,' he chimed. Around strangers and on the telephone, he sounded like the most easy-going bloke in the world.

'All right, Spud. How's it going?' It was SP. He'd called Phil Spud for years, but nobody remembered the origins of the nickname. 'What's going on, Bro? Mum's furious.' It was only around Violet that they spoke with cut-glass pronunciation. 'What's all this about you getting married? Bit of a rush, isn't it? We haven't even met the girl yet.'

'You've heard then? Listen, SP, are you going to come?'

'Whoa. Slow down, man. In fact, that's what I've rung up to say. Why not just slow down? Mum say's this girl—what's her name? Julie? Mum says she's not pregnant, so what's the rush? Why don't you wait a while? You haven't known her for five minutes. We're worried about you, Spud, and don't want to see you made a fool of.'

'Made a fool of? What are you talking about? Who's making a fool of me, SP? You're judging her before you've met her because of what Mum says.'

'I don't like my Mum being hurt, Phil. She cried to Ros for two hours today. What are you playing at?' His voice had taken on a hard edge.

Phil's voice echoed his resentment. 'I don't like Mum being hurt either. All I want to do is marry the girl I... All I want to do is marry Julie, and if you don't want to come, then bollocks to you, that's fine, but the marriage is going ahead. Sod the lot of you.'

'Come down off that bloody high horse of yours a minute, will you? If my littlest bro is getting married, then we'll be there. All the lads will, you know that.'

'And Mum and Dad?'

'That might not happen, Spud.'

'Stuff them then.'

'She's pretty raged up, and the old man just wants a quiet life. My guess is he'll try and talk her around, but you know what she's like. What's the big hurry, Phil? Why are you digging your heels in on this?

If you waited and gave everybody a chance to get to know her, I'm sure things will calm down. Why do you have to get married in a rush? You've only known her six months, for Christ's sake, and six weeks is a short space of time. How can you arrange a marriage in six weeks? Doesn't it make sense to do things properly? Why not set a date for next summer, and we'll have a bash to be proud of? Or are you hiding something? Come on, tell us the truth. Is she up the duff?'

Phil spent the next ten minutes convincing SP that Julie wasn't pregnant. He blushed as he admitted that they hadn't slept together and that they had separate bedrooms for the time being. He said he wanted to do things properly—the catholic way—to please Mother. Julie was furious and could have hit him for talking about their personal life so openly.

'Let me be honest with you. We're worried. What's this with the mental illness thing? What exactly is wrong with her? I'm not judging or anything, but if we can understand, maybe what you're doing won't seem so mad.'

'What?' Phil spluttered into the telephone. 'There's nothing wrong with her. What are you on about? Who's saying that? What the fuck? What mental illness?'

'Mum says she's been in Dale View. Said she thought it was drugs-related, something to do with heroin, or something.'

'Oh, she's gone too far this time. She's talking a load of bollocks, man. Heroin! I've never heard anything so ridiculous.' He was shouting. Julie had been following Phil's side of the conversation, and at that moment, just until the shock set in, she thought the situation was hilarious. She laughed.

'She said what?' she spluttered. 'I've never done drugs in my life.'

On the other end of the telephone, SP heard what Julie had said.

He lowered his voice to a whisper. 'I'm guessing she hasn't got AIDS either, then.'

'No. She has not got bloody AIDS.' This time even Phil could see the funny side, and the three of them shared the joke.

SP tried to persuade Phil and Julie to change their plans and have the reception at the hotel, but Julie wouldn't hear of it. She wanted this to be her wedding, organised her way.

She asked to speak to SP before Phil hung up. 'Hello, Simon Peter.'

'Sod the formalities, love. Call me SP. Everyone does.'

'Look,' she went on. 'I know you think this is too soon and all that, but I love your brother. I suppose I just want to say thank you for giving us a go. It means a lot to Phil, well, to both of us. Thank you.'

Julie was hurt. She wasn't a bad person. How could Violet make up those horrible lies about her? She went into the garden and dug around the plants in her herb garden, looking for miscreant weeds. She talked to her baby chives. They were growing well but were tall and leggy, bolting for the sun until they couldn't sustain their own weight and had slewed to one side. Julie didn't want them to look untidy. She supported them with fresh soil and asked the more robust Basil why anybody could be so cruel. Phil brought her coffee, and they sat at their table on the patio, enjoying the garden. It was bitterly cold, and he put his cardigan around her shoulders.

He praised her efforts in the garden and said that she was doing a good job. She basked in his compliment. He told her not to worry and that everything would work out. She tried to believe him.

James rang the same evening. He began the conversation with, 'Way to go, bro,' and then continued, 'have you lost the plot, or what? It's okay shacking up with a drug-crazed loony for a bit. Hell, I've bedded a few of them myself, but hell, man, wanting to marry one? If you were here now, I'd shake your hand. It's the first time you've ever bested me as the black sheep of the family. When did you grow a pair of bollocks? I bet the old girl had a cow. Wish I'd seen it. Is she a goer then, this Julie?'

For the second time that night, Phil explained the situation, and James was disappointed. But he assured them that he wouldn't miss the wedding for the world. 'Hell, there's bound to be a punch-up some-where along the line, bud. Count me in. I'll travel up from London the night before with John if he's coming. You can guarantee he won't want to miss the party.'

Andrew was the next to ring. SP had already filled him in on the anti-climax of their mother's vicious tongue.

'Hey, Phil. I'm sorry about all the hassle you've had, bruv. I've just called to say that I hope there's an invitation to this wedding for us.'

And so, it was arranged. The wedding was going ahead, and all the Woods' boys would be in attendance. Julie didn't feel accepted by the hostile family, but maybe a few bridges had been mended before too much damage was done.

They didn't hear from Mother Woods again until soon after the invitations had been sent out. Phil had invited friends in Windermere, and word spread that the youngest of the Woods boys was getting married and, what's more, it was taking place in a registry office.

People stopped Violet in the street to fish for gossip about this startlingly low-key marriage. She flew home in a rage that day. She tried to get Donald to do the dirty work for her, to let it be understood that this was his idea and that he'd put his foot down to make his wife comply.

Donald had done his damnedest to make Violet change her mind about not attending their son's wedding. It broke his heart to think he wouldn't be there to shake his youngest son's hand and wish him all the best. He didn't approve of the girl, either, but it was Phil's choice and, rightly or wrongly, he had made it. Violet had been immovable, and Donald resigned himself that if he wanted a continued peaceful life, he would have to stand beside his wife and boycott the wedding. He wanted to go against her wishes, but this was too big a fight for him to take on.

The gossips were already out in force. It wouldn't do to be seen to be at war with his wife, and if he went against her, he knew for a certainty there would be war.

She flounced through reception in a fury. Mrs Hughes-Norris was knocked out of her path as Violet muscled her way through the WI brigade with elbows out and murder in her eyes.

'Something must be done about this wedding,' she said to her husband when she reached their suite.

Donald was rarely immovable about anything, but on this point, he faced his wife down and flatly refused to do her grovelling for her. Had

Violet been less involved in herself at that moment, she might have seen an unusual expression tiptoe across her husband's face. He listened with his arms folded across his chest. His mouth worked hard not to let the minuscule curl at the edges of his lips turn into a full-on grin, and his eyes shone. He'd never seen Violet eat humble pie before and wanted to see if it could be done. He was going to enjoy this. He tried to push for a run out to see the couple and sort this silly mess face to face, but that was going too far, and Violet was having none of it.

'Hello.'

'Philip, My darling. How are you both? How is Julia?' Violet enthused in a voice flooded with insincerity.

'What is it, Mother? If you want another fight, we're not interested. You said some vile, terrible things about Jules. How could you?'

'I know, dear,' her voice remained bright and not in the least repentant. 'Your father and the boys have told me off already about that silly misunderstanding. You must tell Julia to be more precise about things, dear, and we won't get the wrong end of the stick. Still, never mind that it's not important. Now then, dear, time is moving on. If we are going to make this wedding the Event of the Year, dear, we're going to have to get on. Now then, the first thing we've got to do is cancel that horrible registry office. What were you thinking, Philip? How beneath you. Sometimes I despair of you boys, I really do. Now, wait until you hear this. It was almost impossible, I grant you, and there had to be some radical changes made. But—are you ready for this, dear? As a special favour to me, Monsignor Burton has agreed to attend your wedding at St Mary's, though, of course, father McDonnegal will lead the service.

We'll have the hotel at our disposal, of course. There now, what do you think of that?'

Julie had her ear pressed against the telephone and was fighting for the handset with Phil to hear what Violet was saying. She couldn't believe what she heard. Phil was like a plank listening to his Mother muscle in. He didn't say a word. Julie was the first to speak. She addressed her comment to Phil but was in no doubt that Violet, and indeed most of the neighbours, could hear her.

'No way. No bloody way is that woman taking over my wedding.'

Violet gave a little chuckle. 'Oh, she's such a one, that Julia of yours. Tell her there's no need to thank me, dear. I'll pick her up at ten sharp tomorrow. We'll have to have her measured for a dress.' Her voice dropped for dramatic effect, 'Given her dimensions. It might take some time, dear. It really is most inconsiderate of you to give me so little time to arrange an entire wedding and not just any wedding. The Wedding of the Year, dear. Now, you two lovebirds, just leave everything to me. Cheerio.' And with that, Phil was left listening to a broken connection, and Violet was gone.

'Thank you very much,' Julie screamed, wheeling round to Phil in fury. 'Why didn't you tell her there's no way I'm going with her to get my wedding dress? She's welcome as a guest, but she's having nothing to do with the organisation. Why didn't you tell her, Phil?' she finished with a sob.

Phil's mouth had stretched to form a thin lipless line. He spoke to her in disgust. 'You're hysterical. Calm down, and when you're ready to have a civilised discussion, we'll talk.'

'She called me an AIDS-ridden junkie with mental problems, Phil. How do you expect me to react?'

He retreated to the quiet of the study.

She was hurt. She sat on the sofa staring at the television but taking nothing in. She couldn't understand why Phil wouldn't stand up to his mother. Her blood pressure dropped, her breathing returned to normal, and she went from rasping sobs to the occasional dry hitch. It wasn't Phil's fault that his mother had rung. She could see that. She had turned on him. She could see that too. She took him a cup of coffee, remembering to knock on the study door and wait for an answer before going in.

'I'm sorry, love,' she said, going up behind him and putting her arms around his shoulders. She felt him stiffen beneath her touch. 'I know this isn't easy for you, and you must feel stuck between us. Can we talk now, please?'

'She's my mother, Julie. Why can't you let her in? Have you any idea how hard that was for her?'

Julie wanted to say that it wasn't easy for her either, but she held her counsel. 'If I go tomorrow, she's going to take over. This is our wedding. It's supposed to be the best day of our lives. I want us to arrange it ourselves. I don't mind getting married at the registry. I like the fact that it's small and intimate and that we're paying for it all ourselves. I don't want her to take over, Phil.'

'Julia, I didn't realise you were the elite when it came to producing a wedding. Have you any idea how many weddings Mother managed? She's done celebrities.'

'What did you call me?'

'What?'

'You just called me Julia.'

'No, I didn't.'

'You did. You called me Julia.'

'Don't be ridiculous. Anyway, my mother's wedding plans might not be good enough for you, but I think it was very generous of her. You're going to make her look a fool in front of her priest if you snub her. And frankly, I won't have that. Either you let my mother in, or the wedding's off. And what's more, I expect you to show some gratitude. What's it to be? Do you want to marry me?'

She tried to keep her temper. He was still angry with her. He had every right to be, but she was angry too. 'I'm sorry, but that's just it. Your mum produces weddings. She choreographs them like a stage production. That's wonderful if it's what you want. But I just want us to say our vows with the people we care about behind us and then have a bit of a do afterwards. I want it to be special. I know we had no choice but to do it on the cheap, but it's exactly the way I want it.'

'Have you stopped to think about what I want? Have you asked me if I want a dirty little two-bit affair? Has it even crossed your mind that unless I'm married in the sight of God, as far as I'm concerned, we won't be married? I went along with you because it was all we could afford, and I wanted to please you.' He omitted the fact that the main reason he agreed to marry her was to keep her out of his bed. 'Things are different now. Mother is offering us a proper marriage, done in the correct way.' The anger went out of his voice, and she felt his shoulders slump. 'That's what I want, Julie.'

She turned things over through the night. Insomnia was a new but frequent bed partner these days. She resisted the thought of that woman having anything to do with their wedding.

Having her make the arrangements was giving their marriage the kiss of death before they made it to the altar. And then some of Phil's words came back to her, 'Have you any idea how hard that must have been for her?' Julie smiled and hugged a pillow to her. The thought of how hard it would be for Violet to watch her favourite son marry a woman she detested filled Julie with a delicious feeling of power. Even better was the fact that she would be paying for it all.

Hadn't one of her main accusations been that Julie was a gold digger? She could learn her part, and, she decided, she was going to play it to the hilt. It would have to be a grand wedding because Julie knew that Violet's position in the community was everything to her. It would be a wonderful, lavish and expensive wedding, with all of Julie's down-to-earth family and friends in attendance, and Violet would be paying for every penny of it. Let the old bitch have her way, Julie thought. I'm going to love every second of it from this moment on. And, while I'm having the time of my life, she'll hate it and be suffering.

She slept soundly and dreamt about stuffing her face with chocolate wedding cake and victory.

Chapter Fourteen

It was six-thirty in the morning. Julie was in the garden as the sun rose on her wedding day. Their house had enormous enclosed back, side and front gardens, and she was on a bench made from two large vertical rocks and a horizontal sheet of black slate. Her coffee was the first of the day, and it was piping hot and calming. She loved this seat in this part of the garden. Phil had made it for her, and he chose the position because it had the best view over the rest of their land. It was a simple piece of furniture, half ornamental and half functional. He'd made it from rocks taken from Roan Head beach, where he found the flat, broad slate that lay horizontally across the top, and then it had taken weeks of beachcombing to find two tall pieces of rock that were similar enough in size to work into legs. She'd insisted that it was put under the boughs of the huge cherry tree in the bottom left-hand corner of the patio. The ground in front of her was littered with thousands of cherry blossom petals. The cherry was her favourite tree. She loved its delicate, pale pink petals but hated that it only flowered for such a short time. She looked forward to the first photograph when she had put her dress on. She'd sit under the tree with her train arranged around her, and fresh petals would fall as the shutter closed.

She thought about Phil at the hotel. Following tradition, he'd spent the night there with his best man and long-time friend, Chris Wattle. She smiled as she imagined his family trying to talk him out of marrying her. She could hear them saying, 'It's not too late to back out, Spud.' But she knew he'd hold firm and be standing at the altar when she walked down the aisle. Her fiancé was a stubborn man. He wouldn't let himself down.

But would he let her down? That was the question as she sat under the tree. Did he really love her? More to the point, did she love him? She thought she was in love when they'd moved in together, but months of sharing a house came with his obsessive-compulsive habits.

She'd met a man who was easygoing and mellow. But he wasn't like that. He was resolute and controlling. The Catholic religion possessed Phil. And then there was the question of sex. She could understand that he wanted to go to his wedding bed, a virgin. She wasn't. And that was a stick he had to beat her with. She understood and respected his religious belief, but a nagging voice told her things might not change after the ceremony. Whenever she'd mentioned him moving into her room—their room—after the wedding, he changed the subject.

Do you love him? She heard the voice in her head as clearly as if she'd spoken the words out loud. She ignored it and thought about her dress.

Do you love him?

She listened to the birdsong as the morning chorus practised singing her to her wedding. She would have smiled at her inner child if that child hadn't grabbed the bars of her cage and rattled it so hard that she couldn't ignore what she already knew.

No, she didn't love him. But she wanted to, so that was something. She felt that with time, she could learn how he liked the cutlery drawer arranged, and she'd remember to turn the labels of tins to the front of the cupboard. They needed to grow together. He'd smarten her and make her conscientious and particular about things, and she'd loosen him up. She believed they could make a good marriage from a troubled start. It wasn't all about flouncy dresses and home-grown confetti trees. If she'd truly believed it wasn't going to be a happy marriage, she wouldn't have gone through with it.

She was cheated. She should have been ecstatic. She'd written this very moment into her wedding plan. *Cup of coffee, sitting under the cherry blossom, feeling ecstatic.* She was excited about the day and the honeymoon to follow but bowled over by true love and excitement at embarking on a lifelong union with her husband. No. It wasn't like that. She made her first vow of the day. It was a private one. She vowed that, no matter what, she was going to be a good wife.

They had hen-night drinks the night before. Several empty wine bottles untidied the worktops in the kitchen. Phil wouldn't like that. He hated a messy home. Lisa and Emma, her sisters, had stayed over, along with Anne Wattle, the best man's wife. She was a guest at Phil's insistence.

Julie had only met her once. She was a quiet woman, almost silent. The three of them had spent all night trying to involve her in conversation and not let her be left out, but it was awkward. Julie hoped one of her sisters would be downstairs before Anne.

An hour later, the kitchen was buzzing with excited conversation. It was only eight o'clock, and she wasn't getting married until one. Phil had asked her not to drink the night before. He said it was for her own good because he wanted her to enjoy her wedding day with a clear head.

It had seemed sensible advice. Anne was teetotal and only drank orange juice. Lisa and Emma had come downstairs with hangovers after being called by Julie two minutes after Anne made an appearance. Emma, the sensible one, suggested bacon butties to soak up last night's wine. Lisa, the forward one, suggested Anne make them. Anne, the silent one, cooked.

After eating, Anne tidied the house and washed up while Julie's sisters fought over the bathroom. Julie was the last to get ready, and Anne said that she'd take her turn after Lisa and Emma, or after Julie, or whenever. She said she didn't mind. The hairdresser was arriving at eleven. Julie spent a long time up to her neck in bubbles for her last bath as a single woman.

Another woman arrived to do their makeup, and when she'd finished, Julie had never felt so beautiful. In fact, she had never once in her entire life felt attractive at all until that moment when she looked in the mirror. She felt as though she'd spent her life masked and had turned into somebody she didn't know. She was shy when she stood in the middle of the living room in her wedding dress. Phil's mother had tried to buy a dress that was frumpy and unflattering to her larger shape. Julie knew she did it on purpose to score points. And to say to her cronies, 'Well, dear, I did the best I could with what I had to work with. Despite it costing four thousand pounds, nothing could make that tramp look anything other than what she is. I did try.' Julie had fought her in the towns and on the beaches. She told her she wouldn't be seen dead in any of the dresses Violet picked out for her. She'd stormed out of the shop,

139

giving Violet more cause to tittle-tattle about her to the bridal wear proprietor. Julie refused to return until her wishes had been listened to. Far from opting for a big fat ugly cloud of netting that made her look like Antarctica, she'd opted for simple, sophisticated elegance. Her dress had a fitted bodice that, when laced, lost an instant three inches from her waistline. The skirt was a shift of heavy satin, straight-lined and flattering to a bigger lady. The train swirled around her feet in a vast fishtail, and she'd chosen a full veil that fell to her waist. On her wedding day, Julie Spencer was beautiful.

Her parents arrived and cried. The wedding party went into the garden, and Julie sat on the bench at the end of the patio with her father standing above her with one hand resting on her shoulder. The photographer arrived an hour earlier and had been setting up his equipment in the garden. It was perfect. How could this wedding not be blessed when everything had fallen into place just as she had wanted? She put the thoughts of that morning down to wedding day jitters.

At twelve-thirty, a white Rolls Royce adorned with deep purple ribbons to match her colour scheme pulled up outside the front door. The neighbours had gathered to see the bride leave. Julie was a princess.

At the church, standing in front of the massive oak doors, she was scared. The knave was cool and peaceful, and her husband-to-be was waiting for her on the other side of the doors, yet she wanted to stay where she was and collect her thoughts. Philip was here. His mother, and the family, hadn't talked him out of it. She was surprised they hadn't succeeded. Nobody gave her the not-too-late-to-back-down speech. They told her how lucky she was and how she'd fallen on her feet. She was amazed that her future husband had turned up to marry her. She was grateful. The organ took up the opening strains of *The Wedding March*, and her father held out his arm to her.

Showtime.

As they walked past each pew, the people turned to look at her. Aunties that she hadn't seen for years beamed their gummy grins, and, on Phil's side, people she'd never met looked at her with curiosity, wanting to see the disgusting, drug-addled creature Philip had taken up with. When they reached the front of the church, her mum had a tissue up to her face, dabbing her eyes and sniffing. Violet's reaction was very different.

As Julie approached the altar, she locked eyes with her future mother-in-law. In that unguarded second, before she rearranged her mask, the look in Violet's eye was one of pure hatred. In that split second, her lip curled away from her teeth in a snarl. Julie knew that no olive branches were laid, no alms arranged in front of her. A veneer may have been applied to their relationship for the sake of appearances, but the battle swords were drawn.

The four brothers and their spouses stared. They were neither warm nor openly hostile, just bland vacant stares. Simon Peter was concerned with his appearance and looked bored. Andrew was disinterested. He failed to keep his feral children under control. James' eyes swept over the yards of satin and lace and then journeyed back up Julie's voluptuous body. They rested on the bodice with a sneer. John's glance only stayed on Julie for a second before straying to Lisa. He looked her up and down with lust in his gaze, and his partner Gaynor's expression hardened and fixed on Jesus nailed to the Cross. Jealousy leaked from her posture, and hatred for Julie, who had the pretty sister, grew in the pit of her stomach.

As the procession reached the altar railing and Richard, Julie's dad, delivered her to her husband-to-be, Philip beamed, and the choristers stood. Philip tried to squeeze out a little tear and nearly succeeded. Julie felt real emotion as the soloist's soprano voice sang *Ave Maria*. At the final refrain, the choir joined in, and the music was striking. At Violet's express insistence, Monsignor Burton had been wheeled out for the day. He hadn't left the Castlerigg monastery in Keswick for over five years. The Benedictine monks cared for him, and the old priest was well into his late nineties. He spent most of his time in service or dozing in the monastery gardens and was as nutty as a squirrel's stash. The clergy refused to turn the poor old gentleman out of his routine. They said it would confuse him, but Violet would hear none of it. As well as writing letters of appeal to the bishop himself, she turned up on the monastery doorstep to plead her case. She told them that the Monsignor had Married Violet. He had served at the Christenings, and First Holy Communion, of all five of her boys. She wept into her handkerchief and said that if he wasn't in attendance at the marriage of her youngest child, then as long as the monsignor was alive, the wedding couldn't go ahead. The clergy pondered this statement at length to determine if the crazy old coot was making a death threat. In the end, it didn't matter because the gilt-edged cheque that she handed over with discretion—towards the monastery funds—salved their holy conscience.

The Monsignor was slumped forward in his wheelchair, conducting his mass in Latin to an audience of none. His voice rose and fell, and

142

during the fire and brimstone parts, it would be impossible to hear anything else. When he forgot which prayer he was up to, he went back to the beginning and started again. Violet said it was most unfortunate and deeply regretted her insistence that he be the guest of honour.

Several times during the service, proceedings had to halt because he'd hit another rousing part of his service and flung his hands up as he incanted Latin at a far-reaching screech. It was only the restraints tying him into the wheelchair that held him in place and stopped him from launching himself out to kneel at the appropriate times. He broke wind, then fell asleep in time for the important bit.

Everybody laughed except Violet, who was horrified when Julie and Philip knelt at the altar, and the brothers had written *HE* on the sole of one of Philip's shoes and *LP* on the other.

The crucial point of the ceremony, the bit that people would talk about for months, was the part where the priest asked the congregation, 'If anybody here knows of any lawful impediment why these two people should not be joined in holy matrimony, then let them speak now or forever hold their peace.' Donald put a restraining hand on Violet's shoulder, manning up to stop his wife from disgracing herself, her marriage and her family. When Violet had changed her mind about boycotting the wedding, she was still ranting and raving. She promised every family member that when that time came, she'd stand up and denounce the wedding. At some point, the chambermaids had heard her making the same threat to Simon Peter, and then the whole village knew what Violet planned to do. Julie and Philip knew because Violet had screamed the threat down the phone at her. Speculation was rife as to whether it would prove to be an empty and meaningless threat. If

Violet did say anything, she would only be making an unholy show of herself.

The moment came, and Father McDonnegal laid down the gauntlet. You could hear a pin drop in the church. The outcome of the next thirty seconds meant a lot to Gary Yardley, one of the regulars in the hotel bar. He was running a book on it. Everybody's attention was focused on Violet.

Julie had plans of her own, and that's when she chose to show the village, and her new family, some of her mettle. As the priest spoke the words, she was in profile to Violet. She removed her left hand from Philip's, lifted the veil from her face and turned to confront Violet. And there she stood, holding her cascading bouquet of honeysuckle in front of her. Her expression was neutral, but her eyes were wide open—and challenging.

Violet had nothing.

On this occasion, she was all mouth. She coloured to the roots of her bronze hair dye. Her face was scarlet and clashed with the Barbara Cartland hat of flowers and feathers spilling over her head.

Julie raised an eyebrow.

Only seconds had passed since the priest finished speaking, but as Julie held her ground and Violet squirmed and flustered, it seemed longer. After Julie raised her eyebrow, effectively slapping Violet across the face with her glove, the congregation loved it, and Maisy Roach said it was better than a soap opera. It was clear that she wasn't going to turn back to the altar until some response had been made.

Violet stared at her, silently imploring her to go back and continue the service. But Julie waited. Violet cleared her throat. She made a sound that might have been a titter or a chortle.

Perhaps she attempted bell-like laughter, but instead, she spat out barbs from the wire she choked on. She smiled a sickly smile, pleading with her still, squirming uncomfortably in her seat, and she turned to Auntie Dorothy beside her, rolling her eyes as though to say, 'Silly girl, she does so like her practical jokes.' Her smile was forced and tight-lipped as she shooed Julie's attention back to the priest with a white-gloved hand. Even the priest was relieved.

Julie lowered her eyebrow, nodded once and with a flick of her hair, she curtsied proudly to Violet and turned back to the altar. Philip was stiff. When she took his hand and asked Father McDonnegal to continue, he allowed it for the sake of propriety, but Julie knew he was furious with her for embarrassing his mother. He went through the motions, but Julie had ruined their day.

Philip played his part. When he spoke the last of his vows, his eyes shone with love, but Julie saw the glint behind the sheen that wasn't visible to anybody else. When it came to exchanging the rings, Julie's fingers were swollen. Philip made several attempts but couldn't push the band past the fat below her ring finger's second joint. They heard the brothers laughing at them in the pew behind. James guffawed. Philip was embarrassed, and Julie was angry. It wasn't her fault that her fingers had swollen in the heat. When the ceremony was over and the register signed, the priest was relieved. Philip was sulking about his mother, and Julie didn't know how she felt. She tried to analyse it while posing for photographs in the archway of the seventeenth-century church. She felt a headache coming on.

Julie looked forward to her reception. She thought she'd be able to relax. But the headache gnawed at her while they ate the roast beef dinner. By the main course, the niggle had turned into a roar. She felt sick and picked at the food that she'd so looked forward to. Desserts were Julie's vice. She loved rich, sticky, creamy desserts. When the trifle was delivered to her plate, she couldn't touch it. The pain in her head was blinding. She needed to lie down. She had only taken one sip from her glass. During the toasts, she pretended to sip the vintage champagne. The noise of clattering cutlery, bustling waiters and conversation was deafening. She barely heard the best man's speech. When her father got up to speak, she pulled her mind past the jackhammer in her head to listen. He spoke from the heart and with love. He told Julie how proud of her he was.

Donald rose. He kept his words brief, welcomed Julie into the family and raised his glass in a toast. He was stoic and dignified. What couldn't be killed and buried in his garden beneath a full moon had to be endured.

Julie's parents had saved to give them a hundred pounds. It wasn't much, but her mum had worked hard for that money, and her dad had gone without. Julie knew it was more than they could afford. Phil's parents had paid for the wedding at a cost of thousands, and that meant nothing. The brothers had clubbed together and bought a cheap trinket.

Julie took the insult and stored it.

After the meal, there was an hour of mingling before the evening entertainment. Julie felt terrible. The headache had turned into a full-blown migraine, and she couldn't bear it. She went around the groups of guests, ensuring that everybody was having a good time. She carried her untouched flute of champagne with her and couldn't face a drop. She heard James' raucous laugh as the words of his conversation drifted to her. 'Yeah,' he said to a group of the hotel staff. 'I wanted to write "Help me," on one shoe and "I'm about to be crushed" on the other, but the lads wouldn't let me.'

Julie took the insult and stored it.

She left her party to go to bed before the first dance, before cutting the cake and before the party. She threw up in the acres of restricting wedding dress and then hung over the toilet bowl, dry heaving for an hour. She fought to get out of the dress, but she couldn't. It was like a straitjacket, restraining her and crushing her diaphragm. Fully dressed, she lay on the marital four-poster and wanted to die. The day was a disaster, and she felt awful. Her head pounded, and she couldn't face the smallest chink of light. She prayed that somebody would come by soon and untie her from the suffocating wedding dress, but nobody did. Philip never came to bed. He stayed up all night partying with his brothers.

Julie spent her wedding night ill and alone.

Chapter Fifteen

J ulie had a terrible night. The wedding dress cut into her, and she couldn't breathe. The migraine had pummelled her until the early hours of the morning when she fell into a fitful sleep. She woke in a fugue. The curtains were heavy and lined and let in no light. It took her a moment to realise where she was. She thought it was still the middle of the night, and it took her another moment to remember she was a married woman. She turned her head to look at her new husband, but he wasn't there. The clock told her it was gone ten. Why hadn't anybody called her for breakfast?

Some of the previous day's misery washed over her, but she refused to let it access her mind. She felt thick-headed but not unwell. The migraine was gone. Today was the first day of her marriage, and they were going to Corfu later for their honeymoon. Things had got off to a bad start, but that was behind them. She was excited. She jumped out of bed, fought with the damned dress and wrestled herself to the window, where she flung open the curtains and let glorious, bright sunshine flood the room. She rang reception to ask them to send one of her sisters. She wanted a bath before she went in search of Phil and needed somebody to untie her from the dress. The girl in reception told her that as her family had to check out of their rooms by ten, they had left to travel home to Barrow. Violet had left word that Julie had asked not to be disturbed.

Violet had thrown her family out as though they were rubbish. How could she be so cruel? Not stopping to check her appearance, she flounced out of the room to either find her husband or confront her bitch of a mother-in-law, whichever came first.

The desk clerk stared at Julie but told her that Phil had passed out and was carried to John's room just before the guests arrived for their breakfast. She turned from the desk. Everybody milling around the reception area stared at her. Sharon paged Simon Peter to report a small problem in reception.

SP strode in, and without saying a word, he grabbed Julie under the elbow and guided her to the lift. As it was already on the ground floor, it only took seconds to open. 'What the hell are you playing at coming into reception like that?' He whispered, pointing at her dress. 'You look deranged. Who do you think you are, Lady bloody Haversham?'

Julie had no idea who Lady bloody Haversham was, so ignored his question to pose one of her own. 'Where's Phil?'

SP pushed her into the lift. 'Make yourself decent, woman, and never come into my hotel if you aren't presentable again.'

The front of her dress was splattered in vomit. Her hair had come down from its wedding arrangement on one side and hung in vomit-stiffened tails. Her makeup, which had been so exquisite the day before, had run down her face. Her breasts, having nowhere else to go, partially spilt out of the top of the tight bodice. SP was right. She looked

149

deranged. As the lift rose, and in the tight confines, she could smell herself. She was ashamed.

On the top floor. As she squeezed her size and her dress out of the small door, three people waited to get in. The lift stank of stale vomit. She sobbed and ran along the corridor to John's room. There were other guests in the corridor. They all stared at her. John took ages to answer. 'All right, I'm coming,' he shouted as she hammered. She burst through the door as soon as it opened. Gaynor was still in bed, but she sat up and pulled the quilt to her chin before curling her nose in disgust. 'Bloody hell, you look worse than we do,' John said, taking in the state of Julie. Phil was asleep on the sofa. His shoes were on the floor, and his feet hung over the edge of the arm. He slept fully clothed.

She berated him all the way back to their room. Phil said nothing. He was tight-lipped and silent. As she struggled with the key, he had his hand over his mouth, and he gruffly uttered one word, 'Hurry,' and then he pushed past her and ran into the bathroom, where she heard him retching. The newlyweds may not have spent the night together, but the toilet had seen plenty of action.

She flumped on the bed to wait. She heard the water running and realised that the selfish man had jumped straight in the shower before releasing her from the prison of the bastard dress which she had come to loathe with a passion. The aroma of his shower gel oozed under the bathroom door. She heard him towelling off and brushing his teeth. If only he'd unfastened her, she might have joined him in the shower. She could have shown him how wonderful it is to be washed all over by somebody who loves you. Cleaning him before they made love for the first time would be an act that was sacramental, and if it was good enough for Mary Magdalene, she had no qualms with it.

He came out and made it clear that he didn't want anything to do with undressing her but undid the multitude of knots that held the laces of her bodice tight. She felt her body screaming for mercy as inches of it were released to spill out of its tether. He told her that he felt better after his shower. She suggested they have a cuddle before packing their things for Corfu. And as he flung the cases onto the bed, he made a feeble excuse to leave the room.

He was gone, and Julie was alone again.

She dragged the underskirts from her and stood in front of the mirror in her wedding lingerie, a second whalebone corset that had punished her for twenty-four hours. He hadn't seen her underwear. The previous day, as she looked at herself in it, she felt sexy and alluring, now she looked with a critical eye and realised that she was ridiculous. Her breasts weren't contained in the cups of the bodice, she had rolls of spare flesh under her armpits, and the areola of both nipples was visible where the garment had failed to hold her up. The stockings, stretched beyond their natural elasticity, were held only at the two points of contact with the suspender clips. The rest of them had drooped. Far from coming up to the tops of her thighs, they barely covered her kneecaps. And she had deep indentations where the tight elastic had dug into her flesh. The partial loss of circulation had caused severe black bruising around the dents. The feeling of relief when she undid the suspender clips was instant, she could have undone them the night before, but the pain from the bodice was so intense that she hadn't noticed the discomfort in her legs.

She struggled to undo the hooks and eyes travelling down the back of the corset. Her fat arms ached, and the effort of reaching high up her back and fighting with the fastenings left her out of breath. She had to stop and rest less than halfway through. In desperation, she took the tiny scissors out of her nail care bag. She cut up the front of the satin between the whalebone. It was almost as hard as trying to unhook it, but at last, she was free. She stepped out of the satin thong at last, and she breathed. Her body had deep ruts where the whalebones had cut into her, and she'd gained inches of girth in ten seconds, but she was free. She ran a bath and let the softness of the hot water ease the pain. She was glad her husband wasn't with her because she was ugly.

She had dried and dressed in a simple pair of black trousers and a blouse when she heard Phil come in. He knocked on the bathroom door and told her they had to hurry to get packed and ready to go because his mother had asked them to join them for a light brunch.

Julie hadn't been asked anything, she was called to heel like a dog, and there was no option of refusal.

In Violet's quarters, brunch had already been served. Violet perched on the edge of a sofa, so Julie took the other end and mirrored her. She sat with one buttock barely on the very rim of the seat, the other half of her backside hung uncomfortably in mid-air, and her thighs had to cling to the leg of the sofa for support. She tried to cross her ankles and twist her lower legs to the left, but they were too large to contort in that way. Julie comforted herself with the fact that Violet wasn't slim, either and looked equally ridiculous. Phil flopped into an armchair across the room. He was nursing his hangover and looked thoroughly miserable.

Lunch was eaten from China side plates, croissants and other sweet and savoury pastries. Julie smelled the warm bread and realised she was starving. She hadn't eaten since breakfast the day before and could have demolished the lot. She took a croissant and a small slice of cheese.

The crispy bacon looked delicious, too. What she wanted was two doorstops of fresh bread, half a pound of butter, a bottle of ketchup and the full plate of bacon with two fried eggs on top.

She made do with the one croissant and the sliver of cheese. She raised it to her lips and bit daintily into it. Flaky pastry cascaded and sprinkled her knee and Violet's cream sofa. She didn't look at Violet to gauge her reaction. After the first delicate nibble caused an avalanche that the Alps would envy, she put her side plate on the occasional table beside her and took her chances with the rattling cup of tea in its delicate saucer instead. They left half an hour later. Violet dropped an icy kiss towards each of Julie's cheeks without contacting her skin and told Phil to 'Uphold the family name,' whatever the hell that meant. Julie's stomach growled after being tricked into thinking it was going to be fed.

Donald drove them to Manchester airport. The journey was long and uncomfortable, and very little was said. He repeated that yesterday had gone well, and both Julie and Phil agreed with him, despite it being one of the worst days of Julie's life. He and Phil discussed herbaceous borders and the predicted weather forecast in Greece.

At the airport, she wanted to get some food, but after a tour of every eatery in departures, Phil said that everything was far too expensive and he wouldn't pay their inflated prices on principal. He refused the in-flight meals because he'd seen a documentary based around a factory where airport meals were produced. After seeing that, he'd vowed never to eat on a plane again. His principals were all well and good, but Julie was hungry, and far from being elated at the prospect of their honeymoon she was in a bad mood, and when she was hungry, she was nasty. Philip had control of their money, including the hundred pounds that her parents had given them. She asked him for enough to buy a sandwich and a bar of chocolate. He refused, saying that it was a waste of money and that they were on a tight budget. She whined that she was hungry, while Phil spent ten pounds on a raffle ticket to win the fancy sports car that was in the middle of the departure lounge.

Julie had never flown before and was terrified when the plane took off. Phil was a seasoned traveller and held her hand, telling her that it was fine and to relax. He'd taken the window seat, and Julie had to strain her eyes to watch the earth slipping away. The in-flight movie was *Shallow Hal*. Philip said it reminded him of her. He tried to explain that he meant it as a compliment, that you shouldn't judge a person on their size. Julie didn't appreciate the compliment or the remark and was embarrassed that the man sitting next to her smirked when he said it. Julie had taken up more than her share of the seating arrangements, and the man beside her had to lean into the aisle for comfort. She was insulted by Phil's words. When the drinks cart came along, he ordered a whisky on the rocks for him and a vodka and coke for her. She would rather have had a sandwich. She asked for a packet of nuts. It was the only food on offer with the drinks trolley. Phil glared at her but bought them. They were tiny, and she wolfed them in three handfuls. They cost one pound seventy-five, and he sulked about it until they circled for landing. They looked out of the window and were excited as they had their first glimpse of the island.

Philip was grumpy when they landed because he had to wait with her to get their luggage from the carousel. He wasn't allowed to have a cigarette until they'd cleared customs and were outside the building. He'd gone three hours without one, and he was as cranky as hell. They left the cool interior of the airport terminal, and an unnatural heat, the likes of which Julie had never felt in her life, engulfed them. It was so hot that it took her breath away. Everything about the place, right down to the atmosphere, was foreign. Julie loved it and was so excited that her former moodiness was forgotten. They boarded the coach and chatted with other holidaymakers for the half-hour trip to their all-inclusive complex.

Julie was devastated to learn that they'd missed dinner when they checked in. They had finished serving half an hour earlier. The intense heat had dropped to a light Mediterranean haze as they'd travelled, and by the time they went upstairs, it was chilly. The room was spectacular. Julie was delighted that there was only one bed. That would save any arguments or upset later. She saw Phil eye it with disgust. The bed was enormous and must have been eight feet across. Philip cast a hotelier's eye over the room. He ran his finger along the skirting, looking for dust. He checked the light fittings for cobwebs, and he checked that the wardrobe had the requisite six wooden coat hangers per person. Julie was entranced, everything was perfect, and she couldn't wait to sink into the deep bath before going to bed with her husband for the first time.

After contenting himself that the room met his approval, Phil went to the French doors and threw them open onto the balcony. He scoured the mini-bar and took out two bottles, whisky for him and vodka for her, with a mini can of Coke. He helped himself to the ice tray. Julie suggested that they go to the hotel bar instead of using the mini bar in their room. She worried that there would be a hefty cost involved. Phil laughed, 'It's all-inclusive stupid. Everything's free.'

'Oh,' She smarted when her husband called her stupid, but her mood was lifted over the wonders of Greece. Their balcony overlooked the beautiful gardens of the resort that led to the beach a couple of hundred feet away. They watched the waves lapping the shore, and she felt a tranquillity and peace of mind that she'd never known before. At that perfect moment, she was truly happy. She loved the resort. She loved Greece, and she loved her husband.

Her stomach, thinking it was never going to be fed again, had given up complaining and far from feeling empty and uncomfortable, she had a sense of not needing to eat every five minutes to comfort herself and find pleasure in food.

She looked at Phil. For the first time in his life, he had grown his hair to his collar. His mother had been telling him for weeks to get a haircut and was horrified when Julie had put her foot down before the wedding and said that she and Phil liked his hair longer and he wouldn't be having it cut for the big day. He was looking at the sea and had a smile on his face. He seemed happy, but she wanted to hear him say it. 'Are you happy, love?'

He turned to face her. His face cracked into an enormous grin, and his eyes crinkled at the corners. 'Happier than I've ever been in my life,' he replied. 'I love you.'

'I love you, too,' she said simply.

'Come here and kiss me.' He leaned over and kissed her, wrapping his hand in her hair and pulling her towards him. His mouth was wide and grinding, and he pushed his tongue into hers when she gave a moan of surprise. His chair grated on the patio floor as he moved it closer and cupped her throat with his hand. He pulled his head back from her mouth and gazed into her eyes. His shone with love as he looked at her. He picked up his glass and drained the last of the whisky, pulling her face to his. He kissed her again, drizzling the fiery liquid from his mouth to hers and chasing it with his tongue. That was the sexiest thing he'd ever done, and she wondered which of his brothers had given him the tip. She waited for the moment when he pulled away and make an excuse to get out of the room. She'd let him go and lie in the bed alone. Then she'd replay the moment when he spat whisky from his mouth into hers. She'd make the rest of the scenario up. The months of waiting for Philip to make love to her left her wanting. Despite being married for twenty-four hours, she doubted her husband would ever make love to her. With every second, she waited for him to reject her.

Philip didn't pull away. He kissed her harder. His breathing altered and became laboured, but Julie had been here before. He often got breathy, and sometimes she'd even felt his erection press against her, but at that point, he always stopped and left her frustrated.

'Julie,' he moaned her name into her open mouth. He'd never done that before either. The word was heavy and rich in her mouth. She felt a roll of butterflies turn a somersault in her stomach. She wanted him more than she could ever remember wanting a man before. Months of being deprived of intimate physical contact other than a few kisses had set her on fire, but she still expected rejection.

Philip lowered his hand from her throat. He cupped her breast. He had never touched her body. He kissed her neck, behind her ear and onto her throat. His hand left the outside of her clothing, and she felt the warmth of his fingers driving into the cup of her bra. She wanted him to take it off, to take all her clothes off, but she didn't dare move or break the spell.

Partly for balance, she put her hands on his thighs. She stroked the skin of his upper leg as he dropped his lips into her cleavage. He kissed the cleft of her breast, his mouth an inch from her. She stroked him, aching, aware of his erection close to her fingertips. She circled her fingers on his thigh, and he grabbed her left hand and thrust it onto the front of his flies. He was in her hand. Bitterly disappointing—but there. He'd put it there.

He took the hand that was manipulating him through his trousers and thrust it away from him. He sat up straight, holding her in front of him so she couldn't touch him. Julie looked into his eyes, the first sting of tears tingling behind her lashes. She wanted him so much, and he was going to reject her again. But she saw his lust mirroring her own. He stood, still holding her hands and went into the bedroom, dragging her with him. She almost fell over the chairs. He stood in front of her by the end of the bed and pushed her onto it. He wrestled himself out of his clothes and was naked in front of her. She could see her tiny husband for the first time, but she wanted him.

He helped her out of her clothes until she lay shy and naked. She tried to cover herself with the bedspread, but he pulled it back, looking at her. 'What about the curtains? Somebody might see,' she said. He told her to stuff the curtains.

He squashed her and forced the air out of her body. He didn't give her any moistening before trying to ram inside her. She'd have liked some more foreplay first. He couldn't find the way in and grunted in frustration. She put her hand down and guided him. He stabbed her hard to the hilt. It was forceful and hurt, but she didn't complain and encouraged him. He'd never made love before, but instinct showed him what to do.

He tried to ride her but over-judged it and fell out. Leading him back home, his wife smiled

'Slowly,' she advised him. 'Take it easy, and it will glide in and stay inside.' That was better. He eased in with calm thrusts for a few seconds as he learned how to control his movements. Then he moved faster until he was riding her hard. She grabbed his back and felt his muscles contracting as he drove inside her. It wasn't the gentle lovemaking she'd imagined for their first time, but if this was how he wanted it, she wasn't going to argue. It hurt, but it was good. He concentrated on his own pleasure, and she didn't mind that. It was his first time, and she'd guide him to please her next time.

He jerked his lower body, and she felt he was close, but she wasn't there. She tried to slow him down. But he wouldn't be stopped. He was sweating, drips falling from his body onto her chest. A droplet fell from his forehead into her eyes, stinging them and making her blink. She forced them open despite the sting because she wanted to watch his first

159

orgasm. He yelled as though he was proud of himself. She wanted to enjoy him too, but she wasn't ready. And he flopped on top of her and slipped from his mooring. He was soaking wet with sweat and heaving exhausted breaths.

He rolled off and turned on his side to light a cigarette.

She was at the point of no return. Her body ached for him. 'Phil, touch me, please.'

'What?'

'Please, will you touch me? She blushed, feeling like a tart for asking him to give her sexual gratification.

'Oh, right.' He moved his cigarette to his right hand and lowered his left between her legs.

She looked at Philip with love. His lip was curled in disgust at what she'd done. He stubbed his cigarette out, still looking as though he'd swallowed something unpleasant, and then he excused himself and went to the bathroom. She heard him washing, and then she heard him vomiting, and then she heard him washing again.

She turned on her side, facing away from the bathroom and cried herself to sleep.

The next morning, she was quiet over breakfast. She nibbled on watermelon. The fruit salad bar was alien to her, and she felt cosmopolitan eating watermelon for breakfast. It was delicious but only water, so she had a slice of toast with scrambled eggs, a rasher of bacon, a sausage and a small spoon of beans. Phil ate twice as much, and she was struck by the unfairness of life that he could eat one potato more than a pig and was like a washboard, while she only had to look at a chip to gain weight. She drank fresh orange, something she only did when she had a hangover, and she followed it with a cup of even fresher coffee. It was bitter and way too strong, but real coffee was on offer with this sumptuous breakfast, and she felt like a princess.

After breakfast, they went for a walk around the complex, it was vast and nothing like Julie had ever seen before. Within an hour and a half of breakfast, they had a beef pancake cooked on a griddle at the side of the path by an ancient lady who sat cross-legged and could turn out a pancake a minute. They found the small all-night restaurant that stayed open after the three buffets, the a *lá carte*, and the three themed restaurants had closed. All the food wastage was re-fried, re-boiled or re-constituted to look like something else and was laid out for the all-nighters coming in from the clubs with a need to soak up some alcohol. Julie chastised Phil for not finding this little gem the night before when they were starving. They could have had a snack in the moonlight. Phil said that it sounded dodgy. He didn't want to get food poisoning. Julie pointed out that when they had a roast at home, they always fried the leftovers and had bubble and squeak. The hotel had four stars. Of course, everything had to be done to a standard.

They took sun loungers by the juice bar overlooking the largest swimming pool. Every hour they indulged in a different variety of fresh juice in a little plastic cup. Julie creamed herself with suntan lotion and smothered some over her husband's back and legs. When she asked him to turn over, he was reluctant. When he buckled under her nagging and turned, he had a sheepish look on his face and an erection. He covered it with his paperback and, given that they were surrounded by other people, Julie left him to apply his own suntan lotion, to his own front, in his own good time. She was flattered about the erection, though, and thought it was sweet when his cheeks burned and he muttered shyly, 'Sorry, but after what happened, I can't help it. I had one earlier, too.' She couldn't have had a better lead-in to the subject that she'd wanted to broach all morning.

'Phil, I heard you being sick last night. You know—afterwards?' He was embarrassed again. He tried to blame it on the dodgy food, but they hadn't eaten anything, and then the weather, but it was cool in the room, and finally, he blamed the last throes of his hangover from their wedding night. She asked him if she disgusted him. He said of course not. He told her not to be so stupid, and then he buried his head in his paperback. The subject was closed.

They had a delicious lunch on the sun terrace. Julie had a salad that seemed to offer a million different dishes, with some potato croquettes and a piece of grilled fish. Philip had a meat feast. He filled his plate with ribs and beef stroganoff and all kinds of seasoned and sauced delicacies. Julie asked him if the food was arousing him, as it had at breakfast. He laughed and replied that it had nothing to do with the food and that it had been down to her. She slid a hand under the table and onto his leg. He stopped her mid-thigh, shocked. 'Julie,' he whispered, 'people will see.' He was shocked but didn't seem angry. 'Oh God,' he muttered, 'here we go again. What have you done to me?'

For dessert, Julie had a spoonful of lemon mousse and half a slice of pineapple gateaux and something else that was pink and indefinable. Phil had more meat. When they left the terrace, the heat hit them like a blanket. It was fierce, and she felt lightheaded after the large meal. She suggested they lie down to let their food digest.

They lay on the bed. Phil had taken off his shirt and lay in just his shorts. Julie wore a loose sun dress. She grabbed his hand, and he intertwined his fingers with hers. She had never been so happy in her life. She was at peace, and any worries from home had wafted away on a Grecian breeze. She felt a new tranquility the likes of which wasn't possible in England. Phil was relaxed too, and she thought she might be falling in love with her husband. She lay on the bed with her eyes closed, listening to the swish of the sea.

She would have drifted off, but Phil was restless. He kept fidgeting, and he was stroking her hand with his thumb. The movement in the same place was irritating her skin, and she opened her eyes to look at him. He was staring at her. His shorts came to a point in the middle, and he had the biggest erection. 'It won't go down,' he said.

'We'd better do something about it then, hadn't we?'

She straddled him and took the waistband of his shorts in her hands. She leaned forward and kissed. He grabbed her by the shoulders and threw her off him and onto her back. Their lovemaking was a repeat of the first time. He thrust into her and came fast, leaving her wanting again. This time he was more willing to finish her off by hand. In fact, he was keen and forced his fingers inside her until she was filled, and he was hurting her. She told him and asked him to be gentle. He was crestfallen but removed two of his fingers. He stared at her face and then at her body and the flesh of her wobbling belly. He wiped his hand on the corner of her sundress and pulled a face, but he seemed pleased with what he'd achieved, and although he phrased the question in different ways, he asked her several times if it had been good. She lied and told him it was fantastic. He asked if he was the best lover she'd had, and she answered him with.

'Of course you are.'

He left the bed to wash, but he didn't throw up.

After that, he was at her day and night. His sexual appetite had been awakened, and he was starving. As much as she tried to inject some variety into their sex life, he bucked against it. He was strictly missionary and always in a hurry. His needs were of greater importance, and he didn't want or need foreplay. He wanted to get in and come. Anything else bored him. He craved the gift without unwrapping the present. By the third time he'd stopped leaving her to wash, he said he liked the smell of her on his fingers and the feel of her on his Old Man. He didn't like the word cock, he said it was coarse. That second night of sleeping in the same bed, he didn't roll over and sleep with his back to her. He spooned her, wrapping one leg over her body and holding her into him so that she could feel his heartbeat through her back. At first, she loved it and went to sleep with her man wrapped tight around her. She woke through the night to find him lying on top of her forcing her legs open and ramming inside her.

She was confused and disorientated. She didn't know where she was, and in a sleep fugue, she tried to fight him off, but he grunted into her neck. He was extra turned on by the way he'd woken her. He grunted twice and came over the top of her legs before he'd even got inside. She cleaned herself, and when she got back into bed, his arm and his leg came over her and locked her in place. She woke again. The bed was soaking with sweat. He had all the sheets, and his body was leaking like a watering can. Her back was dripping wet and freezing cold. She took a blanket from the wardrobe and wrapped it around her. Julie finished the night, dozing in a chair on the balcony. The sunrise over the ocean was the most beautiful thing that she'd ever seen in her life. Her husband was crazy with desire for her, and her world was good. Phil woke at eight and dragged her back to bed for more sex.

During the holiday, they jet skied and went horse riding. The jet skiing was great fun, but she was nervous about the sea. She loved the speed of the ski and the sensation of bumping on top of the ocean with the sea spray cooling her from the vicious heat. But as much as she loved it, she feared falling into the cold water and was cautious when it came to turning. Phil looked good on the water.

The man at the stables looked them up and down and said he had a special horse for Julie—one with six legs. She didn't appreciate this jibe about her weight, but Phil thought it was hilarious. If she hadn't loved horse riding so much, she'd have taken her affront and left without giving them the benefit of their custom. They brought her a big horse, and she had to be given a leg up to mount. The guide expected her to be as accomplished in her riding skill as she was at mounting. Her weight did hamper her being able to vault into the saddle, but it didn't prevent her from being able to ride. When he asked if any of the riders wanted to break away from the pack and follow him for a gallop, she pulled her horse to his side. He told her it might not be a good idea as the horse she rode was very fast and needed an experienced hand. She held back, letting the man gallop across the sands with two other members of the trek, and then she nudged her mount on. Her seat was accomplished. She shortened the reins and dropped her hands, allowing her posture to fall forward so that she was looking between the ears of her horse. The

165

ride was exhilarating, and the steady pounding of the horse's hooves beat in time with her heartbeat. The sand flew by in a blur beneath her, and the wind blew strong around her, giving the impression of even greater speed. She was flying and drew expertly alongside the leader of the trek bringing her horse to a steady canter, then a trot and then she stopped.

Back at the stables, the man praised her, and she said that perhaps he shouldn't be so quick to judge a book by its cover, but he didn't understand her. He responded by drawing her away from the crowd as they dismounted and suggesting she join him the following morning for another ride, just the two of them. She declined and returned to her husband. She wasn't sure whether the guide had wanted to make another few quid from her and was offering a one-on-one session at an elevated cost or if he was coming on to her and was offering more than a horse ride.

They hired a car and drove all over the island. Philip discovered a love for sex al fresco and joked that he fancied being caught in flagrante. They took a carriage ride through Corfu town and ate in a seafood restaurant outside the bustle. The next day they drove to the beautiful monastery at Paleokastritsa, where they listened to the choristers at evensong. Most of the tourists were long gone by early evening, and they followed a meandering path to the votive room, a small cave away from the main courtyard. The room was set with hundreds of red votive candles giving the place an eerie glow. She whispered in his ear. She told him that she could slip out of her panties and put them in her bag. She was wearing a loose skirt and whispered that she would hear anybody coming long before they got to the cave. She told him how much she wanted him and felt him stiffen against her leg. He had very strong catholic beliefs. He said it would be a terrible sin. 'Lovemaking should be confined to the bedroom,' he said. But he was a hypocrite after he'd taken her three times in various beauty spots the day before. 'And then only for the procreation of life,' he went on. He was a pompous arse sometimes. Julie pulled her panties down and stepped out of them. She wondered how much he believed his crap. She could hear his mother in his voice and very nearly went off the idea of being sexed in the monastery. It was religious in a way. She felt that making love in such a holy place would cement their relationship. It was a blessing from above. He put his hand up her skirt. 'But I want to be inside you so much.'

'Do it.'

He had her against the wall. He'd lowered the front of his shorts, and he drove into her. A trickle of ice-cold water fell on her back from behind her as it travelled down the cobbled stones of the ancient wall. She gasped as the coldness took her breath away. She felt the trickle travel to her waist, and he rammed her hard against the wall. He was inside her and hammering into her harder than he ever had before. It was the first time he'd taken her in a standing position, and he seemed to like the extra leverage that being upright gave him. She was so turned on that she couldn't breathe. She bit into his neck, stopping only short of bruising him to stop her from screaming. He was grunting, and she felt he was close to orgasm within seconds of entering her.

This time, she was right there with him. She had gone from cold to coming in less than two minutes, and the orgasm that ripped through her at the same moment as he came inside her was the strongest of her life. It was all over. He pulled out and covered himself. She went to the ladies to clean herself with baby wipes.

It was the best sex of her life.

She found him in the cloisters. He had his head bowed and his hands lifted in prayer. Tears streaked his face. He lifted his head when she came, and they walked back to the car in silence.

He still didn't speak as they drove away, and they were halfway down the mountain when he said, 'You shouldn't have made me do that. It was wrong.'

'Darling, that was the best sex I've ever had in my life. How can that be wrong?'

He turned and snarled at her, 'Do you have to be so coarse?'

'I'm sorry. I didn't mean to be flippant. I know your religion means a lot to you, but how can it be wrong when two people, who love each other, come together in the sight of God.'

He turned from the twisty mountain pass and looked to see if she was being smutty with her last remark, but she had never been more sincere. 'But don't you see? That's just it. We were in the house of God.' he moaned. 'I've committed a mortal sin. How am I ever going to be able to atone for my wickedness? You don't get it, do you? I'm going to have to go to confession and proclaim my sin. Have you any idea how ashamed I feel? I can't go to our church. I'm going to have to find one that's miles away. I wonder if it would count if I found a church here and confessed to a Greek priest who couldn't understand me.'

Julie searched his face for humour, but he was serious. She wanted to laugh at the ridiculousness of the situation, but she knew it was important to Philip to salve his conscience.

She wanted to think of something positive to say that would make him feel better, but she battled her sympathy against the feeling of hypocrisy that surrounded the incident. He didn't care about his shame when he had her up against the votive room wall banging the arse off her. She tried to lighten the mood before the hand of God appeared through the fluffy white clouds and lifted them, car and all, off the road and dumped them in the sea. 'I wouldn't confess here if I were you. They'd take us into the town square and stone us. I'm sure they'd take a dim view of fornication in their Votive Room. I'd take my chances in England and maybe say a few extra Hail Marys before you get there, just to work off a bit of the penance in advance.' It worked. He grinned at her and squeezed her hand.

'You're a minx, you know. You're very naughty and a terrible influence on me. Was it really that good?' he asked.

'Hell, you bet. It was amazing.'

They ate at a roadside taverna on a balcony overlooking the Aegean. The excellent food assuaged Philip's guilt, and he relived every second of their adventure in whispered tones. He confessed to her that it was the most exciting thing he'd ever done and would never forget it.

On the way home, he pulled the car off the road by a secluded copse and took her from behind over the bonnet of the car. It was a deviation from his strictly-missionary moral stance, and for the second time that day, despite being sore and tender deep in her cervix, she came in unison with her husband. When he wanted her in their room after drinks in the hotel bar, she just wanted to sleep. She begged him for a respite, but he nagged and whined and groped until she gave in. He took her on top, brutally, and she moaned and writhed and pretended that she was enjoying it to speed him up. It was over quickly, and when he tried to trap her in their sleeping position, she suggested she spoon him, so she could stroke his back. He fell asleep, and she moved away from him and cocooned herself in the sheet to avoid his dripping. She was dry and comfortable all night, and she slept well. That was what she called success. Victory to the tired people.

Chapter Sixteen

They got back home from their honeymoon, tanned and happy. Donald picked them up from the airport to take them to the hotel. Julie felt as though she'd been away from their house forever.

As every mile took them closer to the Halcyon Woods, her mood dropped. The honeymoon was a wonderful, sexy, loved-up dream, but now, sitting in the car, it was as though Julie had ceased to exist. She reached for Phil's hand, but he shook her off to indicate a point about jet skiing to his father.

Phil recounted every minute of their time away, bar the intimate stuff. He told him every conversation he'd had, every meal they'd eaten, and gave a blow-by-blow account as though he were under police interrogation. When they got into the hotel and met for drinks with Violet and the two brothers who were there, he went through it all from the beginning again. Julie didn't want to share the details of her honeymoon with his family. It was theirs. It was special and private. She realised she was being petulant, but Phil barely spoke to her all night. Julie couldn't resist butting in when he told his Catholic parents about the monastery on the hill above Paleokastritsa. 'You should have seen

171

the votive room. It was amazing, so spiritual. Something entered me in that room.' Violet seemed pleased with her spiritual birth, but Phil didn't see the funny side. His lips straightened into a single thin line. She'd seen the look before and knew he was angry. He was sensitive about Julie's humour when it was aimed in his mother's direction.

That night, Phil stayed up late with SP and James. He drank too much. Julie was tired and wanted to go to bed, but the alcohol flowed, and she left him to his drunken revelry and went to bed alone. She woke alone and bar the foo-foo dress and stale vomit. It was a repeat of the last time they'd stayed at the hotel. This time Julie breakfasted alone in the dining room and then went in search of her husband. Again, she found him laid out on a brother's sofa in a brother's room. This time he was in James' quarters. James sneered at her when he opened the door. 'Well, well,' he said, leering. 'Aren't you the dark horse? I've been hearing everything about you. Let me know if you ever fancy giving the more experienced brother a run around the monastery.' He winked at her, and Julie felt sickened by his smutty innuendo. Of Phil's brothers, James was the one she liked the least. He was hard and nasty. He didn't like her and made no secret of the fact.

Julie glared at him but otherwise ignored his remarks. 'Is Philip here?' she asked.

He opened the door wider to let her in and gestured at the sofa with Phil sprawled across it. 'Don't worry, love. I was only joking. You're not my type.' His lip curled away from his teeth as he watched her kneel beside Phil and shake him awake.

'I suspect anybody willing to give out would be your type. I feel sorry for Tammy being married to a pig like you.'

Phil was waking and only heard Julie's response to James's slur. He was defensive of his brother. 'Julie, why are you speaking to James like that? Don't blame him for keeping me out all night. I did that of my own accord. Please apologise to James.'

'Yeah, Jules, don't blame me. I'm a good influence.'

'Go screw yourself,' Julie said and regretted it when she saw Phil's face. He went into one of his moods and didn't speak to her for the rest of the day.

It was good to get back to their house, even if Phil only answered her when he had to. Julie had given her mother a key, and she'd come in to clean up while they were on honeymoon. The house was gleaming. Not realising that Julie and Phil didn't share a bedroom, Zoe had only cleaned the master bedroom. But it was made with fresh bedding, and Julie couldn't wait to get into it. She wondered if her husband would be moving into her room now or if he would continue to sleep alone. After sharing a bed with him for ten days in Corfu, she hoped he would go back to the privacy of his own room. She'd only had one decent night's sleep since before she got married.

Phil dropped their cases in the hall and wandered around the house. He went into the downstairs bathroom and turned in a circle. 'Julie, somebody's been in the house. My things have been moved around.'

'Yes, isn't it lovely and clean? I gave Mum a key and asked her to give the place a once over while we were away. I thought it'd be a nice surprise for you to come home to.' Julie's voice came and went in clarity as she set to making coffee and tea in their immaculately clean kitchen. She was thinking about the last time she'd seen it, with champagne bottles, makeup products, the remains of a cooked breakfast—even though

Anne had washed up—and all kinds of other general untidiness that Phil would have gone mad about.

'Mind you, considering the state of the place when we left. She's excelled herself. We can go and visit her tomorrow, and we'll take her some flowers to thank her.'

Phil came into the kitchen. His face was scrunched up with rage and bright red. He slammed a can of deodorant onto the marble island with such force that Julie wanted to check beneath it for damage. In his other hand, he had one of his shirts, presumably dirty, perhaps taken out of the downstairs wash basket. He threw it at her, and when it hit her full in the face and hung there, covering her like a Muslim lady's niqab, she could smell her husband in the material. She pulled it away, astonished. Phil was yelling. She'd never seen him so angry.

'Don't you ever, ever let anybody into my house without my permission again. Who do you think you are?'

'Your house?' she said, repeating the question for good measure. 'And here's me thinking we were an equal partnership, and this is our house. What's the matter with you? Mum's done a fantastic job for us.'

'She's been through my things. I don't like anybody touching my things, do you understand?' His voice had dropped in decibels as he explained how he felt, but as he got to the end of his rant, it rose as his sense of injustice engulfed him. 'What right have you got to give somebody I barely know a key to my house? Anything could have gone missing.'

'Phil, you're talking about my mother. I can't believe that you've just accused my mum of stealing from us. What the hell are you talking about?'

'They're always hard up, aren't they? I want that key back. Today,' he emphasised. 'In fact, no, don't bother. Let her keep it, along with whatever else she took. You do realise that I'm going to have to have all the locks changed, don't you?'

'Don't be so ridiculous. She's my mum. I'd trust her with my life. How can you say such horrible things? She only did this to help us. I don't know how I'm going to get past the fact that you've just called my mother a thief. She wouldn't dream of stealing.' Her bottom lip quivered, and she pushed past him to go into the lounge. It was spotless and smelled of orange zest. 'You, horrible, nasty man? It's my family you're slagging off. We might not have much money, but how dare you.' She sat on the end of one of the plush red sofas and curled her feet up beside her. She held the cup of coffee between her hands and sipped it without tasting the comforting bitterness of the beans. She wanted to throw it at him.

He'd followed her and stood above her, still yelling. 'Come on, Julie, look at them. They live in a council flat. Christ, it's not even a full house with two storeys. It's not as though I'm saying that she took something, all I'm saying is they need the money, and she might have been tempted, that's all. And I'll thank you not to swear. You know how it makes you sound like a cheap trollop, which goes to prove my point about the council flat mentality.'

'You snob. You're a disgusting snob.' She put her coffee down on the table, not forgetting to take a coaster from the dispenser first. The mug felt too much like a weapon. 'Leave me alone.' She was working hard to keep herself under control. 'I don't want to be anywhere near you.'

'See? Can't take it, can you? You can say what you like about my mother. My mother, incidentally, paid for our wedding, but the moment that I dare to criticise the glorious Zoe, you take it personally. People in glass houses shouldn't throw stones.'

He stalked out of the room.

'You get back here. Don't you dare walk out on me, you pompous dickhead. I have barely said a thing about your precious mother, considering that she called me an AIDS-ridden, gold-digging heroin addict. But look at you. Showing your true colours. Like mother, like son. She's a money-minded, pretentious snob, and you're just like her. You're your mother's son. Go on, sulk like a crybaby. Mummy's boy.' Phil straightened his back. Jutted his chin and left. Julie heard him going into his small bedroom. She burst into tears.

The next morning, Phil knocked on her bedroom door. He came in without waiting for a response. He had breakfast on a tray and an erection. He apologised and admitted that he'd overreacted. Of course, I trust your family, he told her. She apologised too. They ate breakfast, had unsatisfying sex as far as Julie was concerned, and put the argument behind them. Phil smiled at her and said he'd be moving his things into the master bedroom that morning.

Julie's heart sank.

It was their last day off before they went back to work. Julie worked in a factory making circuit boards, and Phil, having broken away from the hotel after the fight with his mother, was a maintenance fitter and team leader in the shipyard. Before they left for their honeymoon, he had applied for a promotion to foreman. He was looking forward to getting back to see if the interviews were arranged. Julie couldn't wait to see her friends and was looking forward to getting back to work, but they were both struck with a bad case of post-holiday blues. Phil took her out to dinner. The food was rich, and he droned on about things that interested him and left her wishing the night would end, and then she remembered that Phil was moving into their bed, and she wished that the night would go on forever. But she'd still rather have been at the pub drinking lager with her mates and having a laugh. She was a married woman now, and all that was behind her. She had responsibilities, and drinking poncy wine in a posh restaurant was one of them. It could've been worse. He might have taken her to dinner at the Halcyon.

She woke up the following morning wet from her husband's sweat, exhausted and nauseous. Philip had left for work, and she felt guilty for not being the perfect wife and getting up to see him off with a cooked breakfast. He hadn't woken her. She met up with her best friend, Karen, at the bus stop. The mid-May morning was gorgeous, and the sun was shining. She told Karen all about their honeymoon, especially the sex, and she felt better.

'At least one of us is getting plenty,' Karen said with a laugh. She caught Julie's anxious expression. 'What's the matter? Isn't it good?'

'Not really. Well, yes, sometimes it's great. If I just want a quickie. That time in the monastery was the best sex ever. But he wants it so often. He's at me for sex all the time, and it never varies. He's in. Wham, bam, thank you, ma'am, and out then it's all over. And he's so rough.'

'Don't knock it. I wish I had a man who wanted me that much. Ed would choose the footie over sex with me any day. Get it while you can because I promise you, that honeymoon period soon wears off.'

The bus pulled in beside them. 'As to it being boring, I wish I had a virgin to play with. If it's boring, that's your fault. You need to show him what you want.'

'I suppose.' Julie changed the conversation because the bus was crowded, and she didn't want details of her sex life spread all over town.

Six weeks after coming home from their honeymoon, Julie discovered she was pregnant. Phil, far from flinging his arms around her in delight, was shell-shocked. 'How did that happen?' he asked in a daze.

'How do you think it happened, Einstein? You don't believe in using any form of contraception. I thought this was what you wanted.' She felt tears stinging her eyes. This wasn't going how she'd imagined it. 'We discussed it. You said you wanted to start a family.'

'Yes, but I didn't think it would be so quick. I thought it would take longer. I've only just got my promotion. I wanted to save some money first. We've only been married a few weeks. How did it happen so fast?'

'God, Phil, it only takes once. If I'd known you were going to react like this, I'd have gone on the pill.'

'That's a wicked thing to say. You know it's against my religion.'

'Yes, but it's not against mine. And now, I'm carrying a baby that you don't want.' She burst into tears.

Phil put his arms around her. 'Shush, don't be silly. Of course, I want it.'

'You do?'

'Yes, of course, I do. It was just a shock, that's all. I'm delighted we're having a baby.' He picked her up, swung her around and whooped in delight. Julie dried her eyes. This was more like it.

They arranged a special dinner to tell their parents. Richard and Zoe were delighted. This was their first grandchild. Zoe cried, and Richard beamed and hugged Julie. Richard pumped Phil's hand, saying, 'Well done, lad,' making Phil blush and glance at his own parents.

After a curt congratulations, Donald didn't react. They might as well have announced that they'd bought a new pan set in the Debenham's sale. Violet's face was grim. Julie had seen the same expression on Phil's face many times. She looked at her with distaste and only applied a false smile when she was asked about her feelings by Zoe, who was trilling like an excited budgie. Julie wondered if Violet was disgusted that she was having a baby—or because her youngest child had lost his virginity.

Every week, Zoe came to the house with a set of vests or a couple of bibs. Violet bought an enormous Silver Cross coach-built pram that took up most of the lounge. 'If I'm going to be pushing it, no grandchild of mine will be seen in one of those modern monstrosities. All of mine had coach-built prams. There simply is no other option.' Julie called it her Big, Fat Gypsy Pram and bought a cheap stroller from eBay for when Violet wasn't around.

Phil was present at the birth when Victoria-Violet Woods was born. Julie was looking at him when the midwife put his child in his arms. His face was sullen. He'd wanted a boy. Despite Julie telling him it could just as easily be a girl, he wouldn't listen. Phil only ever thought of his child in the male gender. Any other flavour wasn't going to happen. If boys were good enough for his mother, they were good enough for him. He wanted a son, and that son was going to have his name, Philip John Woods Jr.

Julie said if it was a boy, she wanted him to have his own name and his own identity, but Phil's ego regarding his future son would brook no argument. At each scan, he asked the technician what sex the baby was. Julie had explicitly had it written into her records that she didn't want to know the sex of their baby. She'd sneakily asked that Phil not be told either. If it was a girl, she wanted him to have time to get used to the notion. Julie knew the second he held his child in his arms for the first time, any thoughts he'd had about gender would fade into insignificance.

Only they didn't.

Phil had planned for a son. And he didn't want a girl.

Chapter Seventeen

S imon was anxious and grumpy, and frightened. Robert was coming to visit today. He was Janet Metcalfe's brother, and he was horrible to Simon and some of the others. Robert was even nasty to Janet and she was his sister. He called Janet a spastic. He didn't call Simon a spastic. He called Simon Mong-boy and pulled his hair when Simon walked past. Sometimes Mother called Simon, 'Mongol.' Simon wondered if Robert had been talking to Mother.

He stuffed all his belongings into his rucksack as if he was leaving home for good. He had to pack everything down very hard. The hanging clothes in his wardrobe wouldn't fit into his bag so he'd had to just stuff them under his bed as they were.

Robert had never been into his bedroom. He wasn't allowed, but Simon went through this ritual every time Robert was coming, just in case. Robert made Simon tell him what number his room was. And Robert said that he was going to come in through the middle of the night and kill him if he said anything to anybody.

He couldn't risk him getting hold of Simon's best cardigan. That had Simon's name inside the collar. It didn't say Robert Metcalfe's name inside the collar at all. Not.

Simon got frustrated when his thick fingers couldn't do up the zip. 'Concentape, Shimon,' he said to himself, but it didn't matter how hard he concentrated. The zip wouldn't fasten, and his best cardigan with the zipper up the front and leather patches on the elbows bulged out of the top of his bag. His mouth was open, and his tongue protruded as he worked on the zip, and he dribbled onto his hand. He looked up to see if Mother had appeared by magic and was very pleased to see that she hadn't.

He wiped his dribbly hand on his cardigan and went back to work. Simon had a short attention span and a short fuse. He needed things to work for him the first time, and if they didn't, he got mad. Now he was mad. Under normal circumstances, he'd ask one of the carers to help him zip up his rucksack, but he couldn't do that. If he told Belinda or Jane about his zip, they would ask why he had packed everything into his rucksack. They were like that. They wouldn't just say, 'Yes, Simon, of course, I'll do your zip for you.' They wouldn't do his rucksack up and walk away. That was too hard for them. Like Simon trying to hide his stuff under the bed. It should be easy, but it wasn't.

Simon had a picture of the end of the zip on his thumb, and it was all red around it. If it didn't have the hurt around it, it might be good to have a picture of a zip on the end of his thumb, but Simon whimpered when he saw it. He heard Belinda walking Janet up the corridor outside. That meant that Robert and Janet's mum and dad would be coming soon. Simon panicked, he grabbed the zip and pulled on it really hard, and then he was holding the end of the zip in his hand, and it wasn't attached to his rucksack anymore. This was bad. 'This is bad,' Simon said, 'This is bery, bery bad.'

Jane came to take him to the dayroom for integration. Simon had stuffed the rucksack under the bed with all his important things and all his not-important things too. Everything was bulging out of the top of his bag, and that worried him a lot. He stood by his desk, moving from foot to foot and making his noise that sounded like a cow. His face was bright red, and his big eyes were bulging out of his face even more than normal. Jane called his name. 'Simon. Come on now.' But Simon didn't answer because he wasn't there.

His big body was there, and his trainers were there, and his brown jumper, which was really green, was there, but Simon wasn't there. Simon was in his own place where he went when the world got too much for him. Matron came and made Simon come back. She gave him some medicine, and he was put to bed to rest. Worrying about this gave Simon a big headache. Simon was happy that he was in bed having a rest because it meant that he wasn't in integration getting his hair pulled by Robert and being called Mong-boy. But Simon wasn't tired. It was only half past after lunch, and Simon wasn't supposed to be in bed having a rest. He was supposed to be in integration getting his hair pulled. It was a big problem, and Simon fell asleep worrying about it.

When he woke up, Nancy was standing by his bed. He'd been asleep for a long time because Belinda and Jane had gone home, and Nancy and Anne had come on duty. 'Hello, sleepyhead,' said Nancy laughing. Simon smiled at her. 'Look, Simon, I've got a surprise for you.' Nancy stepped to one side, and Simon wasn't smiling anymore. Robert was smiling. He was smiling his nice smile, the one that was supposed to show that he was good. Nancy was still talking, but Simon wasn't listening.

'Robert has stayed a little bit longer today because Janet's mum and dad have taken her to the hospital to get some special shoes for her. Isn't that nice? When we told Robert that you were under the weather today, he asked if he could come and see you for a bit. Isn't that nice?' Nancy winked at Robert and said, 'Robert says you're his favourite. Isn't that nice?'

It wasn't nice.

Robert had already pulled up the chair from beside Simon's desk. The chair doesn't go beside the bed. It goes beside the desk. That's where it goes. Robert sat down. Simon was frightened. He could feel his heart going thump, thump, thump.

Simon closed his eyes and made a big snore.

Nancy laughed again. Simon made all the carers laugh. They said he had a good sense of human. 'Will you look at that, Robert? He's having a joke with us. Come on, you. Sit up. I've brought you a nice cup of tea and two Jaffa Cakes. They're your favourite.'

Simon loved Jaffa Cakes, and he hadn't had a lot of lunch because his tummy felt icky. Simon's tummy always felt icky when Robert was coming. He got upset on a Wednesday when Mother came too, but he didn't feel icky in his tummy then, just worried. Simon looked at his two Jaffa Cakes. 'Right, I'll leave you two for a bit. Robert, if you come to the kitchen when you're ready, the cook will rustle you up a cuppa and a slice of cake.'

'Thank you, Nancy,' Robert said in his talking-to-the-staff voice. 'I will.'

Nancy shut the door, and Simon wished that Mother was there. Mother was scary and would shout loud at Robert and call him stupid. Mother would make him go away. Robert grabbed Simon's two Jaffa Cakes and stuffed one into his mouth, not taking time to chew and swallow before he rammed the second one in too. 'Hey Mong-boy, aren't you pleased to see me?'

Simon didn't answer.

'That's not very friendly when I've gone out of my way to come and sit with you. What have you got in here then?' Robert reached over and pulled open Simon's underwear drawer. It was empty. He pulled open the drawer underneath that one and then the last one on the bottom. 'Hey, where's all your shit?'

Simon didn't say anything. But he was scared that Robert would look under his bed.

But it was all right because Robert had got bored of looking in drawers and cupboards. He looked at Simon's cup of tea. 'Aren't you going to drink your tea, Monger?' He called Simon Monger, too, sometimes. Simon didn't want his tea. He was still worrying about his stuff and just wanted Robert to go away.

'Here, let me help you.' He picked up the teacup and came towards Simon. Simon was frightened. Robert put his arm around Simon's head and hauled it up from the pillow, and then he rammed the cup into his mouth, hurting him. He forced him to drink the tea. It was still too hot. Simon knew to wait for five minutes and then blow on his tea before taking a sip to see if it was the right tempica. Robert

185

didn't care about the temperature. He just poured it all into Simon's mouth. It wasn't boiling hot at all. Not. But it was still hot enough to make Simon struggle. The tea spilt all down Simon's front, and Simon was upset. Some of the others spilt their tea and their food down their fronts, but Simon was *high-end retardation*. Simon was very careful not to spill anything down him because he liked being *high-end retardation*. It made him feel special, but he would never be unkind and tell Janet and the others that she was low-end and that she had to get her shoes from the hospital. That would be unkind. He just kept his specialness to himself and looked at his everybody, white trainers sometimes.

Simon choked on the tea and started coughing. Robert sat back in his chair and laughed. 'Ugh, look at the mess you've made, you dirty bastard. You can't even drink from a cup like normal people. You make me sick.'

Simon thought he might be sick. He couldn't stop coughing. Not. And he was all wet. His pyjamas were all wet. His bed was all wet. And he couldn't tell. Nancy would think he was turning into the a low end retardation.

Simon was still worried about his stuff. It was bery bad to tell lies. But it would be bery bad at all if Robert found Shimon's stuff. It had Shimon's name on it on a special label what Mrs Taylor, the housekeeper, did sewed in, 'There's no thing under the bed. Not,' he said.

Robert laughed and knelt to pull Simon's stuff out. 'You moron,' he laughed. Robert was sixteen, but Simon didn't think he ought to use dirty words like that. 'I didn't think you'd hidden it. I just thought they took it off you to stop you shitting all over it or something.' He was laughing very hard. 'You shot yourself right in the foot there, me old son.' Robert flung Simon's clothes all over the floor.

'Clothes do not live on the floor, Shimon. Clothing lives on hangers in the wardrobe.' Simon was distressed. He repeated this phrase on a loop. Robert was opening Simon's red pencil case. Simon didn't like nobody touching his red pencil case. It had his name on it on the inside. Robert could see Simon's name when he opened it. It wasn't sewed in on a label, but it was wrote in black marker pen so that it wouldn't come oft. Robert started taking everything out of his red pencil case and looking at it. He put Simon's parker pen in his pocket.

Simon stopped talking about his clothes and changed his chant to, 'Shimon's red pencil case. Shimon's name on it. Marker pen. Not come oft. Not.'

'Will you stop rabbiting on like an idiot?' Robert came up to Simon with a red felt tip pen and waved it in front of Simon's face.

Simon thought he was going to draw a picture right on him. 'We draws on paper, not on walls. Not,' Simon said.

Robert laughed. If he had been going to draw on Simon's face, he changed his mind. He pulled the duvet back, and Simon grabbed it and pulled it up to his chin. Robert slapped Simon across the face, and tears came into Simon's eyes. 'Don't do that, Monger. Play nice.' Robert pulled the covers back again.

This time Simon didn't do anything. A tear ran out of his eye, but Simon wasn't really crying. He was too frightened to cry. It was a tear from the sting in his eyes after Robert slapped him. He looked down at himself, and the front of his pyjama top had come up a bit, showing his big tummy.

Robert grabbed some of his tummy and pinched it hard. Simon cried out because it hurt. 'Got a dick under all this flab, have you?' He flicked Simon hard on his tummy.

Simon was confused. Dick was the handyman and gardener. He came three times a week on Monday, Wednesday, and Friday, but he had his own bed in his house somewhere else. He lived with Missus Dick and didn't sleep in Simon's bed.

'Well, have you? Have you got a dick?' he pulled the front of Simon's pyjama bottoms down.

'No,' Simon said, hoping it would make him stop.

Robert thought this was very funny and laughed a lot. 'Oh Mong-boy, you are grade-A priceless. Haven't got a dick.' He kept laughing. And then he took hold of Simon's willy. This was bery bad. If a stranger touches you *there,* you have to tell. But Robert wasn't a stranger, and Simon couldn't tell.

Robert started writing something on Simon's willy. Simon couldn't read it, but he knew his letters c-o-c-k and then a gap, s-u-c, it tickled, and Simon's willy got big like it does sometimes, and then they had to up his tablets to stop it from getting big. Robert got very angry. He yelled as though Simon had hurt him.

'Oh, Jesus Christ. You filthy queer.' Simon hadn't got mad and punched him. Maybe Simon's willy had got hot as well as big, and it had burned him. Simon was too frightened to get mad. Simon just wanted him to go away.

Robert got angrier. He made a big fist and grabbed a bunch of Simon's pyjama top in his hand. He was going to punch Simon right in the nose, and Simon knew it was going to hurt a lot. He screwed up his eyes and waited.

Robert grunted and threw Simon back into his pillows. He turned around and punched the wall beside Simon's bed, making his picture of sunflowers nearly fall off. He leaned over Simon and ripped his Pyjama top open. One of his buttons flew off and rolled under his chest of drawers. Mrs Taylor would be mad with Simon and would tell him off for not looking after his things. Simon didn't have his eyes closed anymore. He was terrified and could hear his heart going thump, thump, thump very fast. 'I want to smash your dirty face in,' Robert said. 'I want to hit you so hard that you never get a hard-on again. I want to ram your teeth down your throat.' He took the felt pen and wrote g-a-y, gap, b-o-y on Simon's bare chest.

Simon didn't feel well. He got a big pain under his armpit. He felt sick. The pain was bad. Really bad. Badder than any bad pain he'd ever had before. His eyes went big and bulgy, and he took a breath in and didn't let it out again. He was rolling on the bed and making a strangled cry in his throat, but he couldn't get any sound out. Robert shouted, 'Oh, Christ,' and grabbed a rubber from the pencil case. He tried to rub the red felt tip from Simon's chest. This wasn't just a fit. It looked like a heart attack. He had to get rid of the writing before he called for help. The rubber wasn't working. He ran over to the sink in the corner of the room and rubbed Simon's flannel with soap under the tap. Simon was bucking, writhing, and still clutching his chest when Robert rubbed his skin hard to get the marks off. He cleaned his chest, repulsed and disgusted, and he grabbed Simon's penis and cleaned the obscene slogan from that, too, before covering Simon up and pulling

189

his blankets over him. He'd left large, dripping wet patches on Simon, and he had red marks on his chest, genitalia, and face. It couldn't be helped. He was going to have to yell for help, or Simon was going to die. He didn't care about that, but he did care about his own safety. He didn't want to be blamed for this. Simon stopped writhing and lay still. His eyes were wide open, and his tongue lolled from the side of his mouth. Robert screamed, and nurses flooded the room.

Nancy pulled Simon's pillows out, laying him flat, and did CPR while Anne ran out to ring an ambulance. Matron came in and took over the chest compressions from Nancy while she covered Simon's mouth with hers and gave him respirations. They didn't notice Simon's wet clothing or the marks on his skin. Robert watched, horrified, terrified, and fascinated. Watching somebody die had been the scariest, most awesome thing he'd ever seen.

Chapter Eighteen

I t was the evening of the annual awards ceremony for the Licensed
Victualler's Association. Violet was nominated for three awards
and was furious because the year before, she was up for four and
had walked away with three of them. This year, the rumour mill had
it that The Lakeside Hotel was going to take the overall *Best Hotel
in Cumbria* award. The die had already been cast, and the decisions
made.

Her invitation had come, and with it, the news that she was only up
for the three nominations. She made her staff's life a living hell. The Best
Hotel award belonged to Halcyon Woods. She had umpteen certifi-
cates and a bloody great trophy to prove it. The trophy changed hands
with each new recipient of the award, but it had been at the Halcyon
Woods for five years running. The previous year, her nomination was
for best restaurant, best bedrooms, best gardens, and overall winner in
the show. She had won all but the bedrooms, and the following day the
housekeeper, all the chambermaids, upstairs cleaners and the laundry
staff were given their notice. Violet told the staff why she was firing
them, and when the unfair dismissal notices came through, she said the
recession had hit. Halcyon Wood's trade had been unaffected by the

great recession. She told concerned guests that in the interim, the family would pull together to undertake their own domestic duties, and they would be performed to exacting standards. How dare the hotel lose a category? The staff didn't have a leg to stand on, and the following day, despite the recession, Violet advertised for twenty-one new members of domestic staff, including a housekeeper.

This year she'd only been nominated for Best Gardens, Best internal floral arrangements and best bedrooms. Violet stormed and blustered. She said that the award for floral arrangements was an insult. She felt it was a made-up award thrown at underachieving hotels when they couldn't think of anything else to award them. It was only a step up from the most original garden gnomes award, which most of the hoteliers saw as a bit of fun and tried to win for prosperity. Eight years earlier, Donald wanted to enter the spirit of things and commissioned a pair of caricature gnomes in the style of himself and Violet. His wife had thrown them at him and threatened divorce if ever a gnome of any description laid its fishing rod in one of her ponds.

From that moment on, gnomes were barred from the Halcyon Woods establishment. Donald noticed that Violet took a dim view of dwarfs as well as Gnomes after she refused to take a weekend group booking of them in July last year. 'All those little people weebling around and looking small,' she'd said. 'It would quite lower the tone.' Donald hadn't acknowledged her from behind his newspaper. He'd given up trying to argue managerial decisions with Violet years before. 'And besides, they always have such sharp, pointed little teeth, dear. They often look quite ready to bite somebody.'

Donald took a moment to ponder this insight. 'Don't they have the same kind of teeth as anybody else?'

'Oh no, dear. It harks back to when they were primordial and had to live by their wits to survive in the forest.'

'Oh,' Donald said. There was a lady who lived on Springfield Lane. Donald once passed her a packet of Fox's mints that were out of her reach in the newsagents, and they'd had a good chat about horses. She bought the mints to feed her horse. She was a dwarf but didn't seem to have sharp teeth and lived in a town semi. She didn't look as though she'd ever had to live by her wits in a forest. Donald felt it best to drop the conversation because he'd never win.

It was important for Violet to create the right impression at this year's ceremony. It had been somewhat of an annus horribilis in the Woods Dynasty. James had publicly split up with Tammy in a bar. Witnesses said they'd had to pull him off her. They got back together a month later, but it was a messy business and involved an unpleasant restraining order that didn't shed good light on the hotel.

Andrew was involved in a misguided business deal. The police called it fraud, and it made the newspapers. Violet said afterwards that fraud is such an ugly word. The watchmaker in question should have been flattered that Andrew so admired his work that he wanted to emulate it himself. Bribes were paid from the top rung of the civil service ladder to the bottom, and Violet took her red lipstick a shade deeper to show her stiff upper lip in times of trouble.

Later in the year again, James, still under the shadow of what Violet called the silly tiff with his wife, found himself the victim of a pub brawl. He'd defended himself against a pack of football hooligans. James stood in the dock for the second time that year, and three teenage boys were awarded thousands of pounds in damages.

When the terrible year was almost at a close, there was further humiliation when James was brought home by the police. He was wearing a dress. 'Soliciting in town,' the Police said, 'picking up men for money.' It was all lies. They had it in for the Woods. Violet screamed victimisation but never very loudly when anybody official was around. That was the greatest scandal of them all. James was a problem sometimes, but seeing her boy in the dock accused of such atrocities when he'd merely been on a fancy-dress night out was ridiculous. Bookings were cancelled that week, and her lipstick deepened by two whole shades and preceded her face into a room. Last year had been a bad one that the family needed to dust off and put behind them. This was the occasion to shine.

It took the combined effort of three of her sons and Donald to talk Violet out of wearing her fox fur for the award ceremony. Yes, it showed a certain prestige, but it also caused consternation whenever she wore it, as people tended to be sensitive around the whole issue of fox hunting.

'Well, I didn't kill the blessed thing, dear,' was Violet's continual bleat. It took all the tact and diplomacy that Ros could muster to talk her down and help her choose something else befitting the grand occasion. Ros was the Halcyon Woods' secret weapon. She was the one person in the world who had a certain amount of influence over Violet. For some reason, Violet liked her eldest son's wife. She would take counsel from her and listen to what she had to say.

She was employed as a bookkeeper for the business, but her real talent lay in stopping Violet from ruining the Hotel with any one of her terrible ideas that could land them, if not in the Court of Human Rights, then certainly shown in an unfavourable light in the local press.

Like the time Violet had wanted to take the hotel upmarket. She instructed the girls in reception to ask visitors for proof of their earnings and said that only people with an income in excess of one hundred thousand pounds a year should be allowed to make a booking or sign in.

Luckily, Beth had rung up to Ros' apartment and asked her to come down and sort her mother-in-law out. Another time, Violet wanted guests to take a medical before using the hotel pool and gymnasium, and she once decided that every guest should have their bags and person searched on leaving to see if they'd stolen anything. Ros was the calming voice of reason on each of these and many more occasions. She understood Violet and could handle her and talk her down. She was an asset worth her weight in gold because, since her retirement, Violet had too much time to sit and think and, these days, although she was still as sharp as a tack in some respects, other ideas were slewed, and her judgement impaired.

The evening was unfolding as expected. Violet, smarting from the slur of her nominations, was the epitome of graciousness, an act perfected over many seasons in hospitality. She simpered and cooed, flattering corporate ego. And she complimented corporate ego's wife before turning to the next bigwig and tittle-tattling about who corporate ego's wife was sleeping with.

The family had their own table toward the front of the room. She had made grand donations to various charities for this place, but she was unhappy with the position, and before they sat for dinner, she had

Donald and two waiters angling the table so she had a clearer runway up to the stage. The salmon floatage starter was too dry, the lettuce too bitter, the champagne too gassy, and the wine too tart. The main course had arrived at their table, and Violet was delivering her opinion of the steak when her phone rang. She coloured because it was the height of bad manners to have one's phone turned on during these occasions. But Violet never turned this phone off. It never rang, but twice a week, she took it out of her handbag and charged it before putting it back in the bag's inside pocket.

That telephone had never rung, and it had never been switched off.

She rummaged in her bag, trying to locate the zip to the inner pocket. In her haste, she was all fingers and thumbs and almost dropped it. She clasped the phone to her breast, trying to still the noise coming from it. 'Excuse me,' she said, scraping her chair away from the table and stepping backwards to collide with a waiter holding a tray laden with plates. The waiter was good and managed to sidestep Violet, maintaining the balance of his load. 'Hello. Yes, this is she,' Violet said, ignoring the waiter and stumbling through the close tables to the exit.

Violet returned to the dining room a few minutes later. She stood at the side of the room trying to get Donald's attention, but he was engrossed in his dinner and had forgotten about Violet and the mysterious phone call. The boys were more curious. Phil was questioning Donald about who it might be. He was more observant than the others. He'd seen how shaken his mother was when the phone rang. Her reaction was more than just embarrassment for her social faux pas. But what made Philip sit up and take notice was when he noticed that the phone she answered wasn't her usual one. She had never mentioned changing it, and Violet never did anything like that without a performance that involved the entire family. It was Phil who saw his mother across the room, jumping up and down in her ridiculous chiffon tent as she spoke into the mobile.

'Dad,' he said, tapping Donald on the shoulder to drag his attention away from the plate. 'Dad, Mum wants you. She seems het up.'

'Son, your mother's always het up,' Donald answered around a mouthful of rare Scottish beef. 'While this hunk of meat, on the other hand, is a rare treat to be savoured and enjoyed without your mother's acid stare turning it to leather under her shrivelling gaze. She can wait.'

Phil tutted in frustration and stood up to go to his mother. He took her under the elbow and led her from the threshold of the dining room, where she stood in the waiter's way. They went to the relative privacy of the corridor outside.

'No, Philip. Go away. I don't want you,' she swatted him with her hand. 'Go and get your father.' She was pale under her powdered cheekbones. She shook and seemed unsteady on her feet. He guided her to a pink velvet chair and motioned to a passing employee, demanding he fetch her a glass of water. 'I've got to go, Philip. I haven't got time for this. Oh, do stop fussing and get your father.'

Having finished the last morsel on his plate and feeling the need to loosen his belt, break wind and perhaps get some air before dessert, Donald was less reluctant to move. 'What is it, woman?' he asked as he got to his wife, who'd risen from the chair and stood by the main entrance to the hotel. 'Are you ill?'

Phil had followed his father out and hovered by his parents. He was curious to know what was going on, as was James, who had come out to see what the fuss was about. Violet pulled Donald away from her sons and spoke to him. 'There's been trouble. The boy. He's in hospital, intensive care. It's serious. I must go.'

Donald's face clouded. Phil and James strained to catch what was being said but only picked up the odd phrase. Somebody was in a bad way in hospital, but the family were all there. James commented that it couldn't be anybody important. They were all accounted for, and yet their mother was shaken. Their father straightened his shoulders. His body was stiff and disapproving.

'You won't come with me?'

'No.'

'I've called a cab,' Violet said. 'You'll have to come for me in the car after you've slept off your excesses. Make my excuses, will you?'

'Where are you going, mother? What is it? Who's hurt?' James shouted, but their mother had turned, opened the door of the taxi and was climbing inside.

It was after ten o'clock when she arrived at the front desk of the hospital. She was directed to the ICU, but nobody offered to escort her. 'Young man,' she said to a porter wheeling a patient covered in blood along the corridor. 'Take me to the intensive care unit immediately.'

The porter didn't realise that Violet was talking to him. 'You. Are you deaf or an imbecile?' The porter turned, confused. 'Leave him there. He's clearly drunk. He'll be quite all right there for a moment, and this is urgent business. Intensive care?'

'Oi, who are you calling drunk?' the patient slurred from behind a face full of swelling.

'What?' the porter said.

'Intensive care. Now.'

'If you follow the arrows to the lift, madam, ICU's on the third floor. You can't miss it.' He came to an intersection and veered off, leaving Violet shouting at his retreating back.

There was a flurry of conversation from the nurses' station when she got to the intensive care ward. The nurses and a doctor behind the desk were discussing cases, and the nurses to the side of the desk were talking about their love lives. Violet burst among them like a German Shepherd into a flock of pigeons. She was out of breath, and her bunions were throbbing in the stiff court shoes. She'd walked further in the last five minutes than she'd done in the preceding month. She flung her handbag on the nurses' station desk and flopped the top half of her body on top of the counter. 'Water. I need water.' She croaked, lifting her head from her arms. One of the clips holding hair piled on top of her head came loose, and a mass of frizzy hair dropped over her face. Her red lipstick spread from her thin top lip to finish below her nose.

The two young nurses beside Violet giggled, and an older nurse struggled to bring her face to order and then glared the girls into silence. 'Can I help you?' she asked, ignoring Violet's plea for hydration and adopting her business-like smile that conveyed compassion and authority in equal measure.

'And you are?' Violet asked.

The nurse was taken aback, and the smile dropped from her face to be replaced by a look that said she was the boss around here. 'I'm staff nurse Jeffries,' she said, motioning to her name badge. 'How can I help you, Madam?'

'You can't. You won't do at all. I need to speak to the man in charge. You there, young man.' She poked her finger towards the doctor, who had his head immersed in somebody's records. He was out of range for her to make physical contact, but he raised his head to stare at her.

'Are you a real doctor, or one of those people who follow the doctors around the wards?'

Adrian Walker smiled. He could charm any old bird out of the trees, and this buzzard was no exception. 'I am indeed a real doctor, Ma'am. They even gave me a certificate to prove it. Now, why don't you tell me what I can do for you.'

'I'd prefer somebody higher, but you'll have to do. Simon Peter,' she dropped her voice on the last word, 'Woods,' she said. At that moment, the pager attached to the doctor's pocket sounded an urgent alarm. He looked at it. 'I'm sorry, Madam, this is important. I've got to go.' He patted her arm. 'Nurse Jefferies will look after you. She's got a piece of paper, too.' He winked at Violet and took off down the ward in the direction of monitors sounding alarms.

'You've come to see Simon Woods?' sister Jefferies asked. 'Are you a relative?'

'I'm his,' Violet faltered. 'He's my. I'm his legal guardian.'

'Oh, right, I guess that's good enough. Only next of kin are allowed in. He's very poorly, but we've got him sedated, and he's doing as well as can be expected. I'll take you to him. Don't be alarmed by all the monitoring equipment. It's keeping him alive. He's asleep, but some people believe they can hear you, so feel free to talk to him.' She was striding down the corridor as she spoke, and Violet was struggling to keep up with her. 'I can't tell you anymore, I'm afraid, but a doctor will be along shortly.' She opened a door and admitted Violet. 'Make yourself comfortable, and when the nurses have a spare moment, they'll bring you a cup of tea. She motioned the bell above the bed. 'Ring if you need anything.' She put her hand on the front of Simon's chest. 'Right, my bonny lad, there's a lady here to see you. Don't you be giving her any of your lip now.'

Jeffries closed the door behind her, and Violet was left alone with the droning beep of the monitor, the loud ticking of the wall clock, and the noise of saline and morphine feeding into a drip bag for company.

The doughy white figure, in the white bed, in the white room, seemed less real than the small noises around her. She sat in the bedside chair. Before looking at her son properly, she eased her feet out of the shoes, raised one fat ankle and rubbed it. She would have trouble walking the next day. She examined the bunion on the side of her big toe. It was visibly red through the thick denier of her tights. She stood up, poured herself a glass of water from the jug on the bedside cabinet, and wondered if the glass had been pressed to her son's mouth. She screwed her face in disgust, lowered the glass without drinking, and sat down. She couldn't avoid it any longer and looked at her son for the first time. His chest rose in time with the machine breathing for him. His face was slack, eyes closed, fleshy mouth open, and his tongue protruded. Violet shuddered, and with all her might, she willed for the heartbeat to stop. She wanted the shame to end.

She examined the equipment, working out what each did, how it worked and what it was for. The drip feed worked by controlling a simple slide wheel. Taking it down would lessen the flow of drugs, and sliding it up increased them. The beeping monitor took its signal from the clamp cradling Simon's thumb and recording his pulse. She looked at the door and listened for footsteps in the hall. Then she removed the finger clamp from his thumb and put it on her own. She watched the numbers rising on the monitor screen, but they didn't sound any alarms. She was ready to transfer the clamp if anybody came down the corridor. Her own elevated but steady heartbeat, within the perimeters of acceptable levels, pulsed out static pictures on graph paper. The machine beeped like a contented robot, and she studied the man that she gave birth to and felt the reflexive, familiar revulsion that she had every time she'd ever looked at him. She could speed up the flow of morphine into his bloodstream and then return it to its original position when somebody approached, but she doubted it would be enough to kill him. She tested the tension on the nasal tube hooked to the ventilator. The tube was fastened under his nose with a piece of Micropore surgical tape. She loosened it enough to allow movement of the tube but not enough to show it had been disturbed. She wondered if she could pull the tube out far enough to suffocate him without it coming right out of his airway. She tested the theory by easing the tube from her son's throat an inch at a time. This was her moment, her chance. She could

202

rid herself of this terminal disease that she'd carried on her soul. God would forgive her.

Surely, she had passed his test of burden after all these years. In almost thirty years, she had only missed two Wednesday visits. Staff had come and gone from the home, but she was a constant. She had greater longevity there than any member of staff. She'd never failed in her duty, apart from the two occasions when she was too ill to attend. And for thirty years, she'd burned with hatred and shame. She pulled the tube another inch, and he opened his mouth wider, although his eyes stayed shut. He was unconscious, but his broken, imbecilic mind had the presence of self-worth enough to send messages to his nervous system to fight for life.

She watched him gasp, choking on the air that he couldn't pull into his lungs. She saw his impaired brain starved of oxygen, and she waited for the stillness that would be her reward for bravery. He reminded her of a fish out of water. A big fat, bloated, ugly fish, gasping and flapping for a life that he hadn't earned and didn't deserve. He was making a gurgling sound. She suffered the first stirrings of panic. What if she was caught? Her reputation would be destroyed. The WI. The Media. She'd scream euthanasia from the dock, but could she take the risk? She might not be the people's heroine for such a merciful and selfless act. And at best, the secret that she'd guarded all these years—the fact that she had a disabled child, would be out. She wanted him to die, but she wouldn't be able to live with herself if the word was out that she'd given birth to that.

She wanted to kill him, but her secret would be out. She couldn't do it. The bastard still had her in his infernal trap.

Later, she didn't know if she was already forcing the tube back down his windpipe when she heard the footsteps approaching or if the footsteps came first. But when she heard the nurse, she had to act fast. The tube was a lot harder to get back down than it was pulling it out. He made unearthly choking noises. The footsteps were level with the door. There was a wet mucus mark on the tube, and it was three inches higher than it had been. She transferred the finger clamp. The monitor dropped, slowed, settled, and was still settling when the nurse came in. Violet flung the top half of her body over Simon and feigned weeping. The nurse glanced at the monitor and rushed to the bed. She guided Violet up by the shoulders. 'Easy, love. You've trapped his monitor.'

She sat Violet in the chair and looked at Simon Peter's finger clamp. The pace was still slowing but was steadier. The nurse adjusted it. After a few seconds, it stuck in a slow, steady, one-beep-per-second rhythm. 'Crickey, I think you'd knocked the wind out of him there. I know it's upsetting, but try not to squash him.' Violet looked up from dabbing her eyes. 'I mean,' the nurse said, 'please, just make sure he's got plenty of air.' She realised this was a dumb statement that highlighted her student status. The patient wasn't breathing for himself, so it didn't matter how much air he had, but having that great lump lying over him had done something to the monitor. It was okay now, and she could see to the matter at hand, 'Can I get you a cup of tea or anything?'

Chapter Nineteen

'Will you please see to Vicki while I put this wash on?'

'Come on, Jules, just a quickie. I'm aching.' He reached for her as she bent to stuff the dirty clothes into the washer. He had one hand around her waist, and the other grabbed her breast. He watched it leak milk over his hand as he rubbed his erection against her buttocks. 'Come on, Mummy. Turn around and give Daddy some titty milk.'

She stood with Phil attached to her. Picking up a packet of washing powder tablets, she crushed them hard in her fist before opening the packet. She wished they were her husband's balls. He disgusted her. If ever a man needed castrating, it was him. 'Your mother's coming any minute now. Get off me, will you.'

She flung him away, pulling her disarranged top and bra down with one hand while she opened the tablet packet and put them into the washing machine with the other. Phil was smelling the breast milk on his palm, and she turned away when she saw his tongue come out to lick it.

She went into the living room, where Vicki was crying against the bars of her playpen. Julie picked her up and cradled her into her shoulder. The child stopped crying, but she gave a great heave every few seconds as the residue of her sobs subsided. Julie stroked her angry daughter's sweaty head and swore that she saw the reproach in the baby's eyes. 'I'm sorry, baby girl. Mummy had to get tidied up for Grandma coming. And as usual, Daddy's no help at all. We don't want to give her anything to crow about, do we, sweetheart? No, we don't.'

'I'll just go and sort myself out again, then, shall I?' Phil said as he walked past the living room door and stomped up the stairs in the direction of the bedroom and his stash of *18 and barely legal* porn. She hated it when he was on the late shift. He'd be pestering her again before he went out at two.

Forgiven for her abandonment to the playpen, Vicki was reaching for Julie's breast. These days it felt as though everybody wanted a piece of her.

Grandma, as she insisted on being called by all three of them so as not to confuse Victoria, was already perched on the sofa, with the baby on her knee, when Phil came downstairs. He glared at Julie in the second before Mother turned around, and then, when she did, he smiled a simpering smile and dropped a light kiss on top of Julie's head. Julie felt a wetness on her scalp. The bastard had spat into her hair. She imagined it burning like acid. He'd be in a bad mood for the rest of the morning because she'd refused him sex, and when he pestered her for it later, he would be rougher than normal. She couldn't refuse him twice in one day.

When she'd made the tea, she washed up the teaspoon, dried it on the tea towel and put it in the drawer facing the right way and ensuring that it sat neatly with the others. Julie had learned a lot since leaving her family home. She'd learned to cook and found that she had a natural flair and enjoyed it. Mostly it was the little things she had to perfect and never slip up on. The first time she'd stirred a cup of tea and left the spoon on the side of the sink, Phil had gripped the top of her arm. He'd screamed at her, called her a dirty whore, and stood over her while she washed the teaspoon and put it away. Her arm was dappled with dark blue bruises for a week before fading to a dirty yellow. He had a similar reaction when he saw Julie drying her hands on a tea towel. He yelled so hard that he damaged his throat. He didn't touch her, but he degraded her and called her names before turning the blame on her family and upbringing. Hand towels were for drying hands. Tea towels were for pots. She only needed yelling at once. She got it.

The house, even with a baby in it, was spotless. Even the dust bunnies were banished to warrens beyond the property. There wasn't a node of dust, not a spot of dirt anywhere in their home. It was immaculate. As soon as something was used, it was cleaned. It was the way he liked it.

The strange thing was, she liked it too. She had changed. At her family home, she'd been untidy. Clothes were taken off and discarded over the back of the bedroom chair until it threatened to tip under the weight. As Mrs Julie Woods, she was a different woman. Lisa came to visit them a few months after they were married. It was so good having her sister there, but Julie found that she had to tidy up after her all the time, so it didn't upset Phil. After the first two days, she was angry with her untidy sister. When she waved Lisa off, Julie heaved a big sigh of relief and couldn't wait to get the duster out to obliterate stray fingerprints that might have been left behind.

She'd changed in other ways, too. Julie had always been a jeans, tee shirt, and ponytail kind of girl. If she had to analyse her change of style, she'd have put it down to becoming a mother and growing up. But lots of women had babies without changing their personalities. She'd taken to buying print dresses and skirts. She was drawn to delicate flowers. Dolly shoes, feminine and dainty, replaced her trainers. She was leg waxing and having six-weekly hairdos. Phil hadn't ordered her to do it. He'd never said a word. But on occasions, he disapproved of her dress sense or lack of it. Julie's change of image was tied up in a Martha Stewart fantasy. She had to be the perfect mother and, more importantly, the perfect wife.

'Nice cake, dear,' Grandma said. 'Did you bake it yourself?' She had. She made everything from scratch. Phil didn't hold with processed food. He said it wasn't proper sustenance for a man to work on. She made roast dinners and baked cakes. She'd given up work at her husband's insistence, and now she cooked, cleaned, and pottered in the garden.

'Guess what?' she'd said to Lisa on the phone soon after her marriage.
'What?'
'I'm doing plants.'
'You're what?'
She was excited. 'Plants and stuff. I'm growing them.'
'It's called gardening, love.'
'Oh, yeah,' she'd said. 'I knew that.'

Phil had come home and complained about the state of the garden. She didn't have a clue what she was doing, but she bought books, and then every few days, she bought blubs or seeds.

In six months, she bought her own poly-tunnel and grew their veg. She had a herb garden, flower beds, and lawns—three in total, including the front—they were so smooth you could play bowls on them. She had a tool shed and a potting shed, and she took advice from her father-in-law. This year, she'd entered her first carrots at the local fête. They hadn't been placed, but her Victoria sponge took third and was awarded a blue rosette.

Since the day she got married, she hadn't taken a single alcoholic drink. Partly because Vicki came along so fast and because she was breastfeeding. She declined all offers of nights out from her sisters and old workmates until they'd stopped inviting her. Occasionally, she went shopping with her sister on a Saturday afternoon, but that was rare. She preferred being at home in her lovely house, in her lovely garden, happy.

Lisa and Emma, and even her mum and dad on occasion, called her The Stepford Wife behind her back—and then to her face. She became Steppy, and she tolerated it with good humour. They never called her it in front of Phil, though, just like they never called Victoria Vicki when he was around. He didn't like it. Wherever possible, he preferred her to be given the full title of Victoria-Violet. Lisa called her Vicki-Vee and said it sounded like a DJ's name, but Julie couldn't bring herself to say that. She never ever used her daughter's hyphenated name.

She felt that calling her daughter Violet, or even a shortened form of it, would sour her child, but she'd stopped shuddering when Phil used the full name because that's all he ever called her, apart from when he was angry, and then he would address her as The Child.

Julie detested her husband. She grew to hate him after Vicki was born. He had no interest in his little girl apart from when his parents were around or there was somebody else he was playing the devoted father to. When it was the three of them, he ignored her. He never woke in the night to change her. He never changed a nappy at all. He resented her and was jealous that she took her mother's attention.

'Victoria-Violet loves her grandma more than anybody else in the world,' Violet sang as she bounced Vicki on her knee. Vicki had enough and was struggling to get down, but Violet held her in a vice-like grip. There were going to be tears. Julie watched her daughter screw up her face in preparation for the first yell. She had her father's temper. She stood up and put a plain biscuit in Vicki's fist to distract her. 'Does silly Mummy feed you those nasty biscuits that are full of sugar? Does she, then? Silly Mummy. Tell her, Victoria-Violet, tell her silly mummy.' Julie thought she might puke if she had to listen to any more of Violet's baby talk.

'Oh, here, dear, take her from me. Grandma really mustn't get this coat dirty. Jaeger, dear.' She held Vicki out to Julie as though the baby was radioactive. Phil stepped in and took her out of his mother's arms. He cradled her in the crook of his arm and kissed her on her cheek.

'Victoria-Violet is Daddy's Little Princess, isn't she?' he said. Vicki flung herself sideways, extending her arms towards her mother. She dropped the sucked biscuit on the floor and grizzled. As Julie stood to take her from Phil, she realised it was the first time Phil had touched his daughter in almost a week.

'You shouldn't give in to her like that, Philip, dear. She's far too clingy for her mother. It's not good for her. She'll be a spoiled brat. Put her down in her playpen and let her be.'

Vicki was grabbing Julie's breast. Ignoring Violet's advice, she left the room, sickened by the act that Phil was performing for his mother's benefit.

When she brought Vicki home from the hospital, Violet and Donald came to visit. The baby was grizzling for a feed so Julie covered her chest with a feeding cloth and put her daughter to her breast. She hadn't given it a second thought—her baby needed feeding, and she was there to provide for her.

'Take the child to the nursery and do that,' Phil said. Julie had never heard him speak to her so coldly, and she thought she'd heard every nasty tone the man possessed. His eyes were smouldering with fury. She looked up, shocked to find Donald pointedly looking out of the window and Violet with her head turned into the sofa with an expression of deep disgust on her frosty face.

'The flowers are looking nice again,' Donald said. Julie hoisted Vicki, covered herself and left the room.

'How dare you disrespect my parents like that,' Phil raged when they'd gone. 'I cannot believe that you brazenly exposed yourself to my father like a fishwife. I will never live this down. How could you? You filthy, dirty whore. I would make you get on your knees and humbly beg their forgiveness if it didn't mean bringing the disgusting spectacle up again.' He was clearly thinking about making her anyway. 'No, it's best left now. But if you ever embarrass me in front of my parents like that again, I will never forgive you. If you were a Christian woman, you'd go to confession and beg for your soul to be cleansed of such wickedness. He stormed out of the room without another word. The upside was that he never pestered her for sex for nearly a month after that. He said she disgusted him, but he still lay in their bed, masturbating beside her at night.

Julie thought back to that incident when she sat in the nursery chair feeding Vicki. She could hear their muffled voices from downstairs, and she was content. How could Phil not love this precious child?

'Grandma and Grandpa are leaving now, Julie,' Phil shouted up the stairs.

'Okay, see you next time. Thank you for the bonnet,' Julie shouted back. She heard Phil's feet pounding up the stairs. She knew from the footfalls he was angry again. He flung the door open, startling Vicki and making her jump in her mother's arms. She whimpered but didn't remove her mouth from the nipple.

'Have you no manners?' he hissed. 'Get down those stairs now and say goodbye to my parents.'

'I'm in the middle of feeding your daughter. I can't just pull her away,' she hissed back.

'Put the child down and do it.' He didn't wait for her to respond and grabbed Vicki from her mother's arms. As the suction from around Julie's breast was released, Vicki's rosebud mouth came away with a loud smacking noise. She drew breath and wailed. Phil almost threw her into her cot. She wasn't finished feeding and hadn't been winded.

If Donald and Violet weren't waiting at the bottom of the stairs, she would have fought against this indignity, but it was better not to make a scene. It would only be held against her by all concerned. She glanced at her screaming baby and left the room, covering her breast as she went.

'No need. Really no need,' Donald said as she appeared around the bend in the stairs with a smile ready on her face.

'Every need, Dad,' Phil replied, hammering the point home that they'd had words, but Philip was the master in his house.

Violet's mouth dropped open to gape as she stared at her daughter-in-law. Julie was about to embrace Donald in the customary, awkward goodbye hug before moving on to Violet, but Donald had also seen what had happened and busied himself with his hat, holding it in front of himself like a shield.

Julie looked down and saw the sticky wet patch on the front of her top. Still full, her swollen breast had lactated. She felt a small river of milk trickle to her navel.

'Clean yourself, woman,' Phil spoke to her like a dog, humiliating her.

Julie went back to Vicki. She lifted her from the cot, crooning to her. Vicki latched on to her mother's breast, comforting them both. Five minutes later, Julie was singing to her daughter, who had hold of her little finger and was staring into her mother's eyes. Out of the blue, Julie remembered the look on her Mother-in-law's horrified face when her breast had leaked onto her top, and she laughed. Not getting the nuance of the joke but finding it funny anyway, Vicki laughed too, and mother and daughter shared a special moment before Julie had to go downstairs to face her husband's latest fury.

Chapter Twenty

J ulie went downstairs in her dressing gown. The smell of toast and percolating coffee hit her before she got near the kitchen. Phil headed her off on the threshold. He had a white tea towel folded over his arm. 'Good morning, Madam. May I escort you to your table, where breakfast is about to be served,' he said, guiding her past the kitchen and into the dining room where the table was laid. He pulled out a chair, and Julie sat. He pushed her chair in. Before going back into the kitchen, Phil bent and dropped a kiss onto the top of her head. No spit. She was honoured. 'Happy anniversary, my darling.'

It was a beautiful May morning, warm enough that Phil had thrown the patio doors wide open. The sun was shining, the garden was coming into bloom, and Julie identified a starling, wood pigeon and a cuckoo amongst the riotous birdsongs. The birds were as happy as she was that the long and bitter winter was over. They were going to Morocco later that morning, but the excitement wasn't the only reason for the little fountain that rose somewhere in the pit of her tummy and burst into a million tiny champagne bubbles of happiness.

She loved her garden, it was her pride and joy, and she also loved this room and the lounge that opened through a door to the right.

The special one that they kept for visitors. The dining room was the only room in the house that was wallpapered. She'd seen it in the shop and knew it was made for this room. It had a pale blue wash with a light-yellow stripe on the bottom of the wall, and above it was a wonderful buttercup print. Delicate yellow flowers sprayed the walls, just like her dresses, and brought the outside garden inside. The dining table sat twelve, was made from solid oak and had matching chairs with high backs that screamed grandiosity.

The chair cushions were upholstered with a blue and yellow print. The dining room displayed her Cappo Di Monte collection. She had more than forty pieces, most of it bought at auction for a song. In stark contrast to the delicacy of the rest of the room, her tableware was Tunisian. She fell in love with the Tunisian style, and over two trips to the country that year, they'd brought back an extensive range of tableware and crockery, all in vibrant red, blue and yellow. Her glassware was lead crystal, and when they had guests for dinner, which was often, Julie's table was always complimented. Her style was an extension of her, and she felt that she wore it well.

Every week they bought three bunches of flowers with their shopping, two large mixed bouquets for the living room and lounge, and a delicate drop of carnations for the dining room table. She alternated the colour of the carnations weekly. This morning, by her place setting, was a huge bouquet of gardenias, freesias and red roses. A card was propped against her juice glass, with a jeweller's box in front of it.

They'd been married for six glorious years, and every single day Julie wished her husband would have a heart attack and die.

She was happier than she'd ever been in her life. She'd taken to being a wife and mother better than she could ever have expected. She loved being married. She just hated her husband and would like to replace him with a better spouse. As she reached for her card, she smiled a smug smile, remembering the voices of doom in the lead-up to her wedding, who prophesied that it would never last.

To my darling wife, with love always and forever, Philip xxx

Her card to him bore similar words of love. She wondered how often he'd wished her dead.

Vicki, who was a blessedly late riser in the mornings, ran barefoot into the dining room and flung herself into her mother's arms.

'Stop running in the house,' Phil yelled at her from the kitchen.

'Mummy, the sleeps are all used up now, aren't they?' At this, the wide smile froze on her tiny face for a second in case it had been a huge grown-up joke, and she still had another five million sleeps to endure before they went on holiday.'

'They have indeed, my darling. And where are we going today?'

'Mocco,' the little girl screeched.

'Yay, Morocco,' Julie tickled her daughter and caused gales of giggles.

Phil arrived with two plates in his hands and a dish for Vicki. 'Proper behaviour in the dining room, please,' he said, glaring at his daughter. 'Go and sit down nicely now, please, Victoria-Violet. Have you washed your hands?'

'Yes, Daddy.' Julie watched part of her little girl's bubble burst. 'Daddy, we're going Mocco today. Would you pass me the Wice Cwispies, please, Mummy?'

'How many times do you have to be told it's Morocco? What are you doing, Julie? Don't give her that rubbish this morning. She won't eat her eggs.'

Julie had taken the cereal dispenser and was pouring a few into the bottom of a bowl for Vicki. 'Can't she have both? It's a special day.'

'No.'

'Why lay them out on the table then?'

'Because it looks good, doesn't it? I wanted everything to be perfect. Aren't you going to open your present?'

'All this effort is perfect. It's wonderful. Thank you for going to all this trouble.' She reached for the jewellery box. This would have been a perfect morning if he wasn't so uptight. Vicki could never do a thing right when he was around. He was always barking at her. Trying to muster her earlier feeling of happiness and forcing down the resentment, she opened the box. A tiny pair of diamond and sapphire earrings winked at her, and she gasped in delight. They were beautiful.

'Why you got a pessant, Mummy. Is it your burfday?'

'No, darling, it's our anniversary. Today your daddy and I have been married for six years.'

'Wish your mother a Happy Anniversary, Victoria-Violet.' Phil was still growling.

'Happy Amme nursery,' her brow furrowed into four little creases as she floundered. 'What is it, Daddy?'

How could he not be enchanted by his daughter's chatter? Julie marvelled every day at each new thing she came out with. Their daughter was bright and her thirst for knowledge inexhaustible. Julie laughed. 'Don't you worry, sweetheart, it's a great big word.'

'And she'll never learn to talk properly if you don't encourage her. You let her get away with being lazy.' He turned to face his daughter. 'Ann-e-ver-sary. Say it.'

Victoria giggled. 'Like Aunty Annie,' she said, referring to one of the helpers at her preschool.

'Say it.'

'Ann-e-ber-sary'

'Versary'

'Versary.'

'Put it together.'

'Put it together.'

Phil sighed and closed his eyes. 'Say anniversary, you stupid child.'

'Anniversary.'

Julie cringed, and pop went another champagne bubble.

Chapter Twenty-One

A fter a different holiday a year later, Lisa checked out Julie's tan. 'Jamaica lived up to expectation, then?'

It was January, and Julie, Phil and Vicki had returned from some winter sun. 'How much longer are you going to live like this, Toots?' It was a familiar question, and Lisa had asked it many times. 'It breaks my heart to see you so broken.' That wasn't enough, so she struggled to find another word. 'And Cowed.'

'Notice you didn't say unhappy or miserable or depressed? You still don't get it. I'm happier than I've ever been in my life. This is everything I've ever wanted and more. You think he bullies me, but I can handle him. He's a small price to pay to have Vicki and all this.'

'But the sex stuff. You've just spent the last ten minutes telling me how bad it was on holiday. You nearly put me off my sandwich,' she said, motioning to her empty plate.

'Even that's not so bad once you get used to it. The thing with sex is not to fight it. I've perfected the sixty-second blow job to an Olympic standard. Honestly, nine times out of ten, that keeps him on an even keel. We rarely have full-on sex these days.'

'It's no way to live. The man's a monster.'

'It's my way to live, and it works for me.'

'But you could divorce him and take him to the cleaners. Why are you so bloody stubborn about it? Your promise to his dragon of a mother means nothing.'

'It means everything.'

'You know it's going to come one day. Are you really going to throw everything away?'

Julie thought back to the golden promise she'd made her Mother-in-law in the early days of the bitter fights and arguments. Violet had called her a gold digger. Said that she'd crawled out of the gutter. And that Philip was nothing more than a meal ticket. Julie promised, on her life, that if ever her marriage went sour, she would leave with nothing more than the clothes on her back.

She answered her sister's question. 'Yes, I am. I'll walk out of here empty-handed and without a second's hesitation.'

'God, you're stubborn sometimes. Bloody hell, girl, for what you put up with, you've earned every chrome washer in this place. It's Vicki-Vee's inheritance. You can't deny her that.'

'I would rather my daughter grew up with dignity and integrity than a silver spoon. If I walk out of here with her, and we have to struggle for a while, it'll be character-building for her, and she'll always know her mother did what was right. A promise like that can't be broken. Anyway, shush, it's not going to come to that. Things are fine.'

Sensing friction building between them, Lisa changed the subject. 'So, how's Woodzilla been?'

'Not so bad. She adores Vicki, and she's taken to calling me Dear, so maybe after six years of marriage, she's realised that I'm not the monster she had me painted.'

'She's such a hypocrite. How can she pull our family to bits when she's got a prostitute in a frock for one son, a fraudster for another, and a frigging sex addict for a third?' She pointed upstairs to where Phil was asleep from his night shift.

'Shush, you'll wake him,' Julie said just as the living room door opened. He'd crept down the stairs and had been listening at the door. As she heard him coming in, Lisa grabbed her cup and side plate off the coffee table. Julie didn't know how much of their conversation he heard. His voice, when he spoke, was cool and gave no indication of the fury he held beneath the surface. 'Well, look at Miss Lisa, sitting on my sofa, eating my food, drinking my coffee, and slagging off my family. I think it's time you ran along home now, don't you, dear?' He emphasised the last word and ripped the cup out of Lisa's hands, throwing it against the far wall. Coffee dregs dripped from the muted mauve paintwork and ran in two trails down the wall to the carpet. Lisa put her coat on. 'Get out,' Phil said in a controlled voice. 'Get out of my house and don't ever come back.'

'Come with me, Jules,' she said.

Julie shook her head.

'Will you be all right? I'll ring you.' Lisa glared at Phil before leaving.

Phil waited for the squeak of the garden gate before speaking. 'Am I such a bad husband?'

'No, of course not.'

'I give you everything you ask for. I work eighty hours a week to keep you happy. And you repay me like this. Don't you love me? You let your family talk about my people as though we're the ones that are stinking filth. How can that be?'

'Please don't start, Phil. Of course, I love you. I don't know how much you heard, but it's just our Lisa mouthing off. You know she's got a big trap.'

He walked over to her, and Julie shrank in her seat. Philip grabbed the front of her fleece and pulled her towards him. 'Liar,' he hissed. 'I could wring your rancid neck right now.' His eyes were blazing, and Julie was scared. Phil worked up some spittle in his mouth and spat it in Julie's face before throwing her into the chair. He stalked out of the room, leaving Julie to wipe the soiling from her face.

She was glad Vicki was at school. She'd been quiet lately, and Julie was worried that the fights between her and Phil were scaring her. She went into the kitchen for a dustpan, for the broken crockery, and a wet cloth to wash the coffee from the wall.

In many ways, Phil was the perfect husband. He was right. He was a workaholic. When Julie met him, he was a fitter on the shop floor. From that, he was elevated to foreman, and now he had a white-collar job in the offices that allowed them an extravagant lifestyle. He worked five twelve-hour shifts instead of three or four and often went into the office on Saturday and Sunday. Phil loved his work and despised his daughter. He kept out of the way.

They had three foreign holidays a year. They'd had already been to Morocco and Jamaica that year. He never denied Julie, or indeed Vicki, anything. If they wanted it, it was available. A tin containing an emergency float of one thousand pounds was kept in the back of one of the kitchen cupboards. It was there to pay for anything that cropped up between visits to the bank.

Julie had never lived with financial security. Her parent's money worries had clouded her childhood. They often had debt collectors and the loan woman at the door, and sometimes there wasn't enough to eat.

Now she had everything. Julie had taken a part-time job working in the kitchen of a nursing home, and she loved it. Her money was her own, and Philip never asked her about it or wanted to know what she did with it. She could help her family when they needed it. She'd take money from the kitchen tin, but she always made sure that she replaced it on payday. Once a month, she went to the mortgage brokers on Duke Street. The mortgage was an endowment and came out of Phil's bank on the fifteenth of every month. He left the finances to Julie, secure in the knowledge that everything was paid up and on time. He never looked at the biannual statements from the mortgage company. At the end of every month, Julie would make a second, equal monthly payment on the house. It came from her own wage and was her secret gift to Phil. It was her kick in the teeth for Violet. When the mortgage came to an end years before the final payment was due, she wanted to be able to say, 'See? I did that. I doubled the house payments so we would be debt-free earlier. Now call me a gold digger.' With every extra payment, Julie felt ten feet tall.

Theirs was a difficult and unhappy marriage, but Julie's life, on the whole, couldn't have been better. She was a loyal and faithful wife and a loving mother.

Mrs Calvert walked across the schoolyard as Julie was re-fastening Vicki's coat and getting the first barrage of words about her day at school. 'Mrs Woods, hang on. Can I have a word, please?' Julie looked up, startled, and rose to meet the teacher.

'What is it? Is everything all right?'

'Oh yes, I'm sure it is. If you'd just like to come to my office, I won't keep you long. I've arranged for Miss Finch to watch Victoria for you.' Despite the head teacher's light tone, it sounded serious. Julie was worried.

In her office, Miss Calvert pointed Julie to a chair and produced a buff file. She looked at it for a moment before speaking. 'Our role as teachers is not just to impart knowledge, Mrs Woods. We are also there to look out for the well-being of the children in our care. We're trained to notice sudden or even gradual behavioural changes.'

Julie had sat forward, alarmed. She clasped her hands in her lap. 'What is it? What's the matter?'

The middle-aged teacher smiled. 'Don't worry. I'm sure it's nothing, but you see, that's why we want to talk to you now so that if something is wrong, we can sort it out.'

'Okay,' Julie said, wishing she'd get to the point.

'Victoria has always been an exemplary student, Mrs Woods. A real credit to you. She's very well-behaved in class, one of the top students. And that in itself is part of the problem.'

'It is?'

'Miss Finch, as you know, is Victoria's form teacher. How can I put this? She's concerned that, in some ways, Victoria is almost too good. Her manners are so tight that they suffocate her. Am I making sense?'

'Not really.'

'Okay, let me read you part of this progress report from Miss Finch. "Victoria is too stiff. She seems too polite, too clean, too well-mannered, too everything. It's as though she only allows two-thirds of herself to come out. I have an impression that Victoria is holding her personality in check." I know,' the head continued, 'this may seem silly to you. How can a child be too good, but it's a worry, and in some cases, it can be an indicator of other things.'

Julie interrupted. 'What a load of rubbish. There's nothing wrong with Vicki's personality. She's fine. How can you haul me in here to complain that my child is too well-behaved? I've never heard such rubbish. And while I'm here, Miss Calvert, perhaps I can draw your attention to what happened yesterday. Millie Green called my daughter a bitch. I won't stand for that.'

'Mrs Woods, you're taking this all wrong. I'm not here to make you feel as though we're criticising you. I just wanted an informal chat with you to see that everything is okay. As to the incident with Millie yesterday, we are aware of it, and I believe Miss Finch has sent a letter to Millie's parents. Mrs Woods, you have a lovely daughter. She's a joy to teach. We've seen how you are with her in the yard, and she talks about you all the time. But she's never mentioned her father. Not once.'

The teacher stopped talking to let the information sink in.

'That's because he works a lot.'

'I see. As you know, Victoria's a chatterbox. But both Mrs Finch and I have noticed that when we mention her father, Victoria gets distressed.'

'That's rubbish. What are you saying? Let me get this straight, are you accusing Philip of something? Are you suggesting that my husband is abusing our daughter?'

'No.' The teacher spoke firmly. 'No, Mrs Woods, please get that idea out of your head. That's not what I'm saying at all. Please don't think that for a second. Victoria is a happy little girl. She's showing no symptoms of being abused in any way.'

'You've been looking for them, then? Signs.'

'We watch every child in the school, Mrs Woods. We observe Vicki no more or less than anybody else. It's our job to be observant. She's showing none of the usual symptoms of being abused, but she is showing signs of domestic distress.' The teacher picked up an exercise book from the desk.

'Because she'd noticed some changes in Victoria's behaviour, Miss Finch set the class an exercise. She asked them to think about the best time they'd ever had with their daddy and write about it.'

'Wait a minute.' Julie was furious. 'The teacher set the whole class a lesson just to trap my daughter into saying something bad about her dad?'

The headmistress didn't answer. She turned Vicki's book upside down so that it would face Julie, and she pushed it across the table.

Vicki had written: *Daddy + mummy + me went to Jamaker. Mummy made sand casuls wiv me. Mummy an me lafed when we got ower feets wet. Mummy and me dansd on the beech.*

Miss Calvert watched Julie's reaction.

'Vicki and I have a lot of fun together. It doesn't mean that she doesn't have fun with her dad, too. She just remembered that day in her head. Philip can be a bit stuffy. He's not the type to play in the sea or build sandcastles. Does that mean he's not a good father?' Julie felt tears stinging the back of her eyes and fought to keep them contained.

Miss Calvert pushed a box of tissues across the desk to her. 'When Miss Finch asked the children to write about a time with their fathers, she expressly asked the children to think of a time when their mothers weren't there, a day when they were having a good time alone with their dads.' She let the implications drift into the room.

'He's a wonderful father. He works all hours to give Victoria the life she has. I'm sorry, I don't know what else to say. I'm hurt that you're making my husband out to be a monster. He's not. He's really not.'

'I don't mean to upset you, Mrs Woods, and we're honestly not suggesting that something bad is happening at home. I assure you that's not the case. If we had any real concerns, this chat wouldn't be happening, and the meeting would be far less informal. We've just noticed some tension between Victoria and her father that we wanted to make you aware of, as is our duty. All we ask is that you speak to Victoria yourself, and maybe we can talk again in a week or two.'

Julie left the headmistress's office, reeling. Half of the way home, she seethed in indignation, mentally defending her husband and resenting the negativity against him. In the other half, she thought about just how much she'd buried her head in the sand where Philip and Victoria were concerned. She acted as a peacemaker between them, always trying to keep the equilibrium. She went through life hoping that Phil would ease up and find the joy in his daughter that she had.

Sometimes she counted days. The week before she counted six days when the only time he'd spoken to Vicki was to tell her off. He was at her all the time, pulling her up on her manners, making her sit up straight, be quiet, talk properly, eat nicely, don't drag your feet, pull your dress down, pick up your toys, fasten your shoes, don't swing your legs into the furniture, sit properly on the chairs, and a multitude of other minor complaints. When he talked to Vicki, he had a tone. He used a disapproving, strict tone of voice when he asked her to do something. He only ever talked to her in two ways, in a strict voice to make her do something or shouting when he was telling her off. He never talked to her.

Since starting work, Julie had noticed a change in Vicki, but she'd swallowed it and pretended it was her imagination. If she was working overtime, Phil would be there when Vicki came home from school. Vicki would throw a tantrum before Julie went to work. It was rare that Phil picked her up. He was always at work, so Julie couldn't take extra work very often. On the odd occasion that he did, she thought that it was good for Vicki. The child would have a tantrum, but that was because of her break in routine. It was out of the norm to have Dad there instead of her mum. Children liked order and bucked against change. She hated Julie for not being there for her. Julie didn't want her growing up spoiled, so ignored her crying. She'd pry Vicki off her legs when she went out of the door. She was grateful when she'd already dropped her daughter off at school when she left for work. She wouldn't tell the child in advance if her dad was picking her up. Vicki asked her every day if she would be there when she came out of school, and every day Julie said she would. Phil only picked her up about once a month, if that. Julie believed it was good for both of them.

When she got in from work, Vicki was always in bed. She'd ask how she'd been, and Phil would always say, 'Fine. No problem.' After Phil had looked after her, Vicki sometimes wet the bed. Julie knew in her heart that something was wrong, but she chose to ignore it. Apple carts were delicate things. The following day Vicki would be clingy and whiney, but that was to be expected. Julie would assure her that she'd be there after school, and Vicki would settle down.

Julie's head was banging. She'd been trying to work through the headache, but it got worse as her shift progressed, and now, she felt nauseous with it, too. She was told to go home and get some rest, an offer she jumped at.

She put her key in the door and went into the living room. The television was blaring in the lounge at the back of the house. Vicki had a little red table that she ate some meals on if they weren't eating in the dining room, or she'd use it to draw and do jigsaws. Julie pulled it into the middle of the room for her, and when it wasn't used, it fit into an alcove at the back of the room. Vicki was sitting bolt upright at the table, facing the wall. She didn't turn around when Julie went in.

'Vicki, I'm home, darling. Don't I get a hug?'

Vicki turned around. Her cheeks were streaked with tears. 'I can't, Mummy,' she said from her plastic chair. 'I'm not allowed to move until bedtime.'

Julie was by her daughter's side. She pulled Vicki into her arms and carried her to the sofa, where she sat with her on her knee. Phil didn't know she'd come home and was watching telly in the lounge.

Julie held Vicki's hand in hers. It was like ice.

'How long have you been sitting there, darling?'

'Since I came home from school, Mummy. Daddy always makes me sit here, and I have to be really still and quiet until bedtime. He watches TV in the lounge, and I'm not allowed to disturb him.' Her voice was even smaller. 'I'm not allowed to move to go to the toilet.'

'Have you had your tea?'

'Daddy gives me a drink of juice when I get in.'

'That's all you've had?'

Her little girl nodded, and big tears watered her eyes. 'Don't tell on me. He'll be mad.'

'No, he won't, sweetheart. Don't you worry? Now you go up and put your jammies on, and I'll make you some tomato soup and toast soldiers before you go to bed. How's that? She held her daughter close and kissed her hair.

'I don't like it when you leave me, Mummy,' Vicki jumped off her knee smiling, and Julie patted her on the bottom as she skipped across the room.

'I promise you, sweetie, I'm not going to leave you anymore. I'm sorry.'

Julie waited for the door to shut before confronting her husband. He heard the living room door opening.

'What the hell? I told you to sit on your chair and be quiet, you disobedient little bitch.' He met Julie at the threshold of the kitchen, and the shock on his face told its own tale.

'What the hell's going on?' she shouted at him. He was wretched with guilt.

'What do you mean, what's going on? Nothing's going on. What are you doing home?'

'I walked in to find our little girl sitting in a corner facing the wall. She was crying her heart out because you'd told her she wasn't allowed to move. What have you been doing to her, Philip? She's your daughter. How can you not want to love her with everything you've got?'

'Is that what she said,' he laughed. 'The little liar. You can tell she's your daughter. Only joking. Look, we've got a problem, sweetheart. Victoria-Violet resents you going to work. She's trying to play us off against each other.'

'Don't blame this on her, you cowardly little man,' she emphasised the word little. 'You have no right to call yourself a father. You haven't even fed her.'

'Don't be so ridiculous. Of course, I've fed her. She's been pushing your buttons, Julie. The little bitch has been lying through her teeth to cause trouble between us.' Julie recoiled and put her hands over her mouth. She couldn't believe what her husband had just called their daughter. Had he ever said that to her face before today? He was still talking. 'She wants a good hiding. I'll sort her out, lying and causing trouble. You've always been too soft, pandering to her every whim. If you want somebody to blame for this, you can start by looking in the mirror, woman. If I don't discipline the child and teach her some respect, she's going to revert to her genes and grow up a low-grade whore like her mother.'

She didn't think about it. She reacted. 'I want a divorce,' she pushed past and pounded up the stairs. Vicki's bedroom door was open, and Julie saw her sitting on the edge of her bed, looking terrified. She'd heard them arguing. What were a nice kitchen and Tunisian cookware in comparison to her daughter's happiness? She pulled a holdall from the top of the wardrobe in her room, mindful of her promise. She would return it later. Julie went to Vicki's room. 'It's all right, darling, don't be frightened. We're going on holiday, just the two of us.' She had a couple of hundred pounds left from this month's wages. It wasn't a lot, but it would buy her a night in a bed and breakfast while she thought about her next move. Of course, she'd have to go home, cap in hand to her parents. But the shame of her failed marriage burned inside. She didn't want to admit she'd fallen short as a wife. She'd moved on from the tired council house on the roughest estate in Barrow. She'd grown accustomed to better, and Vicki had never lived the way she had. Her parents didn't even have central heating. As she threw clothes into the holdall for Vicki, she realised her family were right. She was a snob. She hated the thought of going back to what she'd left behind. She worked hard for what she had. Her mind was racing as she threw Vicki's clothes into the bag and told her about the wonderful time they were going to have.

'I'm hungry, Mummy,' Vicki said.

'I know, sweetheart, and you know what, forget silly old tomato soup. When we get to our hotel, we'll order a takeaway. Anything you want.'

'Takeaway, wow.' Vicki said it as though it was Cinderella's castle. They didn't eat processed food. Phil insisted that the food was cooked from scratch. Vicki had only ever eaten takeaway at her auntie's house, and because it came in exciting packages, it was like the Holy Grail. She jumped and chatted, trying to decide between a Happy Meal or chicken nuggets or pizza, or sausage and chips.

Maybe they could afford a rented house. She only worked part-time, but Emma was at home with a small baby. Perhaps Julie could pay her to have Vicki after school. Her mind was reeling with possibilities as she zipped their daughter into her warm winter coat.

She went into the living room with Vicki in one arm and the holdall in the other. Phil was watching the television and didn't bother looking up.

'You think you're leaving me?' he sneered.

'No, Philip. I am leaving you.'

'You'll be back with your tail between your legs, begging me for forgiveness. I give it twenty-four hours. You're pathetic. I'm trying to discipline the child to avoid situations like this, and you namby-pamby her. Go if you want. I'll be better off without the lot of you. You only hold me back.'

She went to the pot where they kept keys and odd coins and took her car keys.

Philip raised his eyebrow. 'You think you're taking your car? Think again. The car stays with me.'

She could have kicked herself for not thinking. He enjoyed his victory. She threw the car keys and caught him on the cheek. Vicki was crying, and Phil wiped the bleeding scratch on his face.

'That's assault.'

Julie had to swallow. She wanted to scream at him to F-off, but she had Vicki in her arms, and the child was already terrified. She had to make do with the less satisfying, 'Get lost, Philip.' She went to the phone to ring for a taxi to take them into town where they could find a bed and breakfast. She picked up the receiver and dialled as Phil walked over to them. Vicki shrank into her mother's arms, clinging to her.

He grabbed the phone out of her hand and pressed the disconnection button before she had finished dialling. 'My telephone, I do believe.'

'You monster,' she whispered and hoped that whispering it would stop it from sticking in Vicki's memory. She had her face buried in her mother's hair so she didn't have to look at her father and see the fighting. Julie's arm was aching from holding her.

'What's in the bag?' Phil asked.

'Nothing of yours,' Julie spat back. 'Some things for Victoria. You can't begrudge me that.'

Phil adopted a mocking sing-song voice. 'I'm telling you now that if I ever leave, I'll walk out of here with nothing but the clothes on my back.'

She dropped the bag. It landed on Phil's feet. Julie straightened her aching back. 'You disgust me.' She dropped her handbag next to the holdall and walked out of the door with nothing but her daughter.

The bitterly cold night air hit them, and she stormed down the road with Vicki. She'd have to put her down soon because she was heavy, but she needed to calm her first. She'd left her purse with her money and bank cards. She couldn't pay for a bed and breakfast or a takeaway. She had three choices. She could go to her parents, Lisa's or her other sister, Emma's. Her parents and Emma lived on the same estate, but Lisa was her port of choice because she was the most likely to have money, so Julie could borrow enough to get Vicki her takeaway. She was annoyed that her stubborn pride meant breaking her word to her daughter, but she was victorious that he hadn't got the better of her. She was the winner. But he wasn't trudging through the streets at eight o'clock in the middle of January with nowhere to go. Lisa lived in the opposite direction of Emma and her folks. What if she wasn't in? Emma had kids and was always in, and there was a spare key to her mum's house in the coal shed. But Lisa was a single woman who often went out at night.

With the takeaway heavy on her mind, Julie went to Emma's. Vicki would love playing with her cousins, Jack, and Scott, and she loved Ruby, the baby. It might take her mind off things until Julie could get her bearings and decide her next move.

Julie let Vicki stay home the next day. At three o'clock in the afternoon, Lisa's doorbell rang. She answered it, and Julie heard raised voices.

'I've told you. She doesn't want to see you. Now do one, or I'll call the police, you abusive bastard.'

'I want to see my wife.'

'She doesn't want to see you.'

Julie went into the hall where Phil stood on the doorstep holding a massive bouquet and a teddy bear that was bigger than Ruby. He held them out to her, grinning.

'Julie, this is ridiculous. You're behaving like a child. Come home.'

235

Emma was ready to tear Phil's eyes out and loaded up on another barrage of verbal missiles to fire at him. Julie asked her to give them a minute and said they needed to talk.

'By protecting my child, I'm behaving like one?'

She saw a flash of anger glint in his eyes, but he controlled it. He took a second and breathed. 'Julie, I'm sorry. I want you to come home where you belong. We were both stubborn. We both felt we were in the right, and it got out of hand.'

'How can torturing a little girl ever be right?'

'You're exaggerating. Come home. We'll discuss it. I'll do anything you ask. I promise you I'll change. I'll be the father you want me to be.'

Half an hour after he arrived at Emma's house, they pulled into their drive. When they got in, at Julie's insistence, Phil sat Vicki on his knee and apologised to her. The second insistence was a takeaway, anything Vicki wanted. They bought enough food to feed an army and had a lovely family night in. Phil played on the floor with her. He bristled but controlled himself when Julie said that as a special treat, she could have more than one toy out at once.

Phil didn't raise his voice or talk to Vicki in his usual tone for five days, and the slip into what they considered normal was a gradual slide.

Chapter Twenty-Two

They'd been summoned. Violet met them in reception, 'Victoria-Violet can go and feed the ducks with her daddy, and you can come to my quarters with me, Julie. We must discuss what you're wearing to my party. I hope you don't mind my saying so, dear, but the dress you wore last year was quite inappropriate. I thought maybe rose organza. Come along, dear. Come along.'

Julie pleaded with her eyes for a save from Phil. None was forthcoming. She bent and kissed Vicki and spoke to her husband. 'Watch her near the water. Hold her hand. She gets excited when the ducks come to the edge. Thinks she can swim the way they do, I think,' she laughed. 'Don't let her get too close to the water. If you spread bread around, the ducks will come to you on the grass.' It was six months since she'd gone back to him, but some hurts go deep and there was no trust between them. Julie followed in her mother-in-law's wake, leaving Phil standing at reception with his excited child.

Vicki put her hand in his, 'Come on, Daddy. Let's go to the kitchens and ask Uncle James for some stale bread and cakes. There's a brown duck called Herbert. He's very greedy, even more greedier than the three swans.'

'Either more greedy or greedier, not more greedier. It's ungrammatical,' he corrected her. He was on autopilot and didn't think about the reprimand. It just spewed out of his mouth because picking on his daughter was sport.

'Sorry, Daddy.'

They went to the kitchen where Uncle James lay a stretch of kitchen roll on the counter and sat her on top of it. 'Don't you pump, Vicki-Vee. My guests have to eat the food I prepare on here.' Victoria giggled. He gave her fresh cake to eat, and four slices of crusty bread and some of last night's cake for the ducks.

'Hey, bud,' James said to Phil after teasing his niece. 'Have you heard what I'm getting?'

'No. What?'

'Only a Ferrari 458 Spyder. The greatest car ever built.'

'No way. How can you afford that?'

'I've got most of it saved, but the old lady said she'd give me fifty grand off my inheritance, now.'

'You jammy bugger,' Phil said. 'SP will be livid if you outdo him on a car.'

'I know. He's well pissed. Hey, come on up to mine and I'll show you the photos. I'm due a smoke break. He told the sous chef where he was going, and left orders for what he expected to be done by his return.'

Phil turned to Vicki. 'You go and wait for me in reception, okay? I'm just going to Uncle James' flat to look at something. I'll only be a few minutes.'

Vicki nodded.

'Hey, man, don't leave her down here on her own. Bring her with you. What's wrong with you, man?'

'She's okay. She knows how to behave. Don't you girl?' Phil was annoyed at having his parenting skills questioned by his brother. They left the hotel kitchen, leaving Vicki to make her own way to the reception. James winked at her on the way out.

In James' flat, he booted up the computer. 'Feast your eyes on this beauty and dream some wet dreams,' he said clicking buttons and links. When the page advertising the car came up, he left Phil looking at it while he put the kettle on. He picked a joint out of an ashtray and lit it. Then he flung the window open. There'd been complaints from guests about the smell of weed infusing the hotel corridors on the third floor. He offered Phil a draw on the spliff, but Phil declined. He'd never done drugs. He took his tobacco tin out and rolled himself a cigarette while James finished making coffee. 'Better knock this down quickly and get out to Vicki.'

'She's fine. Chill. What's this about you lamping some bloke in the Sawn last week? Andrew was telling me about it.'

'Tosser. He thought he was hard,' James said. They settled into opposite armchairs while James told his version of events.

Philip put his cup in the sink. He was irritated that he had to leave his brother because of the child. He only left because James said he had to get back to the kitchen.

Phil wandered to reception. It was a Tuesday afternoon, and the hotel was quiet. He wasn't worried to find Vicki wasn't there. He was just mad. He asked where she was.

'I don't know, Mr Woods,' Natalie said. 'She was here ten minutes ago.'

'Weren't you watching her?'

'No. I was sorting out the stationery order. Nobody asked me to watch your daughter.'

'Even an idiot could see that she was unattended for a moment.'

'I'm sorry, Mr Woods, but she was down here for over half an hour sitting in that chair,' she pointed. The receptionist raised her chin. 'I'm only the receptionist here, not a babysitter. I don't think it's my job to be looking after children.'

'You impudent slag. If you want to keep your job, get to the ladies' now and see if she's in there. I'm going to check the kitchen.'

She wasn't there. 'I told you not to leave her by herself,' James said. 'She likes the music room. I'll look in there, you see if she's wandered outside.'

Phil left the hotel by the kitchen door and veered to the left. As he walked towards the south side of the boating lake, he saw a guest running hell for leather across the lawns towards the front door. He felt the first prickle of apprehension crawling up the back of his neck.

He was still out of sight of the lake when he heard somebody screaming. He broke into a run. Time slowed, and the faster he ran, the less ground he covered.

A man was standing in the lake up to his thighs. There weren't many people around—two or three others standing on the bank, somebody with a mobile phone to his ear, a woman screaming— his daughter floating face down in the lake. The man in the water was fighting with weeds that had wrapped around her body. Phil had stopped, and couldn't move. Ten seconds turned to twenty. Victoria was free and the man was striding towards the bank. Phil broke out of his trance and ran down the hill to the water's edge. The guy on the bank, helped to pull the other man out of the water. They lay Vicki on her back in the grass and Phil watched as they knelt beside her and did CPR. Somewhere far in the distance, he heard an ambulance siren.

Chapter Twenty-Three

P hil coped after his divorce. Julie left him with everything, and life continued as before. He worked less, drank more, and spent a lot of money on prostitutes. One of his brothers taught him a long time ago that if you wanted sex, an easy way to get it was to pay for it. John had paid a schoolgirl five pounds and some cigarettes and oral sex. Phil was still a virgin then. He'd interfered with himself sometimes and burned with shame and self-disgust afterwards. He didn't want to have sex. He had no interest in it back then—it was dirty—but his slut of a wife turned him.

Even then, he liked having money. He'd sent notes to Suzie Philips, telling her he knew what she'd done. He'd threatened to write to her parents and made her bring money to the clearing where she'd knelt in front of his brother. He was sad when the Philips family moved away, and his cash cow was gone.

Phil's regret was that he came to sex so late. Julie was his first, but he soon experienced others and found that Julie wasn't very good at it.

He'd grown up with so many hang-ups and had missed out on years of sexual gratification. He wondered what Suzie Philips was doing now. Maybe she'd made a career out of prostitution.

He couldn't believe that his bitch of a wife blamed him for the death of their daughter. It was a terrible, tragic accident. Everybody said so, especially the coroner. She could go bang herself. If he was lacking as a father, why had she left Victoria-Violet with him in the first place?

Picking the material for stupid bloody dresses was more important than their child's wellbeing. If she wanted somebody to blame, she should have looked at herself.

In the six months that followed, you'd have thought she was the only one who lost a child. He was grieving, too, you know. He told his mother that he doubted he'd be able to look at another duck again. Violet said that duck phobia was a terrible thing to suffer and wrote a note telling Chef never to serve duck when Philip was home.

Violet would miss Victoria, of course, but she had grandchildren coming out of her ears, what with James' flower-power brood. Losing that one was a small price to pay to have her baby back in her arms. Philip came home a lot more often, and without that awful low-grade woman dragging him down, he was so much like his old self. He was happier. Violet was philosophical and reasoned that everything had worked out for the best, really.

Phil was distraught when Julie left him. But for a different reason altogether. He was beside himself with grief. Julie almost kept her promise of walking out with nothing—but not quite. When his wife walked out, she took something very precious with her.

A lifetime of his hard work was gone, and he'd never get over the loss of it. The trollop had hired somebody to break into his safe. She'd stolen his books and the folders of incriminating evidence and proof. Violet couldn't see why a load of old diaries mattered so much. Let her have them. It was only a bunch of books. But Philip couldn't get over it.

'It was my life's work, Mother.'

'But, darling, who's going to care about what you did in December 1986 or March 1992? At least she didn't get away with any money or your house. Let it go. Write some more little stories.'

'Little stories. Mother, they were historical documents. There were lists of people who owe me money.'

'What kind of people?' Violet asked. 'Who owes you money? What for?'

'That's not important. The fact is that there were things in that safe that can't be replaced or replicated, and now she has them.' Violet didn't see what all the fuss was about, she could have taken everything, and at least he still had the house.

In truth, Philip was a man waiting for the hammer to fall. He stayed at his own house as little as possible, terrified of the knock on the door. He jumped every time the gate squeaked in the wind. On the rare occasion that somebody did come, he wouldn't open up. He'd sneak upstairs and look out of the bathroom window, but it was only ever the postman or some bastard wanting money for charity.

As the months after Julie left passed, and he was still at liberty to walk the streets a free man, he feared his arrest less. He saw no reason not to continue where he had left off. He cleaned off his trusty cameras and spent a couple of thousand pounds on one of the new office computers.

He taught himself how to use it and put a password on new documents that he could bury deep in files within the system. He liked the new way of working. It was far superior to ledgers and books. He opened spreadsheets and kept his books just as he had with his special fountain pen.

He lost a lot of business due to the theft of his evidence, but he managed to re-snare some of his old customers. In a small Lakeland town, there was always somebody doing something that they shouldn't. New business grew as it always had. The eavesdropper was back in business, and the figurative sign above his door read open.

Two years later, in 2004, the biggest scandal to hit the Woods family since James had been charged with cross-dressing prostitution broke out. With SP and James in charge, the men worked well together. SP ran the hotel side of things, and James enforced full control over the kitchen and restaurants, as he had for the last ten years. That year, one of James's favourite recipes came to bite them on the backside.

It was called cooking the books. SP and James had been defrauding the tax man and creaming from the hotel profits for years. The auditors arrived mob-handed to undertake a thorough investigation. The books were taken, computers seized, and every receipt, every wage slip and every penny in and out was scrutinised for discrepancies. SP and James were arrested and taken in handcuffs to the local station.

Violet called Graham Bradson, the corrupt but trusted family solicitor. He met with Violet the same day in her quarters. James had already been in a lot of trouble. He was looking at a long stretch. Over a family dinner, ramifications were discussed and re-discussed. Tempers frayed, and some broke. When the summit concluded, it was decided that SP would take the fall for them both. They couldn't both be saved, and James had the most to lose.

SP covered for his brother. They'd been stealing vast sums of money since they'd matured from shorts into long pants, but SP had never had any serious criminal convictions. Even so, the Crown Prosecution Service wanted to make an example of him. The case was referred to Crown Court at Preston. He stood trial in front of twelve men strong and true, though four of the jurors were women.

One of them fancied him and wouldn't opt to convict. She couldn't believe that a man with such a kind face could commit fraud. She said that perhaps it was an accident and that he'd fully intended to declare their income but forgot. A couple of the other jurors commented that it was unfortunate they were selected randomly and not on the merit of intellect. It took ten minutes of negotiations around a table for the lenient juror to change her mind and come to the same decision as the other eleven.

Simon Peter Woods showed no emotion when he was given a three-year custodial sentence. He was away for just over a year and a half with time off for good behaviour but had a terrible time inside. His upbringing meant that he stood out from the other prisoners. He was bullied and victimised, beaten up on more than one occasion, and his spirit was broken. Three months into his sentence, he tried to hang himself, and after spending three days in the hospital wing, he was transferred to a different prison. The problem was never the other offenders. It was him. He was still different. The bullying picked up where it left off, and SP had little choice but to change. He grew hard skin and learned to brawl. He undid years of elocution lessons and taught himself how to drop his aitches.

He grew accustomed to food seasoned with spit.

Violet told the guests that her eldest son was in Hong Kong setting up another hotel and would be home when their Asian enterprise was strong enough to fly without a Woods figurehead at the helm. The locals knew the truth. The town knew the Woods boys were rotten to the core. One after another, they fell by the wayside and turned to trouble.

When SP went away, Andrew wasn't given a choice. The family business needed him, and as he was next in line to the throne, the role of office fell to him. He still managed his own business, though he passed on the legitimate stuff to Beth. Andrew was rich beyond measure. Nobody knew how much he had stashed away. When he made his first timepiece forgeries in his early twenties, it was a game. It was art reproducing the watches and clocks from history. He had an aptitude for imitating Rolex and the modern greats. He saw his work as a compliment to the originals. He never did, and never had, cared about money, and most of it was unwanted.

He hid it in secret offshore accounts, not to evade paying tax but because he didn't know where else to put it. The better he was at forging, the more he was in demand. As his name spread in the underworld, he came under the scrutiny of Maurio Rizzla, a mafia boss with a keen eye for business. It was said he could fillet a man faster than a butcher could hang a beef.

Within weeks, Andrew wasn't working for himself. He was forced into the Rizzla stable and was an employee of Maurio 'Razor' Rizzla. Razor fed him commissions and impossible deadlines to complete them. Andrew had never been a nine-to-five man. He'd worked when he wanted to work. He slept when he wanted to sleep, and he made love to free-spirited women as his loins led him. He didn't like answering to somebody else. The money was vast, each commission giving him more to swell his secret bank accounts. Razor paid him extortionate sums but demanded his loyalty and subservience.

When Andrew was frightened and tried to quit, Razor had him hustled into a van, driven to a disused warehouse at the centre of his operations and beaten up by four heavies. He got away and fled under the cover of darkness to the continent, where he lived in the communes, met Beth, and had his children.

After years in exile, they came back into the country, but Andrew drew attention by spending large sums of money on the expansive farm with acres of land and all his workshops, studios, and outbuildings.

He wanted to be an honest man, bringing his kids up well in love and compost and making Beth proud of him. He had his home. It was everything he needed. His plan was to keep the farm as a working venture of dairy, meat, and arable land. He set the west of his property up as a commune for wayward travellers passing through, allowing them to earn their keep for as long as they wanted to stay and work the land.

It didn't take long for Razor to find them. He'd always known Andrew would return to the happy homestead and family pile. He'd been waiting. He reeled Andrew back into his employ.

Beth was pregnant, and Razor bided his time before leaving Andrew a reminder, something that would stay with him. Just in case he ever forgot who was in charge.

One night, when Beth was tending a calving cow, she was jumped from behind and taken to Razor. He kept her prisoner and raped her several times over a period of twenty-four hours. Afterwards, he rang Andrew to tell him that Beth was in his bed. Beth pleaded with Andrew to help her. He could do nothing, and when Beth returned with only minor injuries, the adoration she had for her husband had left her eyes.

Henry Stephen Woods was born nine months later, and his parents peered at him, looking for resemblance. He wasn't given a fanciful name like his brothers and sisters or named after the elements. He carried a traditional name. He grew up darker than any of his siblings, but Andrew didn't hold that against him. He didn't blame Henry for who he was—or who he came from.

Beth didn't want any more children. She wasn't as sweet. She loved less, complained more, and grew bitterness along with the herbs in plant pots on her windowsill. Andrew wanted to live the life of an honest farmer, but Rizzla owned him, and he couldn't buy his emancipation.

When he was called to take on the hotel as well, it was his duty to rise to that rite of passage. He worked all hours to manage his life and fulfil Rizzla's demands as well as those of the hotel.

The tax returns were filed correctly, and the takings and profits had never been better, but Andrew didn't cope with the responsibility. He'd shaved his beard, cut his hair, and wore a suit that made him feel like a corporate loser. He was used to wearing sandals because shoes pinched his feet. He hated the pomp of the hotel and longed for his land. Andrew lived by a calendar in as much as he did what the seasons told him to run his farm. He counted the days until his brother reclaimed his position, and until then, he worried that he had another wage to deal with. Andrew knew money was the root of all evil, but as hard as he tried to denounce it and live a simple existence, he just made more. It was his personal curse.

Time dragged on in the Woods Empire. It was ten years since Julie and Philip had divorced. Violet had grown closer to Ros and relied on her more to keep her grounded in reality. SP still stole and lined his pockets from the business. James still got into fights, beat his wife, and wore women's clothes, seeking his sexual deviance wherever he could. Andrew still forged. John's gambling was out of control. And Philip blackmailed the people of the town and was a rich man on the back of people's misery.

In the cycle of sausages, beef was beef, and nothing much had changed.

Donald died while tending his garden. He'd have liked that. The gardeners had knocked off for the day, and he was digging out a few vegetables to make a hamper for the Legion raffle that night. The pain came suddenly, and he leaned on his spade, waiting for the twinge to pass.

And then he was gone.

It was as fast as that, without drama, anybody knowing, or any fuss. Just the way he would have wanted it. Dinner was eaten without Donald attending, and Violet pursed her lips in annoyance. She had the waiter transfer her meal from the dining table to a tray and ate it on her knee in the lounge. Donald's food was covered and put in the kitchenette oven to keep warm.

After eating, she picked up a paperback and read for a while. It was only when the shadows lengthened and she had to turn the reading lamp on that she realised the time. Donald should be getting ready for his lodge. The feeling of foreboding settled around her from the top of her head. It swathed over her shoulders and down her body. Something was wrong. Donald was never late for the lodge and wouldn't dream of going without showering his garden mud away first. A fastidious man, he went to the weekly meetings in slacks, and a blazer, with a small bowtie, cinched tight at his neck. She called Ros. She was always her first point of contact in any dilemma or crisis.

Ros sighed and dragged herself from the sofa. She was watching the concluding part of a crime drama on TV and resented that she wouldn't be allowed to see the ending. She had wasted her time making sure she was cleared of duties and ready to watch the first two episodes because now she was going to miss the last part. She might as well not have bothered. Violet's call was insistent, and Ros hated her.

She assured Violet that Donald wouldn't be far. Yes, she'd go and find him right away. She had to dress, as she was just out of the bath and had settled for the night in her pyjamas. Poor Donald. She didn't blame him for sloping off for a bit of clandestine time alone. He wasn't in the reception or lounge of the hotel. She stopped the porters and asked them to search for Donald outside.

The doctor who signed Donald's death certificate estimated that he'd been dead between three and four hours.

The gammon had dried up in the oven.

Violet was lost without him. He'd been there the majority of her life. He kept her grounded and reined in her colourful ideas. He had been her stake in the ground, the anchor that kept her fancies earthbound. After his death, she leaned on Ros for emotional support.

•

Chapter Twenty-Four

They say that life goes on. Julie went through the motions of going on. In the days after Vicki's death, there seemed little point in anything. She moved out of the marital bed and into the spare room. She was unapproachable, and Philip never touched her again, not even so much as a tap on the shoulder. At the funeral, she refused to have him near her. His family flanked him on one side of the grave, and she by hers on the other.

This time, instead of bolting and leaving him on gut instinct, she planned her move with precision. After three months of intense, debilitating, suicidal grieving, she went back to work full-time. The home meant nothing to her, and the garden lay neglected to overgrow. Her role in life was to work. When she worked, she stopped thinking, and that kept her alive when she had nothing to live for.

She thought about taking her life every day. She took an overdose and had to have her stomach pumped, leading to a three-day stay in the hospital and a compulsory six-week counselling course. The counsellor was vapid, with huge eyes that said, 'Wherever you are now, I've been in that place and come through it.'

It might have helped Julie to rant about how much she hated her husband. She could have discussed the ways she fantasised about killing him, but she didn't. She talked about herself just enough to fulfil the terms of her course and keep her from being sectioned.

She was her own counsel. The only thing keeping her putting one foot in front of the other and taking the next breath into her body—was revenge.

When she was strong enough to deal with it, Julie sought legal advice about her divorce. She had an appointment with a solicitor who gave her a consultation and then refused to represent her.

She sat in front of the power horse's desk where a black granite plaque announced a black granite woman, *Miss Monica Dupont.* She was hungry, a self-confessed man-hater, specialised in representing women in the divorce courts. Julie told her story, and with each point against Philip, Monica's smile was wider as she totted another thousand on the final settlement. Julie didn't exaggerate or embellish. She just told the story of their marriage from beginning to end.

'The bastard,' Monica said when Julie finished. 'You want revenge?'

'God, yes. He killed my daughter. I want revenge more than you can ever know.'

'Lady, we are going to nail this bastard to the wall by his balls. I swear to you, by the time I've finished with him, he won't have a pot to piss in.

We are going to take him for every penny he's got. You want the house, the car, half of his pension. What else has he got?'

'No.'

'I beg your pardon?'

'I want a divorce. I don't want a penny of his stinking money. I'll deal with the revenge side of things my own way.'

'I don't understand.'

Julie went on to tell Monica about the promise she'd made to Violet. She spoke in a flat monotone when she talked about the horrible things that Violet had done to her.

'My God, all the more reason to hit them where it hurts. Listen to me. You are not a gold digger. You've earned every penny of what I'm going to get for you. For goodness sake, woman, you can't keep a promise to that monster. All bets are off. You must see that. Do it for your daughter.'

Julie was taken aback. She hadn't expected a solicitor to speak like that. 'I'm sorry. I don't want anything. All I need is my own surname.'

'Then I can't help you. I'm sorry, you have an excellent case, but if you won't let me do my job, I won't take it on.' She'd already stood up and was walking to the door to show Julie out. 'If you change your mind, please get in touch and let me at him.' She smiled as Julie passed, but Monica's contempt for her was visible. A woman, who wouldn't financially strip a bastard husband to the bone, was a lower life form.

The second solicitor Julie spoke to was an impassionate man. He had no qualms about representing her. He wasn't interested in hearing her tales of woe. He wrote the salient facts, just enough to show irreconcilable differences, and ran with it. It was the easiest divorce he'd ever dealt with. There were no kids involved and no assets to split. Julie had clear grounds for divorce.

The papers would be served quickly, and then, six weeks and one day from the Decree Nisi, the Absolute would go through without question. Roland Johnson would file a few forms to the court, send out a couple of papers to the spouse, write a, *Thank you for your custom and congratulations on your divorce*, letter to the plaintive, and take his nine grand, plus expenses.

For his part, Philip didn't make waves. While they still shared a house, he was considerate enough to leave his coming week's rota out for her on a Sunday night. They spent ridiculous amounts of time at their respective jobs. Julie arranged her shifts to fit around his, so they were rarely in the house at the same time. She worked in the same nursing home as before Vicki's death but had come out of the kitchen to work as a hobby therapist. She didn't need any qualifications but took courses as another way of being away from home and bettering herself. Learning was a soothing balm and helped stop her from going mad.

When it was impossible to avoid Philip, their lives collided. She'd make something to eat and take it to her room. She wouldn't come out until he'd gone. Julie didn't look at him. He made her puke. Soon after Vicki's death, when she made eye contact with her husband, she felt her gorge rising and had to run to the toilet and purge her stomach. There was no need to accuse him verbally or lay blame for their daughter's death at his door. Her stomach did it for her—but needing to or not, that didn't stop her from doing it.

When she passed the threshold of his room and knew he was in there, she'd stop at his door and rattle the handle to get his attention. Sometimes she'd do it deep in the night when she could hear him snoring. 'What's going on?' he'd say, snuffling himself out of sweet dreams, and she'd hiss through the door, 'Murderer.' Just to keep it fresh in his mind.

She stopped the secret mortgage payments to his account. She stopped helping her family out of their financial crises. She ate at work, and apart from her basic living expenses, almost everything she earned went into her leaving-Philip fund. She only had one extravagance. Twice a week, she studied. She used her office at work, and from seven until nine in the evening, she hired a private tutor who worked with her and set complex exercises to complete as homework.

She bought newspapers to help with her study and read them cover to cover during her lunch breaks and when she got home in the evenings. Her life was full and busy. She had no time to dwell on things that were gone.

Three months after going back to work and six months, to the day, since Vicki's death, Julie went into her daughter's old bedroom. She remembered it as a nursery. She thought back to sitting in the peacock chair with her child at her breast during the early morning feeds. It was her favourite time. Some parents hate that feed, but Julie loved it. It was when she felt at her most peaceful, with the radio playing soft music and Vicki all warm and cosy, staring up at her with blue eyes as she fed. The baby made greedy gulping noises as she took from her mother, and Julie had thought that Vicki would always be there for her to nurture for the rest of her life.

She remembered when Vicki was five, and they were lying on her Barbie bed together. Vicki's eyes were heavy as she fought to keep them open until the end of the chapter. 'What happens next, Mummy? Will Violet Beauregard be a blueberry for ever and ever?'

'I don't know. Wait and see.'

'Violet Beauregard's very bossy, isn't she, Mummy?'

'Yes, darling.'

'And she's called Violet, like Grandma.'

'Yes, she is.'

'And Grandma's very bossy, too.'

'Yes, she is.'

'Does it hurt being a blueberry?'

'Oh, I shouldn't think so. Now then, where were we?' Vicki's face was screwed up in thought, and she wasn't for being derailed in her ruminations.

'It would be very funny if Grandma turned into a blueberry.'

Julie laughed with her daughter. 'It would love. Especially if she kept her bright red lipstick.' Vicki got giddy after that, and Julie had to settle her again. Inevitably, Phil shouted up the stairs that she should be asleep by now.

That was way back when Vicki was five, and it was another week before they visited the hotel. Julie nearly choked on her teacake when Vicki piped up, 'Grandma, do you like blueberries a really, really lot?'

'What a strange question, child. Where on earth did that come from? You say the oddest things out of the blue, dear.'

'Yes, but do you like blueberries, Grandma?'

'Vicki, tell Grandma about the horse that we fed on the way here,' Julie said.

'No, Mummy. I need to know if Grandma likes blueberries.'

'I suppose I do. I don't dislike them,' Violet said, humouring Vicki.

'Bloody horrible things, dry all your mouth out,' Donald muttered from behind his paper.

Vicki gasped and put her hands over her mouth in delight. 'See, Mummy? She is, she is.'

'I am what? Victoria-Violet, do start making sense, dear.'

'Grandma is Violet Beauregard when she was a little girl. What's it like turning into a blueberry, Grandma? Does it hurt?'

Now, Julie smiled as memories of her daughter flooded her mind, and tears of regret flooded her eyes. The room was packed up after Vicki's death. Most of her things were taken to the charity shop, and it was used as a storeroom. She picked up a small material doll with yellow hair from the top of one of the boxes that hadn't been closed properly. Bringing the doll to her nose, she was sad that she couldn't smell her daughter. She almost took it with her, but that would mean breaking her promise and taking more than the clothes on her back. She didn't need a cloth doll to remind her. She put it back in the box, pressed the flap, and looked around the room. Julie didn't see boxes. She saw the mobile over the cot and the Barbie bed. And she saw Vicki's brow furrowed in concentration as she struggled to tie her first pair of lace-up shoes. Julie closed the door behind her so as not to disturb the ghosts of times gone by.

She went out of the front door and posted her keys back through the letter box. She would miss her family, but she could live without them. The only real love in her heart was for her dead daughter. She hadn't told a soul she was leaving. She had her handbag over her shoulder. Her handbag was bought with her money. It contained her purse, driving licence and passport.

At check-in, the girl raised her eyebrows, though checking in without luggage was more common these days, what with skinny baggage allowances and obese fines for exceeding them.

Julie's only regret was that her divorce would take a while, so she couldn't change her passport back into her maiden name. The papers were being served on Philip that day. She'd arranged for them to be handed to him at work, hopefully in front of the entire shop floor. She may legally have the curse of the Woods' name hanging over her, but she intended to live her life as the uncomplicated and very free Miss Julie Spencer. But the unexpected happened.

Julie found that the Spencer name didn't fit her either.

Chapter Twenty-Five

She touched down at El Prat airport in Barcelona and thought of her husband. While in flight, she'd closed her eyes and spoken to Vicki with her mind's voice. I love you with all my heart, my darling. You know I'll never ever forget you. You gave me the happiest years of my life, and I can never tell you how sorry I am that I let you down. They'll pay Vicki, the lot of them. If it's the last thing that I do, I am going to make them pay in your name, my love. If I squeeze my eyes shut really tight, I can feel your little hand in mine now. I know you're here with me, chattering in my ear. But my darling, this is where you have to be a big brave girl. It's time for Mummy to move on. I will always love you, but I'm not going to be able to have these chats with you anymore. It's time for you to go forward, too, my love. I love you, Vicki. And then she whispered aloud, 'I love you.'

The fat man in the seat next to her said, 'Excuse me?'

Julie glared at him.

She waded through the barrier of dry heat as she left the airport. She'd left England at the drab beginning of another unpleasant winter. Along a wall to the left, furious pink bougainvillaea grew from the floor to the roof, and a little greenhouse lizard winked at her from the stem without taking fright or preparing itself to run. The scent of mimosa from the flowering baskets tantalised her, and she felt a wonderful, butterflying surge of adrenaline-filled excitement at the beginning of this new life.

She'd allowed herself three glorious days to reacquaint herself with her favourite city before she got down to the serious business of building a life. She'd booked into a cheap hotel away from the tourist quarter, right in the heart of the real Barcelona. Later that week, she had an appointment to meet with a rental agent who was going to show her around some flats and even one modest villa within her budget. Then she had three interviews already lined up, and later, a meeting with an employment agency in case none of the interviews offered the right job for her.

She'd miss her family, but she thought of herself as a tree standing alone with neither blossom nor berries to offer. She didn't have a friend in the world or a soul to talk to. Nobody knew where she was, and she expected not to be found. Nobody would believe she had the confidence to set up life in a new country. They wouldn't consider looking for her at airports, and even if they did, they would automatically search for the flight details from Manchester. It was the only airport that they had ever used. For that reason, she'd taken the train to London where, hopefully, any trail they were following would fizzle to nothing. She flew from Luton. If she was ever found by some miracle, it was no big deal, but she would prefer not to be. She wanted a sanitary cleansing from her old life. The date was 11th November 2002, and she felt as though she was reborn.

On the day of her job interviews, she went into a newsagent to buy *Fama* and *20 minutos*, the same newspapers she had been reading daily at home. As she left the shop, she noticed the rack of scratch cards. She had never bought one in her life, and neither had she ever done the lottery, though Phil had bought tickets a few times at the beginning of their marriage before the novelty had worn off. On impulse, she bought one and handed over a euro. '*Buena Suerta, Señora,*' said the lady behind the counter, wishing her good luck with a wide smile.

'*Gracias,*' Julie replied before telling the woman that she had come to live in their beautiful country. She loved any opportunity to try out her new language. They chatted for a few minutes in Spanish, and Julie felt as though she belonged. She couldn't imagine wanting to be anywhere else but here.

Outside the shop, she took a coin from her change and scratched off the panels on the card. She checked the three matching symbols, and then she checked them again. She turned the card over and read the instructions, in Spanish, on the reverse. And then, she looked at the front again to see if, during the last minute, the three matching symbols had changed. She got a cab to the hotel in a daze. She had to ring a number to verify the win. She relayed the reference number on the scratch card, waiting for the call-centre employee to tell her in a dispassionate voice that she had made a mistake. When he did reply, surely something was lost in translation. She spoke Spanish slowly but fluently. However, having a college professor enunciating every syllable with exaggeration was far different from hearing rapidly volleyed words spoken in a regional dialect. She couldn't have just won five hundred and fifty thousand euros. She only believed it when the money had cleared her new bank account, and she drew out her first twenty euros to buy lunch in a pavement café in the heart of the tourist quarter.

Over the next six months, Julie's divorce came through. The first thing she did was toast herself with a slippery nipple cocktail in a beachfront bar, which she found that she really didn't like. Then she changed her name by deed poll. On 6th May 2003, Julie Woods signed her new name on a legal document proclaiming her to be Señora Consuela Vengarse. Vengarse translated into English as 'To be avenged.' The name pleased her.

On her arrival in Barcelona, she'd rented a modest villa. Nothing ostentatious, but she loved it with all of her heart. With the five hundred- and fifty-thousand-euro winnings from her scratch card, she had enough capital to secure a mortgage on business premises for a bakery.

Returning home in the evenings to her villa was a joy that filled her. She was never lonely, not even in the early months before she made friends. The villa was typically Mediterranean, in an open-plan design, with tile floors throughout to cool the air. She had decking outside the colonial doors on the ground floor, and a balcony along the first floor, front of the building. Her garden was modest, with established fruit and olive trees and ample beds ready for planting, and she shared a pool with other tenants in the complex. She furnished it with beautiful things, and it was a very different home from that which she'd shared with Philip. It was far more expensive and splendid.

In retrospect, Julie wondered how she had loved such a stuffy, enclosed space so much when the villa was so open, cool, and spacious. Her life came together in ways she could never have expected, and God loved her.

Her love of baking flourished as her shop made money. The desserts in Barcelona were very different from a traditional English bakery. Consuela didn't try to introduce English baking. She merely pulled on what she already excelled at. She made Victoria sponge cakes, and in the early days, before she became too busy to think, as she beat the ingredients of each one, she thought about her daughter, and, though her life was perfect, she remembered her hatred for the family who murdered Vicki.

She made trifles and cheese scones. Once she was established, she had products flown in from England—English sausage, bacon, and double cream. She extended her bakery to include a dining area for customers and produced full English breakfasts in her traditional English café. She made time-honoured meat, potato pies, Cornish pasties, and sausage rolls. The Spaniards couldn't get enough of Victoria's Kitchen, and her till never stopped ringing.

Consuela had never been afraid of hard work. She rose every morning at four and didn't get home until seven, and the weight fell from her obese frame, her skin coloured, turning deep brown in the sun. In six months, she made enough money to move to bigger premises with a larger bakery out back. Her life, she noticed, was moving in six-month increments, each heralding a new change in direction and circumstance. She hired staff, and soon the kitchens were operating twelve-hour shifts, seven days a week. Soon she had to hire more staff and was selling her products wholesale to other businesses. She bought a factory with offices above and opened seven more Victoria's Kitchen bakeries across Spain. Victoria's Kitchen became a recognised brand, and Consuela Vengarse was a wealthy multi-millionaire company director with enough profit in the bank to secure her future a hundred times over. Cinderella stories don't happen to everybody, and she felt chosen and truly blessed. God wanted her to reap vengeance. She'd moved into her own villa with expansive gardens and her own pool. A woman in her own right, she had paid back her mortgages and owned her own corner of the world. All of this made her happy, but it was only ever the means to an end.

Consuela made friends. She went out for drinks in the evening and discovered a taste for Martini. She had dinner parties, and while she missed having her distinctive Tunisian tableware, she bought less flamboyant but nonetheless exquisite crockery from the kilns of Barcelona. She had wines from the Montserrat vineyards less than twenty miles away and cooked splendid meals for a growing mismatch of new friends.

While browsing an art gallery one Sunday, she met Jorge Vasquez. He took her to dinner, and she thought about taking him to bed. She imagined his mouth roaming her body as she had her second drink, and after her third, the fantasy became reality when Jorge Vasquez took

Consuela Vengarse to his bed. She called herself Whore-Hay's Whore, which amused him.

Consuela was good at sex. She knew that. But she had never loved it before. Philip had always been an unsatisfactory lover. For the first time, she bathed in her sexuality, danced in it, and covered it in diamonds and gold. She could have let the past go. She could have just blanked it from her memory and lived out her days in blessed wealth and luxury. She had good friends and a good life. She was happy and successful beyond her dreams, but she had taken her new surname for a reason, and vengeance had to be hers.

The day she opened the telephone directory on Plastic Surgeons, her life changed again.

Chapter Twenty-Six

E ngland was cold. She had forgotten how much. Ten years under the Spanish sun had made her soft.

She'd sent a gilt invitation, and there was never any doubt that he'd come. It was delivered in a classy black envelope to his office so that suspicions wouldn't be aroused at home. *You've been selected at random*—etcetera. She knew the five-hundred-pound gift voucher, redeemable for casino chips, would bring him like a child to the Pied Piper, and just like the fable of Hamlet, she would make Violet's children follow wherever she damn well led them.

Consuela was already at the roulette table. John took a seat three stools away from her. He looked nervous, and a thin line of perspiration moistened his upper lip. He rolled the top chip across his palm as he studied the board. The ball was spinning through the game in progress. He stared at it greedily, eyes dancing, body tense. The wheel slowed and dropped into number eighteen. The croupier dollied the losing bets home, and a Japanese businessman collected his winnings. His friends jabberwockied in Japanese and they jumped up and down like an annoyance of Furbies. They walked away from the table, heading for the bandits.

Consuela sat the next few spins out. That's what separated a seasoned player from a stag party. She watched the board and scrutinised the other players. Of the five men left in the game, she knew who the chancers were, playing straight up, thirty-five to one, and who was playing it safe with outside bets. She had John Woods pegged for a rouge-noir initially, leading to four corners when he started losing. He'd be a big man in the bookies, playing bravado on the gee-gees, but put him in a situation where the stakes were lethal, and his bollocks would retreat like a kid's in a rugby scrum. He'd play even bets.

John bet on two spins, betting rouge-noir and odds-even. She knew he would. Ten-pound stakes, and he lost both. He upped the ante, adding a second twelve, making his next bet thirty pounds instead of twenty. She was aware of him staring at her when he thought she wasn't looking. She didn't even have to put in any effort. He wanted her, simple as that. He wouldn't have the balls to make a move, though. Her extensive plastic surgery saw to it that she was out of his league. Consuela was unrecognisable as his former sister-in-law.

It was time to be noticed. She felt his eyes rest on her. It was only ever a matter of time. Gambling and women were his vices, as she'd learned from reading Phil's diaries, and he couldn't concentrate on one to the exclusion of the other. Although it wasn't necessary, she stood up to place a three-hundred-pound straight-up bet. His eyes were on her legs. She posed for him for a second before resuming her seat. She heard his intake of breath. Three hundred on a thirty-five to-one shot was ridiculous money. She lost with a matter-of-fact shrug of her shoulders.

When the croupier had cleared her chips, she placed five hundred on the same number. She lost.

She had drawn the attention of every man at the table. She was the only woman and was playing a suicidal game. A debonair suit on the other side of the table walked around and indicated the seat next to her. She had to get rid of him.

'Do you mind? Miss, I can't help but be impressed by a woman so stuck on her lucky number that she can lose big and not cry.'

John glared at him. The look wasn't lost on her. The brash man with the American Accent had just done what John would never have the guts to attempt.

The Yank put his chips on the table and went to sit down. Consuela put her hand on the chair to stop him from moving in. She stared at the American. Her expression froze him in his tracks.

'I mind,' she said in a heavily accented voice.

'Jeez, sorry, Ma'am,' he tipped an imaginary hat, gathered his chips, and walked away, shaking his head.

Consuela turned to look at John Woods. He was caught in the trap of her stare like a naughty boy caught peeping into the girl's changing rooms during a PE lesson. He lowered his gaze.

'Won't you join me?'

She knew he'd heard her, but he kept his eyes on the board, playing with his chips, focussing on the spinning wheel and the ball blurring in front of his eyes. She knew him well—the husk in her voice was probably enough to give him a boner. Consuela cleared her throat to get his attention. She was waiting for a response, looking at him with an open expression. He raised his head, feeling the weight of her gaze penetrating his.

'Excuse me?'

'Come. Sit next to me. Keep the wild dogs at bay.'

He might as well have done the comedic Stan Laurel gesture of pointing at himself and looking around to see if she was really talking to him, and couldn't have looked any more ridiculous. In his own environment, he was a peacock. He was brash and confident, wooing the local girls and the guests in his parents' hotel. He bedded plenty and flirted with more. Here, he was like a child thrust into an adult environment. He didn't belong, and his bravado fell to his feet while his dinner jacket suffocated him and his tie pinched at the collar.

'Maria Callas.' She held out her hand palm downwards. He had no idea whether she intended for him to shake her hand or kiss it. In his confusion, he clasped her fingertips and then didn't know what to do.

'John Woods,' he introduced himself, and just a hint of his swagger returned as he realised that the other men, croupier included, saw that he had just pulled the most beautiful and probably the richest woman in the room. 'You're very beautiful,' he added, attempting his killer smile.

'And you are very,'—small is what she wanted to say, but she amended her words—'kind,' she finished, removing her hand from his.

They played three more rounds. Consuela lost them. He won two modest fifty-percent chance wins, barely worthy of note.

'You're lucky for me.' He asked her to kiss his next chips. She obliged and then laughed as though he amused her. He lost, but she had emboldened him. He wanted to show off. He collected his meagre stash of

271

remaining chips, three hundred and eighty pounds, it was small change in a place like this. He placed them all on his next bet, Two eighty on black, one hundred on evens, fifty-fifty all or nothing.

The ball span, and he sweated. His eyes bore into the spinning wheel, willing the ball to land on black. He'd chosen it, he said, for the colour of her hair. They were playing *La Partage* rules. Zero was the devil's rut. The ball span. Once that little sphere of luck, good or bad, came to rest, he'd either be puffing his chest like a peacock, or he'd have to retreat to the cashier for more chips. Consuela had done her homework. He'd be drawing on his credit card. It was already overdrawn. He may have to face the embarrassment of it being refused. If that were the case, he'd walk away humiliated. She knew he'd want to impress her. And then he'd expect to get her into bed. She'd been all over his finances. He already owed a fortune to Monty Wheeler, his bookie. Gaynor was whingeing about his gambling and the debt they were in. She was breathing down his neck and breaking his bollocks, and if he didn't win big soon, several other guys from town, big guys with pickaxe handles, were likely to be calling. All of his juggling batons were up in the air at once, and soon he'd be out of his depth. Mother would have to bail him out—again. But tonight, Consuela watched him wanting to forget. He needed Lady Luck to smile at him with favour.

The roulette ball stopped spinning. It landed on number four. Black and Even, two wins. He'd just doubled his money. Consuela lost her stake and told him she was bored of losing and was sitting the next game out.

The croupier dollied her chips away and passed John's winnings back. Piling them up in front of him, he held the top one, a hundred chip, in front of Consuela's lips for her to kiss before sliding the lot onto black. The croupier set the wheel spinning and dropped the ball. 'No more bets, please.' The ball rotated until it was a spinning line, and John looked dizzy. He closed his eyes, waiting for the click-click-click of the ball settling, willing it to fall into a black slot.

'Ten black,' the croupier said. John opened his eyes.

Consuela smiled. 'You are having good luck, my friend. I like to surround myself with lucky people.'

In two spins, he won one thousand, five-hundred and twenty pounds. He should take his money and walk away. But he was a fool. A wise man deducts possibility from probability, while a fool commits to folly. He pushed his winnings across the board. This time he put his entire stake on the second twelve. 2-to-1 odds. For every pound he bet, he would take back two pounds if he won, but winning on the second twelve was less likely. To take the money, the ball had to land in a slot between number thirteen and twenty-four.

Consuela purred like a cat. 'So daring. So reckless.' She ran a red talon along the inside of his wrist, and he shivered under her touch. There was twice as much chance of him losing as winning this time. Consuela bet he felt sick. The night worked like a dream. Everything about it must have felt surreal. From his stammering, she knew he'd forgotten her name as soon as she'd told him. A couple more spins in his favour, and he'd be into serious money. It was just a case of having the balls, just being able to hold your nerve long enough.

His future was spinning in the wheel. Consuela made a show of being bored with the game. She took a file from her purse and worked on her nails. John was strung out, his adrenaline causing the equivalent of a synthetic high, and he couldn't stand still. Sweat had dappled his forehead in polka-dots.

The ball stopped, and he heard Consuela gasp before opening his eyes. Number twenty-one. He'd won again. Four thousand eight hundred pounds. One more spin, and he'd be walking away with twelve grand. If he could hold his nerve for two more runs, he'd leave the table with thirty-six thousand pounds that would go a long way to clearing his debts. 'Two more spins. Two more wins, and I'll quit while I'm ahead.' The odds of five wins on the bounce were almost impossible.

He counted his chips. He'd had better wins on the horses, but there was skill in that. Winning on roulette was a potluck, and this was a good night's work. The way things were looking, there might even be a shag at the end of it.

As he moved his arm to place the next bet, Consuela laid a cool hand on it. He looked at her.

'I'm bored.'

Her appeal faded as the addiction to his gambling fought and won over his loins. 'You run along and be bored somewhere else, sweetheart. I'll catch you up in a few minutes. I'm on a roll here.' He'd just won five grand. Gambling was the only woman turning his head, and Consuela was invisible to him.

'You're a fool, is what you are.'

He pulled his arm back and looked at her. How come she wasn't impressed? 'A minute ago, you said I was daring.' He sounded like a sulky twelve-year-old.

'A minute ago, you were playing the game. Now you're a desperate man. Your eyes are flashing green, the colour of desperation, and the table has its hold on you. If you walk away now, you leave a winner. The next spin, you will lose everything because the table knows it has you in its power. At first, you bet for fun. Now you bet in desperation, and that's an ugly thing to watch in any man.'

She was talking bollocks but had a point about him losing. She took his super-human confidence in her palm and shook it. He was hesitating, unsure. He'd won nearly five grand. It was a lot of money to lose.

She shrugged and turned away from the table, knowing he'd follow.

'Hey, wait. Lady, hang on, I'll come with you.' After stuffing his pockets with his winning chips, he regained his composure. This way he had winnings and might still get that shag. He walked in the direction of the bar, but Consuela hooked her arm into his elbow and led him to the exit.

She kicked her shoes off as he closed the door behind them. Looking around the room, he whistled. 'Wow, this is some hotel room you've got.' It was a suite comprising a bedroom, bathroom, dining room, lounge, and balcony. They were standing in the lounge, and she motioned to the sofa. A gold hostess trolley was laid with a bottle of champagne on ice and several lead crystal decanters filled with amber liquids. 'Champagne?' she asked, lifting the dripping bottle from the bucket. 'Or would you prefer whisky? Brandy?'

She knew what he wanted was to get back to that lucky table in town. 'Whisky, please, Maria. That'll be great.' She'd reminded him of her false name in the taxi on the way to her hotel as he stared at her cleavage.

She poured him a large one, a smaller one for herself, and sat at the other end of the sofa, curling her feet up underneath her. His arm stretched across the back of his seat, and she stroked him, making his arm tingle and clearing thoughts of gambling as his other primal desire took control.

The hotel telephone on the side table rang. 'Who can this be, ringing me at such an hour? I'm not expecting a call. Excuse me.' She put the phone to her ear. '*Si, Señora Callas. Si?*' She spoke for a moment in Spanish before breaking into English, 'Thomas. My darling,' She rolled her tongue around the R and spoke in a richly accented voice. 'Of course, I was going to answer your call. You know how busy I've been.' She motioned to get John's attention. In a show of good manners, he'd picked up a magazine when Consuela answered the phone. She lowered the receiver to speak to him, 'Please excuse me one moment, I must take this call in the bedroom. It's business.'

John stood up. 'Do you want me to go?'

'No. Please wait. Make yourself comfortable. I won't be long.' She went into the bedroom, pushing the door behind her but making sure it was ajar.

'Now Thomas, you *vieja cabra*, what is the great urgency?' She saw John's shadow fall across the room. As she hoped, he was listening at the door.

'Thomas, it is not a problem. *Si*, let me put up all of the money. You are too stubborn, *Cabrio*. Why won't you let me? We don't need the third person. What does it matter that my interest will be greater than yours? It means I will protect our combined interests better—okay, you win. I have a friend. I will talk to him. I'll get back to you with an answer by tomorrow night—*Si*, I know it's a perfect deal, five million turnover? Are you sure? And that's guaranteed? Yes. I know all that. Now go. I'm busy, and this is no time for business. *Chao, chao, caro mia.*' She hung up and stabbed a new telephone number into the handset before putting her finger on the disconnection bar before the connection was made.

'*Hola*, Gregory? Darling, it is I, Maria, you have missed me, *si*?—I know it is very late, and I'm so sorry, but this can't wait. Time is running out on this deal, and I have a proposition for you that cannot hold even until the morning. Do you remember Thomas Barrington? That's right, one squiffy eye that doesn't know where it's looking and the other eyeing up any piece of skirt that's around.' She paused as though listening and then laughed. 'The thing is, Greg, we need an investor—I know—it's amazing that we've got the first refusal. Yes. The Farquaad account. The one I told you about. Yes. It's a massive payout, but we have to move fast. I need an answer now—that's the good part. Twenty down and two million return by the end of the month, guaranteed—you will? Oh, that's wonderful. Will you do a bank transfer?—Oh, that's going to be a problem. You see, I can't get back to Spain in the next couple of days—Darling, you cannot afford to lose out on this. Oil prices are through the roof. We can't fail—*Si*, I understand, but that's no good, it has to be immediate— Okay. *Si*, we will have to leave it, this time. Don't you worry about it. There'll be other deals. I'll speak to you soon, kiss, kiss.'

She sighed, giving John plenty of time to get away from the door before she walked into the lounge. Sitting on the sofa, she picked up her glass, her brow furrowed. She clicked her long nails on the side of her glass, distracted. 'I'm sorry about that, a small business problem that I had to deal with.'

John moved forward in his seat and smiled at her. 'All sorted now?'

She sighed again. 'No.'

John laughed. 'I've got nearly five grand if it'll help you.'

Consuela laughed too. 'Unfortunately, my friend, it doesn't work that way.' She slugged off her whisky in a swallow and moved cat-like to the trolley to pour them a second glass.

John's mind was working fast. He could get the twenty grand she mentioned. It would be risky, but he was sure he could get access to the old lady's accounts. He'd borrow from the hotel and have it paid back before anybody noticed there was a deficit. The accounts weren't tallied until the month's end. It would be a simple loan. Maria was kissing his neck, but all he could think about was clearing two million pounds in less than two weeks. 'Do you like that, Jonny?' she asked, trailing her lips across his neck and onto his cheek.' Nobody had ever called him Jonny before. He liked the way the name dropped from her lips in a husky Spanish accent. She was the sexiest woman he'd ever pulled. He tried to concentrate. John turned his head and covered her mouth with his. She tasted of whisky and lipstick and all things women. Her hand dropped onto his chest and stroked up until she was undoing his shirt buttons. He should have been like a rod of steel by now, but he couldn't get those two million pounds out of his head. He pushed her away and looked into her eyes. 'Let me invest, Maria. I can help you.'

'Don't be ridiculous.'

'Why not? You want an investor, and I've got the money.'

'Darling, I've already told you. Five is not enough.'

'I can get twenty. I heard what you said on the phone. I'm sorry. You want a bank transfer.' He didn't care that he'd just given away his snooping. 'I can have the money in your account by the start of business in the morning. I'm a sound investment. I own a large hotel in Windermere. Twenty grand is nothing.'

'It's out of the question. I don't know you. I might take you to my bed for a little pre-dawn workout, but I don't conduct my business with strangers. You have me all wrong, Jonny boy.'

'My name is John Woods. I'm a major shareholder in the Halcyon Woods Hotel in Windermere. Check me out. I'm good for it.'

'My business partner would never go for that. It's absurd. Out of the question. No. I'm sorry. I shouldn't have been so indiscreet.'

'I want in. What do I have to do, Maria? Tell me, and I'll do it.'

She screwed up her eyes in thought as though she was considering her options.

'I'll think about it. Go now. It is late.' She all but shoved him out of the door. He leaned in to kiss her, and after a brief peck, she pulled away. She had him wriggling on the line. She didn't have to tolerate him slobbering all over her.

'How will I know? Shall I call you tomorrow? Can you give me a number?'

'No, come to my room at six. A banker's draft will not prove to me that your claim is a valid one. We have no business history, so I'm afraid that it will have to be cash. Will that be a problem?' He shook his head. 'In that case, I'll speak to my partner. Bring the money, but I'm promising nothing. He may refuse your offer. We'll see.'

'You're promising nothing except that the two million is guaranteed if we do go ahead, right?'

'Jonny, my dear one. I thought you were a businessman. Surely you understand that there are no guarantees where money is concerned. But oil is liquid gold, prices have never been better, and we have the deeds of passage. Your two million is a beginning dividend in the first month. After that, it will rise, and nobody knows when the balloon will burst. Once you're in, you can reclaim your original investment in the first week or two as agreed and let your profits accumulate for as long as you please, or you can withdraw completely with one clean deal.'

He kissed her again before she got him out of the suite, and she tasted the sour tinge of greed on his breath. Shutting the door behind him, she rested her back against it. A smile played around the corners of her mouth.

Violet yelled at Graham Bradson with her mouth open. 'Don't be preposterous. That's impossible.'

Bradson looked at SP. The accusation was clear from his expression. 'I'm sorry, Violet, but I've been through the books a dozen times. There's nothing to account for that money going missing. On the fifteenth of the month, it was a Friday. You signed for an open banker's draft at nine forty-six in the morning. That was processed and rerouted to the hotel's cash flow, where it was taken from the safe, on the same day, in cash. The balance in the safe was correct because the banker's draft had covered the shortfall.'

'I did not. I tell you, I did not.'

'Somebody did. They used the password.' He stopped short of repeating it in front of her son. 'They used your username and password and had your mother's maiden name to clear security.'

'It could have been any one of a dozen people.' SP was angry. 'Her password's The Old Rugged Cross. We all know it. I wouldn't be surprised if half of the girls at reception have been told. Knowing mother, she's probably given her details to one of the guest's brats and asked them to draw money out for her so that Ros doesn't find out about it. Are you aware that she donated three hundred pounds to The Sisters of Mercy's raffle last month?'

'Quite.' Bradson looked uncomfortable.

'Now maybe you can see why I wanted Power of Attorney. It's for her own good. She's a liability. I knew it was a matter of time until something like this happened.'

'I am here, you know,' Violet said in her most refined voice. She took a small sip of her sherry and hummed, *O sacred heart, O love burning.*

The police were brought in to investigate. It was a far cry from when the boys were young and impervious to blame. Apart from the youngest, the rest all had police records. Violet's sons, and SP especially, were under suspicion. This had SP's previous form all over it. Despite being questioned, SP came out of it squeaky clean, but one of Violet's other sons appeared on the radar.

He was taken to the station for questioning. His fingerprints were all over the company safe. John had no excuse for why he had been in the office, let alone the safe. He appeared on the CCTV cameras when he went into the bank to collect the banker's draft. His crime was amateur, and it wasn't executed well.

Fergusson, the investigating officer, peered at him from the other side of the Formica table. The only sound in the room was the hypnotic whirring of the tape machine recording the interview. 'I ask you again, Mr Woods. Why did you steal the money?'

'I didn't.'

'Stop playing games. We've got you on camera at the bank. For the purpose of the tape, I am passing two colour photographs for Mr Woods to look at.' He slid the A4-sized photographs across to John. They showed him striding out of the bank with a stupid grin on his face. 'Why don't you save us some time and tell the truth?'

'Okay. I took it. But you're wrong. I didn't steal it. I borrowed it. It was a loan. I was going to put it back before anybody noticed it was gone.' He rubbed his sweaty palms on his trousers.

'Taking money without the owner's consent is not taking out an agreed loan. Did your mother give you permission to go into the company safe and help yourself to the money?'

'Not exactly.'

'Define, "Not exactly" for us, Mr Woods,' Fergusson was an old hack and didn't mind applying pressure when he had to. In this instance, he didn't. The posh boy was going to sing like a canary.

'No. She didn't know.'

'You didn't consult her?'

John looked at the table, ashamed. 'No.'

'You stole twenty thousand pounds from the family business.'

'Borrowed.'

Fergusson sighed. 'We've already established that, in the eyes of the law, it was theft. What did you do with the money?'

John squirmed in his seat. 'There was a woman.'

Mark Fergusson and his partner, a younger copper called Silas Nash, exchanged a look. If they had a pound for every time a perp confessed that a woman was at the root of their problems, they would be rich men. 'Go on,' Nash said.

'I'm a married man. Gaynor, my wife, wouldn't understand. I have children. If I tell you what happened, can we keep it away from her?' He looked at the whirring tape recorder.

'Indeed,' Fergusson said. 'Women, eh? They rarely understand. However, this is a police investigation, Sir. We have no interest in your inability to keep it in your pants. We just want to know the facts.'

Nash seemed keen to bag a conviction and was quick to reassure him. 'Tell us what you know, Mr Woods, and we'll do our best to keep your wife out of it. We'll decide what's relevant to the case and what doesn't have to become public property, so to speak. You'll feel better for getting it off your chest.'

'I received a letter through the post. Not the usual bill demand in a brown envelope.' He told them about the casino and meeting the Spanish woman.

'What was her name?

'Maria. Maria Callas.'

'The famous opera singer?' Nash smirked. 'I thought she was dead.'

'What? What are you talking about?'

Nash chuckled. 'You met Maria Callas, the deceased opera singer?'

'She didn't say anything about opera, but she was rich. I didn't give it a second thought.'

Both policemen were laughing. Nash composed himself. 'I think you've been duped. She saw you coming a mile away.'

John told his story, and it sounded ridiculous spoken aloud.

'And that was it?' asked Fergusson. 'You handed over the hotel's money and never saw her again?'

'I was supposed to meet her two nights after I paid.' He shifted on his seat and felt the heat rising in his face. 'She never turned up. She'd invited me to a party and said she wanted to introduce me to the other business partner in an informal setting. There'd be lots of contacts and good business for the hotel. I wanted to do it for my mother. If I brought some business in, money people. I'd be doing something right for once.'

The police officers exchanged a look. 'Go on.'

'The event was at the Adelphi Hotel.' He reddened further and dropped his voice. ' There were eighty high-powered businessmen there for a conference. She told me it was a fancy-dress party. She was going as

Jane and wanted me to go as Tarzan, like a couple.' He paused. 'Security threw me out.'

The policemen tried very hard to maintain a professional demeanour, but the thought of this joker prancing about in a loincloth was too much and they fell about laughing. 'There was no fancy-dress party?' Nash asked.

John shook his head.

'You've been entertaining, lad, I'll give you that,' Fergusson said. 'John Woods. I am arresting you on suspicion of theft.'

The investigation was conducted over the following weeks. Violet, on discovering that her son had stolen the money, tried to drop the case, but the police overruled her and said they had enough evidence to bring their own case to court.

The croupier that night was paid off by Consuela. He remembered seeing the gentleman but had no recollection of a lady, Spanish or otherwise. Consuela's money had bought his silence. The hotel checked their records and found the gentleman was mistaken. Room 703 was not occupied on the night in question. The police searched their computer's data for a businessman under the name of Thomas Barrington. They found Thomas Barrington III living in a nursing home in Suffolk, but he was addled with dementia and made even less sense than John Woods.

Fergusson, who had taken a dislike to Woods, made a point of interviewing his wife. She had no information to give except to confirm that her husband had gone out that evening and hadn't returned until the early hours.

Gaynor filed for divorce. She was used to his affairs but wouldn't tolerate stealing from his mother. The brothers turned against him, though there wasn't one of them who hadn't swindled money from Violet. He rented a dingy bedsit on the wrong side of town. Before his backside ever touched a jail-cell bunk, his creditors got to him first, mean men who didn't stake their claim through a court. He was beaten, left for dead in an alley and found stinking and unshaven.

Even Violet didn't want to see him. Alone in his bedsit, hounded by his creditors for his gambling debts, his decline escalated. He drank as much in the mornings as in the evenings, and he was broken, skeletal and depressed.

Three weeks after coming out of the hospital, and two weeks before his trial, John Woods' flat was burned to the ground. A loan shark scored a name from his list. John Woods' body was wheeled out on a stretcher and taken to the morgue.

Violet was inconsolable. She blamed herself for not visiting. She never forgave herself. A verdict of murder by arson was carried out at the inquest, and the perpetrators of the crime were never caught. For thirty pieces of silver, Violet could have paid her son's debts. She always had before. If she'd bailed him out, he would still be alive. She roamed the corridors of the hotel at night, calling his name and disturbing the guests. Ros left the marital bed and slept in the guest room in Violet's suite to keep an eye on her.

One down.

Chapter
Twenty-Seven

Two acts of sabotage brought about the closure of the hotel that year. The person responsible would have done them a favour if it hadn't heralded the end of an empire for Mother Duck and her brood. The hotel hadn't had a complete makeover since Violet had bought it. The Halcyon was inviting an older clientele. It was all about high tea and scones with strawberry jam and clotted cream. It was classic, vintage, boho British, art deco, and maintained with impeccable cleanliness and taste, but it needed some new life breathing into it.

Every year, a run of bedrooms would be decorated, and every ten years, the reception, lounge, and kitchens would be done on consecutive years. The hotel had never been gutted and given a new, fresh feel. It had been in SP's mind for years, and the saboteur gave him the push he needed.

Consuela signed in using a credit card in the name of Grazia Martinez. She wore muted clothing, had her wig of blonde curls pulled back into a knot, applied little makeup, and was hunched to belie her stature. Her aim to be inconspicuous was impossible—she was the type of woman to be noticed, even when she tried not to be. Her trunk was noted, too. Nobody carried trunks anymore, not in these days of lightweight designer baggage. It was as over the top as she was beautiful. She went to her room. Insisting that she take her own luggage had caused eyebrows to rise at Reception—that's what they employed porters for—but she had timed it to coincide with the arrival of a coach tour of pensioners. They needed a lot of assistance, and Consuela had managed to tuck into the general mêlée, check in at the desk and drag her trunk to the lift with a minimal amount of fuss. An old dear yelled that she was about to faint in the heat, and Consuela slipped away while the staff were distracted.

Once inside, she set to work fast. She had chosen her room with care and specifically requested it when she'd booked. It was a large corner suite on an outside wall, but the beauty was that it was above the hotel kitchens.

She pulled the wardrobe away from the wall. It was heavy, and she struggled, panicking because time was running out. She was sweating, and it took precious minutes to move the furniture far enough from the wall to enable her work. With a cordless circular saw, she cut away two lengths of the skirting board before she dragged the shipping trunk to the wall. The rats were packed in individual pet boxes so that they wouldn't suffocate under the collective body weight. She had ventilated the trunk well, and they'd been in there less than half an hour. She hoped none of them had died, especially the pregnant ones.

Consuela opened each of the one hundred boxes and talked softly to the occupants before pushing them into the holes in the skirting board.

She was long gone, riding in a taxi to Lancaster for cocktails, when the first guest screamed.

She rode hot on the heels of that incident, not letting the hotel draw breath before she hit again. This time was easier. She didn't have to be seen at all and had no need to take a room. The hotel worked around the clock, night staff manned reception, and a core of kitchen staff was kept on all night to work on the veg prep and other jobs that could give them a head start on the day to come.

Connie was banking on the good old routine, which had kept the hotel moving for thirty years. She laid her bets on the fact that little or nothing would have changed. Between two and three in the morning, the kitchen staff took their break and went into the staff room with trays of leftovers from supper service. The kitchen was unattended at this time. It was easy to wait for the night porters to have something to attend to and then slip in while they were away from Reception.

It was a hell of a risk, but she wasn't scared of them. Staff lockers were kept in the anteroom of the kitchens. She was banking on the fact that the night workers eating their supper already had everything that they needed. This wasn't the time for one of them to get a craving for horseradish sauce on their pasta.

Consuela slipped in and worked fast. She hit the storerooms first, moving boxes and packing cases to empty her cartons of maggots where they would do the most damage. She dropped cockroaches in cupboards and along the floors where there were gaps in the skirting. She'd only brought a small holdall with her, which was all she needed

289

this time. She dropped another box around the sink area, ensuring the maggots had crevices to burrow into so they wouldn't be noticed immediately. She opened the catering drums of soup mix, coffee, flour, salt, sugar, gravy granules, pulses and beans, which were in use and had their seals broken. Working fast, she dug maggots and weevils deep into the core of the contents. Anywhere that she could hide them and release cockroaches, she did. It had been so easy. She left as inconspicuously as she arrived.

At nine the following morning, she used her old British accent and called the Environmental Health Agency, explaining that she was a concerned member of staff. She told them that the kitchens at the Halcyon-Woods were alive.

Chapter Twenty-Eight

He was a very happy Simon. In the last ten years, life had changed in so many ways, and it was scary at first. Simon didn't want to move out of Great Gables. It was his home. And it was his people. And it was his room. And it was his desk with his stuff in it. But it had been a long time now, and Simon was h a p - py.

He had his own flat. He was very proud. To get into his flat, he had his own key that he kept on a neon green spring that was attached to his belt loop so that he couldn't lose it. He had his own flat and his own front door. If somebody came to visit and he didn't want to answer the door, he didn't have to. He did that once when Cheryl, his social worker, called. He just wanted to see what it was like to not answer the door. He'd done answering the door when people had come to visit, and he liked that a lot, but he'd never done not answering the door.

Cheryl knocked, and Simon sat on his red sofa with a big smile on his face. Cheryl knocked a lot and then she shouted through his letter box, 'Simon? Simon, love? Are you in? Simon, it's Cheryl. Are you all right in there?' And Simon still sat on his red sofa with a big smile on his face. Simon heard Cheryl's high heels clicking down the path, and he didn't like not answering the door. It wasn't fun like answering was.

He wanted to wonder who was there. That was the fun bit before you opened it. Cheryl was his friend, and he wanted to see her. He could tell her all about work and Jimmy and all the others. But now he had a big problem, Cheryl was leaving, and soon she'd get in her blue car and drive off. Simon had to stop her, but he had his brown slippers on, and you don't wear your brown slippers outside, do you? Brown slippers are for in the house, and shiny black shoes are for going outdoors. Outdoors is just another way of saying outside, but Simon likes saying outdoors because it sounds posh in his new flat. Simon had to run down the path in his brown slippers to stop Cheryl. He didn't think he'd not answer the door again. He was out of puff when he ran down the path and grabbed Cheryl's arm. He said, 'How do you do?' because that's a posh thing to say in his new flat. 'Won't you come in?' And Cheryl laughed.

Simon was living in an Assisted Living project. It was very grand. Mr and Mrs Pickering had the last flat on the row. They were wardens and looked after everybody. All the other flats were full of people just like Simon, but they didn't all have brown hair. Some of them had blonde hair. And Billy Wright didn't have any hair at all. He was bald and didn't even have any eyebrows. Simon lived at number six, and his door was red like his sofa.

Mother didn't visit Simon anymore. She came to his flat once and then said that he was a big man and didn't need her to visit. Simon was glad. She put money in his bank account, and Cheryl or Mrs Pickering would get it when he needed it. Mrs Pickering sat with him every month when he paid his bills. Simon paid all his bills himself, but Mrs Pickering had to make sure he did it right.

The other big change in Simon's life was that he had a job. He worked at the Cosy Kitchen café on Bridge Street and had lots and lots of friends. Sometimes the customers teased him. On yestersunday, Jimmy—he's a workman and wears a yellow jacket—put two salts on lots of tables and two peppers on lots of other tables. And then he said a big complaint to Annie, who is Simon's boss. Simon likes having a boss called Annie. He loves her. And Jimmy said the big complaint and said that Simon had mixed the cardi mats—that's a posh word for salt and pepper—all up.

Annie smacked Jimmy with her tea towel and said, 'Get away with yer,' and then she gave the tea towel to Simon, but before Simon smacked him, Billy—that's one of all the others who wears a yellow jacket—showed Simon how to twist up the tea towel first and flick it. Simon ran around the café chasing Jimmy, and when he caught him, he smacked him with the tea towel and shouted, 'Get away with yer.' Jimmy laughed and gave Simon a pound coin, and Simon put it in his tip jar.

Simon has a lot of tips. And he can leave them at work until he wants to take them because the jar says Simon on it, and nobody touches it. Jimmy and Joey and Billy and Jack— they are Jimmy and all the others— tease him about his tip jar. They try to make Simon say that it's his tits jar, but Simon won't say that because it's a bad word. Even if they say they'll give him a pound if he does because Simon's very clever, and he knows that they are going to give him a pound anyway. Simon likes to tell people about all his friends, but there's an awful lot of them.

And then the new lady came. She was called Consuela—but Simon couldn't say that, so she told him to call her Ayla. She came in one day and sat at the table by the window. And then she came in every day and sat at the table by the window. She talks funny and is very pretty. Simon was scared of her at first because she was new, and Simon is always scared of new customers. Annie said that he had to serve her just like she was Jimmy and all the others, but she didn't look like Jimmy and all the others. Simon got red. He carried her mug really carefully and then went back again for her plate. Annie said Simon was a one-plate-at-a-time kinda guy.

'Here's your latte and your currant bum, be careful of course, because it's bery hot. Can you I get anything else? Thank you, please.'

The lady, because he didn't know that she was called Ayla then, smiled all big at him and said, 'That's perfect, thank you very much. It looks delicious.'

Every day she came in, and every day she talked to Simon when he served her. Soon Consuela was Simon's friend, too, just like Jimmy and all the others.

One day Simon was walking for the bus. He had his head all the way down because he didn't look up when he was going for the bus. Sometimes people weren't nice and scared him. He heard somebody shout his name, but he kept his head all the way down and kept walking. He heard high heels clicking faster to catch up with him.

Sometimes girls with clicky heels on weren't nice, too. It's not just boys who were horrible people. The voice sounded like Consuela from the café because Consuela from the café talks funny. But Simon wasn't taking any chances. Simon kept walking. Somebody grabbed his arm.

'Simon, it's Ayla. Aren't you talking to me today?'

Simon stopped and turned around. Simon talked to Consuela in the café when he served her. Simon did not talk to Consuela in the street when he was going for his bus. Consuela had an awful lot of shopping bags.

'Simon, my car's just around the corner. You couldn't be a love and help me to carry some of this shopping?' Simon didn't know if Consuela was asking him to help her or telling him that he wasn't allowed to help her. Simon likes helping people. It makes people smile. But Simon likes getting his bus, too. He didn't want to miss his bus and have to wait at the bus stop for another one in case the horrible people came and teased him. Simon didn't know what to do. He didn't say anything.

'Please, Simon. If you could help me, it would be doing me a big favour.'

This was bad. 'Miss bus,' Simon said.

'Oh, right. You know what? One good turn deserves another. If you can help me carry my bags, I'll give you a lift home afterwards.'

Of course, it was worse. Of course, it was even badder. Consuela had taken some of her bags and passed them to Simon, and his hands had taken them before his mouth said yes. 'Not get in car. Not. Of course, no lifts from strangers. Not,' Simon mumbled.

Consuela laughed, and it was a nice laugh, 'Oh, come on, Simon, I thought we were friends. I'm not a stranger, am I? I'm your friend, Ayla. You'll hurt my feelings in a minute.'

Simon didn't want to hurt her feelings in a minute, or even tomorrow, or at yestersunday, so he walked along the street with Consuela, worrying. He got into her black car, worrying. Consuela leaned across him and fastened his seatbelt. She smelled very nice. Like flowers. Simon sniffed her hair. He sat without talking all the way home. Consuela talked all the time, and she told him about a place called Spain. Simon thought it must be a long way away. She said that's why she talked funny and then she did the best thing. She winked at Simon, and then she spoke to him just like a normal regular person. Just like Annie or Shirley, who comes in on a Thursday after the shops. She didn't speak from the Spain place anymore. Simon was so surprised that he forgot to worry. Consuela said it was a secret and he mustn't tell anybody. She tapped the side of her nose. When she pulled up outside Simon's house, she undid his seatbelt and leaned all the way over him to open his door. He sniffed her hair again because she still smelled good.

'Bye, Simon. See you tomorrow,' she called after him.

Simon didn't look around.

The next day, Ayla didn't mention giving Simon a lift or about not talking funny. When he put her mug and her currant bum down carefully, she tapped her nose and winked at him.

That night, Simon was walking for his bus. A car slowed down beside him and went very slowly. Simon kept his head down. He saw an arm winding the window, and he was scared. 'Simon, come on, get in. It's raining,' Ayla said to him. He got into her black car, worrying. Ayla told him that she drove past his house every night and she might as well give him a lift home to save him from getting the bus. Simon was still awkward, but after a few days, he liked going home in Ayla's black car. It was even better than getting the bus, and the horrible people didn't tease him or hurt him.

Soon Simon looked forward to going home with his friend Ayla. And Annie knew about it, too, because Ayla told her it was on her way, and Annie didn't mind Ayla taking Simon home. She never told Annie that she could talk normally, though. That bit was still the kind of secret that you tapped the side of your nose about. In the car, they talked about everything. Ayla gave Simon a money plant. But it wasn't a real money plant. It was just a plant. Simon watered it every week just like Ayla told him to, and it grew big.

One day they were talking about *High School Musical II*. Simon knew all the songs and could do the dances just like on the DVD. Ayla asked him if he'd like to go to the pictures to see it. Simon was very excited and put on his best blue jumper. He didn't have dandruff because Mrs Pickering made him buy Head & Shoulders when they went shopping. Ayla said that she'd pick him up at half past seven. Ayla didn't come at half past seven. Ayla didn't come until seven thirty-nine. Simon thought that she wasn't coming and took his big coat off and hung it up in the cupboard. He was very sad until Ayla knocked on the door.

In the cinema, Ayla bought Simon some popcorn and some fizzy orange that made Simon burp, but she had to hold them when Simon needed to clap his hands to the songs. He knew all the words and sang along. Ayla smiled big at him and sang some of the words, too, but she

297

didn't know all of them like Simon did. On the way home, Ayla and Simon went to Pizza Hut and bought a big pizza and fries and then Simon had room left for ice cream. Ayla said he was going to pop, but Simon hoped not. It was the bestest night of Simon's life. Simon didn't know that Wednesdays could be good.

The next week, Ayla came around to Simon's flat. She brought all the ingredients, and she said that she'd teach Simon how to bake a chocolate cake. Simon didn't sleep on Tuesday night because he was so excited. Jimmy and all the others teased him because they said that Ayla was his girlfriend. They sang Ayla and Simon sitting in a tree, k-i-s-s-i-n-g. Simon got red and went into the back room to wash up. Sarah Wallace at Great Gables was his girlfriend, but Simon thought she might be deaded now because Simon hadn't seen Sarah Wallace for a long time. Ayla was his friend.

She didn't come to the café as much anymore. She told Simon she had a business to run, and sometimes she had to go back to Spain and couldn't come for coffee every single day. She still popped in though. And she was waiting to give him a lift home when he left work. Simon knew that she was a really busy lady and that some nights she couldn't pick him up. He had to get the bus then and didn't like it. But Annie and Ayla told him that it was good for his independence to take the bus sometimes.

The chocolate cake was good. Simon had two slices, and Ayla said that he mustn't eat too much or he'd be sick, and then she wouldn't be able to come and bake with him again because it wouldn't be good for him.

'Shimon not eat more until tomorrow,' he told Ayla. 'Of course, Shimon be bery good, of course.' And even though it wasn't a secret, he tapped the side of his nose and blinked in an attempt to wink.

Ayla came to see Simon every Wednesday night when she was in England. It was their night together. Sometimes they baked cakes, sometimes they watched films and sometimes they went out somewhere. Ayla took Simon to the pub. Simon liked the pub. Simon drank half a lagers, please, and it made him burp, especially if he had three half a lagers, please. Simon sang Elvis Presley's *Teddy Bear* on the karaoke. It was his song. David, who was the karaoke man, said that Simon was better than Elvis Presley, and Simon swung his hips and got down on one knee to sing. Mostly somebody had to help him back up again, though.

Simon took Ayla to the Rainbow Club once a month. Cheryl always had to ring up to remind him when it was on, or he forgot. Simon had his own telephone, and when he picked up the receiver, he said, 'Hello, Woods redisenth. How may I help you?' When it was Ayla on the other end, she always used to say, 'It's Ayla. I'm in the Batmobile. You can get the kettle on.' And he always laughed.

Ayla liked it at the Rainbow Club. She wore trousers so that she didn't ladder her stockings and no high heels so that she could crawl on the floor. She always brought things for all the people there, like Simon. But when they had a disco, Ayla danced with everybody and Simon didn't like that. Ayla was his friend. He'd sulk in the car on the way home, and she'd call him 'Sulky sod,' but then she'd start singing a song, and Simon would join in, and then he wouldn't be sulking anymore. Wednesday used to make Simon sad because it was Mummy Day—but

299

now there was no mummy, just a good Ayla. It was the bestest day of the week. Simon had done a lot of baddest Wednesdays to get all the way to the good ones.

One day Simon asked, 'Ayla? Of course. Why Ayla normal?' She stopped with a jigsaw piece in her hand. They were working on the edges, and Ayla said it was part of the chimney pot.

'What do you mean, *Cielo*?'

Simon knows Spanish now. *Cielo* means honey. The horrible people of course don't know Spanish, and Ayla wouldn't call them Cielo at all. Not. 'Shimon is normal. Not. Ayla is normal.'

'Simon, you are a lot of things that other people aren't. You're kind and funny and sweet and a very good singer.'

'Shimon good singer, yes, but not normal. Not. Ayla? Why Ayla not get a normal friend?'

'*Cielo*, I have lots of friends, all different kinds of people. You are just one of them.'

Simon thought about this. He couldn't decide whether this was worthy of a sulk or not. He didn't like Ayla having lots of friends. 'Shimon not like Ayla have lots of friends. Not.'

Consuela laughed. 'Well, that's not very nice, is it?'

Simon had thought about it, and he was definitely sulking. 'Ayla likes normal friends, not of course like Shimon.'

'Hey, sulky sod, I like you lots, like jelly tots. Stop being silly. What if you weren't allowed to see Annie, and Jimmy and Joey, and Billy and all of your friends at Great Gables, you'd be very lonely, wouldn't you?'

Simon didn't answer. He had turned his back on her and didn't want to talk. So Ayla talked to herself.

'Oh dear, Ayla. Now we have a problem. See, there was me going to take Simon to the lake to buy ice cream, but Simon's not talking to me. Do I just buy one ice cream for myself? That would be lonely, just like we were talking about, wouldn't it, Ayla? But if Simon's sulking and doesn't want to come, I can't bring his ice cream home for him because it will melt, and how on earth will I drive with only one hand? It's a problem, Ayla.'

Simon had turned around with a big grin. He went to the cupboard to get his coat. It was sweltering outside, but Simon never went out without his coat. Simon wasn't sulking anymore.

Chapter Twenty-Nine

The nearest bus stop was a mile and a half away from the farm. Consuela sorely regretted not bringing her car and just dumping it in bushes close by. She trudged up the dirt track in the heat of summer. It was uphill, and she was wearing bloody Jesus sandals. She wore a flowing skirt in purples and reds. It came to her ankles, with bells on a string at her waist that tinkled when she walked. She had on a loose vintage top with no bra and had to admit that part did feel very liberating but to be authentic. She had no deodorant or perfume. Bloody hippies, why can't they be at least half-civilised? I bet there's no champagne on ice when I get there. She'd developed a taste for it and could distinguish which fruit had been used on which label.

When she got to the enormous farmhouse, she gave a low whistle. She wasn't the only one who'd done well for herself. Consuela knocked on the door and was told by a pretty girl with a baby at her breast that Beth was in her studio. The girl pointed her in the right direction.

'Hi there, come on in. Take a seat if you can find one.'

Beth had aged. Although Consuela recognised her, if she had to describe her in one word, it would be passionless. The enthusiasm she'd had for life was gone. She smiled, but it was just a smile. Beth, like the rest of them, had always looked down her nose at Julie, but she was the best of the lot. They had talked sometimes, and she knew what it was like to be disapproved of by Violet.

Her work had changed too. She still painted animals, recorded the seasons in oil and was inspired by the elements in her pottery, but there was a dark art amongst the fluff. She'd created sculptures of tortured metal reflecting pain and suffering. Connie bought a lot of art. She knew what was good, and Beth was excellent.

'Connie,' she extended a hand.

'Not from around here, then? Spanish, Basque, right?'

'Not bad. Barcelona. I'm just bumming around your island for a few months, heard there might be some work going on here. I'm a good worker.'

Beth gave a dry laugh. 'There is plenty of work, and we can always use a good worker. We don't pay.'

'*Sí*, that's fine.'

'Just do what you think your stay is worth and come and go as you, please. We don't use locks. I hope you've got a strong back. It's potato picking this week. If you go back to the house, someone there will show you to a dorm and get you something to eat. Good to have you aboard. Welcome, Connie. Stay as long as you like.'

Some women buy fragrances in tiny bottles for vast amounts of money. Consuela brought Listeria, which had cost a fortune. When you have money, you can buy anything. There's nothing that doesn't have a price tag.

She worked in the fields for the rest of that week until she never wanted to see another potato. In the evenings, she singled Beth out to chat to, showed an interest in the farm and wormed herself a week working in the creamery. She was impressed by the size of the operation. Their brand was called *Nature's Riches,* with an impressive turnover of cheese, milk, cream, yogurt and ice cream. Their cheese won awards and was stocked in the organic section of leading supermarkets. She had imagined a couple of women turning handles on a churning bucket, but in fact, the operation was modern and extensive. The machinery was floor-to-ceiling high, and it took the strength of several men to do the manual work. The women were used for packing, labelling and order processing.

This suited Consuela's purpose. She wanted control of the placement of stored cheeses. What she planned to do was risky. If one cheese was taken out of rotation, she could have the death of many people on her hands. That was never her intention. She wanted to bring down one family, not innocent people, and she didn't want to kill anybody.

She took no responsibility for John's death. The people he owed money to got to him. They would have without Consuela's tip-off. If he didn't owe money, he wouldn't have died. It was that simple. However, she took credit for his misery, and the state he died in. He left this world estranged from his family. And she admitted to herself that she'd pushed him into stealing twenty grand from his mother with no means of returning it. He'd have been killed anyway. But his death was down to his greed and rotten nature. He drew his last breath, a lonely man. That was the vengeance Consuela sought.

Andrew singled her out. He wanted to sleep with her. The last time he'd seen Julie, his lip curled. She disgusted him, though he was civil to her when he had to be. But he wanted Consuela. She stirred his blood. His eyes were inflamed with lust. He brushed against her, made excuses to consult with her, and did everything he could to woo her into bed. And she flirted with him. She was disappointed when his obvious desire elicited no reaction from his wife. Beth didn't care. They'd practised free love since the day they met. But this was different. The love had left her eyes. She didn't love or desire her husband. Andrew slept with members of their community. Beth slept alone.

Since the rape, she preferred it that way.

When Consuela took Andrew to bed, it was because she wanted to. She could have had any man on the farm and many women, but Andrew captivated her. His body was lean and taut; he was more animal than man. He turned her on, and she wanted him. She wanted to know if he was as good at satisfying a woman as swinging an axe.

She tipped the vial of listeria into the first basin in the production process. Every piece of equipment in the creamery would have to be destroyed. Listeria affects the young and the old, and it's dangerous for pregnant women because it harms the unborn. Consuela had never had children, but Julie had a little girl—once.

305

Victoria-Violet was murdered.

After the tip-off, the investigating authorities arrived fast. They locked down the farm and took samples. None of the contaminated products left the first storage room, but nevertheless, all of their outlets had to remove the *Nature's Riches* stock from their shelves. It went Nationwide and was featured on the evening news. Woods' Kibbutz Farm was finished. Andrew was depressed. He grieved for the children he'd have killed if it wasn't found in time. Consuela watched his sorrow and revelled in it. He hadn't grieved for Julie's daughter. He was besmirched in the press, and his lifestyle was open to public scrutiny. The intimate details of his sex life were examined when his concubines sold their stories. The vice squad raided them, and a massive cache of drugs was seized. Most of the adults in the commune used them, and their high of choice was as varied as a sweetshop Pick 'n' Mix. The haul was for personal use, but it was worth hundreds of thousands at street value. Social Services descended on the community to investigate how the members looked after their children. Many of them, including two of Beth and Andrew's, were taken into care. His family rallied, but he felt their disapproval for besmirching their name again.

After his ruin—and he was hewn at the knees, Andrew smoked less marijuana and more opium. He turned to Beth for solace, but she had none to give. They'd always liked the Cedar tree on the back lawn, where the little ones played.

It was their children who found him.

Chapter Thirty

She dripped gold and favoured sovereigns, the travellers' currency of old. Her clothing was the best, with Louis Vuitton shoes, and her perfume costing five hundred pounds a bottle. These people, shunned by many in society, knew quality. They wouldn't be fooled by anything less than the best.

It was a semi-permanent site outside Lancaster. She'd done her research. Her car was modest, so she'd hired an expensive sportscar for the day and pulled onto the site in a squeal of tyres. Two men tending horses rushed over.

'This is private property, miss. You have no business here,' the first man was in his twenties.

'I'm here to see the owner of this site.' She spoke with authority.

'Are you from the council?' The second man was the same age but thicker set and less attractive.

'Don't be soft, Wilfred. The 'cil doesn't drive a car like that. What are you here for, Missus?'

'I have a business proposition.'

'We don't do business with gorgas.'

'Excuse me?'

'Outsiders. We only deal with our own kind.'

A trailer door flew open, and a man came out. 'You've lost your way, Missus.'

'I don't believe so. Are you the owner?'

'Who would be wanting to know?'

'As you defend your privacy, so I'm defensive of mine, Mr Lowther. Who I am is not of importance.'

He raised an eyebrow. 'Is that so?'

'Let me convince you that we have some business to discuss.' She opened her clutch bag and gave him a glimpse of a wad of cash.

'Are you alone?'

She nodded.

'Junior, Wilfred, why are my horses not on the snaffle? Stay close to the gate and see we aren't disturbed.' The men leaned in close, trying to see in the gorga's bag. 'Begone with you,' Jacob Lowther roared and the men scattered. 'You'd best follow me, then.' He led her into the trailer.

Jacob motioned Consuela to a seat in the bay window. She'd done her research on the correct etiquette and removed her shoes before entering, but she was canny enough to pick them up and put them inside the door where she could see them. The trailer was immaculate. It was dressed in porcelain works of art. She smiled when she saw the same Royal Doulton tea set that Violet was so proud of. It was displayed in a China cabinet. Violet would be horrified to know that she shared her taste with gypsies.

'Sheila. Get the pibe on, woman.' A voluptuous woman with hair as black as Consuela's made tea. Neither spoke again until Jacob's wife had served them. She didn't ask Consula's taste and the tea was given with sugar and lemon, 'Go on and visit with your sister, begone woman.' Sheila looked Consuela over. Her eyes flamed with jealousy and she glared at her husband. Jacob raised the flat of his hand to his wife, and with lightning reflexes, Consuela grabbed him by the wrist before the slap landed.

'That won't be necessary, Mr Lowther.'

'To be spoken to like that in my home. By a mort, too. I should strike you to the floor. Missus, you've got balls, and you've got my interest. I'll tell you that much.'

Consuela watched until Sheila entered a trailer across the yard.

She took her time, opened her bag, and took out the wad of money. With the handle grip facing her, she put a small derringer pistol with a mother-of-pearl inlaid handle beside her. Jacob straightened but recovered his composure.

'That is ten thousand pounds. If we can strike a deal, I'll leave it with you today. I believe you're a man of your word, and if you say it'll be safe until you claim it, then that's good enough for me. On completion of our business, it will be doubled, and you will not see me again. If you proved not to be a man of honour, Mr Lowther, I'd hunt you down and shoot you like vermin. Do you believe me?'

Jacob played through a gamut of expressions from anger to affront until a grin spread across his features. 'Aye, lass, I believe you would. And it'd be a rum fool that'd cross you. Talk.'

'I've done my research. You and your family engage in bare-knuckle fighting?'

He gave nothing away to confirm or deny the statement. 'Go on.'

'I want a fighter. Several, in fact.'

'We don't do security. Hire a firm.'

'Let me elucidate. I want you to organise a tournament to take place over one night.'

'Travellers don't fight for the entertainment of gorgas.'

'I know that. I want some bouts amongst your own, but I want you to fight an outsider.'

'You've got us wrong, Missus. We don't fight gorgas. They tend to die. We fight for the family name and honour or for prize purses, but always within our own. If this is a bookmaking deal, you've had a wasted journey.'

'I think not. You will be paid twenty thousand for running the event. I'll cover the purse for your fighters. Anything you make on the book is yours.'

'Are you mad? For an event like that, the stakes would be thousands.'

'I have no interest in financial gain. Anything you make on the side is yours.'

'This mush of yours must be a hell of a fighter for you to put him up against the best in Britain.'

'I don't believe so.'

Jacob looked confused. 'You're putting a fighter against the best, but don't think he'll win?'

'My reasons are personal.'

'We don't deal in hired hits. People die in these fights, but we aren't murderers. If you want to off your old man, get some other sucker to spend the rest of his days in prison for you.'

'He'll be a willing participant. He has an ego the size of Britain. You'll enjoy him.'

'Lady, I see to my horses and play with my grandkids. I'm a busy man with no patience, so you'd better talk. You can start with a name. It seems only polite when you're sitting in my home, drinking my tea.'

'My name is not important. Call me Maria.'

'That's not your real name.'

'Here's the deal. I need a location. If you want money to hire somewhere, that's not a problem. I trust you to do what you do and arrange the necessary privacy, et cetera. There'll be several bouts in the competition. The man I bring will fight in three of them, and your men will throw the first two fights.'

'Missus. There'll be no fight-throwing. We fight fair. This is our pride, our culture. We are a proud people. We don't throw fights. If your gorga isn't up to it, you'd better hope he has some powerful life insurance.'

'Our business here is finished. I am sorry I wasted our time.' She opened her bag and put the money away.

'Wait. Leave it with me, I'll find somebody, but it'll cost.'

'Fine.' Connie breathed a sigh of relief, and Jacob copied less visibly. 'Your men will throw the first two fights. Let him win. He'll crow. On the third bout, I want you to beat the living shit out of him. I don't want him walking away.'

'We talk the same language.'

'Maybe. Maybe not. There's one more rule. If my demands aren't met, I go back to Spain, and from there, I call the authorities and blow you wide open. Do you understand?'

'That's an ugly threat.'

'My final, and most important, rule—he must not be killed. I want him alive at the end of it.'

'So be it.'

'The venue must be arranged on a floating date, cancellable and re-organised at short notice if he's not willing on the first date.'

'I can put it up and shut it down with an hour on either side.'

'Perfect.'

'We'll exchange numbers, and when he's taken the bait, I'll be in touch.' Consuela spat into her hand and held it out to Jacob.

The deal was sealed.

Chapter Thirty-One

H er business needed her. Leaving her managers alone for too long led to sloppy standards and a decline in honesty. She had good people, but every army needs a general. She'd been back for a week, and the second she'd stepped on Spanish soil, she knew it was—home. But she couldn't settle. Everything was ready to step into the wonderful life she'd built, but her real work was in England. And she missed something else—someone. Ayla missed Simon. She rang him most nights, and he was so angry with her for leaving him that he didn't answer the phone sometimes, but curiosity always got the better of him. It was good to be on his own. When he answered, she got a buzz out of hearing him say, 'The Woods Redisenth. How may I help you?'

She was sorry she couldn't answer, 'I'm in the Batmobile. You can get the kettle on.' So she made do with, 'I'm in Spain, and I miss my Simon smiles.'

Simon was ten years Consuela's senior, but he filled a hole that Vicki left. Consuela had a child-sized crater, and while Simon couldn't replace Vicki, he filled the hole and spilt out over the sides. She'd taken on the role of a mother figure, and she'd never back away from that. She welcomed it.

Simon once asked why Connie had befriended him. She was careful with his fragile emotions. She couldn't let him be too attached to her. He'd spent years gaining his independence, and forming an unhealthy bond with her was a concern. But Consuela was lonely without him.

She was in her spare bedroom, wondering if Simon could be happy. He struggled with English, and bringing him here could isolate him. For the first time, she let the thought flood in that, when this was over, she could buy a plaque for his door saying *Sala Simón*, and he might like to move here permanently. But Simon loved his flat and his new friends. He was happy there. He might not want to move to Spain. It was just something to talk to him about—in the future.

She'd been in Spain for the aftermath of the Andrew scandal, but she was going back. Her flight had been arranged for a week later, but she'd brought it forward. During one of her routine phone calls to Cheryl, Simon's social worker, she'd said that he had to go to the hospital. It was for his annual barrage of tests to assess the long-term damage from his heart attack several years earlier. He'd panicked and was frightened. The aftermath of his attack was a terrifying time. He didn't like hospitals and refused to go. And they knew how stubborn he was.

The women had grown to be friends due to their concern for Simon. One drunken night, over two bottles of wine and after swearing her to secrecy, Consuela told Cheryl her story, from beginning to the sorry end. The only part she kept back was the ongoing saga of her revenge.

Cheryl was sceptical of her motives, but Consuela showed her that her intentions towards Simon were good. She cared about him and wanted to be a positive influence.

Consuela wanted to be there for the appointment and would fly in to surprise him. She'd meet Cheryl at the hospital the next day, and they could speak to Simon's consultant together. Consuela had no legal or hereditary right to be there, and the consultant would never speak to her without the social worker's blessing. Simon had already had a significant heart attack, and his life expectancy wasn't a long one. Consuela wanted to make sure it was good.

She knocked on the door.

'Surprise.'

Simon's shock caused him to stagger. His eyes were huge in his round, confused face. He ran away from the door and left her standing there. It wasn't the greeting she'd expected. She sighed and followed him into the kitchen.

'Simon, it's me. Aren't you going to say hello?'

'Shush,' he replied, putting one finger up to his lips and spraying saliva over it. Simon studied his calendar. He had his finger over a tick. Connie saw it was today's date. Simon ticked the date off every morning when he got up. The next square had a blue star in it, and Cheryl had written, *Hospital Appointment*, underneath for Mrs Pickering's benefit.

The next five squares were empty, and then on the day Ayla was due to arrive back in England, there was a big gold star.

She smiled. 'I've come home early, Simon. I've come specially to see you.'

His agitation was profound. He hopped around and pointed to his calendar. 'Not six sleeps. Not. Not gold star. Not. Ayla, go back.' He went into the lounge and picked up the telephone handset because that's how he talked to Ayla when Ayla was in Spain. He pointed at it. 'Ayla in Spain. It's hot, and ever-a-body say, Hola.' He looked at the handset, put it to his ear, and said, 'Thank you. Goodbye, please.' and hung up. She seriously thought Simon was going to throw her out for being early.

'I missed you, Simon. I wanted to see you. Haven't you missed me?' She put her arms around him and gave him a hug.

Simon stiffened. 'Shimon miss Ayla in six sleeps,' he was in a grump.

Consuela sighed. It was going to be one of those days. She went back to the kitchen with him trailing behind her. She peeled the gold sticker off the calendar and put it over the last tick. 'Hooray,' she said brightly and waved her hands in the air. 'It's Ayla day.'

'Hooray,' Simon agreed. His arms wobbled and nearly came up, but he didn't look convinced.

'I swear, Simon, sometimes you're like the fly around a horse's backside.' Simon had to stop and think about that. He was frightened of horses and didn't want to be a fly or a horse's backside.

'Put the kettle on, *cielo*,' he said, picking up the kettle and remembering to fill it with water before putting it on to boil. This was his third kettle, and Mrs Pickering said she wouldn't buy him another one. She said he was a liability. Simon didn't know what a liability was, but it had to be better than a fly or a horse's bum. 'Put the kettle on, *cielo*,' he repeated, flicking the switch.

This wasn't a request for Consuela to make the tea. He parroted what she always said as soon as she came in. And he spoke in the flat monotone reserved for when he was coming to terms with changes to his routine. He turned around with an enormous beam on his face. 'Consuela, Shimon, go for ice cream in a little minute?'

'Why not,' she agreed before broaching the subject of the following day's hospital appointment.

Mr Bell, the consultant, looked up from Simon's records. He took a moment to order his thoughts, and his eyes went from Cheryl to Consuela and back again. 'The results aren't as optimistic as we'd hoped, I'm afraid. Downs sufferers have a shorter life expectancy than the rest of us as it is, and Simon's heart complications have compounded the issue.'

'Is he going to die?' Consuelo asked. Her throat had dried, and she was sick with worry.

'We have no way of knowing how long Simon will live, Ms Vengarse. His heart attack has affected the function of his aortic efficiency. There's some decline in kidney function, and his white cell count is on the low side. The muscles working his heart are weakened. The best I can tell you is that he could die tomorrow or, with a good headwind, he could live for another ten or twelve years. I'd anticipate his life expectancy could be somewhere down the middle. The good news is that his weight is lower than six months ago. He's lost ten pounds. That's going to help alleviate some of the pressure on his heart. He doesn't smoke or drink, his job keeps him active, and perhaps the greatest thing on his side is that he's a very positive man. We aren't as happy with the results as we'd like, but it could be worse. I don't think he's ready to leave us just yet.' He smiled.

'Thank you, doctor.' Cheryl offered him her hand to shake while Consuela nodded and attempted a smile. Once released, the tears wouldn't stop. She couldn't bear the thought of losing him—not now. Cheryl took her for coffee in the canteen before they picked Simon up from the dayroom. She was hard on Consuela and told her that Simon wouldn't die at any second and to pull herself together for his sake. Any doubt that Consuela's feelings for Simon were genuine was long gone. Consuela was like any mother being told she'd outlive her child, something she'd known all along but hadn't come to terms with.

Chapter Thirty-Two

The bar was awful, the staff surly, and the clientele a mix of drunken men and loose women on the pull. She'd watched him for a week, and he'd been to this pub twice.

When she walked into the bar, everybody stared at her. She was like a peacock in a crow show and would never blend in. She tossed her hair, straightened her shoulders, and walked to the bar. 'Gin and slimline tonic, with ice and lemon, please.'

'No slimline, just ordinary. The ice we got. We don't do lemon.'

'That'll be fine. Thank you.'

She paid, gave the barmaid a pound tip and took her drink. Ten minutes after buying her first drink, she went for another. The girls behind the bar fell over themselves to get to her first. The other one served her this time, and her demeanour was curious and greedy. 'Same again, love?'

'Yes. Thank you.' She paid and gave another tip.

'Not from around here, are you?' Now that she had her tip, only the curiosity remained.

'Gracey, over there,' she gestured with her hand. 'She reckons you're from Poland. 'But I said you're Eastern European. You wouldn't have a tan like that, and not a fake tan, either. The real kind that you get from the sun.'

'I'm from Spain.' She hadn't expected ingratiating herself to be so easy. 'I'm here for a week or two, visiting friends. They're an elderly couple, and you can only take so much *Coronation Street*, so I thought I'd see what the town offers in the way of nightlife.

'Wow, you're brave. Isn't she brave, Gracie? I couldn't walk into a pub on my own. Could you, Gracie? Could you walk into a pub on your own?'

'Shit, no. I could never do that. You know what I'm like, Tina. I lack confidence, me.'

Consuela laughed. 'All you have to do is stick your chest out and say, 'I'm good, and if you don't like it, to hell with the lot of you.' She had to play it just right. Be interesting enough that they'd talk to her, but not too over the top that she alienated herself. She moderated her language to their level. 'I'm Consuela. I like it here,' she lied. There weren't many customers. A couple in their fifties were the only people sitting at the tables. Three men and two women were drinking at the bar. 'I fancy a shot. Sambuca, Will you join me, ladies? In fact, I'd like to buy everybody one.' It was a risky move drawing attention, but she had that cross to bear, anyway. She didn't want to appear desperate enough to buy people's company. In a place like this, being flash wouldn't get you anywhere—except mugged.

Tina lined up shot glasses and filled them with Sambuca. 'You know something? You looked like a right snotty cow when you walked in, but you're all right, you are.'

That was all it took. She was accepted, an outsider, allowed in the bar under the banner of passing trade—with money—who was all right.

It didn't look as though he was coming in that night.

On Saturday night of the following week, she went back.

'Hey Consuela, what are you having?' Gracie asked before she reached the bar. They had karaoke that night. Connie remembered a girl called Julie who liked Karaoke bars. Like the bar staff, the hosts introduced her to the regulars as they came in and bullied her to sing in a good-natured manner. She had a good time but never lost sight of her purpose.

She was singing when he came in after work. The unfamiliar voice with the thick Spanish accent made him glance at the stage. She sang well, which was a rarity in The Pheasant. By ten, most of the punters could barely stand.

James Woods' mouth dropped open. Consuela spent a vast amount of money to look this well-designed. She was extraordinarily beautiful. She'd bought her body, confidence, class, and sophistication. She wore them exquisitely. When Consuela wanted a man to look at her, he did.

James' head turned, and he looked like a comical fool. It was a momentary reaction before he resumed his pace and ordered his first pint of the ten he'd have before fighting his way out of the door.

She went to the bar and high-fived Gracie. 'Way to go, girl, you rocked that one.' Consuela drained her gin and ordered another. She caught James' gaze and smiled.

321

'*Gracias*, Gracie, I'm going to sit down.' She picked up her glass, turned to James and smiled at him a second time. He returned it.

She sat on a bench beside a couple she'd spoken to the last time she was there. Two young girls were murdering *The Climb*.

Every man in the pub flirted with Connie, and she'd fended them off gracefully. She gave off vibes of wanting to be a friend to most, lover to none.

She passed a few words with Eddy and Maureen. She was a few years younger than him. Eddy was a mouse of a man who wanted two things on a Saturday night—a pint and a quiet life. God knows, he didn't get them the rest of the week. Consuela noticed spite and venom made up his wife's blood supply. She was a gossip and had an opinion about everybody. Maureen had no interest in talking about herself. She wanted to talk about you, your life, your details, your bits of salacious scandal that she could impart to a third person later. She was a sweet middle-aged lady until the conversation flowed, and traits of a weasel appeared along her brow line.

Barry Mosley was a big man in his early fifties, more fat than brawn, but his vanity told him otherwise. Years of karaoke singing had taught him bar-singer habits, and his wail on words was painful. He came to Connie's table and serenaded her. Consuela felt a dig in her ribs.

'I don't like him, do you?' Maureen had screwed up her nose in distaste. 'Thinks he's God's gift, he does.'

'He's having a good time,' Consuela said.

'You won't get rid of him now. You watch.'

'I can soon put him back in his box if he oversteps the mark.'

'I wouldn't encourage him, that's all.' As far as Connie was aware, she hadn't encouraged anybody.

Sure enough, Barry strutted over. He'd been in last time, and she'd stopped him pawing her then. 'Consuela, my darling. You look ravishing tonight. Can I buy you a drink?'

She motioned to her full glass. 'That's kind of you, but I'm okay.'

'Just a little drink. Make an old man happy.'

'Maybe later.'

'Go on, one drink.'

'No, thank you.'

'I'll have half a lager, and he'll have a pint of bitter if you're buying,' Maureen said.

Barry didn't acknowledge that she'd spoken. His voice changed. 'I asked you to have a drink with me. I asked politely. In England—where I come from—it's rude to refuse a polite request.'

'And I said no, thank you, just as politely. And in England, where I'm originally from, it's rude to pester somebody who wants to be left in peace.'

'She said no, Barry. Leave her alone. You're making a dick of yourself,' Tina shouted from behind the bar.

He ignored Tina, too. 'You whore.' Spit flew towards her face as Barry spoke. 'Think you're better than me, with your fancy clothes and your money? Not good enough to buy you a drink, am I? Who do you think you are, coming in here like you own the joint?'

James Woods was behind Barry. 'Move, Barry. You're out of line, man. Come back to the bar before you upset the lady.'

Barry wheeled around to James, his cheeks reddening, and anger twisted his mouth. 'And here's another one from the same stable. Another rich swine who thinks they're something special because they've got money and a fancy job. I'll show you.' Barry swung his fist, but James' reflexes were fast, and he caught Barry's fist before it made contact. He used the other man's momentum against him and twisted Barry's arm high up his back and used it as leverage to walk him out of the pub, where he threw him to the pavement and told him not to come back that night.

James went to Connie. 'Are you okay? I'm sorry about that. I hope it doesn't spoil the rest of your night.' If Connie didn't know him, she'd have been impressed. He hadn't used excessive force against Barry. A far cry from the James she knew, who loved flexing his muscles whenever he got the chance—especially against his wife. 'Let me tell you about Barry,' he said, and he sat at her table.

'There's no need. It was nothing.'

He turned up the charm. 'The thing is,' he continued, 'Barry's a good bloke. He worked hard until a couple of years ago when he was made redundant from the shipyard. Then his wife left him for somebody with money. It made him bitter. He's got a chip on his shoulder about people judging him for being on benefits. He drinks to forget, and he's a proud man. I hope he didn't upset you.'

'No, he didn't. Can I buy you a drink to thank you?' She gave him the benefit of her immaculate veneers and gazed in an expression she hoped looked impressed but fell short of adoration. She had to give his ego something to work with.

'I wouldn't hear of it. In England, where I come from,' he winked at her, 'ladies do not buy drinks for blokes. Same again? Or am I being presumptuous?'

'That'd be great.'

Whispers at the bar were rife when Consuela and James spent the next two drinks together. They chatted and played the flirting game the way it was meant to be played.

'And now,' Consuela insisted, 'it is my round.'

'Or,' James looked unsure for the first time. 'Maybe we could go somewhere else. I know a nice bar,' he lowered his voice to a whisper, 'somewhere better than this. We're in a goldfish bowl here.' He motioned his head towards Maureen, who had spent the last half hour hanging on their every word. 'If we hurry, we can make last orders.'

He took their glasses to the bar, and Maureen was in like a shot. 'Watch him. He's trouble. You think Barry was bad. He's a teddy bear compared to him.'

'Don't worry. I've got his card marked.' She tapped the side of her nose and thought of Simon. He loved karaoke, and she knew, with absolute certainty, that she couldn't bring him to this bar. He'd be laughed at. Simon wouldn't fit in here, and while she'd had a good time and had surprised herself by having fun, neither did she. Consuela waved goodbye as they walked out together. She wouldn't be back.

In the next pub, James took a sip of his pint and laughed. They were sitting in a secluded booth in a wine bar a few streets from The Pheasant. 'Promise me you won't take this the wrong way. Cheesy chat-up lines aren't my style. But you seem familiar. You probably remind me of someone on the telly. Ah,' he blushed, 'told you it was cheesy.'

No, thought Consuela, you haven't seen me on TV. You've told me I'm ugly in a hundred different ways, but that was another lifetime. She remembered the sting of his insults and wanted to smash his face in. She'd like to put him in a wheelchair and see him bleeding. She smiled. 'You're a lovely man.'

The bar was open late, and the drink flowed. As he always had, James became a maudlin drunk. This was the stage before he turned into an obnoxious and violent man, and she'd be long gone before then.

He told her about his financial worries. His salary was generous without allowing for what Consuela knew he creamed off the top. But the more money he had, the more he spent, and the more of it he wasted on beer and women. He'd totted up some debts, and he whined that his mother, rich beyond her needs, had refused to bail him out. He sank into self-pity, and if she was a stranger thinking of taking him as a lover, he couldn't have been less appealing. 'I just need to find a way of making some fast money,' he moaned.

Consuela furrowed her brow as if in thought. He caught the look, and it piqued his interest. 'What?'

'No, nothing. Ignore me. It's a stupid idea.'

'What? What is? Tell me.'

'It was nothing.'

'Come on. You can't do that. If you have something to say, then say it, don't mess me about.' It was the first time he'd let his guard slip, and the James she knew peeped through his façade of being human.

'I can't tell you. It's one of the ways I've made my fortune in the past, but it's not above board. Please don't make me say any more.' She touched his forearm. 'I like you, James, and I don't want you to think badly of me.'

She had him by his unpleasant, nasty scrotum. He worked through the possibilities, and she guessed where his thought process took him—lap dancer, escort, whore.

His charm was in place as though he'd straightened his tie. 'Consuela.' He took her hand and stroked the back with his thumb. 'There's nothing you could say to make me think badly of you. You're an amazing woman. And if you're naughty, it makes you an amazingly interesting woman. One's secrets are an enormous turn-on when they're shared with a stranger, such as me, for instance.' He leered, and she felt sick. 'Go on, tell me your dark secret. I dare you.'

Consuela giggled and recrossed her legs to tease him. 'I am an entrepreneur back in Spain, and I admit, occasionally here in England, too. I have been responsible for organising,' she halted and took a sip of her drink, letting him see how nervous she was, saying without words that this was difficult for her, that she didn't discuss this kind of thing outside her business circles. 'Promise me that this is strictly confidential, James. If word got out, I'd be in trouble.' He nodded. 'I organise bare-knuckle fighting for the top underground organisations in the world. It's made me a rich woman.'

He exhaled and let out the air with a whoosh. 'Blow me—I mean, good Lord. I didn't expect that. You're full of surprises, aren't you?' He dropped her hand, and his rested on her thigh. She gave him a moment and watched a range of emotions cross his face.

'I want in.'

Consuela laughed. 'Out of the question. It's impossible. I shouldn't have said anything. It's a fast way to make a lot of money, and my mouth got ahead of me. This isn't the way for you.' He'd moved her hair away from her shoulder as she talked, leaned in, and was kissing her neck. Consuela felt as though a slug was crawling up her throat. She had to hold steady, so she didn't recoil.

'We're made for each other, you, and me. I knew it the second I saw you. You captivate me. You're the sexiest woman that I've laid eyes on. Think bad of you? Darling, what you've told me has inflamed my passion. You're like nobody in this backwater—Get me into a fight.'

His wet mouth stinking of beer attached to hers. He slobbered all over her. She wanted to knee him in the crotch but returned his kisses. 'I can't. You don't understand.' She was breathless from his kiss, her voice more husky than normal. For an accomplished actress, this role was worthy of an Oscar. She was repulsed by him. 'These men are animals. The fighters I've lined up for next Monday are the hardest men in the country. You'd get hurt. Forget it and kiss me some more.'

His gaze toughened. 'I'm hard. I run this town. Ask anybody.' He flexed his muscle and presented his biceps for her to feel. He was nothing if not predictable, and she was right to attack through his vanity. 'I'm the hardest man around here.' He lowered his voice. 'I've been away for it. In prison. Get me into a fight.'

'Are you sure you can handle it? It's a tough game.'

'I'm a tough man. Let me take you home, and I'll show you the animal. I'm gentleman on the outside and caveman in the bedroom.'

She convinced him she wasn't that kind of girl. That he'd have to woo her first. She poured iced water on his ardour, raised his ego by saying she'd get him in the ring, and arranged to meet him at five thirty the following Monday. She told him to train in the three days before the fights and that sex was off the menu until after Monday, and blue steak was the order of the day. She kissed him before jumping in a taxi and speeding away.

She needed to shower.

Chapter
Thirty-Three

James trained all weekend. He'd cut down on drinking and ate a load of lean red meat and raw eggs for breakfast. He could have done with a couple of months to train and had to make do with two days, but a good right hook is a good right hook, and a killer instinct is something that you just have. No amount of gym hours or fancy sweatbands can teach you how to floor a guy with a single punch. You're born with it, and James had it in abundance. He'd beaten up many a scrawny kitchen hand in his time. He never wasted a thought on the possibility that he wouldn't win. He was a lover and a fighter, and James Woods was a winner. When he'd taken the purse for the tournament, he intended a post-fight work down in the bedroom with the lovely Consuela. He was out to impress. It wasn't just about the money.

Jacob Lowther strode up to James and Consuela. James didn't like the way the man's eyes travelled over her body when she wasn't looking. She was his woman, and he didn't want any dirty gipsies giving her the glad eye. He had a low opinion of gypos. Thieves, the lot of them, dirty pikeys. They were a scourge on society, put on earth for the purpose of lowering the house prices of decent folk who paid their taxes. James had been questioned over tax evasion, and it was only his brother taking the fall that kept him out of prison.

He didn't like the way Consuela was talking to Jacob. They discussed the evening and how it was organised. She seemed to have a level of respect for the sewer rat. She laughed with him, and they were familiar. James put a protective arm around her shoulder, and she glared at him and shrugged it off. He felt a familiar itch in the palms of his hands. He wanted to make them into fists. He wanted to smash the gipsy man's face in. He didn't like the way they were talking as though he wasn't there. He didn't like being ignored.

The event was in a warehouse deep in the maze of a disused retail park. Jacob had put a ban on people arriving in vehicles. He laid on buses to ferry them in from town. The success of the evening relied on discretion. There was a ring in the centre of the makeshift arena and no seating. Hundreds of people from the travelling community were attending, and there was standing room only. This was a big-money event, and word had travelled fast. There were eight fights, and James was competing in three. He didn't know that. He expected to work through the heats to finish overall champion. He'd be taken out in the semi-finals.

Jacob turned to him. 'So you reckon you can handle yourself, eh, sonny? It's a great honour for you to be here. We don't invite Gorgas to our soirées.' He laughed at his joke.

James said. 'Don't call me sonny, old man. I'll take you out any day of the week.' His hands were balled at his sides, and he had an ugly snarl on his face. He took a step towards Jacob.

'Save your energy for the ring, lad. I'm not going to cock fight with you. The days when I had something to prove are long behind me.' Jacob and Consuela shook hands, and he indicated where James should get changed to prepare for his fight. He didn't offer his hand to James, and James spat on the ground in his wake, the fury of being snubbed by a man so beneath him throbbed with the adrenaline in his blood.

The crowd parted as he came out to fight. His opponent came from the other side of the ring and was patted and egged on by his community. James danced, and air punched to the ring, bringing on an array of catcalls and raucous laughter.

He wore red knee-length shorts and new red wrestling boots. He had a bright red, satin dressing gown with a white towel around his neck.

Charlie McMeekin only wore a pair of cut-off denim shorts and was barefoot.

James did a lap of the ring, punching the air and trying to stir the crowd in his favour. They laughed at him and jeered until the referee went over the rules.

'Right, lads, a three-second count-in. Two minutes. No biting, no eye gouging, no concealed weapons. A knockout or surrender signals the end of the bout. If you get a knockout, you stand clear of your opponent, and he'll be counted out for ten seconds. All clear?' Both men nodded.

'What the hell's that in your gob, laddie?' the ref asked.

James removed his gum shield so he could speak. 'Just a gum shield.'

'We don't use them here, boy. Get rid.'

'Piss off,' James said. 'Have you any idea how much I paid my orthodontist for these teeth?'

'Let the ponce have it,' Charlie said. 'He's going to need it when I lay into him.'

James lunged, and Charlie swung in retaliation. James ducked his head, and Charlie had him in a headlock, swinging his fist to hit him in the face before the bout began.

'Separate. You pair of bloody idiots. I've worked in dog fights where the opponents had better manners. In your corners.' The ref broke them up.

When he called them to fight, they came out angry. Charlie's pride was hurt, having to throw the fight and not taking the gorga bastard down. Ten grand was a lot of money for the twenty-five-year-old. His reputation meant a lot to him, but not as much as ten grand. He couldn't even get any decent digs in. They wanted the gorga to go three bouts, so he had to keep him pretty. Charlie had a pair of kids to bring up, and money was tight. It was a lot of money to him, but it was also a lot of pride to lose.

James came out with an axe to grind. He'd been in many a bar brawl, and this was no different. He got the first punch in. Charlie's lip split, and he sprayed blood in an arc when he shook his head. He came back at

James with a mild kidney punch. James felt his temper burst. He could give it out, but like all bullies, he didn't take it. The pain in his side made him see red, and he felt the vessels burst in his eyes as his blood pressure rose, and the last of his temper exploded. With a roar, he tore at Charlie. He hit him with a barrage of punches, and Charlie gave little back. James was flying high. He'd beaten harder men in the pub. This gypo had nothing about him. He hit him again. Charlie got him in a headlock, and they circled the ring. James felt and grabbed Charlie by the balls. He went onto his knees. James swung and kicked him in the face. He fell onto his back, out cold. The ref told him to break, but James ran forward and kicked the unconscious man hard in the kidneys. The crowd went mad, baying for James' blood. It didn't follow the code to kick a man when he was down. They wanted him disqualified from the competition. The ref knew the score. He'd been bought, too. He allowed James to qualify for the next round.

● James cleaned up after the fight and joined Connie to watch the last contestants in the first round of heats. He wasn't interested in the fighting and didn't watch to see if the man he was taking on next made it to his heat. He was too cocky to study their game and was secure in his ability to win. He crowed like a peacock, and Consuela fed his ego, telling him how wonderful he was and how the other man didn't know what had hit him.

The quarterfinals played out as the first round. James was an easy victor and came away high on his win. He had a split to his right eye that bled and obscured his vision but was elated and unaware of the cut. He did a lap of the ring, skipping and waving his hands. The crowd booed him off. There were calls of 'fix' screamed at the referee.

His third opponent was smaller and lighter than him.

'For God's sake, send me a man,' he shouted. 'Make some pretence of it being a sport.' His opponent's fighting name was Terry 'The Bull' Terrier.

'You're going to get hurt, young man,' James said.

'And if I hadn't been told to leave you breathing, you'd be going home in a coffin for that kick you gave my cousin.'

The ref called them, and James held his hand out. Terry snubbed him and spat at his feet. The ref called him out. 'Shake hands, lad. We'll have sportsmanlike behaviour. Shake or be disqualified.' They shook, and Terry glared at James.

When the ref's hand dropped, James came fast. He was on the attack, with his previous bouts making him bold. Terry had studied his opponent. He knew his weakness and strengths. It was an easy takedown, but he wasn't in a rush. Let the crowd have their sport.

James led with a right uppercut. Terry saw it and spun away. He could have had three jabs in with a fast circle of James, but he didn't. James struck at him again. Terry swerved him, ran up the corner post and did a back flip over James' head. The crowd went wild. Terry ran from diagonal corners of the ring every time James came with a punch. He hadn't landed any, and Terry hadn't thrown one. James was tired. His feet were stomping on the canvas. He was angry, which made him dangerous. Terry squatted to the floor, crossed his arms, and did the Kossak dance. James panted, with his fists raised, waiting for Terry to come for him. The bugger was fast.

Terry scampered across the ring on his haunches and bit James on the ankle before scurrying into the opposite corner. It was his trademark move, and the crowd were pumped with excitement. It took James by surprise, and he yelped.

Terry stopped playing.

James roared and ran to kick Terry in the face. Terry had guided him into it. James swung his leg, and Terry grabbed it as he ploughed the kick forward. He twisted the leg and used it to overbalance him. James sprawled on the canvas, and Terry backed off, giving him time to stand. James rested his hands on his knees, gasping when he was on his feet. The wiry man leap-frogged him from a squatting position.

'Shall I take him?' he roared to the crowd.

'Take him. Take him,' they took up the chant.

James was raging. The tendons stood out in his neck like bands, and his temper broke, leaving him out of control and dangerous.

Terry ran up the corner post and took a flying leap at James, a confused and enraged animal. He landed on his opponent's back and stuck to him with his legs around his waist like a monkey. Leaning forward, he pummelled James' face until it was hidden behind a mask of blood. James roared, trying to dislodge his attacker. Terry pulled his feet in and ran up James' back to flip off, somersault, and come to a standing position facing him. He punched him once, twice, three times in the face. He followed with a roundhouse kick to the kidneys. 'That one's for my cousin,' he yelled. James bent over, and Terry kicked him in the face. 'And that one's for me.'

James' head came up with an arced curtain of blood surrounding it. His body followed the momentum of his head, and he landed on his back in the ring. His skull made contact first with a crunch. His head bounced up and hit the sawdust a second time. He was out cold.

Later, a stolen white Ford Transit van with false plates pulled up to the doors of Accident and Emergency at Lancaster General Hospital in a squeal of tyres. The back doors opened, and two men launched a third onto the pavement before the van screamed away.

He was barely alive.

Chapter Thirty-Four

S P sulked.

Ros said, 'Please don't drink too much tonight, love. You've been late for work three times this week, which sets a bad example for the staff.'

'Stop nagging me, woman. Why shouldn't I have a drink after work? I'm here from first light until two or three in the morning. And you're never there to warm my bed.'

Ros had heard it all before. She heard the razor edge to her voice and hated it. 'Eleven is hardly first light. And you stay until the early hours because you're in the bar drinking with your maudlin brother. It can't be fun with self-pity floating in your whisky glasses.'

'You never used to be a hard woman, Ros. You've changed.'

'Years of babysitting your mother have made me bitter. Don't drink with James all night. Get to bed.'

'He's broken his neck, Ros. He's in a wheelchair and won't walk again. I think that entitles him to be angry.'

'His story's a load of rubbish. Five men jumped him for fun when he was on his way home. He's turned into a self-pitying alcoholic, and he's dragging you along for the ride.'

'Go to bed. You're a Harpie, woman. Leave me alone.'

SP dropped his key card and fell picking it up. It took three attempts to get into his room. He staggered to bed and landed, fully clothed, on his back. Within minutes he was snoring.

The cold water brought him around. He felt funny. Not just drunk, but odd. He couldn't focus. The room spun and swirled, twisting inside itself. Colours were shapes, and shapes were sounds. He couldn't differentiate one from the other.

And that's when he saw her.

The Lord God Almighty had chosen him.

Just like Bernadette, he was a lowly servant, chosen from above to receive a visitation from the Virgin Mary.

She stood at the end of his bed dressed in black and had a golden halo shining over her head. She'd appeared to him in the form of an angel, extending her resplendent wings, and golden dust shimmered in their loveliness. He wanted to get up and fall to his knees, but he was paralysed and couldn't move. He couldn't so much as swallow. He tried to ask her what her message for the world was, but he couldn't speak.

He felt pressure releasing on his upper arm. She spoke, but it was in Hebrew. She said the message would be clear when he woke up, and he'd know what to tell the world. He was a prophet, just like his mother told everybody. Simon Peter Woods was the next Messiah.

The Virgin Mother went out to his balcony. He'd left his balcony doors open to cool his room during the sweltering night. He didn't see the Mother of God spread her wings and fly away because he couldn't turn his head. The paralysis restrained him, but he wasn't worried. The Messiah was euphoric.

He didn't sleep again that night. He watched the magnificent light show the Virgin had left for him. He was shown the stars in his room and all the planets and the galaxies of God's wondrous creation. An extended tape measure appeared in a corner of his room with a giant apple balancing on the top. He watched a caterpillar crawling up the inches to fall back to the ground before it ever reached the apple. It climbed many times before morphing into a herd of gazelle that ran across the walls and into his bathroom. His mouth collected with saliva, but he couldn't swallow. This was drowning. He was aware of his throat, but it had thickened, and he had no reflex ability. The Messiah dribbled down his chin.

The duck pond was in his bedroom, and the beautification turned ugly. A little girl swam towards him. She was covered in waterweed. He panicked, and the swirling colours on the walls turned dark green and deep purple—and black. He calmed himself, safe in the knowledge that the Divine Virgin of Virgins would never do anything bad to him. With that knowing, some orange and yellow crept onto the walls. And he smiled, watching the traces of colour swirling from the lampshades.

Ros found him in bed. After getting Violet up and dressing her, she checked her husband was up and had a clear enough head to work. The employees were gossiping, and she had to stamp on it before it reached rebellion.

SP was on his bed with his mouth open. He'd urinated, and a wet, stinking stain spread on the quilt. The smell of urine, stale whisky and his unwashed body in the stifling room were overpowering. She worried when she couldn't rouse him and went to find James. His brother wheeled himself to the bed. After trying to wake him, he said SP was breathing and to let him sleep it off.

SP appeared shame-faced and sheepish in his mother's quarters at four in the afternoon. He was showered and well-groomed. When he lifted his teacup, a tremor made the cup rattle in its saucer. Otherwise, physically he seemed fine. He told his mother about the visitation from the Virgin Mary and implored her to interpret the event. Violet fed his mania. It was her destiny to be the vessel that carried greatness. She rushed to tell Clarissa Grainger about the miracle that had occurred in her very hotel. A shrine would be built in an arbour on the side lawn as a more appropriate place for The Mother of God to appear. She'd be sure to catch Simon Peter in a state of undress, which would be most unfitting. When the Virgin materialised again, Violet said he must ask her to appear in the summer house by the lake as a temporary measure until she'd had the shrine built. And could she please come at a more appropriate hour. 'However,' she said. 'Best to avoid three o'clock when the guests take high tea on the lawns.'

Ros couldn't speak to her husband and went downstairs to do SP's job. When he appeared in the bar after dinner, James said SP had flipped and poured him a large whisky.

That night, she appeared again. He was going to ask what she was doing to him, but a feeling of well-being carried him into orbit, and the beautiful colours came.

On the fifth night of her visitations, there was a thunderstorm. The rain lashed outside his window. SP hadn't drunk as much and arrived at his room semi-sober. He ran to the balcony and shut the doors against the rain pelting his carpet. And he sat in his winged armchair to wait.

He'd stopped talking about the visitations to everybody except his mother. He made it to work on the second morning of Our Lady's appearances but not the third or fourth. He was distracted. His concentration was poor. Nausea possessed him like a demon, and he vomited in the waste bin behind reception. He was sent to his room. His appetite left him, and he had to be forced to eat. Tremors ripped through his body, and in the evening, he burned with a fever that dulled with whisky. Violet refused to let them call a doctor. It was his divine suffering and His Lady's test.

That night she didn't come.

The clock turned. His condition worsened. He was delirious. He moved to his bed and crawled beneath the sheets. Within minutes they were soaked with sweat. SP shivered and burned until—instead of the Virgin Mary— sickness and diarrhoea came to him.

Ros found him the next morning. His bed, pitted in excrement and vomit, smelt so bad that she gagged. He was soaked in sweat and burned with a fever. He told her he was dying.

Ros hated him as she helped him into the shower and turned the hose on. Her cheeks burned with shame as she took his soiled sheets and fastened them in rubbish sacks to go in the refuse skip. She dealt with everything while he lay in bed feeling sorry for himself.

She fed him weak broth and rang the family doctor. To hell with Violet Woods. Dr Adler asked if SP had taken anything. She assured him he hadn't—only whiskey. Ros told him about the amount of whisky. The doctor recognised addiction, and this wasn't alcohol. He suspected heroin, took a blood test, and kept his mouth shut until he knew.

That night she came.

Ros missed her by seconds. She was exhausted and going between Violet's and her husband's room. When she went to him, the tremors had stopped, and the fever had broken. He had a smile on his face—and he was out of it.

A needle hung from his arm, the plunger spent, and blood dropped in the carriage. The tourniquet was fastened to his upper arm, and Ros sank to her knees and cried.

When Consuela came for vengeance, she'd done her homework. Phil had remarried four years ago. He had two sons, Thomas, three, and a baby, Oliver, who was four months old. She followed him, watched him, stalked him. He was happy. His wife was a mouse, pretty enough in her own way but carrying some baby weight. His children seemed happy, too, but then, to the outside world, so had Vicki.

Sometimes she thought about taking the boys. She fantasised about taking them with her to Spain and keeping them for her own. In her darkest hours, she imagined killing them like Vicki had been taken, watching them drown, and knowing Phil would suffer. The sins of the father shall be visited upon the son a thousand times.

But Vicki had been an innocent child, just like those two boys. They didn't deserve her vengeance. They were beautiful boys. Consuela knew them. She watched them play, listened to Thomas' games, and saw Vicki's features on their faces.

Thomas pretended he was a spaceman and walked around his garden as though he was walking on the moon. She pictured Phil, the first time the little boy had shown an interest in space travel. He'd have lectured the boy and forced him to look at pictures and documentaries beyond his years. But he hadn't killed the child's love of space or his imagination—yet. Connie couldn't hurt their father through the boys.

Two men were dead, and another was in a wheelchair because of her. John and Andrew wouldn't be dead if she hadn't come back. But she didn't kill them or put James in the wheelchair. He did it himself. His vanity, and a good kicking, broke his neck. All she did was present him with an idea. He'd welcomed and wanted it.

John's greed and Andrew's loose lifestyle led to their deaths. She didn't have any responsibility for them. They could have turned and altered their ways. They chose not to. Whoever resists the authorities resists what God has appointed, and those who resist will incur judgment.

344

She did make SP a heroin addict. She assaulted him while he slept, pushing the needles into his vein without consent. She regretted that. Better if he'd done it through choice, as the others had chosen their paths. But she righted it by giving him the power to choose on her last visit. It was a new addiction and could be cured with a short rehabilitation. He could have put it right. On the fifth and final visit, she injected him with heroin and left his next fix. It was filled and ready for use on the dressing table. She left an appointment card beside it for a five-day detox in a private clinic that she'd pre-paid. He had to ignore the needle and turn up for the appointment.

He was weak.

SP saw the syringe, and a different picture came into focus. His visitations weren't from the Virgin Mary. He'd been stupid. Ros must have done this to him. Somebody had. He rang the clinic and was told that a lady had booked the appointment with a credit card. The name was false, and the card led to an untraceable dead end.

He knew what he was doing when he depressed the plunger. He was a weak man. He yearned for pretty colours. Six months earlier, a member of his staff had been sacked for drug use on the premises. He went through the staff records and hunted him down. The junkie was SP's new supplier.

SP was unfit for work. He couldn't hold his job. His wealth meant his addiction grew fast, and he spent his waking hours incapacitated. He was unwashed and dirty. He kept himself away from public areas and avoided the guests.

Philip was called to run the hotel but wasn't up to it. He couldn't give up his own job to run the hotel further into the ground.

Ros had to hire an outsider to run it for the first time since Violet took the Halcyon Woods Hotel. The empire crumbled and was on its knees. James oversaw the running of the kitchen from his wheelchair but only went in a couple of times a day and screamed at everybody. The Empire was a damaged wreck, and Violet's ducklings were drowning—like Victoria.

Chapter Thirty-Five

He was working the back shift, from three until eleven. She watched him leave home at two-thirty on Monday, Tuesday, and Wednesday, and he got home at twenty past eleven those nights. He'd moved from the old house—from *her* house—and he'd bought a much bigger detached property with stables for his new wife's horses and large gardens on the Roan Head road. It suited Consuela's

p   u   r   -

pose.

The road they lived on was a country lane. There were no streetlights, and traffic after his backshift was light. She'd visited Jacob. Money had changed hands, and for this business venture, they used Wilfred because he ran faster than his brother, Junior.

Consuela Vengarse walked along the tree-lined lane. She had a kitbag of expensive photographic equipment and a high-end Cannon on a webbing strap around her neck. In this incarnation, she was a keen and accomplished photographer, commissioned to take scenic shots for *Country Life Magazine*. She had easels at her studio with arty prints to confirm her story should she ever entertain him there. In real life, she couldn't take a decent photograph for toffee. Every snap had the subject out of focus or decapitated.

At eleven-twenty, as headlights shone further along the road, a man jumped out of bushes at the roadside and grabbed her. They were beside a gate leading into a field of cows. He rammed her into it and brought his body up against her. He had a day's growth and kissed her hard to ensure that her lips were swollen and she had an inflamed stubble rash when she was rescued. He pulled her top, tearing the zip on her fleece and ripping her blouse open. Two buttons flew off as he exposed her cleavage and lacy, teal-coloured bra. 'Nice,' he murmured before burying his mouth into her breasts and neck. He sucked her flesh until it bruised and left marks on her arms where he mauled her.

She smiled when she felt his erection. 'Pull the camera strap around my neck and twist it tight.'

He stopped groping her. 'Missus, I'm good with all the kissing and the cuddling. Hell, I'm enjoying that, but I don't hurt women. Never have, never will.'

The car was closer. She pulled her arm free and struggled. He fastened his mouth on hers and kissed her, then moved to her neck, leaving her free to scream. She thrashed and cried out as the car pulled into the side of the road with care, avoiding brambles that might scratch the finish.

The attacker broke away and ran, pumping his arms and legs to cover the ground fast. Consuela was weak in the knees and wilted to the floor sobbing as the man ran to her.

'Are you all right?' He knelt beside her, and she turned tear-stained eyes to him and nodded. The tears were genuine. When Wilfred ran

348

away, and Phil stopped the car, she tightened the camera strap around her neck and strangled herself. It was only for a few seconds, while her ex-husband fiddled about, hiding something important in the glove box before getting out to rescue the woman being assaulted. She'd pulled the strap hard, and it would bruise. The inside of her throat was raw. She'd bitten her lip at the same time to make it bleed. When Consuela made eye contact with her ex-husband for the first time in ten years, she almost lost control of her hatred and had to suffocate the desire to stab him.

'Can you stand?' he helped her to her feet, but she didn't move. 'Stay there a second. I've got a blanket in the car.'

'Don't leave me,' she cried.

'It's okay. I'm here. I won't leave you.'

She flung herself into his arms. Her blouse was open, and her exposed cleavage pressed against his chest. He might be a loyal man and faithful to his wife, but she knew his body would respond. He was addicted to sex.

She'd spent many thousands on surgery and was unrecognisable, but he hadn't altered. Time had been good to him, and the feeling that he was like a memory foam mattress repulsed her. Phil fitted against her perfectly. He looked the same and even smelt the same. She sobbed into his neck, and she felt his heartbeat through his shirt. She moved her body as though she suffocated in his neck, and her breast pressed against his arm with her inhalations. She'd screwed this man a thousand times and knew how to arouse him. That was all that she needed—for now.

'Thank you. You saved my life.'

'Anybody would have done the same.' He used the same line on the day they met when he'd rescued her from danger. 'I live just down the road. Don't worry. My wife's in. It's safe. She'll look after you, and we can call the police and get you to the hospital to be checked over.'

She smiled at him. 'I've been a nuisance already, I'm okay. It was the initial shock. I'm not badly hurt, just bruised. I can walk home. Thank you.'

'Rubbish, you can't walk on this lonely road in the dark. What if he comes back? I don't want to scare you, love, but you've got a nasty bruise on your neck. Let me take you to A&E. I can have you there in five minutes.'

Hero on the outside—and bastard within.

She fingered her throat and winced, it was agony, and when she spoke, her husky voice was raspy and hoarse. 'I don't want to be any trouble.'

'It's no trouble, my dear.'

Twat.

His hand was already under her elbow. He guided her to the car. 'I'll ring my wife to let her know what's happening.'

As he reached for his phone, it rang. 'Hello. Yes—something's come up. I'll ring you back in a few minutes and tell you, darling. Yes. Put it in the oven, and I'll have it when I get back. Won't be long. Yes. Love you, too.' He made pathetic kissing noises. He never did that with her.

Bastard.

He was close to his new wife. Consuela knew that. He seemed to be in love with her, and getting her ex-husband into bed again wasn't going

350

to be easy, but he'd made the next part simple. She didn't even have to play up to him.

Consuela was examined, and the doctor filled out a prescription for painkillers. Phil insisted on driving her home from the hospital. He'd rung his wife while Consuela was with the doctor and brought her up to speed.

Guiding her into the passenger seat, he avoided too much physical contact. She directed him to the flat she'd rented when she was in England. This was the first of the brothers, except Simon, she'd had in this home, and she hated opening her front door to him. He didn't suggest buying brandy for the shock, so she suggested it, even though she had a bottle of Courvoisier in her small bar. It was a calculated move. She recreated their first meeting of twenty years earlier, though this time she had lead crystal glasses instead of chipped Easter bunny mugs.

He didn't take over or put her to bed as he had the first time. He was intimidated by Consuela and her surroundings. He was uncomfortable, and his manner was different to the way he'd been with Julie.

She poured drinks and excused herself to change in her bedroom. She contemplated lingerie, but Phil was already squirming, and she didn't want to frighten him off. She opted for a skirt that finished just above the knee and a simple fitted T-shirt. He'd had a good look at her bra, so she did away with it. She checked her appearance in the mirror to ensure the T-shirt wasn't overtly sexual—she was aiming for irresistible, not slutty. The seduction would be his idea. No matter how faithful, he'd come to her willingly. She gave her nipples a tweak. She paid a lot for them. It was time they earned their keep. They were prominent enough to get his attention.

She offered him another drink when she noticed his glass was empty. He was driving, and although she tried to tempt him, he'd only have a soft drink. Sitting next to him was too obvious, so she took the armchair facing him. She crossed her legs, flashing her thigh. Her skirt rode up when she sat, and she pulled it with modesty. Trapped beneath her, the hem sat at mid-thigh. His eyes were fixed on her as she pulled the barrette holding her hair in a loose bun. Her black hair fell in long curls to spill over her shoulders. He cleared his throat and crossed his legs.

She pandered to his ego and cooed about how he'd rescued her from the clutches of death. 'You were so brave. You came just when I needed you like a knight in shining armour,' she laughed beautifully. 'I can never repay you. But I must think of something to show my appreciation. In Spain, it's a matter of honour to refund kindness given.' She made sure it was implied as a financial proposition rather than a sexual one.

'Honestly. There's no need. This isn't the first time I've come to the aid of a damsel in distress, so to speak,' he laughed. 'I once threw a pint over a young lady who'd spilt a bowl of boiling pasta over her. Otherwise, it could have been nasty. She'd have been scarred for life. I'm a first aider, you see, so I knew what to do.'

'Really? How fascinating. Was she all right?'

'Yes. Thanks to my quick thinking, she was unharmed. In fact, I married her.'

'It was your wife?'

'Not this one. I've been married twice. Danielle's my second wife. She's far prettier—slimmer, too. Second time lucky, eh?'

'I thought it was third time lucky?' She gave him a coquettish smile. 'So, was the first one a demon?'

'I wouldn't go that far, but you have no idea. She was highly strung.'

'You don't miss her, then?'

'Her. Never. Danni's ten times the woman she was.' He looked her in the eye, 'We're very happy.'

She changed the subject. 'What do you do for work, Philip?'

'Call me Phil. My mother's the only person who calls me Philip and trust me. You are nothing like her.' He laughed again—flirting. 'I'm an HR manager for a large car manufacturer.'

'Impressive. Do you like it?'

He always did like talking about himself. 'I used to. I worked my way up from the shop floor and took this position nine years ago. But I'm bored. I've taken it as far as I can, and I'm at the top of the ladder. To improve my status, I'd have to go somewhere else, and it'd be too much of a gamble. You know what it's like, the pay's good and I'm comfortable. I provide for my family, and although the company shows me no appreciation, the salary reflects my value.'

'Sounds grim. If the circumstances fell into place, you'd like a new challenge, though?'

'God, yes. I used to go to work with such a buzz from doing a good job, but now, it's just work. I'd love something to get my teeth into, but I'll stay where I am and plod along, probably until the day I retire.'

'You've got twenty years in you yet. Could you stand that?'

'I'll take the early retirement option when it's offered. If the pay-out is good enough.'

'Interesting.' She ran a manicured fingernail around the rim of her glass, caressing the bowl of the snifter, and then she masturbated the stem. She made love to the brandy glass with her fingertips, feigning distraction, knowing he was thinking about sex. He was fantasising about having sex with her.

'Well, I'd better be going, I suppose. Danni will be wondering where I've got to.'

'Will she be waiting up for you? She must love you very much.'

He laughed again. 'And I love her very much, but I doubt she'll wait up. It's late, but she's a light sleeper and won't settle until she knows I'm home safe.'

It was now or never. She stopped fingering the glass and went in for the kill. 'Give me five minutes of your time. I have a business proposition, which you'd be a fool to turn down.' He'd listen, and he'd accept. He wouldn't want to be seen as a fool.

'I own a large company primarily based in Spain, just outside Barcelona. However, I have eleven subsidiary businesses in England. I'm constantly flying in from Spain to oversee them. I've been on the lookout for a trustworthy businessman to run my British operation. It's a big deal. Do you think you would be up to it?'

'Me? What—are you offering me a job?'

'No, I'm a businesswoman, Phil, not a fool. I'm offering you an opportunity to apply for a job. And not just any job. A massive job. So I repeat. Are you up to it?'

'Yes. Of course, I am. I have twenty years of managerial experience.'

'Save it for your CV.' As you say, it's late. She took a pen and paper from her writing desk and scribbled down an email address and mobile number. 'Here. Email me your CV. I need two references, and I want you to write down why I should hire you. Why are you the best man for my operation?'

'I'm flattered, thank you. But I don't know.'

'What do you earn?'

'A hundred and ten thousand, plus a new car on contract, every two years.'

'If you're the right man to run my office, it pays a hundred and sixty and, within reason, your choice of car, not on contract. I'll replace it every five years, and you get to keep the old one.'

'Why would you do that for me?'

'Because you saved my life, Philip. I told you, in my country, that is a debt of honour. But you haven't got the job yet. You still have to prove yourself worthy. This is the job of a lifetime, Phil. Don't let it pass you by.' She had led him towards the door. She extended her hand for him to shake. Instead, he took it and kissed the back, maintaining eye contact with her the whole time.'

She was in business mode. She didn't flirt with him. She wanted him to go away thinking about her offer first and sex second. But she knew that when he got home to his wife, he'd wake her and force her into hard sex, and she knew, with one hundred per cent certainty, that in his imagination, he would be pounding an exotic Spanish woman called Consuela, not his mumsy wife.

Chapter Thirty-Six

Things moved fast. It was better than she'd hoped. While Phil was serving his months' notice, she set up the business ready for him to walk into. Consuela had snaked her way into his life. She spent her weekends barbequing with Philip and Danielle. The second time they invited her to the house, Philip told her his mother, two brothers, and their families would be there.

Consuela said she was looking forward to it, but when the day came, she had an unfortunate business crisis that took her away from the country for the weekend. She knew she'd be discussed and hoped her nationality wasn't mentioned. She didn't want the brothers swapping stories. SP's vision had never spoken to him, so he didn't know she spoke with an accent. She hoped he still thought it was the Virgin Mary or that he'd been spiked with heroin by a known enemy. James had met a Spanish gangster's moll, a far cry from the high-flying businesswoman Phil would be working for.

Danielle wasn't the simpering mouse of a mother Consuela expected, and she liked her. The women were friends, and Consuela was sorry that she was going to hurt her. Sacrifices were unavoidable in taking down her ex-husband. His boys were sweet. Thomas could be a sulker and petulant like his father, but he was mostly a good kid. Oliver was a little sweetheart and loved his Auntie Ayla. She saw Vicki's face in both of them, and it hurt.

On the third weekend, when it was just the five of them, Connie wished she could have brought Simon. He'd have got a buzz out of it and would have loved playing with the boys. Phil was the only one of the Woods brothers who knew about Simon. He'd seen him going from the bus to his school once. Connie had read about it in his diaries. Phil wrote that Simon was ugly and stupid, 'Deeply entrenched in his disgusting mongolism,' he'd said. Connie wanted to kick him in the balls for that statement alone. Simon was ten times the man he could ever be.

The office set-up went well. She rented property in a designer complex with air conditioning and plate glass windows. Consuela had eleven subsidiary branches of Victoria's Kitchen in England. She was shutting three of them, they weren't doing well, and she brought over enough of their stock to validate the Barrow office. It was Connie's idea to give Danielle a job. She took her on as a receptionist from ten until three, Monday to Friday, with total flexibility for illness and school holidays. She was generous and gave her an eighteen grand a year salary with no deductions for the time taken off for necessary childcare. When this was over, she wanted Danielle and the boys to be okay.

Philip was her Head of Operations, and they interviewed the rest of their staff together. Phil surprised her. She'd wanted to take on a plain woman of dim intelligence to be his PA. He fought Consuela and said he wouldn't be able to work with a woman like that. Connie gave her reasons for wanting to hire her. She said that she would be honest and she seemed reliable. Her references were adequate. Phil said that she had no drive. He fought her to hire a man in his late twenties called Max Oaks. Phil said that he had ambition and balls. He could work with him and said that even his name sounded steadfast and reliable. He stood up to her, wouldn't back down and backed his horse well. She was impressed. Max was the man she'd have taken on had she been hiring for real. To complete their staff, they hired a general assistant, responsible for the admin and odd jobs. She was an ordinary girl, more than capable of the job, called Debra Thomas. Their team was established.

The surprises didn't stop. In his first week, Phil insisted on meeting all the staff at the three failing factories. He'd begged a stay of execution and said he could bring them up from their knees. Connie hadn't anticipated this. It was too close for comfort and too close to home, but Phil was determined to do a good job. He came back from his week brim-full of ideas. Most of them were good, and Connie had a newfound grudging respect for the way that the man did business. If things were different, and he'd seen her potential when they were together—and if she had seen his—they could have been formidable in the business world. His aptitude and enthusiasm made the thought of bringing him down sweeter.

In the ten years since she'd seen him, time hadn't been hard on him. He'd spread across the middle, and he had some greying at the temples, but he still had a head of black hair. Whereas she had grown six whole inches, and he was still short.

She'd had her legs broken in Russia and rods inserted and grafted into the bone to lengthen her legs. The one thing that prevented her from being recognised above everything else was this increase in her overall height.

Philip's stature was unchanged. He wore the white sports socks that had infuriated her. She remembered having sex with him and staring at the socks as he hammered into her. The white socks with sandals turned her stomach when they were abroad. She remembered his small penis and the way he'd sweat over her. He'd dripped perspiration from his forehead into her eyes, stinging them. She'd ball her fists and put them under her backside to stop her from punching him while he rode her. She thought about it all while she watched him at his desk in his crisp white shirt.

While his wife was yards away at the reception desk in the foyer, she'd flirt with him. There were days when his tiny erection had so much wood it would almost lift his desk. She knew him and how to lean over him, displaying her body when she was reaching for something. She knew how to brush against him in passing and how to insert images, ideas, and fantasies into his brain. And she knew that he got off on thinking about having sex with Consuela while his wife was working in sweet oblivion. Consuela tortured his imagination.

The office was only going to operate for a month. It was a shame, given time, Phil and Max could have turned the failing businesses around. They worked well, and Phil was hard to the point of brutal in implementing changes and making things happen.

They'd worked together for three weeks and had known each other coming up eight weeks when Connie told Phil she needed him with her on a trip to Spain. Danielle was the needy type and didn't like him being away from home. She sulked until Connie promised that if they made good time, he'd only be away for a couple of days. Connie knew it would be a week.

Danni drove them to the airport and cried when she waved Phil away. Despite leaving his wife in tears, Phil was in good humour. She knew he liked travelling because they'd done enough of it together. Phil said he had fond memories of Barcelona and was happy to have a working holiday away from his family. On the plane, he was in an excellent mood, and when the drinks trolley came around, they ordered two whisky and cokes each, all on company expenses. They travelled First Class and had leg room to stretch. After the excellent in-flight meal, Connie feigned sleepiness and dosed as the plane prepared for the descent. She pretended to sleep and let her head fall onto Phil's shoulder. She was surprised when he let it rest there. Through slitted lids, she saw him peer down her top, and when she nuzzled into his body, she saw the definition of his erection through his suit pants. He disgusted her.

When they landed, Phil woke her. She pretended embarrassment for resting on him, and he swept her apology away. Max had booked them into single rooms in the Hotel Omm. Consuela knew how to manipulate him into believing it was his idea that they stay instead at her villa. It would be easier if they worked late or very early in the day. And it was geographically more convenient to the hub of her enterprise. They could eat when they wanted to and not be disturbed by other diners. They were ideas she insinuated into his head, but he thought he'd suggested them. He rang Danni as soon as they dropped their cases in their rooms to let her know about the new arrangements. Consuela had expected fireworks, but Danni trusted her husband, and she accepted the changes without complaint. Her beef was that he was away from home, not who he was with. She trusted Consuela.

They freshened up in their ensuite bathrooms. Phil would almost certainly masturbate under the hot water, and the thought of it turned her stomach.

To start immediately, they worked from home that afternoon. Connie had arranged meetings at some of her plants for the following day and throughout the week, but they were at her villa for their first afternoon. The blistering temperatures suited her purpose. She wore a gold bikini with a sheer kaftan over it to work in. The kaftan was see-through and covered nothing, but it added titillation. She didn't need suncream and had a Mediterranean skin tone. She'd adjusted to the Spanish sun but wanted to evoke memories. She used the cheap coconut cream she had when they were together. She knew the smell turned him on. In Ibiza, on their fourth wedding anniversary, he'd bought her a perfume that was branded especially for the island. It was low-end. Nothing like what she wore now, but it was a scent that he associated with sex. She'd had some delivered from Ibiza to use that week. She pulled her mane of thick black hair into a single plait that left her shoulders bare. She was going to spend the afternoon driving him insane.

Her housekeeper and cook, Anita Castillo, had been given her hours for the following week. When Consuela was in England, Anita came in to water the plants and clean the villa, and when Consuela was home, they worked her hours accordingly. Anita produced a fantastic lunch of grilled salmon with a light salad and baked potatoes. Desert was fresh fruit, much of it from Consuela's garden. They washed their meal down with a bottle of La Rioja Alta.

She worked Phil hard in the brutal sun from one until four. She had one glass of wine, and he had drunk three. The effects of the alcohol showed, and she saw him striving to maintain a professional demeanour. He wore shorts and a tee shirt and was covered in a sheen of perspiration. His shirt was stained with wet, dark patches. He repulsed her. The office was air-conditioned, but the windows were open, and the scent of mimosa and oleander came in with the sun's heat. She was brusque and business-like as she swished around the office, and his eyes followed her like a hungry raptor.

At four, she called Anita to bring them iced tea on the terrace, and they went into the sun.

He complimented her on the garden as they sat in comfy furniture next to an oak table. She never tired of looking at her garden. Every week there was something new to see. The bougainvillaea covered the back of the villa. and trailing Wisteria hung in grape-like bunches of blooms over a trellised arbour that led to the pool. Rich scents hung in the air, and the colours were magnificent. She was truly blessed. She only needed two more things to make her life perfect. To avenge the death of her daughter and have Simon with her for at least part of the year. When they talked about her garden, he mentioned that his first wife had been a keen gardener.

They sipped their tea and relaxed in the afternoon haze. Connie took off her kaftan. She let it fall to the chair in a shimmer of gauze and stood in a skimpy bikini.

'Come on then,' she said before leading the way to the pool. She stood on the edge and dove in. Consuela had surfaced by the time he made the edge of the pool and got rid of his pathetic sandals, white socks, and wet shirt. He dove in without elegance, but not before she saw the bulge in his shorts, and he'd seen her rise with nipples erect and goose pimples on her breasts from the cool contrast of the pool against the afternoon heat.

She swam underwater and came up to duck him. They splashed and frolicked in the water, and she laughed, happy and fake. She remembered past times of playing in pools with Vicki, and Consuela wanted to hold his head under the water and watch the bastard die.

There was skin-on-skin contact. She rose in front of him, and he grabbed her roughly. His face was inches from hers, and water dripped from his fringe. He was going to kiss her. His head moved towards her. She opened her mouth a touch, and then in the second before their lips met, she splashed him and swam away. It was too soon. They would kiss, and he'd be eaten with guilt, and that would be it. When Consuela took Philip Woods to bed again, she wanted him ripe to explode so there could be no going back.

She pretended she wasn't aware of his intention. She played with him as though nothing had happened. The next time she floated up behind him. She wrapped her legs around his body before pushing him underwater and swimming the length of the pool without either of them coming up for air. At the deep end, they rose against the edge. To get to the ladder, she had to pass in front of him. She could have swum clear, but she clung to the edge taking her hand across his body to grab hold of the other side. Her knee came up with the buoyancy of the water and brushed against the front of his shorts. His manhood was like iron and stuck straight out in front of him. Her fingers travelled across his chest, a red talon grazing his nipple as she transferred from one side of him to the other in the deep water. The touch was a mere brush, but when her leg grazed his penis, he gasped, and when the pressure was lifted, he groaned, unable to stop himself.

She was satisfied with her opening gambit and swam to the ladder. As she pulled herself out of the pool, the water cascaded off her body in pearl droplets against the barrier of the sun cream. The weight of water captured in her bikini bottoms pulled them down, showing him that she had no tan lines. If he noticed her perfect scarring, he never made comment. He stayed in the pool.

When he joined her in the office, he was calm and in control. She knew he'd ejaculated. She'd been with him for ten years. She knew nothing calmed him until he'd had sexual release when he was horny. She hoped he'd gone to his room to do it and hadn't contaminated her pool. He was freshly showered and dressed in a clean shirt and shorts. They worked until dinner time.

Dinner was served at eight. They ate fresh fish with vegetables, followed by a dessert of mangos in a light torte. Their wine selection included a vintage Marques de Caseres, followed by sangria on the terrace and ending the night with vodka and brandy. They stayed up late and talked about work, about family and life. He'd changed a lot. He was a better human being, but she still hated the man that he'd been, and Vicki wasn't given any second chances. Why should he have them? She would destroy him. They were drunk. When he kissed her goodnight, she allowed him to kiss her on the lips, not on each cheek as was normal. She let his lips press against hers for a fraction of a second longer than was polite before she was the one to pull away. He dropped his hands to cover the inevitable erection.

Chapter Thirty-Seven

The next morning he was all business. She knew from the efficient way that he spoke to her, that the kiss was at the forefront of his mind. He was guilty. Since kissing her on the mouth, he'd blown sweet kisses down the phone to his wife.

They had a busy day. She listened to Phil's opinion and pretended to care. The meetings were staging, the trip a fabrication. She didn't need him there. But as with the business in England, what he said made sense. She saw ways of cutting costs and increasing productivity without alienating her workforce, who she valued and treated well in return for loyal employment. She intended to use some of Phil's suggestions going forward.

The next night, after returning to the villa to shower and change, they went out. Connie took him to an excellent Cantonese restaurant, and they bar-hopped before falling into a club and dancing until the early hours. Connie kept fit with Zumba. Twice a week, she found it a great release of work tension to dance the Zumba. She was lithe and danced well, and she was sexy without being slutty, outstanding without being exhibitionist, and Philip strutted like a king next to her. Every man's eyes were on the woman he was out with. Connie doubted he thought about his wife once.

When the music slowed, he took her in his arms, and they swayed into a rhythmic waltz. After a few bars, she dropped his hand and let her arms slide around his neck. She pressed her body against the length of his. Hello, how did I know you'd be there? She swayed her hips, and with each sashay, her pelvis brushed against his penis. Her head was against his shoulder, and she sang in Spanish as they danced. She was driving him wild, and his breath, hot against her ear, was raspy and uneven. He was drunk, his inhibitions were compromised with alcohol and his feeling of well-being. She hadn't pushed him away, and he was led by his cock. He didn't try to hide his erection. He knew she'd felt it and that he was being played with. He was powerless to resist.

As they danced, he was bolder. He let his hands drop from her waist to her bottom. When she didn't resist, he increased the pressure under his hands and pulled her to him while thrusting his pelvis into her body. They wore thin clothing. Consuela was in a sun dress with no bra and only a tiny thong. Philip was in a pair of linen trousers and a dress shirt. She was aware of every vein and contour of his penis as it thrust against her. She maintained the rhythm of her dance while he dry-humped her on the dance floor. His breath was in full sexual flow, he moaned twice when his sensitive glans rubbed against her pubic bone. He even dropped a couple of disgusting, wet kisses onto her neck. The dirty bastard was going to come in his shorts if she didn't pull away.

Thankfully, the song ended before he did. 'I think we'd better get a drink to cool down,' she muttered in his ear.

'One more dance,' he whined.

One more molestation was closer to the mark. 'I think we've had too much alcohol,' she laughed. 'We need a soft drink to allow the mood to soften, don't you think?'

He blushed. She was cool and in control. He was erect, hot, sweating and on the point of losing his load in his pants. He gained enough control to get to the bar. His erection dwindled, and he wiped his sweaty face with a hanky. But his mind and his imagination were still turgid. She knew that. Danni was the last thing on his mind, and she could have had him if she'd wanted to.

She didn't, not yet.

He tried to paw her at the bar, in the taxi on the way home, and in the living room when they were at the villa. She laughed him off, flirting with him while keeping the mood light and him at arm's length.

The next morning he came to breakfast shamefaced. She was the first to speak. She touched his arm as he sat at the table. Anita was in the kitchen, but she kept her voice low. 'I want to apologise for my appalling behaviour last night. My only excuse is that I was drunk. It's been a long time since I had a strong, virile man in my arms, and I was caught up in the moment. If you want to cut the trip short, I can book you a flight home today, but I can assure you, it won't happen again.'

He let her take sole responsibility and blame the utter bastard. 'Oh, think nothing of it. I don't want to leave before the work's finished. We came out here to do a job, and that's what I'm going to do. We'll just make sure you have one less vodka tonight so you don't get carried away again.'

He'd ply her with as much alcohol as he could get down her throat. Like a hypnotist, she'd inserted triggers into his brain. He all but forgot he had a wife, apart from the pathetic and insipid duty calls home. His master was lustful, and he was in his master's grip. Consuela wiggled her hips, and his penis dripped like a tap.

She was ready to take him when the time was right.

She fended his advances until their last night in Spain. She couldn't bear the thought of more than one intimate night with him. By the time dinner was finished and Anita had left for the night, she had him panting like a dog. She didn't need to brush against him any longer. He did enough of that for both of them. She was pouring after-dinner drinks when he came up behind her. She wore a backless evening dress and felt his fingers on the bare flesh across her shoulders.

He mistook her shudder for one of arousal. She fought every instinct in her body that wanted to smash her glass on the hostess bar, then spin around and ram it into his face. She envisaged striking once, pulling back, striking again to his eyes, and pulling back. And striking a third time into the carotid artery in his throat and watching him bleed out. Consuela leaned back into his hand, giving him the encouragement he sought.

Bingo!

Let's do this.

His lips dropped to the nape of her neck. When they lifted, he left a saliva imprint of his mouth on her skin. She remembered him once filling his mouth with saliva and mucus. He purposefully spat it into her hair when she'd annoyed him in front of his parents, and he couldn't do anything about it in the open. He kissed her, and she pushed her bottom into his groin. His hand moved to the front and grabbed her between the legs. He was raising her skirt with his other hand. He hadn't learned any finesse in the years that they'd been apart, whereas she was an excellent lover with no shortage of partners to hone her abilities. He was going to take her right there bent over her designer bar.

She swung around and kissed him on the mouth. His filled with saliva and it dripped from his mouth into hers. She fought the urge to gag. Vomiting in his mouth would be payback for the slaver in kind and would give her immense satisfaction but wasn't the way forward when she had filthy sex in mind.

She led him to the bedroom where the recording equipment was already filming.

Chapter Thirty-Eight

S imon had folded his underwear, his six pairs of shorts and six vests and six tee shirts and two hats and one pair of sunglasses and two pairs of sandals, six pairs of underwear and six pairs of shorts and six pairs of underwear and six pairs of socks and six tee shirts and six pairs of underwear and six pairs of socks. Simon worried that he wouldn't have enough clothes to wear in Spain. Ayla told him that she does have a washing machine, you know and wanted to take nearly all of Simon's clothes out of his big blue suitcase. They had a big argue. Simon had a seizure, and Simon won. Simon was worried that he wouldn't have enough clothes to wear in Spain. Ayla worried about breaking her back. She'd taken him shopping because they were going on a big plane to Spain the next day, but first, they were going to a really posh party that night, and it was very special. When they were shopping, Ayla said he only needed six pairs of underpants, but Simon was worried, and every time she turned her back, he put another six pairs of underpants and another six pairs of socks in the trolley. He had a big lot of underwear.

Simon sang, 'Oh my dear, I'm ob to summy Spain, Eh biba Esbanya,' until Ayla told him that if he sang it just one more time, she'd put him on a different plane and book him into a villa in Tahiti. But Simon knew she was only joking. He was very excited. Ayla had her own swimming pool, and Simon could swim in it every day. She said she'd shout at him if he peed in it. He peed when he went swimming in the sea, and he sometimes peed in the shower, but he didn't tell Ayla that. He'd never been on a big plane before, and he was going to go right up in the sky. Ayla said he'd be all the way up higher than the clouds, and when he looked out of the window, the clouds would be on the bottom of him and not on the top. That was very strange indeed. Ayla said he'd have to sit on his head in the plane to make the world come the right way up again, but Simon didn't think that was true. He thought it was another joke, but he packed a cushion to put under his head, just in case. Ayla took the cushion out of his suitcase and told him he wouldn't need it, and said he wouldn't need all his big cardigans and jumpers and he wouldn't need his parka coat. She said she'd buy him lots of new Spanish clothes, in lovely bright colours, when they got there.

Simon was big excited about going to Spain on a big plane, and he was big excited about the posh party tonight he had all this big excitement inside his tummy getting all mixed up, so he didn't know which excitement was the plane and which excitement was the party.

He farted, and his tummy felt better, and Ayla called him a *cerdo sucio*, which means dirty pig. Simon was a bit sad because when he was younger, there were a whole lot of people that he'd like to have said *cerdo sucio* to. But now he only knew people who were nice to him. He had a brand-new thing to say to the horrible people, but the horrible people had all gone. Ayla laughed and said that only he could worry about having a good life. Then she sang, 'It's like rain on your wedding

371

day. It's a free ride when you've already paid,' but Simon didn't know that one. He didn't think he was getting married. So he sat down when he was supposed to be packing, and he had a big think about it. Ayla told him he'd have his choice of *cerdo suckios* to choose from that night. Simon was worried then, and he hadn't even finished worrying about not having enough clothes to wear in Spain yet. Was it going to be a bad party with horrible people? Being Spanish, maybe Ayla didn't know what a party was. Simon was good at knowing parties. He'd been to lots of parties, and he knowed them all. He knowed jelly and ice cream and party hats and balloons that made you spit when you tried to blow them up—but they never went up. Simon didn't want to go to no place where 'Horrible People' meant 'Party' in Spanish.

Ayla spent a lot of time telling Simon what she wanted him to do at the party. They'd been practising for ages. She made him happy by telling him that they were going to do a kind of play and he was going to be the main actor man. She said they'd have a wonderful time and if there were any horrible people there, it didn't matter, because they'd be together and they'd laugh at the horrible people and make them go away. Simon had never laughed at horrible people, but with Ayla, he thought he could do it in a kind of play when he was the main actor man. He felt bery ibporbant.

Ayla laid out his black thirty-six-inch-waist trousers that went back to the shop to be exchanged for new ones, and now they weren't a thirty-six-inch-waist anymore, they were thirty-eight-inch-waist trousers, but they were still black. And she laid out his new blue shirt with silver pinstripes. And she told him to make sure that when he got in the shower, he washed all of himself and didn't try to get away with one of his two-minute cat licks.

Simon didn't want a shower. He was going to have a long bath, and he was going to put soft bubbles in it. They were peach, and when they were in the bottle, they were a kind of orange and pink colour mashed together like ice cream. He was going to use his blue shower gel and his shampoo and conditioner. And then he was going to put aftershave on and his silver chain and his black shoes that were shiny and good for dancing in. Ayla would tell him he looked good enough to eat and that she was proud of him, and then she'd call him *cielo*.

Simon was ready to go to the party at four o'clock. He knew it was a long time until half past seven when Ayla was coming to pick him up. He said oops and sat very still so that he wouldn't crease his new shirt and trousers with the thirty-eight-inch waist.

It was the day of the garden party, and Phil was in the bad books as he left for work. Danni had wanted him to take the whole day off to be with her and the boys, but he had a backlog of work on his desk and insisted on going until lunchtime. When he got to work and pulled his car into his personal parking space, with his name painted on the floor, he found that his was the only car there. The blinds were drawn on the office windows. Max and that dim admin girl were supposed to be in from eight, and it was just short of nine o'clock. He put his key in the lock, and the door opened into a space that was empty. Literally empty. There was neither a potted plant nor a stick of furniture in the building. Desks, computers, filing cabinets and whiteboards—were all gone. He thought they'd been burgled. Until he saw the note pinned to the toilet door.

My Darling Philip. Your services are no longer required. I have dispensed with the staff and have cleared the office. Your employment is terminated with immediate effect. On a personal note, I should return home straight away if I were you. Your world is about to crash down around your ears, and your wife needs you.

Vengeance will be mine, Goodbye.

Yours never, Conseula xxx

His mind was racing. He thought it was an elaborate joke. Consuela wasn't answering her phone. It rang with the discordant tone of a phone withdrawn from service. He was reeling. He'd never been a man of keen wit. The subtleties of Consuela's joke trickled into his mind drop by acidic drop. His world had turned upside down.

They'd arranged for Danni and the boys to go to the hotel early. Phil was worried sick when he turned into their drive and saw her car was still there.

In his haste to find out what was wrong, his key got stuck in the door. Danni promised she'd go to the hotel to help with the last-minute arrangements. She was good at organisation and very reliable. Violet liked her. She'd never have let her mother-in-law down or faced her disapproval unless something was wrong. Something must have happened to one of his boys. He felt cold dread gripping his stomach. 'What is it?

What's the matter? Are the boys all right?' he yelled, bursting into the lounge.

The children weren't there. Danni sat on the sofa, her face red and swollen with heartbreak, tears distorted her face, and she was ugly crying, but she didn't say a word.

A DVD was running on the recorder when he'd gone into the room. Danni stopped it, pressed rewind, and set it playing again. He was frozen to the floor. And he was transfixed on the TV screen—horrified. She pressed stop, and rewind. The movie halted and then ran backwards, and Phil saw the foul images running in reverse for a few seconds. She hit stop and play. The same section of the movie played again.

Phil was lying on a bed. His mind raced, wondering if he could say that it was a superimposed image of his face on somebody else's body, but he couldn't. It was him, and there was no escaping it.

He was naked on a bed with Consuela's head between his legs. He watched himself bend forward so that he could watch her. His screen face was contorted in ecstasy—his real one in horror. His wife was watching the exact moment that he came, and Connie pulled her head away at the last second. Danni didn't say a word. She pressed stop, and rewind. She hit stop and play, and the sequence began.

'Honey, it meant nothing. I can explain.'

Danni spoke like a robot. Her voice sounded as though her larynx was made of metal. 'Get your things and get out.'

He saw the note from Connie on the arm of the chair. Presumably, it had come through the post with the DVD. He picked it up, and the note informed Danni that her employment had been terminated and

375

her husband was crap in bed. Philip couldn't take it in. He wanted his Mother. She'd make it better.

'It's Mother's garden party,' he said in a pathetic voice. 'You should get ready. You're not dressed yet.'

'Get out.'

Philip left the house without another word. He'd go to the party and wouldn't say anything today. It would spoil Mummy's big event. Danni needed time to calm down, and then they'd move forward and put this behind them. It wouldn't be too bad if he had to buy her a new car or something to get over her silly tantrum.

He'd pretend everything was fine when he got there. It might be fun. He'd have a laugh with James. He could pretend. He could do that. Danni would be okay, and he'd deal with her tomorrow. Consuela had shown him that Danni was boring anyway. It had been good up to now, but if she was going to get heavy—like the last one, he was better off without her. Phil liked being single and was more worried about his job than his marriage. He felt that he might have a nervous breakdown.

But it could all wait until tomorrow.

Chapter Thirty-Nine

When Consuela picked Simon up, she took him to Burger King, which was one of his favourite places on Earth. She wasn't sure they'd be at the party long enough to get anything to eat. While he grinned from behind a massive burger, Ayla delved in her bag for wipes and adjusted the serviette at Simon's chin to make sure he didn't spill down himself. She wasn't going to give that family any excuse to mock him. Simon was happy, and nothing was going to fracture that.

In the limousine on the forty-five-minute drive to Windermere, Ayla broached the subject of Violet. She'd been picking her moment to tell him. She had to prepare him for seeing his mother again, but she didn't want him to melt down and had to handle it delicately. Consuela had too much at stake in the night to risk Simon blowing his stack. When he faced his family, she wanted him to do it tall and proud. A man with dignity, just as they'd practised.

'Simon, I've got another surprise for you.'

His face lit up, and he turned towards her. 'A subride? Ayla, Shimon's all full up with Burger King and subridesis. Shimon's gonna go pop. What new subride?'

Consuela laughed, but anybody who didn't have Simon's simplistic view of the world would notice the tremor and nervousness. 'Your Mother's coming to watch our play. Isn't that fantastic?' It broke her heart to see his face fall. He hadn't seen Violet in two years, and those had been the happiest years of his life.

'Shimon not know. Not.' He spoke with such sadness. 'Shimon miss Mummy, some little times, but all some big times, Shimon not miss Mummy. Shimon scared.'

She put her arm around him. 'Simon, you don't have to be frightened. We're doing the play, and you're the star of the show, just like we said. Yes?'

'Yes,' his eyes were solemn, 'Shimon Scared.'

'When you stand in front of all of those people and do your play, your mummy is going to be so proud of you.'

Simon smiled but looked doubtful.

'Let's go through it again, just how it's going to be so that you're happy to get it right and make your mummy proud.' To distract him from thoughts about his mother, Consuela took him through what would happen when they got to the hotel.

The party was loud. It had been going since eleven that morning. A tradition built over the years was the Halcyon Woods Summer Garden Party, second only to the Queen's garden party, and coming second place to that was debatable in Violet's opinion. The day was the main event in the Windermere calendar. Everybody would be there.

During the day, anybody with a fat wallet was welcome. There was entertainment, stalls, and food, all at a healthy financial premium. They

378

had tournaments, archery, It's-a-Knockout, the X-Factor, face painting, donkey rides and food enough to sink a ship.

The evening was a genteel affair, with the Windermere elite dining in the banqueting hall. There was an elegant sit-down meal with after-dinner speeches, followed by a string quartet and a ceilidh for the lively who wanted to dance.

Consuela timed it so they'd arrive in the middle of the speeches. Her special delivery arrived on time, and while everybody was occupied inside the banqueting hall at the back of the hotel, she talked to the pallbearers and explained what they would do. It was a shame the four black stallions pulling the white casket had gone unnoticed, but the detail was everything. Giving a cursory glance at the coffin and the flowers, she made sure everything was in order.

She peeped through the door, waiting for Violet to position herself behind the podium for her speech. Mother duck headed the proceedings, in a prime position to see—and be seen.

Consuela motioned to her helper for the music and gave a nod to the four men holding the tiny coffin.

Showdown!

As it had on the day of the funeral all of those years earlier, the strains of *All Things Bright and Beautiful* played to the people. She'd gone to great effort to recreate everything exactly as it had been that day. The flowers were identical. The brass plaque on the top of the white coffin with gold furniture read, *In memory of our lovely angel.* And the sandbag inside the coffin was similar, if not identical, to the one giving weight to the proceedings so long ago.

The pallbearers walked in a slow, dignified death march down the centre aisle of the banqueting hall. At the head of the walkway, they stopped and waited for Consuela to catch up. When the music was turned off, a deadly hush fell over the room. You could hear a pin drop.

'What's going on? What's the meaning of this outrage? Who are you?' Violet seethed with rage. She didn't grasp the implications of what was happening—until she did—and the colour drained from her face.

'That's Maria Callas,' James shouted.

'Consuela, what are you doing here?' Philip said, jumping to his feet.

Consuela waved him down, and he sat like an obedient puppy. 'I need to talk to you,' he hissed. 'You've ruined my marriage, you bitch.'

'You got off lightly, mate,' James said. 'She put me in a wheelchair.'

Connie held up her hand for silence, and everybody, Violet included, stopped speaking. The old crone blew out of her mouth hard like a distended fish.

Her helper was Paul Morley, the brother of a young chef who once had the misfortune to work under James. Paul wheeled a trolley beside her, and Consuela picked up a frame protected with a midnight blue velvet cover. She took her time revealing the portrait before kissing it. She showed it to the audience and placed it on top of the white coffin, facing Violet.'

The colour left the older woman's face. She was bleached of tone and bluster, and the makeup stood out on her cheekbones. She stared at the portrait of the handsome man, horrified. Groping behind her for the stability of a chair, she wilted into it in a swoon. Violet's dramatics amused Consuela. Excitement, as the culmination of her ten-year plan, came to fruition and made her skin glow. There was no pity in her heart for these people.

The crowd had enjoyed their day, feasted on the meal, and resigned themselves to the inevitable speeches. They asked what was going on in confused whispers. SP bent down beside Violet, and the crowd were thrilled by the unexpected entertainment. You could always rely on them Woodses'es to put on a show. There wasn't a family like them for scandal. Consuela cleared her throat, and a reverent hush fell over the room.

'Some of you will remember attending a funeral long ago. The tragic funeral of a baby on the third of November nineteen sixty-three.' There was a whoosh of whispers around the room, and a few of the older people nodded their heads, wondering what was going on.

'Violet Woods was very young. She had her first child, a boy, born in wedlock, but only by a matter of weeks. He was stillborn, and some of you attended his funeral.' She indicated the coffin with her hand.

'Jesus, sweet mother of God, she's only gone and dug 'im up.' One of the locals drew the sign of the cross on her body as she spoke.

SP helped Violet up. He was taking her away from this nonsense and called Ros to hold her arm. Consuela swung on them, 'Leave her alone. Sit down. She's not leaving until I've had my say.'

'That woman's mad,' James shouted. She put me in this wheelchair. Somebody call the police.'

Nobody moved.

Consuela rested her hand on the coffin. 'In memory of our lovely angel,' she read. She picked a flower from the wreath forming the word *SON* and smelt it. She smiled before speaking. Nobody moved.

'Ladies and Gentlemen, you must be wondering what this is about. I'm here to introduce you to the baby that was buried back in nineteen sixty-three. He's not a baby any longer. He's a fine man. It is with great pleasure that I introduce to you the eldest child of Donald and Violet Woods. I give you, Mr Simon Peter Woods.'

The doors at the end of the great room opened with a creak, and Simon walked through them. He was beaming and stood very straight, just as Ayla had taught him to do. He held the white, word flowers that Ayla told him spelt out *Mother*. He walked carefully and slowly, counting one elephant between each step. It took a long time to stop saying, 'One elephant,' out loud, and he had to walk up and down his living room a lot of times until he remembered not to shout it. His feet hurt a lot, and he worried that all that walking up and down on his nice carpet would make there be no nice carpet left. He was walking on a wooden floor now, like his name. That was funny, but he didn't laugh because that wasn't part of the play. Not. His feet made a big click, click, click noise, but he wasn't worried about it because Ayla told him that it might be quiet in there, and it was good if his shoes made a big noise because that was dra-mat-ic for the play. He was worried because in the car Connie had changed the play. He was supposed to put the white flowers that spelt the word *Mother* on the white box. But now she said he had to walk up to Mummy and give her the flowers. If she wouldn't take them, he had to put them in her lap, and it didn't matter. Not. If she threw them on the floor because that might be part of the play, too. It was a bery confusing play.

Simon walked up to his mother and offered her the wreath. Violet made a strangled noise in the back of her throat and lifted her hands in the air as if the flowers were a snake. Simon was beaming at his mummy. He wanted to make her proud. He really wanted to say hello to her, but Consuela was very strict about that. She said he wasn't allowed to say anything unless she spoke to him with a direct question. That was part of the play.

Just like he was told, he turned around by putting his heel down on the floor and lifting his toes up and spinning on his heel. He liked doing that. It was the best bit of the play and bery dra-mat-tic. He walked over to Connie, but he couldn't remember if he had to count, one elephant. He was going to worry if he got worried. And if he worried, he might throw a fit and ruin the play. But before he got worried, he had an idea. He'd count one kangaroo, instead, because they were smaller than elephants. He nearly ruined the play because he was used to counting elephants and wasn't used to counting kangaroos, so he counted them out loud, and most of the people watching the play laughed. Some old ladies gave him a big clap, and so he did a big bow. Then Ayla came over and took his hand and calmed him down, and walked him to the white box.

Simon beamed.

When Consuela announced him as Simon Peter, SP stood up and demanded to know what the hell was going on. Consuela told him to have patience and that all would be revealed. Then she spoke to the crowd.

'This man, Ladies and Gentlemen, is Violet's first-born child. But as you can see, he isn't dead. Look at him. Isn't he magnificent?'

The row of three old ladies clapped again, and Simon felt bery important. It was a bery good play, and he was a bery good actor as well as a bery good singer.

'Shall we see who's in the casket?' There was a collective gasp around the room. The replica coffin wasn't nailed shut and opened easily. She swept the flowers off the top and opened the lid. Several people at the back of the room stood up to get a better view.

Consuela lifted the bundle of white lace from the casket as you'd lift a baby, and a woman five rows back fainted. Consuela pulled a 4lb sandbag from inside the Christening gown and held it up for the people to see. 'This bag of sand, or one just like it, is what Violet Woods buried. It was in the grave she tended so lovingly for the last forty years. And this fine man,' she pointed at Simon, who grinned even bigger, 'is the son—Violet was so ashamed of. She packed him off to an institution, where he spent most of his life. He has a condition that I'm sure you are all aware of. Simon has Downs Syndrome,' Simon said the words with Connie. It wasn't part of the play for him to say them too, but he liked saying that he was a fine man with Downs Syndrome, so he said those words when she did. He wanted to be big in the play again.

'Simon's condition makes him different to other people, but if wealth was measured by good attributes in a human being, Simon could buy and sell any one of the Woods a thousand times over.' Simon didn't understand all those words, but he knew it was a bery important part of the play. The old ladies clapped a lot this time, and one of them shouted, 'Hooray.' Simon thought the ladies liked him bery much. Maybe they would invite him to their house for tea one day and cakes because he was such a good actor.

It was the next bit of the play. Simon thought this was a boring bit and had suggested an awful lot of times that Connie let him sing a song instead of this bit. He wanted to be centre stage, but he didn't have another big bit in the play until the end. All he was doing was passing pictures to Ayla. Anybody could do that. You didn't need to be a good actor to do it. He wanted to sing a song, but Ayla brought a chair over for him to sit on until it was his time to get up.

Simon sulked, but the old ladies kept smiling. The man in the wheelchair, like the one that Bernie Roberts had at Great Gables, was staring at him. He looked really mad at Simon, so Simon didn't look at him at all. Not. Maybe he wanted to be a great actor man, too, and to get up at the front and do the play, but he couldn't on account of being in a wheelchair. That was bery sad, and Simon wanted to smile at him, but the man was too angry.

Ayla pulled four pictures out of the cloth. They were smaller than the picture of Simon. That's because Simon's picture was the specialest one. She showed the pictures to the people before giving them to Simon to hold.

The man in the wheelchair, the man standing beside Mummy, another man who was drunk, and some ladies were arguing with Mummy about the baby what didn't die—and about Simon. Simon was confused. Ayla didn't tell him if this was part of the play, and Simon needed to know. People shouldn't argue in the middle of the play. Not. That was rude. And if they were being rude, Simon wanted to tell them to shut up. But he didn't know if it was part of the play. Simon decided to tell them to shut up anyway, so he put his finger over his lips. He looked at the people arguing with Mummy and made a loud shush noise without getting too much spit on his fingers.

The old ladies clapped.

Simon wanted to see if they would clap if he did something else. So he got the pictures of the boring people, and he jiggled them on his lap to make it look like they were dancing. The old ladies clapped like mad and beamed. Simon grinned at them. Ayla came over to whisper in his ear that he was spoiling the play. Simon thought that was not fair. Not. The people arguing with Mummy were making a lot of bad noise, and she didn't shout at them. Ayla whispered that it was her bit now. She held her hand up and said, 'Ah, ah,' when he was going to argue, so he didn't and shut his mouth. She said that if he did anything else that they hadn't practised, he wouldn't be able to stand up at the end, and that's when he got to take a big bow. Ayla told him to act out 'sitting quietly on a chair.' And then she went back to the people.

Connie took another large picture from the cloth and held it up to the people. This one wasn't framed like Simon's picture was, so he thought it might be a little bit special. Connie held the picture in front of her.

Every trace of the Spanish accent disappeared from Consuela's voice. She spoke in her old accent—like Julie Spencer. She saw it as Julie making a cameo appearance in her life for the last time before she was banished forever. Her voice was deeper than before, but those who knew her as Julie recognised it.

'Some of you will know the person in this picture. Her name was Julie Woods. Ten years ago, she was married to Philip Woods. He was a bad husband and a bad father. He took their little girl and murdered her.' She wheeled on Philip and screamed at him, 'You killed our daughter, you murderer.'

Nobody understood what was going on. The drunken man came over and grabbed the picture out of Consuela's hands, and looked from it to her.

'You're not Julie. It's impossible.' He heard but didn't believe what was in front of him. 'You look nothing like her. You can't be. You're taller.' He motioned with his hand to show how tall Julie had been.

'I have had twenty-seven operations to look like this. I lay in traction in a Russian clinic for six months to gain six inches in height. I've had my larynx operated on and almost every part of my body. I learned to speak a new language, and I became somebody new. I'm somebody that I like. When you were unfaithful to your new wife and had sex with me three nights ago, rutting in my bed like a disgusting animal, you had no idea you were sleeping with your ex-wife.'

The crowd gasped. This was the best thing they'd seen in the long, scandalous run of the Wood's time in the village.

When Consuela told the brothers to bring Violet to the front where they could see and hear what was said, they did. James shouted obscenities, but he wanted to know what this was about as much as the rest of them. SP had taken heroin that morning to get him through the day. He'd slipped off to his room at lunchtime to top up, and he'd had a lot of alcohol to carry him into oblivion. The image he'd seen was indistinct in his memory, but a cold feeling crept through his addled brain cells, telling him he'd seen the woman by the coffin before. He was high and had trouble grasping what was happening. He was happy to sit in an addled daze. Philip was drunk and in shock. Like James, he shouted comments from the peanut gallery, but mostly he was sullen and listened to what the woman who had wrecked his life—again—had to say.

Simon arranged the photographs in order and passed Connie, one of the men with the black glasses, first.

'Simon Peter the Second, Ladies and Gentlemen. A fine upstanding pillar of society—wouldn't you agree?' The crowd looked at SP. His head slumped to one side. He was trying to focus, but her moving hands made it difficult.

'He was born an imposter. He was given the title of heir to the Woods' estate. A title that wasn't his to own. What kind of sick woman gives her second child the same name as her challenged firstborn? Simon Peter was raised, educated, and groomed throughout his childhood to take over the family business. Simon Peter has taken the right of his older brother's inheritance. He's taken his name. And while he's lived with his mouth around a silver spoon, the original brother has mouldered in a facility away from prying eyes. Simon has never known one moment of maternal love. His mother visited once a week out of a sense of guilt and duty. She resented him for it and hated him for what he was. Look at the second Simon Peter and compare him to the man sitting over there.' She pointed at Simon, and every head in the room turned to look at him except Violet. She hung hers in shame. It was supposed to be her special day of the year. She was in shock and hummed a hymn to herself.

Simon beamed with pride, but he kept laughing at Ayla talking in the funny voice. 'Aye, lass, tha knows.' He shouted in a northern accent so that everybody could hear, and he tapped the side of his nose. One of the old ladies clapped her hands in delight.

Consuela carried on talking. 'Which one, do you think, is the thief, Ladies and Gentlemen? Which one has stolen from the business for years? And which is a pathetic heroin addict? On the other hand, which one do you think is a son any mother would be proud of because he's sweet and funny and kind? Which is a good man, would you say?'

SP slurred, trying to get to his feet and failing, 'That's slander.'

'Shut up, or get out,' Consuela spat at him. 'You're a worthless human being. What kind of husband have you been? What kind of man?' SP sank into his chin. His outburst took the last of his energy, and he had nothing else to say. James shouted in defence of his brother, but Consuela told him to be quiet, or she'd have him wheeled out of the room.

She handed the photo of SP back to Simon, and he passed her the next one. This man had a red jumper on.

'John Woods,' Consuela said. 'Thief, gambler, swindler, and womaniser. Are we seeing a pattern emerging? He conned his mother out of thousands, and still, she bailed him out when his gambling was criminal. What kind of father was this man when he was out bedding hundreds of women during the course of his marriage? He's dead now. And good riddance.'

The next picture was of the man with the long hair and the beard.

'Of the five Woods' boys who were allowed to grow up in the wealth and splendour of the family home, Andrew is the best of the rancid lot.' Several of the crowd nodded, and some muttered their agreement. 'He's no longer with us, but the world is a better place without him.' Somebody made a comment about not speaking ill of the dead, but Consuela continued.

'This man was also a thief. He forged watches and made vast amounts of money. He was involved in gang crime, and the money he brought to the mafia bought arms and drugs. He was a drug addict. He brought his children up in a commune, sleeping with women who weren't his children's mothers. He grew drugs on his property and lived a life of loose morals. This one immersed himself in crime until the day he died.'

Philip wept for his dead brothers as though Connie had read out a touching eulogy. 'Andrew was a good man,' he shouted.

She took up the second to last photo and glared at James. The crowd looked at him too. 'This man is a thug. He's gone through life beating his wife and brawling. He thinks his evil temper can carry him through. He's bullied to the point of breaking people of a weaker character. He has driven people to suicide. James Woods has to wear a dress to come down from the pressure of always being the hard man, bawling people out, and fighting. Inside, he's a frightened little boy. Every time he hurt somebody, Mummy signed a cheque and got him off the hook. He's scum, pathetic.'

'You put me in this wheelchair, you crazy cow.'

'No, you fool. You put yourself in it. I didn't force you into illegal backstreet fighting with Neanderthal thugs. You begged me to set it up. You're a vain, egotistical, pathetic human being.'

Chapter Forty

C onsuela replaced James' photo with Phil's. Simon, playing to the audience in general and his old ladies in particular, spread his hands to show they were empty because he'd been putting the used pictures under his chair so they didn't get mixed up. When he spread his hands and made a surprised face, he looked at his ladies, but they didn't clap. They were staring at Ayla and listening to every word she said. Simon went into a big sulk. If they weren't going to give him no more big claps, he might not even bother getting up and doing the great acting in the play. He might not even take his big bow at the end. And when they send the invitation to go to their house for tea and cakes, he might just tell them, 'No thanks you,' and not go—but that all depended on what kind of cakes.

Consuela had the picture of Philip but looked at the man in person before turning the photograph around for the people to see. 'Thank you for bearing with me because I've almost saved the best until last. I've run out of photos, but there's still one left to tell you about after Philip Woods, my ex-husband. Philip Woods,' she repeated the name as though she was tasting the words in her mouth, and it was sour. 'I've told you he took my little girl and killed her. She drowned in the pond a few feet from where you're sitting. Accident, they said. It was no accident. It was murder by way of neglect.'

Phil jumped out of his seat, and although he'd sobered since Consuela's entrance, he staggered and almost fell over. 'You're evil. You're the devil coming here with a coffin and all your games. It's sick.'

'And who made me sick, Philip? Who spread the evil and infected me with it? Who took sweet Julie Spencer and turned her into somebody filled with hatred and rage? You did, you bastard.'

Simon made a surprised face and covered his mouth with his hand, it was partly because he wanted to get back in the play, but it was more because Ayla used the dirty word. 'Dirty word,' he shouted, and some people laughed. He felt better, but most people were still looking at Ayla and the drunk man. 'Dirty word, dirty Bird,' he tried for another laugh.

'Be quiet, Simon,' Ayla said, and she sounded annoyed with him, so he put his head down and thought about going on a big plane to Spain and then he forgot all about being in a sulk. She'd turned back to Philip.

'That's not all you did, though, is it Phil? Should we tell Mummy about the blackmail?'

Phil's eyes darted around the room. Consuela thought he was going to run for it. He was more worried about conning a few quid out of his mother than he was about taking his daughter's life.

'Shut up, and get out, you evil witch. Haven't you upset my family enough?' He didn't wait for a reply, which Consuela felt was a great shame because she had an answer ready for him.

'Yes, make her go away, Philip. I don't like her,' Violet spoke for the first time and raised her head to examine Consuela and see if she really was that Julie from the past.

'That was the problem, Violet. You never did like me? You never gave me a chance. You looked at my background, found me lacking and did everything in your power to stop Philip from marrying me.'

'Simon Peter, Philip, she's being nasty to me. Make her stop.'

'Oh shut up, I'll get to you in a minute,' Consuela said.

'Why's she saying she's going to get to me? I don't know her.'

'Shush, Mother and listen,' James said. 'This is getting good.' Philip glared at his brother, and SP was beyond caring. He'd passed out in his chair.

'You did like confrontation, didn't you, James? Always there waiting to stick the knife in me. You ready with a hateful remark about my figure.' James was still having a hard time equating the stunner who'd shafted him with his chunky ex-sister-in-law.

'What figure? You didn't have a figure. You were an ugly Weeble. Mind, I've got to say you look fit enough now. And see me in this wheelchair? I can still smash your plastic face in and put it back to how it used to be. Think I won't?'

She looked down at James. 'I have no doubt that if you had the intelligence to find me, you'd inflict violence on me. That's all you're good at, hurting women. But come on, James, let me play. You like a bit of salacious gossip. I bet you a fiver that you want to know what your little brother's been up to.'

James gestured to give her the floor. She took it. 'Philip has known about Simon for a long time.'

Violet's head shot up. Consuela had her attention. And Violet was still shrewd enough to pull out of her weakening mind when she needed to. She stared at Consuela with rapt attention.

'Philip's thing was watching people, listening at doors, spying, and turning his nasty, sly character into an object for poking into other people's lives. Violet used to visit Simon every Wednesday afternoon.'

Simon sighed. He was bored. He didn't expect the play to be this long, but he couldn't stop himself from piping up, 'Shimon not like Webunsday. Not.'

'Wednesdays weren't pleasant for him. His mother was cruel and bullied him.'

'Oh, you wicked girl. I most certainly did not. I did what I could for the boy. How can you say such a horrible thing?'

One afternoon, Philip followed Violet to see where she went. He did some digging, asked some questions, and learned everything he wanted to know. At thirteen, he knew he had an older brother with Downs Syndrome. He hid outside the home one day and watched Simon getting on his school bus.'

'Is this true, Philip, and have you really been having an affair with this vile woman? Is that why Danielle isn't here?' Violet asked.

Consuela talked over her, doing Philip the favour of not having to answer his mother. 'When Philip found out he had another brother, he didn't confront his mother and beg her to bring the lad home, so he could be with his family where he should have belonged. Like Violet, he was ashamed of what Simon was. But he didn't ignore it. He used the situation to blackmail his mother. It's all in the diaries, Violet. Philip was the one who blackmailed you with your dirty secret all those years ago.'

'That can't be true. The blackmailer threatened to ruin me.'

'I know. He wrote about it—bragging. And that's exactly what your youngest son did. You weren't his first. John used a girl in his class for sex. Philip blackmailed her. It's in the diaries, those stories, and hundreds more. Unbeknown to anybody, Philip has blackmailed the people of this town for thirty years.'

Pennies dropped all over the room, and customers, present and past, saw their blackmailer and rose from their seats. Phil ran from the room with half a dozen men behind him. Violet was weeping. James, who was violent to the point that it had damaged his brain, was grinning. Sensing a fight and still fancying his chances despite the chair, he wheeled to the door in Philip's wake.

Consuela looked around and recognised people from the blackmailing diaries sitting next to their spouses, looking terrified. They didn't move or say a word. She caught the eyes of them all and empathised with them.

SP was unconscious. The brothers were either dead, passed out, or out of earshot. Ros was there, and a couple of Andrew's grown-up kids, but for the final showdown, it was just Consuela and her nemesis.

Consuela looked Violet in the eye, and the other woman looked away.

'Why are you doing this to me?' Violet was pathetic.

'Come on, Violet. Don't make this a battle of the weak against the strong. You might have this lot fooled, but I know there isn't a weak bone in your body. You're as tough as old boots, so let's see you put up a fight.'

'I'm an old woman.'

'You're an old fool. Your reputation means everything to you. It's more important than any of your children, than your marriage, maybe even your God, but do you know what you are? You're a joke. People laugh at you. They always have. Mother Duck and her five ugly ducklings.'

'I'm highly respected in this town.' There were a few titters. And somebody shouted, 'Quack. Quack.'

Simon liked doing farm animals, and he took up the quack and quacked several times more before dropping into a deep moo. Consuela didn't bother shutting him up.

'When I met Phil, I was a kid myself. I thought I was in love. You were right about one thing. I didn't love him. He's impossible to love. Before you met me, you decided, I wasn't good enough. It didn't even have anything to do with Philip. I wasn't good enough for you, and you were vile to me. You made my life a misery. You called me a heroin addict when I'd never touched drugs in my life. Well, Violet, look at your son passed out and dribbling. That's what an addict looks like. Did you ever once see me like that? You called me a prostitute. Your precious James was imprisoned for prostituting himself to men in a dress. You called me a gold digger. Your children have dug gold from you from the moment they could walk. That's why you never breastfed. They'd have had the silver out of your fillings while they sucked.'

'You filthy woman. See everybody. See what she is, with her dirty mouth?'

'Go'arn, lassie,' one of the men said.

'You were nothing when my son met you.'

'That's right, Violet. You said he picked me out of the gutter.'

'And so he did. He should have left you there to be eaten by rats.'

'Look at your family, Violet, and then look at mine. You've got money, but pound for pound, you've got a lot more gutter than me.' Some of the crowd laughed.

'She tried it on with my dear late husband once,' Violet shouted. 'She exposed herself to him.' that shocked the crowd, and they straightened up to see what the outcome of the allegation was.

She laughed. 'I breastfed my hungry child in his presence.'

'Ah,' the crowd were disappointed at the anti-climax.

'Why are you here, Julie?'

'I have a clear reason. But Julie isn't here, Violet. She died with her daughter. My name is legally Consuela Vengarse. You can call me what you like, but I know who I am.'

'You're a trollop and a hussy. That's what you are.'

'As you've told me many times, Violet, but you asked why I came back.' She called Simon over and held his hand. Simon did the twist and tried to moonwalk but got tangled up in his feet.

The doors at the back of the room banged open, and a tall lady in a tailored suit and high stiletto heels walked up to Violet. The lady was called Monica Dupont. She was a solicitor, a ballbreaker, who only went after men, but she was happy to take this family out, from the rotten matriarch to every putrid apple on the tree. In ten years, she never forgot the story Julie Woods told her about the way the family treated her. Monica had looked down on Julie. She thought her weak and turned her business away because she wouldn't financially destroy her husband.

Monica was wrong, and that was a seldom-felt experience. She was astute when it came to people and was used to being right. The women had become friends, and Monica admired Consuela for what she'd made of herself, despite the Woods' repression.

'Mrs Violet Woods?'

'And you are?'

Monica handed her the envelope. 'You can open it later, but to let you know what it contains. That is a summons for you to appear in court two weeks from today. I am representing Mr Simon Peter Woods,' she paused, '—the elder.' There were some titters around the room. 'We are bringing a case against you to have Mr Woods affirmed in his rightful title as heir of the Halcyon Woods Hotel. With an independent injunction against you granting Mr Woods his one-sixth share, of all assets, in the event of your death. Further to this, we are seeking to claim a like amount, based on an approximation of everything your other sons have had over the years, to be paid to Mr Woods immediately. You will find all the paperwork and reports relevant to our case inside the envelope.'

Violet smiled and looked around the assembled people smugly. 'My dear woman. I would like to see the credentials that declare you a competent solicitor. You must know you can't represent that man in court.'

Consuela cut in. 'He's your son Violet. Say it. Say he's your son.'

'That man is no son of mine. I denounce him.'

'You wicked woman,' somebody shouted.

'And as I was about to say before the guttersnipe interrupted me, you can't represent him in court because he isn't of sane mind. He's incompetent and not capable of knowing what's in his best interests. That, my dear, is why I am his legal guardian.'

'You've got me there, Mrs Woods. I bow to your superior knowledge. It's true. Indeed you were. But last Tuesday, Senora Consuela Vengarse applied to the court and laid before them the extenuating circumstances of Mr Woods' maternal neglect and cruelty. She applied for—and was granted—the position of Guardian ad litem to Mr Woods. A guardian ad litem is an independent person appointed to take on the best interests of her ward. Ms Vengarse is responsible for Mr Wood's welfare, and that includes his financial well-being. You'll find that, as well as my excellent credentials for the post I hold, everything in that envelope is legal and binding.

Ten years ago, I wanted to take your weasel of a son for everything he had. Consuela wouldn't let me have him, so I've waited a long time for this Mrs Woods. I'm going to take you for everything I can legally get on Simon's behalf. And when I've finished with you, I'm going to spit you out like a dirty rag. I've been looking at every loophole in the law. At the moment, it stands that your assets must be split six ways, between your living sons and the surviving offspring of your dead ones. But believe me, lady, if there's any way I can take this whole pile of rubble for my client. I'm going to find it, so you'd better have a good solicitor because I'm looking forward to meeting him.' Monica hugged Consuela, high-fived Simon, and left the room with her high heels clicking all the way out of the door.

Consuela smiled, and Violet looked done in. The people who paid a ticket price for entertainment that night weren't disappointed. 'Thank you for your time and patience, everybody. I'm going to leave now, but I'll let Simon have the last word.'

This was Simon's big moment.

He stood with a huge grin on his face and looked around at all of the people. Mummy didn't look very proud of him yet, but she would be when he'd done his great acting.

'Shimon Woods, is I?'

'I am Simon Woods,' Ayla corrected him.

Simon cleared his throat and started again. 'I am Shimon Woods. Shimon is a bery great singer. Shimon is a bery great actor. Shimon is always good to other people. Shimon is a fine man.'

He stopped and puffed up his chest. He put one arm behind his back and bowed low. When he rose, he shouted out above the noise of the crowd clapping him and whistling.

'I am Shimon Woods.'

Printed in Great Britain
by Amazon

34312827R00229